I0768903

EVERY *heartbeat* AFTER

By Hannah Bird

Copyright @ 2025 by Hannah Bird. All rights reserved.

No part of this book may be reproduced in any form or by any electronic or mechanical means, including information storage and retrieval systems, without written permission from the author, except for the use of brief quotations in a book review.

This is a work of fiction. Names, characters, places, and incidents are either the products of the author's imagination or are used fictitiously. Any resemblance to actual persons, living or dead, businesses, companies, events, or locales is entirely coincidental.

Editor: Lea Ann Schafer

Formatter: Kristen Hamilton at Kristen's Red Pen

Cover Design: Y'all, That Graphic

Published in the United States.

Also by Hannah Bird

Loveless Series

The End and Then (Book 1)

What's Left of Me (Book 2)

Standalones

Promise Me This

The Cost of Forgetting You

Novellas

That Christmas Kind of Feeling

Love in the Time of Conversation Hearts

Author's Note

Dear Reader,

While *Every Heartbeat After* is mostly a love story, there are a few themes which may be hard for some readers. Your mental health is important, and if these themes are difficult for you, I recommend picking up another story at this time.

Every Heartbeat After includes themes of parental death, drug abuse in a family member, divorce due to infidelity (past, not on page), and car accidents resulting in bodily injury.

Please take care of your heart first. And as always, thank you so much for choosing to read any book of mine. Your support means the world to me. I hope Tess and Kit's love is as much a buoy for you to read as it has been for me to write.

With love,

HB

For anyone who's ever wondered, "What would they think of me now?"

And for Andrew, who taught me how to be silly in love. Everything is better since you.

Chapter One

Kit

THE NUMBER one libido killer has got to be your ex grimacing at you from across the bar while you attempt to flirt with someone new.

And not because she wants you instead. Because she thinks you have no game.

I watch the tall redhead I'd been attempting to charm walk away, silently cursing Zoey Allen for being unable to mask her emotions.

"Have you considered unscented hair cream?" Zoey asks as soon as I'm within earshot. Without waiting for the request, she tucks a glass under the seasonal IPA's spout and pulls. "Or maybe change into your uniform, if that's allowed. Women love a man in uniform."

I drop my empty glass onto the countertop and take a seat. Propping both elbows on the bar, I catch my own terse gaze in the mercury-glass wall behind her. "Have you considered keeping your opinions to yourself?"

She deposits a coaster in front of me, then pins it with the freshly poured beer.

"Believe it or not, I have." Eyebrows raised, she drums a riff with hot-pink fingernails against the wooden countertop. "But then you do something stupid like pretending to write a woman a ticket for being too beautiful, and I lose all faith in your abilities."

I snort, rippling the surface of my beer. "Worked on you."

Her blue eyes narrow. "I'm still claiming temporary insanity on that one."

"Of course you are."

We went on a handful of dates when I first moved to town a couple years back. She quickly realized she had feelings for her now fiancé and I wasn't in the mood for anything serious, so it made sense to cut things off. No harm, no foul. We've remained friends ever since. And what kind of friend would I be if I didn't seize every opportunity to remind her she's no better than any other woman I've seduced in this bar?

Her bar. Even if I wanted to avoid doing this in front of her, I couldn't. Zoey owns Nomads. It's the only decent place to get a drink and potentially meet someone in all of Loveless, our quiet little town at the foot of the Colorado Rockies.

I thought moving somewhere so small would bring me peace of mind after leaving the Air Force and ending my broken marriage. And in some ways, it has. Life as a sheriff's deputy here is none too eventful the majority of the time. Mostly traffic duty and the occasional drug bust. But I'm pushing thirty-two, and while I have no desire to remarry, it'd be nice to have a slightly bigger pool of dating prospects.

A deep chuckle sounds from my left. I turn, realizing Chase Taylor, who owns the small outfitter next door, is sitting a few stools down. He raises his glass and points a finger at Zoey. "Give the man a break, Zo. Just because your sense of humor is too highbrow for his jokes doesn't mean every woman's is."

I'm about to thank him when the implication catches up to me. "Wait—"

"You're right." Zoey blows a stray blonde curl off her forehead and offers me a satirical smile. "Surely there's someone out there who finds Deputy Llewellyn's unique combination of uncontrollable lust and pure male ego to be incredibly enticing."

Chase takes a sip to cover his laughter. I sit up straight, gaze slicing from him to Zoey. "Thanks. Glad to have you both in my corner."

Chase's smile is cheeky and loose. The man is happiness incarnate, even exhausted as he is from caring for his newborn twins. And he *is* exhausted, if the purple bags beneath his eyes are any indication. "Happy to help, man."

Whether it's a growl or a groan that putters off my lips, I couldn't say. "When is your wife coming back to bartending? She's much nicer to me. Or Zander. Where is he tonight? Anyone who doesn't delight in my failures, please."

"Eden's a bit busy keeping two infants alive, but I'll send her your regards." Chase's face goes soft, eyes dopey. An expression of pure adoration if I've ever seen one. "I'm actually just picking up dinner; then I'll be headed that way, too. Believe me, I'm sure she wishes she were here. Adeline's going through a sleep regression."

"Oh man, I forgot she mentioned that." Zoey winces sympathetically. "I'll have Santi throw in some extra snacks for the midnight power hour."

Chase nods his appreciation. As if on cue, a bell chimes from the kitchen, signaling an order is up. He downs the last of his beer as Zoey tucks the towel she'd been using to wipe the counter into her back pocket and points at me. "And Zander is on one of his field courses for the alpine rescue team training. You're stuck with me, so be nice."

With that, she disappears into the kitchen, and I sink lower into my seat.

"It's okay, man," Chase offers. "It took me giving up on looking to find Eden. I'm sure it'll happen for you, too."

A frown I'm embarrassed to admit is rooted in the early stages of self-loathing threatens to take over my face. What *is* that? It's been roughly three years since my marriage imploded, and in that time the balance of flirting enough to get laid but not so much that it becomes something more has worked well for me. It's been fun. Easy. And after Courtney knocked the breath out of me with her affair, lighthearted was exactly what I needed. So why is disappointment tickling my already tense jaw at the fact that I suspect Chase is wrong?

I never wanted it to *happen for me* again, so why do I care if it doesn't?

"Order's up. I threw in two extra skillet cookies for Eden." Zoey forgoes the bar and rounds its corner instead, wrapping Chase in a hug before depositing the to-go bag in his outstretched hand. "Give my love to those babies, would you?"

"You know I will. See you around." Chase meets my gaze over the top of Zoey's head and salutes me. "Give 'em hell, Kit."

"Or give 'em a gentlemanly approach and a nice compliment that doesn't involve the threat of jail." Zoey pinches my cheek as she skirts past me. "See how that works out for you."

"Don't you have other patrons to bother?" I grumble.

"Yeah, yeah. I'm going," she tosses over her shoulder. She heads for a table of bankers in the corner booth, all dressed in polos and pressed slacks that have lost a bit of their crispness thanks to a long day of desk warming.

I scan the rest of the crowd. Mostly locals, which is surprising for a Friday in the dead of summer. The far wall is filled with booths, and high-tops dot the expanse of hardwood between them and the bar where I sit. In lieu of normal decorations, plants fill every bit of open space. If there's one thing I know about Zoey, it's that her thumb is evergreen.

The room buzzes with energy. Everyone's excited for the weekend. Ready to hit the mountains or go soak in a lake or just waste away in front of their televisions. They've all got somebody. A coworker to nudge while animatedly recounting the day's watercooler talk. A partner to wrap an arm around and pull in close. A friend to send cookies home for while she cares for her newborns.

Loveless and all its lovely people have welcomed me in as much as anyone. Still, I can't help but feel other. Set apart.

I rub at the knot in my chest. It's this fucking day that's got me all sentimental. Every year I feel it coming on like a migraine. It's probably for the best if I don't bring anybody home with me. What I need is a cold shower and a nightcap. Then I can ignore the inevitable pity text from my parents as I scroll through the pictures I only let myself look at once a year, to remind myself why it's better this way.

Better she cheated, so I could end it before we did something stupid like add a kid to the mix. Better I don't visit my parents, so I can't see the disappointment written all over their faces. Better to be alone, so I can't be hurt like that again. On what would be our wedding anniversary, it's important to remember all the reasons this is the way things have to be.

"What are you moping about, Rookie?"

I blink away the haze that had filled my vision, revealing my boss, Tomas, and his best friend, Gary. The two of them together are a show in opposites. Gary, with his shiny, bald head, short stature, and white Santa beard. Tomas meanwhile stands nearly as tall as me at six feet, with close-cropped dark hair that's gone silver at the temples and deep wrinkles embedded in the tawny skin of his face. He's still in his uniform, though he should've been off hours ago.

"Not moping. Just thinking." I drag my gaze over his person pointedly. "Didn't have time to change?"

"Had to take this one to PT a few towns over." Tomas elbows Gary. "One step closer to getting that boot off."

My gaze drops to said boot, which is currently propped on one of those orthopedic scooters that someone—I'm betting Zoey—has decked out in plant stickers. "How'd you do that again?"

"Fishing incident." Gary waves a hand, rolls over, and takes a seat on the stool beside me. His right foot is more of a club than an appendage at the moment, with the medical boot immobilizing his leg from toe to knee. "I don't like to talk about it. Real traumatic."

I quirk a brow, and Tomas snorts.

"Is the trauma more closely related to snapping your ankle tripping over a fallen log or the size of that trout you let get away?"

"It would've broken records," Gary mock-cries, slamming a fist against the counter.

"Funny how all the fish that got away were record setters," I goad, elbowing the old man.

"Same with women," Tomas says.

I scoff. "I don't know about *that*—"

"He's right," Zoey interjects as she reclaims her spot behind the bar and begins assembling drinks. She meets my gaze and winks. "For example, that woman earlier set the record for fastest to reject you."

"*Ouch,*" Gary says just as Tomas makes a sizzling sound through his teeth.

Satisfied with herself, Zoey tucks a curl behind her ear and cocks a brow at Gary. "You boys want anything?"

"Tomas's wife is making dinner, actually," Gary says. "So we can't stay. Just wanted to check in that you're still good to pick up Tess tomorrow?"

"Who's Tess?" I ask.

"His niece," Tomas explains.

"Shit." Zoey grits her teeth, swiping a hand over her brow. "I'm so sorry, Gary. I completely forgot. What time does she land? Zander's got this training course all weekend and that other guy we hired quit with no notice, so I'm covering the bar tomorrow."

"Let's see, her flight gets in at…" Gary plucks a pair of glasses from his shirt pocket and places them low on the bridge of his nose. The light of his phone screen is reflected back, and I read the display at the same time he says, "Three thirty."

"That's right in the middle of dinner prep. I don't think I can slip away," she says, panic flashing in her blue gaze.

"Kit can go," Tomas offers. "He's covering a night shift for me tomorrow, so he's not in till seven. And he's got all night to get a head start on sleeping."

"What if I have plans?" I ask, indignant.

"Do you?" they all ask simultaneously, with at least three eyebrows raised in my direction. Maybe more from my boss.

I press my lips together, which is the closest thing they'll be getting to a response.

Tomas grunts. "Knew it." He turns to Gary. "Just text me the details and I'll get them over to the rookie."

"The rookie has been working for you for two years now," I grumble.

"I have his number," Gary says, speaking over me. He unlocks his phone and starts typing.

"I haven't said I'll go." My phone chirps in my pocket before the words have died on my lips. I retrieve it, scanning the text Gary just sent. Tess Monroe. Delta Airlines. Three thirty in the afternoon at Denver International. "Since when do you even have a niece?"

"Since about a month ago." His chest puffs out, and a big smile overtakes his face. No further explanation is offered. "I appreciate you doing this for me, Kit. I'd go, but, you know." He gestures to his imprisoned foot. "A bit incapacitated at the moment."

Guess that settles it then. I pocket my phone and meet Zoey's gaze. "Can you get me the bill?"

"It's on me," Gary offers. "To show my appreciation."

"As if you pay," Zoey chides. Nomad's was Gary's before it was hers, and though I suspect him not paying is something she insisted on more than anything, as a thank-you for selling the place to her, she does a convincing job of pinning him for it.

Tomas chuckles. Gary ignores her and presses on. "She's staying at the motel up the street. I told her I'd meet her here for dinner after she's settled. She's a delight. You'll like her."

"Didn't you say you've only known her a month?" I ask, interest officially piqued.

He wipes a hand down his beard, gaze faraway as he says, "I can just tell. She's something special."

"Noted. I'll pull up at the gate and keep an eye out for *something special.*"

"Oh, right." Gary plucks his phone from where he'd set it on the counter and taps through a few screens, then turns it my way.

Tess *is* something special. It's a selfie, with poor lighting and an even poorer angle, but there's something about her that dries up my throat the minute I see her. Shoulder-length blonde hair curls away from her pixie-like face in loose ringlets. Bright green eyes meet my gaze, feeling as alive and animated as if she were right in front of me. Her smile is infectious. Before I know it, I'm wearing one, too.

The phone drops, and Tess's face is replaced by Gary's decidedly less attractive one.

"Don't even think about it," he warns.

"Don't worry." Tomas claps my shoulder and winks. "Llewellyn will be on his best behavior."

Zoey hoists the tray of drinks onto her shoulder with a grunt. When she speaks, her voice is strained. "Not sure that's the vote of confidence you think it is, Sheriff."

She walks away, leaving the attention of both men fully on me.

"I will be," I finally manage to choke out, wondering why the air in here is suddenly so much thicker. "I mean, erm, I'll be there. No problem, Gary."

"There better not be a problem," he says, brow raised. Too bad he's as threatening as a mall Santa with his cherub cheeks and twinkling gray eyes. "Don't you scare off my niece before I've even had the chance to meet her."

"Hell, Gary, if she looks anything like you, you've got nothing to worry about," Tomas teases. "Come on, can't keep the wife waiting much longer."

"I'm watching you," Gary says, but his clipped tone quickly dissolves into laughter. "All right, I'm starved. Let's go."

Together, Tomas and I help him from his seat and back onto his scooter. The two of them begin their slow hobble toward the exit. Meanwhile I'm racking my brain, trying to figure out when was the last time a woman stole my breath like that.

Not even a woman. A *picture* of a woman. And a long fucking time ago, that's when.

"Uh-oh," Zoey teases, plopping her now empty tray next to me as she scans my face. "Someone's in trouble."

Trouble, indeed.

Chapter Two

Tess

"You've got to be kidding me."

I roll my head back and pinch my eyes closed. We've been taxiing on the runway for at least thirty minutes, waiting for our gate to open up. The man beside me—midfifties, big belly, bigger attitude (you know the type)—is losing the cool he never had. And with no one riding in the middle seat between us, he's decided I'm the best person to receive his aired grievances.

He leans closer, assuming I somehow didn't hear his first groaned complaint. "I paid good money to be on the first flight, and at this rate I could've slept in and taken the second. So fucking ridiculous."

The flight attendant, who wears the kind of empathetic expression that tells me she hasn't been at this long enough to become jaded, pauses by our row. "Sir, we understand delays are never ideal, but—"

He cuts her off with a sound caught somewhere between a scoff and a snort, followed by a muttered, "Oh, fuck off."

A little of the light behind her amber eyes dims. She shuffles past, realizing this is a battle that's not worth fighting.

I'm beginning to wish I'd driven.

Never mind that the drive from the small town where I live in Alabama to Loveless, Colorado, would take the better half of twenty-two hours, when I've only scheduled a few free days off work. Flying next to this asshole is worth it solely for the precious extra hours it gains me with my uncle.

Uncle. I roll the word around in my head, trying to familiarize myself with it. It's no less strange than the moment it popped up on my LineageDNA results. Gary Barbeau is in his late sixties, with no kids and a family that's all but gone, much like mine. Yet somehow, a shimmering thread stretched between us in the form of a college fling my late grandfather never knew resulted in a child. The woman married a different man, who raised Gary as his own. My grandfather went on to marry my grandmother, producing a daughter who would one day have me.

And the rest, as they say, is history.

Briefly I allow myself to wonder what Mom would think if she were here. A half-brother she never knew she had. After generations of only children, what a surprise that would've been.

It aches more than I'd like, so I shove it down into my heart and lock the door. Another time. Today is a happy day.

Finally the plane rolls into place at the gate and all aisle seaters, apart from myself, shoot up like a light. I mostly refrain because it irritates me to no end that everyone's in a rush to go nowhere, but I'd be lying if I said there wasn't a part of me that revels in the waves of agitation rolling off my seatmate at the perceived delay I'm causing him.

"You can go," he says. Or grunts. His anger-honed tenor makes everything sound less like words and more like an animalistic insistence that I *move.*

I consider holding the line, but Gary mentioned a friend of his would be waiting to pick me up, and I'm already running behind. The Southern manners in me win out in the end, and I force myself to rise and grab my bag from the overhead bin. The weight of it slaps against my spine as I slip the pack onto my shoulder. The kind flight attendant is tucked into a row of empty seats a few feet ahead, watching as each passenger marches single file down the aisle. I offer her a genuine smile as I pass. "You're amazing. Just ignore the assholes," loud enough for said asshole to overhear.

It earns an indignant huff from him but an appreciative nod from her, so it's worth it.

Denver International Airport was designed to maximize step count while minimizing efficiency. By the time I make my way out of the building, exchanging insufficient AC for balmy summer air, sweat adheres my flowy trousers to my thighs. I'm grateful for the sliver of skin showing beneath my crop top, especially when the mountain breeze rushes in to kiss it.

I scan the row of vehicles parked along the curb outside baggage claim, searching for the blonde woman with wild curls from the photo Gary sent me a few weeks back when he first broke his ankle and realized he wouldn't be able to pick me up. When I don't spot her, I retrieve my phone from my pack. I know Gary texted me her number at some point.

I find our thread (ensuring it's Gary B instead of Gary Z—my boss from an ill-fated endeavor as a diving instructor a few summers back) buried beneath a slew of unread messages from various people I swear I'll get back to eventually. My uncle, too, has a blue dot next to his name indicating I've missed a text. I click on it and tuck my sunglasses onto my head.

GARY B

Zoey has to work, so I've tapped into my local resources and found a replacement. Look for the sheriff's cruiser.

I fire off a reply, letting him know I've landed and will be en route shortly, then I dial the number he sent in a follow-up message. The first ring rolls through just as my gaze lands on a black SUV with *Sheriff* emblazoned along white door panels. A man leans against it, his chin tucked and his phone in his hand. I'm already walking toward him when he lifts it to his ear and his voice reaches through the line.

"Kit Llewellyn speaking."

A grin spreads across my face for no reason. "Kit Llewellyn, are you here to pick me up?"

His gaze lifts and our eyes meet. My body reacts to him before my mind can even process his sharp jawline and violence-bent nose. Despite the oppressive heat, a chill runs through me. My steps falter. I capture more details, like his tousled blackish-brown hair and thin lips that form a tense line beneath high cheekbones. His hazel eyes have entered my field of vision by the time I remember to hang up the phone.

His mouth opens and then closes. A corner lifts. I feel more than see the path of his gaze as it travels over me, gone just as quickly as it comes.

When he once again settles on my face, the crooked grin becomes a genuine smile. "You must be something special."

I pause, hand on my bag's strap where it rests against my ribs. "Excuse me?"

He coughs. Clears his throat. Red rises from the collar of his tan uniform shirt. "Sorry. You're Tess, right? Gary's niece?"

Some small part of me sparks at that. Belonging to someone. How long has it been since I was somebody's daughter? Somebody's anything?

Since my grandfather—my last living relative—passed two years ago, I've only been Tess. Completely solitary. Utterly alone.

"That's me." I answer with a smile that's only semi-forced. The embarrassment has reached his cheeks, dyeing them scarlet. For some ungodly reason I'm tempted to rise up on my tiptoes and kiss the flushed skin.

What the hell, Tess? I may be outgoing, but I'm not *that* outgoing.

All around us, engines rumble and exhaust floods the air. Doors slam and people embrace, their excited chatter adding to the cacophony. Kit and I stare at each other, and I wonder briefly if he feels the same strange inclination to reach out and touch me.

Doubtful. I'm simply succumbing to the heat and my long day of travel. In an effort to distract myself, I point behind him. "Do I get to ride up front, or am I under arrest?"

He chuckles, and it's like he transforms right in front of me. Whatever awkward energy was plaguing him before, it passes. I take a note from his book and shake it off my shoulders along with the pack. He's just attractive. I can deal with attractive. No reason for my brain to short-circuit over some broad shoulders in a deputy uniform.

"I'll forgo the handcuffs if you promise you can restrain yourself."

I quirk a brow. First he's stumbling over his words, and now he's going to flirt? Perhaps it wasn't just me, then. "Somehow I'll manage."

His gaze flits over me once more, this time so obvious I have to assume he wants me to notice. "Yeah, we'll see." He pulls the door open for me, then holds out his opposite hand, palm up. "I can take your bag."

It's the first time I've noticed his drawl, mostly because I hear them on a daily basis. Everyone in Fly Hollow speaks with a twang, myself included. What I hadn't expected was to encounter one out here, so far from home.

"Where are you from?" I ask when he climbs into the driver's side after depositing my bag in the back seat. The traffic monitor tips his hat to Kit as we pass. No wonder he was allowed to hog the curb while everyone else was whistled at to move.

"Mississippi. Near Pascagoula, if you've ever heard of that."

He's facing the road, but I feel his attention on me. Like a secondary awareness. A hand at the base of your spine when the person holding you is looking away.

"I have. I'm from a small town in southern Alabama."

"No shit." The corner of his mouth twitches. "How on earth did you and Gary end up living so far apart?"

I relax into the seat, letting my gaze drift toward the window. In the distance the Rockies stand sentinel over the city below. Denver is all shiny metal and moving cars, surrounded by nature so vast my mind can barely comprehend it.

"His mom and my grandpa went to college together at the University of Alabama. She must've gotten pregnant right before graduation, but she never told him. At least as far as I can tell. My grandpa passed away, so I can't really ask him for details." I shrug, still staring at the changing landscape around us. "Anyway, I guess she married someone in the military when Gary was a baby and never bothered to tell him that wasn't his dad. Gary joined when he was eighteen to follow the guy's footsteps, and that's how he ended up in Colorado."

Kit nods. "That's how I ended up here, too."

My gaze cuts from the window to his profile, which is cast in early afternoon sunlight, making all his edges more harsh. "What branch?"

"Air Force." He glances at me with a head tilt, measuring my reaction. "Security forces. Basically I was a cop on base."

I wave a hand around. "Fitting."

The corner of his mouth lifts. "What about you? What do you do?"

"This and that. Whatever I'm in the mood for at the time."

He huffs a laugh. "What are you in the mood for lately?"

It's almost sensual, the way he says it. I draw a deep breath. The scent of sandalwood comes off him in waves, filling my lungs. "I took a job managing a gym recently. I sometimes teach classes there in the evening hours, too."

"Let me guess." He rolls to a stop at a red light leading to the highway, then angles a smirk at me. I'm fully prepared for him to say something stupid like naked Pilates based on that look, when he surprises me by saying, "Kickboxing."

I snort, which earns a smile that stretches across his whole face. "Do I strike you as a kickboxer?"

"You strike me as someone who could bring me to my knees."

"*Boooooooo!*" I point both thumbs down, and laughter erupts from him in quick spasms.

He finally catches his breath while shaking his head at oncoming traffic. "Come on, as far as pickup lines go, that was an excellent one."

My skin heats and I drop my hands to my lap. Purse my lips. I'm here for a reason. Seeking out what is quite possibly the last family tie I have this side of the grave. Do I really have time for this man to be trying to pick me up?

No. But it fills my belly with fire all the same.

He glances at me sideways, apprehension pinching his eyes at the corners. It's a hole in the flirtatious facade, and it makes him all the more enticing. A little self-doubt is good for a man. At least I've always thought so.

I decide changing the subject is in both our best interest. "How'd you get roped into being my ride?"

Kit shrugs. "I was available."

I peruse his uniform. "You didn't have to work?"

"Not till later. I took an overnight to cover for one of the other guys."

"Well"—I fold my hands together—"I appreciate you sacrificing your time off for me."

"Hardly a sacrifice," he murmurs. I barely catch it beneath the country music that fills the cab as he turns the radio up. "Feel free to take a nap. We've got about an hour and a half drive back to Loveless."

"I'm not even tired," I say on the tail end of a yawn.

"Mhm." He reaches into the side panel of his door and retrieves a jacket with the sheriff's logo on the chest. "Well, just in case."

He passes it to me, our hands brushing for only a second. I close my eyes, pretending I didn't feel it all the way to my toes.

He turns up the volume, and I wonder if he's pretending, too.

The Horseshoe Inn is two stories with all outdoor entrances that have doors painted turquoise and a small Adirondack chair outside each room. I wash off the flight and the smell of Kit along with it, though I swear I'm still catching whiffs as I walk in the direction of the bar where I'm supposed to meet Gary for dinner.

I shove thoughts of the dark-haired deputy to the back of my brain, where they'll hopefully remain to gather dust. It was a strange start to an otherwise really important weekend. Maybe I just needed to latch on to a distraction, any distraction, so as not to be riddled with nerves. A misguided coping mechanism. Nothing more.

People shuffle past me as I move closer to what appears to be the heart of all the hubbub. Loveless is nestled in a valley, with massive mountains looming all around the picturesque town. Its main street is pedestrian-friendly, all manicured sidewalks and bustling businesses that have window displays meant to entice shoppers. I spot the Nomads sign—black lettering atop a neon geometric design—just past a coffee shop that's closed for the evening. I pause at the entrance, steeling myself with a deep breath.

I shouldn't be nervous. I've talked to Gary multiple times

since I contacted him about our match. Still, the age-old fears creep through. What if he doesn't like me? What if my grief sits like a cloud overhead, casting shadows over all the things that used to make me lovable, so dark that he cannot see them?

No. Today is a happy day. And I will be happy, damn it.

Nomads is filled to the brim when I enter, adding myself to the mass of bodies crowding each cocktail table in the center of the room. Booths line the right wall, and a wooden-topped bar mirrors them on the left. I recognize Zoey from her picture. She's slinging cocktails in front of a mercury-glass wall with shelf after shelf of liquor mounted on its reflective surface. Plants overflow from every nook, cranny, and ceiling beam, giving the place the feel of a warm hug when it would otherwise seem overwhelmingly packed.

"Tess?" I somehow hear over the cacophony of voices.

Gary appears from the fray like a knight on his steed, only my uncle's horse is actually a sticker-coated scooter. He offers a hand to steady me when a man passing by knocks me sideways. I stumble more than step into my uncle's waiting embrace. He's shorter than me, but that's not altogether unusual at five foot ten inches. He smells of Irish Spring soap and beer. I drink it in as he squeezes me three times fast.

"You made it!" When he pulls back, his eyes are red-rimmed. I imagine mine are, too. The crowd parts to let the man on a scooter pass through as he guides us away from the black-and-white-tiled entrance, closer to the bar, where Zoey glances up and offers me a welcoming smile.

"Of course I made it! I had a police escort."

He chuckles, the apples of his cheeks turning rosy. His eyes are slate gray, as kind as they are unfamiliar. I search his face for any hint of hers, but my mother never looked much like her father anyway.

The loss still hits me square in the chest. I got my hopes up when I should've known better. I've never quite figured out how not to do that.

He must see the disappointment in my face, because his grin disappears into the fluff of his beard. "Come on; Santi made us to-go plates. We can find somewhere quieter to catch up."

"Welcome to town, Tess!" Zoey calls as she passes a tied-off bag full of Styrofoam containers to Gary. "Hope Deputy Get-in-Your-Pants didn't, well, you know."

Gary grunts, pinning Zoey with a stare. "My niece would never."

Wouldn't I? Guilt throbs at my temples. I certainly contemplated it more than once on the drive over, when I wasn't dozing in and out. Turns out Kit was right. I was absolutely exhausted.

I still feel the tingle of his thumb rubbing my elbow to wake me when we finally made it to the Horseshoe. I cup it, suddenly certain they can all see the place where he touched me like a scarlet letter burned into my skin.

"You two enjoy dinner," Zoey says, humor alight in her eyes.

"Hopefully we can actually meet sometime this weekend when it's not so…" I wave a hand at the chaos.

She laughs, already fisting two glasses and depositing them beneath their respective beer nozzles. "I'm counting on it. You're part of the family now."

You hear that, Mom and Dad? I'm part of a family again.

I smile because I don't trust myself to speak. Not until Gary and I have made it out of the bar and are safely headed back toward my motel. Our pace is slow, impeded by his less than reliable steering of the scooter supporting his booted foot. I glance at it, my eyebrows pinched together, but decide that if he's not bothered by it, I'm not going to question it.

"Thank you so much for inviting me out here." The night is cool and breezy, easing the heat of the day out of my system. It's so much better than the scorching humidity of the South. "I can see why you love it so much."

"Oh, any place can be a good place. It's the people that make it so lovely." He smiles up at me. "Wendy and I never had any kids of our own, but boy would she get a hoot out of Zoey and the rest of her friends. You'll see tomorrow. They keep me young."

"I'm glad you have them." I genuinely mean it, but my voice is thin. Too much want stripping it of life.

When my parents died, I'd never felt more alone in my life. My grandparents took me in, sure, and my friends still called, but none of them knew how I felt. I let myself wallow in it for a summer. Really tempt the grief to drown me. But then fall came and I'd somehow managed to survive, so I decided if everyone around me's life had gone on like normal, I'd pretend that mine had too. Soon I'd pretended for so long I even tricked myself. Until the first time my grandparents brought me back to the Carmen.

Gary nudges me with his shoulder, stealing me away from the memory. When I meet his gaze, he smiles. "You have them now, too. They may not have popped up on that DNA test, but they're my family, so that means they're yours."

My smile is weak and watery but present nonetheless. "That means more than you know."

He points to a bench along the sidewalk. "Let's take a seat here and eat. I know we've talked so much, but there's still more I'd love to know." He passes me a foam container when I sit down, then opens his own in tandem with me. The scent of spices and fresh, chargrilled meat makes my mouth water.

"What can I tell you that I haven't already?" I take a bite and swallow it down, sucking a dribble of green chili off my thumb. The delicious substance has soaked through the burger bun and poured onto my fries, which is pretty much ideal.

"Well, first you can tell me about your ride with Kit. He can be a real charmer, or at least he thinks so." Gary chuckles, pops a fry in his mouth, and hums his satisfaction. "And then, if you're willing, I'd love to hear about my baby sister."

Despite all the moisture, my mouth is suddenly bone-dry as I contemplate which is worse. I lean into my uncle, gaze fixed on the lamppost across the street. But I'm not really seeing it. I'm seeing my mother in a casket, my father in a matching one five feet to her right.

And I still feel Kit's thumb brushing my skin.

Chapter Three

Kit

THE OFFICE IS QUIET. Save for myself and Tomas, everyone else is on the road. He'll be out of here soon, and then I'll be left alone with my thoughts.

My very unwanted thoughts.

If her picture was enticing, Tess in person is irresistible. I've spent the hours since I dropped her off poring over every word exchanged with a fine-tooth comb. Did she like me? Was I too much?

Was I not enough?

I shake my head at nothing, willing the intrusive thoughts to go away. She's here for a weekend. She's Gary's niece and, from the sounds of it, his only surviving family. There are a million reasons I should forget Tess Monroe.

And yet...

"Shaking some marbles loose over there, Rookie?"

I glance up from the paperwork I admittedly was not reading to find Tomas leaning over my desk, eyebrows raised, with a toothpick pinned between his lips. His dark eyes are warm with mischief, not to mention a level of understanding that has my skin crawling beneath its scrutiny.

"Sorry. Not used to this schedule, and I'm a little off-kilter," I say, hoping I sound the least bit convincing.

The corner of his mouth twitches. "So you're saying it has nothing to do with a certain niece of a certain old man?"

"I'm saying exactly that," I deadpan.

He's poking at my defenses, the same way he does when we bring someone in for an interrogation. Tomas might be jovial on the surface, but he's a damn good sheriff. An even better boss. When he's not giving me hell about women, that is.

"I have it on good authority that you drove away from the Horseshoe Inn with hearts blocking your vision." He removes the toothpick from his mouth and tosses it into the bin beside my desk. "That true, Llewellyn?"

"What have I told you about listening to Marcy Davis?" The owner of the inn is nine parts gossip to one part truth. So what if this time she was on to something?

"That I should only do it when it aligns with a theory I already had." My boss's eyes narrow to judgmental slits. "You dug your own grave, so spill."

"She's a beautiful woman. I'm not blind." I lean back in my chair, folding my hands behind my head. "So what?"

"*So what?*" Tomas rests his chin on steepled fingers, sheer glee rippling the tan skin on his face. "So you, my man, never get defensive about a beautiful woman. But suddenly you're keeping your mouth shut about this one? And she's related to Gary? This is a gold mine of opportunity to rib you for the rest of your days."

I force my gaze to harden, the way it does when I'm dealing with the more unsavory folks we run into on occasion. "It's nothing, okay? And shouldn't you be going home?"

He slaps the top of the cubicle and rises to his full height, glancing toward the door and then back to me. "Yes. I'm actually just supposed to mention to you that you need to schedule some PTO. Alice is on my ass about it."

Alice, his secretary and resident busybody, is on everyone's ass. I'm tempted to say, *Welcome to the club.*

"You know I don't have anywhere to go. Can't I donate it to someone else?"

A line forms between his dark brows. "Why not visit your parents? They're still living, right? I'm sure they'd love to see you."

My parents *are* still living. Whether or not they'd love to see me is another topic altogether. I haven't been home since the divorce finalized. We talk on the phone occasionally, mostly for holidays I'd forget exist if it weren't for all my coworkers requesting off. But I can't bring myself to make the trip to Mississippi. Can't face the disappointment on my parents' faces when they talk to the son who was supposed to make them proud but ended up divorced and miserable all the same.

"I'm good, Tomas. Promise. Just let it roll over if I can't donate it."

"That's the thing. You've accumulated too many hours by not taking them, and they can't risk you cashing them all in at once." He shakes his head, one eyebrow lifted. "You might be the first person in the history of this department to go their whole tenure without using a single personal day. Don't you go to the doctor?"

I wave a hand down my meticulously pressed uniform. "Healthy as a horse. Why would I need to?"

"Because you need a life." He sucks on his teeth—a habit of his when a perp gets too stubborn or one of his deputies toes the line of his patience. "Just please make some plans. We're budgeting for this coming fiscal year, and you've got to take at least ten days before next July. That's not a request, either, Rookie."

I salute him. It's half serious, half please-get-off-my-ass.

If Tomas can tell that I'm just brushing him off, he doesn't show it. "Night, Kit. Let me know if anything gets too crazy."

I grin up at him. "Not a chance. Get some rest. Hug your wife. Maybe even your kids, if you're so inclined."

He snorts, completely tired of my shit. Then he's gone, taking long strides toward the exit, abandoning me and the rest of the empty desks. He opens the door to the department, allowing in a fleeting ray of evening sunlight before it closes and I'm left in the quiet.

I fucking hate night shift.

Too much time to be left to my own thoughts, my own devices. In a half hour or so, I'll pile into my cruiser and roam the roads. Jamie will be here shortly to man the phones, once he drops his kids off at their mom's. The county is quiet at night, so long as the patrons at Dooley's—a dive bar in the next town over —keep their shit together. I'll have nothing to do but stew on Tess's bright green gaze, so attuned to every word, every move I made.

And now, the thought of visiting my parents to boot.

It's not that I don't miss them. I do. Terribly. But my brother has always been the fuckup. The drug addict. In and out of rehab, sucking them dry of an already meager retirement fund. I was supposed to be the golden child. College graduate. Military veteran. Happily married, with two-point-five kids and a white picket fence on the horizon.

Except one long deployment and a fucking affair swept that all out to sea in an instant.

How do you face your parents after that? I haven't figured it out yet, so I just don't. Face them, that is. Not to mention if I go home, I have to somehow smile and nod while they talk about Gage like his last rehab stay cured him; meanwhile he and I both know he still hits me up for money every few months under the guise of keeping the lights on at whatever run-down rental he's camping out in at the time. A part of me is certain he uses the cash to fund his addiction, yet I can't bring myself to ignore his calls.

To let him fail. Not when I've seen how much it devastates our parents when he does.

Tess is another problem for which I have no solution.

It was one car ride. A simple conversation. It shouldn't matter, in the grand scheme of things. Only I still feel her presence like she's curled up beside me, despite her insistence that she wasn't tired. I still see her when I close my eyes, no matter how much I wish I didn't.

It's stupid, I'll admit. But the only thing I can think to do is call Zoey.

She picks up on the fifth ring, just when I've decided she's probably ignoring me. "I thought civilians were supposed to call the police, not the other way around."

I roll my eyes, though I know she can't see. "Hello to you, too."

There's a dull roar of conversation buzzing through the line. Nomads must be packed. And not for nothing—if I could be there instead of heading into an overnight on too little sleep and even less sanity, I would. One of Santi's green chili burgers sounds amazing right about now.

"We're a bit busy, Kit. What do you need?"

I scrub a hand down my face. The bell over the door chimes, announcing Jamie's arrival. I can't say the things I want to in front of him. I'm not even sure what those things are, just that there's a strange feeling in my chest that I want to be rid of.

"Is this about Tess?" Zoey presses.

My chair groans as I lean forward, balancing elbows on knees. "Why would you think that?"

Her sigh is barely audible over the noise of the crowd. "Because I know you. You can scent a vulnerable woman like a bloodhound."

"I resent that."

"But do you deny it?"

I close the file I'd been pretend-perusing. "Why did I call you?"

"Because I'm your best friend, no matter how weird that seems to both of us." There's a telltale squeak of the saloon-style door that leads into Nomads' kitchen, and suddenly conversation is replaced with the metal clang of food prep in the background. "Look, from what little Gary has told me, Tess has been through a lot. And this weekend is important for both of them. So maybe just keep it in your pants this time, yeah?"

I close my eyes, blocking out the bland sheriff's department and Jamie's perfectionistic organizing of the front desk since Akita, who works the day shift, left it in a disarray as usual. I know Zoey's right, at least about the importance of this weekend to Gary and Tess. And her assumption about my intentions is fair, given that's all she's seen from me in the years we've known each other. Hell, it's all I've wanted anyone to see.

What I can't figure out is how to explain that the draw I feel to Tess is not merely physical. It hardly makes sense to me, this piqued interest. Maybe she's right and I'm thinking with my dick without even realizing. And if she's wrong? Then it's best for both me and Tess that I don't acknowledge it.

"Yeah." My voice is gravel. Mulched wood. Everything part and parcel. "Thanks for talking me off the ledge, Zo."

"Anytime. Now go roam the streets and keep the citizens of Loveless and the greater valley safe."

"Deal, so long as you don't get them too drunk."

"You got it, Deputy Dickwad."

I laugh, and it shakes something loose inside. It feels like relief. "Bye, Zo."

"Bye, Kit." Her laughter is the last thing I hear before she hangs up. A reminder not to take myself, or these feelings, too seriously.

Good fucking luck.

Chapter Four

Tess

THE WATER PRESSURE at the motel is abysmal, but I manage to wash the remnants of sleep off in record time as I prepare for the day. We didn't have long to catch up last night, between the jet lag and Gary's insistence that I get some rest. But today there's a festival taking over downtown Loveless. Which means a chance to explore the town with my uncle, and to formally meet some of the people he calls his family. Calls *my* family, now, too.

Plus, there will be food trucks. Say less, am I right?

I drape a flowy sundress over my body, aiming for comfort rather than structure. A random thought flits through my mind —*would Kit like it?* Then I remind myself he's likely sleeping off his overnight shift. And, more importantly, I shouldn't care.

I study myself in the mirror as I apply a thin layer of sunscreen to my face. I'm my mother made over—same green eyes, same white-blonde hair. But is that Gary's twinkle in my eye? Did my grandfather's nose make it onto both our faces?

You don't realize how precious it is to see yourself reflected back in the faces of your loved ones. In their mannerisms and in their stories. Not till they're all gone and there's no one around that carries a piece of you with them. It feels like you're the tree falling in a forest without a soul nearby to listen. It's easy to suspect you might not exist after all.

The woman who checked me in last night stands outside the office building, giving me a once-over as I pass. "You headed out to the festival, miss?" She pushes her glasses up the bridge of her arched nose, a half-burnt cigarette dangling between two fingers. I can't tell if she's the only worker or just owns the place, but I haven't run into anyone else since I arrived, so I imagine she's both.

I nod and offer her a smile. "I am. Want me to bring you back anything?"

"Well aren't you sweet." She knocks off the gathered ash on the tip of her cigarette, then takes a long pull. When she speaks again, smoke frames her exhaled words. "No one's ever offered something like that. Half the time I'm not sure guests really even see me, you know? They just grab their keys and go."

Boy, do I know how that feels. "What would you like?"

She shrugs. "Surprise me."

I pop my sunglasses over my eyes. It's early yet, but the sun is already beating down. It'll be another scorcher of a day, though the breeze takes the edge off enough to breathe. "I can do surprises."

"You going to see that cutie cop who dropped you off yesterday?" Her smirk is a little too knowing for my taste. I feel exposed, like she can see right past my skin to a heart that beats a little harder at even the allusion to Kit. "I tell you, sometimes I'm tempted to report a nonexistent crime just to get a look at him."

I bite the inside of my cheek, letting the sting recenter my thoughts. "Oh, I don't really know him. He was just doing my uncle a favor."

"Who's your uncle?"

I stand a little straighter, grateful for the change in topic. "Gary Barbeau. Used to own Nomads?"

What starts as a laugh morphs into a raspy cough. As if it's personally offended her, she drops the remainder of the cigarette and squashes it beneath a well-worn tennis shoe. "I'm familiar. Even if he hadn't run the only decent bar in town for years, everyone in Loveless knows everybody else."

"Sounds familiar," I mutter. My hometown, Fly Hollow, is no better. I still get piteous expressions everywhere I go, even more than a decade later. It's as though people take one look at me and all they can see is the headline about my parents' car accident. Which is why I try so hard not to be the grieving orphan they expect. I keep thinking if I can make myself bright enough, the rest will be hidden by my shadow.

"You have fun, all right? And don't worry about getting me anything. It's enough that you even thought to ask."

"Have a good day…Marcy," I say, reading her faded name tag. "And it's no bother. I'm really just buttering you up in the hopes of getting extra towels."

She laughs, what must be years of smoking turning the sound to a strained sort of music. "Consider it done."

It's only a few blocks from the motel to the first row of metal barricades marking the border of the festival. Traffic has been diverted to allow for pedestrians to roam the streets safely. Food trucks and vendor tents line each side of the main road through town. Businesses have their doors propped open despite the rising temperatures. Water bowls have been set up for the dogs being walked around by their owners. I scan the faces of the deputies manning the perimeter almost without realizing it, until disappointment at not recognizing them sinks like a stone through my chest.

I spot Gary on the same bench where we ate dinner last night, just like he promised. Zoey's next to him, and a Black man with short hair and mirrored sunglasses sits at her other side, arm slung around her shoulders like it's the most natural thing in the world.

She leans back and kisses his cheek, earning a smile that takes over his entire expression. It's only a snapshot of a life, but it's a happy one.

"Aren't you a vision!" Zoey unravels herself from her partner's arm and stands, stepping toward me with a raised brow. "I'm a hugger. Are you a hugger?"

"I'm an everything-er." I open my arms and squeeze her when she fills them. A few strands of curly hair get caught on the breeze and fan across my face, tickling my nose. "So Zoey, and this is…?"

Her partner rises to his feet and offers his hand. "Aaron, her fiancé."

She beams at that, and I borrow a bit of her sunshine for my own grin. "So nice to meet you both."

"Chase and Eden were going to come, but with the heat they don't think it's a good idea for the babies to be out," Gary explains. "But that's the crew. Zoey bought the bar from me, allowing me to retire. Eden is her best friend and my second adoptive daughter." He winks. I remember the photo he sent from Eden's wedding, where he had the honor of walking her down the aisle. Seems like it's his forte, taking care of people who need a father figure most. "If you're up for a coffee, you can meet Rose. She and her husband own the cafe next door to the bar."

I raise both brows, crumpling my forehead. "Marcy wasn't kidding about everyone knowing each other here."

"Your uncle just loves to take people under his wing. Father to the fatherless, this one," Zoey says with an affected tone.

Gary chokes on his own spit, glancing at me nervously as he tries to clear the blockage. I'm not sure how much he's told Zoey about my past, but concern pinches her expression in a flash. "Oh my God, Tess, I'm so sorry—"

"It's really okay," I say, smile so wide it makes my cheeks ache. I learned a long time ago that if you fold your face in a grin, it disguises all the cracks you don't want seen. "I knew what you meant."

"You shoving your foot in your mouth again, Zo?"

A shiver runs down my spine at the sound of a familiar voice. I glance over my shoulder. Kit's legs are long, and he manages to close the distance before I have the chance to fix my expression. I'm grateful for the sunglasses guarding my widened eyes. There's nothing I can do to take back my popped-open lips, which his gaze lands on immediately.

He's still in his uniform, which is a bit worse for the wear after a night spent working in it. Wrinkles galore, and a badge that's a tad askew. Purple bruises have taken up residence beneath his eyes, which are more brown than green this morning, much to my chagrin.

I have a weakness for brown eyes.

"Shouldn't you be asleep right now?" Zoey's tone is taut. When I glance back at her, she's shooting daggers at Kit that I don't quite understand. Aaron elbows her, a laugh bubbling over his lips.

"Just wanted to take a stroll through the festival before getting some shut-eye." Kit tilts his head, one brow raised. Whatever silent standoff they're having, I think he's winning on nonchalance alone. "That okay with you?"

Before Zoey can respond, Gary claps Kit's shoulder. "Thanks again for giving Tess a ride, son."

Surprisingly Kit's expression turns sheepish. Not something I thought he'd be capable of feeling, but what do I know? I only rode in a car with the guy for a couple hours. I'd do well to remember that he's hardly more than a stranger to me, albeit a handsome one.

"Happy to do it." He meets my gaze once more, and any attempt at brushing these feelings off goes out the door. I don't know how to describe it, the way I feel so stripped bare and also wrapped up tight. He looks at me, and I'm pinned in place, unable to breathe, waiting for the next words off his lips to set me free. As though he senses as much, he clicks his tongue and breaks our stare, glancing instead at the row of booths behind us. "Enjoy your day, Tess. Pretty sure there's a booth for the local kickboxing place across the way. You know, if you're interested."

The giggle that spills out of me is embarrassingly high-pitched. "Noted."

Aaron, Gary, and Zoey are looking at us like we've each grown two heads.

"Bye, y'all." Kit tips his chin toward us, gaze flitting from face to face. It settles on mine for the longest heartbeat before darting away.

"That was so fucking weird," Zoey mumbles.

Aaron flicks his fiancée's hair. "Be nice."

"Oh, Tess." Gary makes a *tsk* sound. The sun bounces off his bald head as he shakes it, and I wonder for a second if he has sunscreen on or not. "You've broken him."

The feeling's mutual, I want to say, suddenly annoyed that I'm this off-kilter thanks to a few interactions with a man who fancies himself charming. It's unfamiliar territory and, I realize, an easy way to distract myself from all the heaviness being here with Gary brings up. The mind latches on to strange things to avoid pain. I should know.

I force my lips into a pleasant smile, stamping down the emotion rising in my throat. "It's just an inside joke, that's all. So where's this coffee you speak of?"

"A block up the street. I'll lead the way," Gary says, the moment with Kit already forgotten.

"Want to sit on your scooter and I'll push, old man?" Aaron jokes.

Zoey snickers and Gary scowls. "Try that and I'll kick you with this boot."

"Don't," Zoey says, voice filled with mock concern as she pretends to hold my uncle back by the shoulders. "The last thing we need is another hobbler slowing us down."

Gary shrugs her off, his bushy white eyebrows furrowed, but his feigned anger quickly morphs into laughter. It's a current that rises up and carries all of us with it. I swallow the momentary sadness down and allow myself to be buoyed. Today is a happy day.

"So what did you think of everyone?"

Zoey and Aaron spent the better half of the morning with us before leaving to give us some one-on-one bonding time. I met the coffee shop owner and her husband, and even their two small children. I also met Tomas, Kit's boss, who greeted me with a bear hug. I met the teller who always processes Gary's military pension checks, and the plant nursery worker who keeps Zoey in foliage. At every turn, there was another friend turned honorary family member whom Gary presented me to with a proud sweep of his arm.

We ate food truck chili dogs and shared a scoop of mint ice cream, which we brought Marcy a cone of, much to her delight. When navigating with the scooter became too exhausting for Gary, we laid in the grass of a nearby green space while the sun sank lower in the sky. For the first time in forever I felt I was a part of something bigger. A community that didn't see me for all that I was missing, but welcomed me for the one thing I had.

Gary.

"They were amazing," I say breathlessly as I help Gary back to his feet. And I mean it. Sure, there are people back home that I'd consider myself close to, including my best friend, Alicia, who has sent a massive amount of texts that await my reply. I know the postmaster and the grocery store clerks and the bank tellers. But today felt different. It felt right in a way I haven't in years.

I'm floating more than walking, whether because of the day I've had or the three hard ciders I drank with our dinner. Gary and I amble slowly down the sidewalk. Any remnants of the festival have been packed up, so our path is clear as we make our way to his apartment, where I'll help him up the stairs before heading back to my motel room.

It's my last night, but I'm already wishing for a thousand more.

He pats my hand, which I've wrapped around his elbow, a soft smile peeking out from his beard. "They liked you, too."

"How can you tell?" I ask, pursing my lips at nothing.

He shrugs. "I just know."

I take him at his word. We may have just met, but I feel like I've known him my whole life. Mom would have liked him. Loved him, actually. Dad, too. And for the first time this weekend, I allow that thought to overwhelm me. Waves of sadness sweep through me, painting the chambers of my heart the deepest shade of blue.

"I wish Mom could have met you," I manage to choke out.

He stills, stopping us just a few feet from the base of his stairwell, and unravels our arms. "I wish I'd met her, too. If she was anything like you, she was surely something special."

Something special. Kit's muttered words at the airport, that I now realize were probably just an echo.

My nose burns, the prelude to tears I don't want to cry. "I miss them both so much. No matter how much time passes—"

"It doesn't hurt any less," Gary finishes for me.

"Exactly." I think of the bridge at the edge of town whose guardrail split my parents' car in two. The river below that buried the pieces. I still go out of my way to avoid it, even so many years after the crash. There's no grinning and bearing it with a grief like that. There's only avoiding it till it catches up to you, then kicking like hell when it does its best to drown you.

"I don't mean to be forward, Tess, but..." Gary's voice is raw with emotion. He takes a moment to clear it, then reaches for my bicep and squeezes lightly. He meets my gaze with one as watery as my own. "I know you have a life in Alabama, but if you ever want... if you'd ever consider..." He wets his lips, then tries again. "Well, I'm just saying that Loveless can be a wonderful place to start over. That's all."

I brush him off with a sharp laugh. It's not the first time someone's suggested that I move. Whether it was my grandparents offering to send me far away from Fly Hollow for college, or strangers who felt like they knew my story enough to suggest I jet off to someplace their cousin-twice-removed lived in and loved. All things that implied my pain was something stationary, that I need only run away from in order to escape. As if I haven't tried.

And though it doesn't quite feel that way with my uncle, I can't kick the instinct to immediately dismiss the idea. Old habits die hard.

It's also impossible to ignore the fear that splinters through me as it always does when I feel tempted to run away from my life. Like a defibrillator shock to my system at the thought that I might abandon the people and places that still remember my parents, even if that memory hurts just as much, if not more, than its absence might most days.

"I can see you turning white as a sheet, so we'll move on as if I didn't mention it." He chuckles nervously. "It's just so good to have family again; I've gotten carried away. I apologize."

"Don't be sorry," I croak, surprising myself. I'm usually so good at keeping these types of feelings hidden from outward view. "It's very kind of you to offer. I just... I'm not sure I'm in the right place in my life for that. You know?"

Because starting over feels a lot like forgetting. As much as I might try to bury the past, I'm also never so far from it that I cannot find my parents if I reach for them. My grandparents, too, now that they're gone. Fly Hollow will always hold the version of me they knew, that everyone believes is real, even when I can't be convinced myself.

It also keeps me close to the Carmen. I think of standing in the airy lobby just two months ago on my annual trip. How close my parents felt, as they always do when I'm at the little seaside resort we frequented. It's strangely similar to the sense of nearness I've felt here in Loveless. A town they never stepped foot in that they're somehow a part of all the same.

"I know." My uncle pats my arm one more time, pulling me from the memory, then turns toward his wrought-iron staircase. "Loveless will win you over yet, Tess. You just wait."

I know it's not what he intended, but a certain dark-haired deputy flashes through my mind in an instant. I reach for Gary's elbow and scoop his scooter up with my other hand, shaking my head at thoughts that don't need encouragement. "I'll try to keep that in mind."

"Would you?" he says, punctuating his chuckle with a whistle. It's the first thing he's done that reminds me of my mother. And it makes me happy to know she's alive in him, too, even if the reminder that I'll never again hear her do the same brings stinging tears to my eyes.

Chapter Five

Kit

HER LAUGHTER PLAGUES my every waking thought for the rest of the day, which in all fairness, there aren't a lot of. I doze intermittently in the recliner in my living room, not even bothering with the bed. It'll take days for my sleep schedule to recover. I'm not as quick to bounce back as I was in my twenties, something that pains me to admit, almost as much as sleeping in this chair does.

The sun is setting on the other side of my blinds, painting my pathetically barren living room in an odd light. My ex made our house in Colorado Springs a home. I, on the other hand, suck at nesting. Even two years after moving here, I've not managed much more than a gaming system beneath the television and a side table for the recliner.

It feels a lot like holding my breath, though I have no clue what for.

As I blink into the settling twilight that leaks through my blinds, Tess's laughter fades into something else. My ears ring with her bright tone when Zoey apologized for the asinine comment about Gary being a father to the fatherless. Everything I've been trained for tells me Tess was covering the truth with too much positivity. One glance at her face when she turned to watch me approach—tense at the corners of an otherwise magnificent smile, green eyes hardened to jade river rocks—and I knew she was compensating for something.

Zo mentioned she'd been through a lot, and if my suspicions are correct, then saying so was short selling it. I picture my father, probably posted up in a La-Z-Boy none too different than this one. No matter how many years have passed since we shared a beer over an Ole Miss game, the idea of burying him hits me square in the chest. "*Fuck,*" I mutter. No wonder this weekend is so important to Tess. If she's lost her father, finding an uncle would be all the more meaningful.

Pain shoots up my back as I rise from the chair and stretch my spine. I stop the dryer mid-tumble and retrieve a clean T-shirt that I pull over my head. The fridge is disappointingly barren. I scrub a hand through my hair. There's only one fast food joint in Loveless, right on the outskirts of town. Looks like no matter how much I'd rather not, I'm hitting the road again tonight.

Part of me hopes going for a drive will help rid my thoughts of Tess at last. And it does, at first. Until I'm meandering home with a vanilla milkshake in hand and spot a tall, blonde figure in a sundress making her way down the quiet sidewalk along Main Street.

Against my better judgment, I pull onto the wrong side of the road and roll down my window. Snarky, offhand flirtations are usually my forte. But suddenly I can't think of a thing to say beyond, "Need a lift?"

She startles. When she glances over at me, her gaze appears red-rimmed in the streetlamp's glow. The vise of my ribs clamps tight around my lungs. I stop the slow roll of the car. She stumbles forward a few steps, then stops, turns around, and walks back to my window.

"You realize I'm only a block away from the motel, right?" She jerks her head in the direction she was walking. "I can literally see it from here."

Whatever sadness drove her nearly to tears, there's no trace of it in her voice. *And I thought I was a good performer.*

I press my lips together and lift my brows. Who am I to blow her cover? If she doesn't want to talk about it, I won't be the one to bring it up. "Just trying to be a gentleman."

She laughs, and it's more genuine than anything I've heard from her today.

"That's the Southern upbringing in you. Thought it would've died off by now." She bends at the waist, arms crossed over her chest, to peer into my vehicle. I've abandoned the cruiser in favor of my new Hellcat, an investment that was mostly wasted since I hardly ever drive it anywhere. The corner of her mouth ticks upward, and I feel the overwhelming urge to kiss her right at its bend. "Is that a milkshake?"

Not what I was expecting her to say. I glance down at the cupholder. "Yes?"

"What flavor?"

"Are you shopping or judging?"

She laughs again. It's by far my favorite prize. I'd exchange every medal I earned in the Air Force for its weight in Tess Monroe's laughter. "You can tell a lot about a man by his taste in milkshake flavors."

I grimace, letting my head fall back against the seat dramatically. "Now feels like a terrible time to mention it's vanilla."

Her spine straightens, and she throws her head back, shoulders shaking as she really gives the laughter her all. I force myself to hold my position, but inside my heart beats rapid-fire. The wind presses her dress against her body. She's all curved silhouette, long, golden legs, and shoulder-length blonde hair whipping in the breeze. I'm nothing but tense muscles, with a hard-on pressing into gym shorts that don't do enough to obscure it.

So of course, that's when she accepts my offer.

"Only if you'll share the rest of the milkshake," she says.

I shift in my seat, sending up a prayer for the first time in forever just to ask God to hide my boner. "Not afraid of cooties?"

She shrugs. "Not yours, anyway."

As she passes in front of my headlights, the wind picks up, nearly losing her the coverage of her skirt. I'm completely enraptured, most likely drooling, when she makes it to the passenger side and steps in.

The space around us is suddenly too small, with not enough air. I roll down the passenger window too, creating a cross breeze that carries the scent of sunscreen from her skin. Before I've even crossed back over to the correct side of an otherwise empty street, she's wrapping her lips around the straw of my milkshake and hollowing out her cheeks.

I'm gonna get blacklisted for the content of my prayers.

She smacks her lips softly and hums her satisfaction, lifting the cup in her hand to study it like it's an ancient tome rather than a fast-food beverage. Gold rings decorate each finger, some stacked three high and others adorned with gemstones in various shades of blue. "Not bad for vanilla."

"Vanilla is a wonderful, versatile flavor," I utter through a tense throat.

Out of the corner of my eye, I catch her smirk. "Spoken like someone who hasn't branched out with his flavors enough."

"I'll have you know that I've sampled many a flavor, thank you very much."

"Oh, I've heard. Your reputation precedes you, Kit Llewellyn."

Fucking Zoey, I swear to God. The Horseshoe Inn appears on our left, but I'm not about to leave this conversation where it's at. "Permission to keep driving so I have time to defend my honor?"

"Permission granted." She offers the milkshake to me, and I take a sip, forcing myself not to consider the overlap of our lips on the straw. "Though there's no need to defend yourself. I don't believe in shaming others for their sampling of the sundae bar, you know?"

I relax a smidge. I don't know why I even care. My ex and I started dating when we were only twenty, but in the years since our divorce, I've made no secret of my *sampling* as Tess calls it. It's not like that with her, though. And for some reason I want her to know I see her differently, even if I don't fully understand it myself.

"Good to know." It's dark out, the only light in the cab coming from my muted radio. I turn onto the county highway that'll carry us to the next town over. She doesn't complain, just goes on sipping. And I can't get her lips out of my mind for the life of me. If I'm going to have any hope of playing it cool, we've got to change the subject. "What's your favorite ice cream flavor?"

She quirks a brow. "Is that a euphemism?"

"No!" I shoot her a stunned glance. Mischief glints in her gaze. She's fucking with me. "Were you specifically sent to torture me?"

Her facial features still. When she speaks again, her voice is low. "Am I? Torturing you?"

I swallow. Something like pleading laces her tone. I recognize it as the same kind I keep buried deep inside, the one that wants someone, *anyone* to tell me that my company's worth keeping. Why does it feel so close to the surface tonight?

"Not at all."

She sighs. I'm not sure if she's satisfied or has just decided she doesn't want to continue down this path in conversation.

Either way, she leans back against her seat and shifts her gaze toward the darkened window. "Where are we headed?"

The road races from the darkness into the path of my headlights, only to be eaten up by my tires a moment later. "Nowhere in particular."

"Couldn't sleep?"

"Not really, no." I scratch the scruff forming along my jaw. I keep a shadow, but this is more midnight than five-o'clock. "How'd things go today with Gary?"

"Really good. It's been so great getting to know him. And everyone else." She takes another sip of the milkshake, and it hits the bottom of the cup. I glance over and she meets my gaze with one of embarrassment. "Oops. I think I finished your shake."

I pluck the empty cup from her hand and deposit it in the holder. "Somehow I'll forgive you."

She fans a hand over her heart. "Oh thank God. I wouldn't be able to face you again if you didn't."

"Afraid of conflict?" I ask, but really I'm thinking, *Will we see each other again?*

"Afraid of being labeled an ice cream bandit."

I chuckle at that, and it unravels some of the knot tying my throat. "You're definitely an ice cream bandit. Who likes vanilla, no less. What does that say about you?"

She straightens in her seat. I feel more than see her gaze when it settles on me. "That I'm wonderful and versatile. Or so I've been told."

I shake my head, and she giggles, the same trill that's been replaying in my thoughts all day. I suck on my teeth, recentering my focus. "You never said what your favorite was."

"Mint chocolate chip. You?"

"Pecan praline. What does that say about me?"

"That you're into nuts," she deadpans.

I make a U-turn on the empty highway, aiming back toward Loveless. "Bad news for you, huh?"

She snaps her fingers. "The good ones are always gay."

This woman is going to be the death of me. I steer the conversation back to safer ground, the opposite of the direction I'm used to going. "Tell me more about your time with Gary. I know he was really excited for you to come out here."

She's silent for so long that I'm beginning to wonder if she's going to answer. I remember the haze in her eyes when I first pulled up alongside her, and nerves pinch my stomach. Clearly something upset her, and I'm suddenly worried I've dredged it all up again.

"It was really wonderful." Her voice is soft as wild heather. Faraway. I find myself shifting closer to the center console, closer to her, in order to hear better. "I needed this, you know. To get away. Be with family."

Her mouth warms the word so much it melts on her tongue. It softens something in me, where I've remained solid as stone for years. "Does your family not live close?"

She shakes her head. I can hear the swish of her hair on her shoulders. "They're all gone."

All of them? I want to ask. But that would make me the biggest asshole on the planet, when the topic is clearly painful. Instead I reach for her knee without thinking and give it a squeeze. "I'm sorry."

She braces her elbow on the center console and balances her chin in her palm. She's so close I can feel her breath on my neck when she peers up at me. "Do you go home often?"

I shake my head, trying with everything I've got to ignore the heat building beneath my skin. "Practically never."

"Do you not get time off with the sheriff's department?"

"I haven't taken a vacation in years." It's a nonanswer, but I'm hoping she takes it.

The lights of Loveless grow brighter. We pass the road that leads to my house. I consider turning. Offering her a drink. But then I remember my pathetic bachelor setup and think better of it.

I want to be good enough for her, I realize. For anyone, just this once.

"Really? I go on a trip every May. There's this resort, the Carmen, about an hour over the Florida state line. I've been going since I was a little girl." Her smile is sad, her voice somber. "Always in the first two weeks, before a lot of the schools up north let out but after the water is warm enough to swim." She lifts off her chin, and for a moment I think she's going to move away. I'm already grieving the loss when she reaches for my hair and runs a hand through it. "It's your hair that smells so good, isn't it?"

A half smile is all I can manage, because my every thought, every nerve is focused on her hand in my hair. On wondering how it'd feel for her to tighten her fist and pull.

I turn onto Main Street, once again bearing down on the end of our night, though I never want it to come. "You like it?"

She draws in a breath and closes her eyes. "Mmm, yes. Smells like driftwood. Love it."

Her words cut through me like lightning. I blow out a breath just to release some of the intensity.

For a man who'd never consider himself a prude, I'm finding myself as horny as a fucking teenager where Tess is concerned. The most innocent touch has my insides in knots. And despite everything I've told myself about leaving her alone, it's beginning to be really fucking hard not to pull over and haul her into my lap.

Does she want that, too? Or is it simply wishful thinking?

"Do you go on your own? To the Carmen, I mean." I force my voice to remain casual while trying to suss out if there's someone waiting for her back home. I won't even consider going down this road if there is.

Her hand retreats as I pull into the parking lot of the motel. Marcy's shut down the office. A few lights glow behind various room curtains, mostly on the second floor, but it's largely quiet. Not the fanciest place—I've had more than a few calls to the Horseshoe for drug activity—but also the only option in Loveless, really. This time I have to fight the urge to invite Tess back to my place, not for sexual reasons but simply to know she's somewhere safe.

"Yeah, I go alone. It's a peaceful place. My little escape from the world."

That same raw tone fills her voice and strikes a chord in me. "I could use some peace," I sigh more than say. I put the car in park along one side of the U-shaped building, hoping it's the side she's staying on. When I turn to face her, she's watching me thoughtfully. It's so much worse than when I was driving. Seeing her like this, wavy hair windblown and lips pursed, sends my thoughts in a dangerous direction. My brain empties, till the only thing I can think of is wanting to taste her. "Maybe I'll check it out sometime."

"If you come in May, I'll be there."

I lift an eyebrow. "Is that an invitation?"

She laughs, green eyes glittering like jewels in the shadows. "If you want it to be."

Images of Tess swimming in the ocean fill my thoughts. Tess sunbathing poolside. Tess laid out on a white comforter, wearing tan lines and not much else. I nod like it's no big deal, though my erection claims otherwise.

Her chin juts toward the motel. "I better head inside. I'm having breakfast with Gary before Zoey takes me to the airport tomorrow."

"You're leaving already?" Am I pouting? This feels a lot like pouting.

"Yeah, just a quick trip. I'll be back eventually, though." A brief smile, then she's reaching for her seat belt. "Unless you tell everyone I steal ice cream. Then I'll have to go into hiding."

"Your secret dies with me." I draw an X over my heart, which pounds through my chest. "Can I walk you to your door?"

"There's that Southern charm." She winks. "I thought you'd never ask."

The night air is cool against my skin. As always in Colorado, the temps drop the moment the sun dips below the mountain peaks. By morning we'll all be sweating again.

And Tess will be on her way home. Why does that thought feel like a physical blow?

I covertly tuck myself into my waistband before rounding the hood of the car. Tess meets me in the middle, looping her arm through mine like it's the thousandth time instead of the first.

I'm on fire everywhere she touches me. She's tall, but I'm taller. From my vantage point, I can see the cowlick on the crown of her head. The slope of her shoulder, which is freckled from the sunshine. Darkness pools between her breasts where her dress cuts into a V, and I look away the minute I realize she's not wearing any bra that I can see.

"This is me," she says, pointing to the farthest door from the office on the first floor.

I could kill Marcy Evans. "Could you be in a less safe room?"

She turns to me, already laughing. "Don't worry. I'm a kickboxing instructor, remember?"

I clench my jaw, scanning the row of rooms between her and my car. Only one light is on in the rooms on this level, and there's no movement to be seen. Still, I don't love the idea of leaving her here.

"Hey." She tugs on my T-shirt, drawing my attention back to her. "I appreciate the concern, but I'll be okay."

"If you say so." But I'm already planning on checking the

property before leaving, just to be sure. As sure as I can be, anyway.

"I do. Say so, that is." Tess tilts her chin up. Her gaze dances over my face before settling on my mouth. My breath hitches.

Yellow light from a nearby streetlamp casts her features in an otherworldly glow. She smells like sunscreen and sugar. Like an addiction and salvation in one. We're so close I'm certain the wild thrum of my heartbeat must be audible. The effect she has on me is that palpable.

I'm on the edge of a very thin rope, barely listening to the voice in my head that tells me this is a bad idea when her tongue glances over her full bottom lip, testing my control.

One touch. How much harm could it really do? I raise my hand slowly, like she's a cornered animal and I only want to offer her safety. She doesn't blink. Doesn't breathe. I brush the backs of my fingers over her cheek, from apple to hollow to jaw. Soft. So fucking soft.

She sinks into it, and that is my final undoing.

"I'm going to kiss you, Tess." My voice is all rasp. Desire has scraped my throat raw.

Her heavy gaze locks with mine. "That a threat or a promise?"

I don't honor that with a response. Instead I tangle my hands in her hair the way I've wanted to since the moment I laid eyes on her. She surges upward at the same time I lean in. When we meet in the middle, the taste of vanilla floods my senses, and *plain* is the last word I'd use to describe it.

Our tongues brush, and she gasps. I take the opportunity to delve deeper, go harder, exploring until I find what makes her go wild. I drag my teeth over her bottom lip, and she throws her arms around my shoulders, clinging to me like I'll escape somehow otherwise.

Except I couldn't, even if I wanted to. I'm too damn caught up in this woman. A fact that'll scare me shitless in the morning, I have no doubt.

I back her into the door of her room and lift, hooking her legs around my hips. Her breasts are soft against my chest, nipples pebbled tight. I no longer care to hide my erection. I hope she feels how hard she makes me. When I roll my hips forward, testing her, her moan is everything I could hope for.

I slip a hand beneath her dress and find lacy underwear cupping her ass. In a stolen moment meant for gasping in air, I meet her gaze with a question in mine.

I watch her come to her senses in real time. I only wish I could say the same for myself.

"You should go," she whispers, our mouths still so close that her exhale is my inhale.

"Are you sure?" I ask, but I already know. A thousand thoughts glow in the emerald depths of her eyes, but they all lead to one conclusion.

It takes every ounce of strength I have to lock down my raging desire. To lower her to the ground. Straighten her dress. Retrieve her purse from where she dropped it on the ground and pluck her key from the outside pocket, then reach around her to insert it into the door. I push it open behind her, and hold. We're still so close that her heaving breaths brush her breasts against me. So close that the uncertainty coming off her in waves tastes bitter on my tongue.

She steps backward, once and then again until the doorknob is stolen from my grasp and she's half-hidden in the shadow of her dark room. A look of shock is frozen on her face. Shock at herself? At me? I have no clue. All I know is that I should've shown more restraint. I shouldn't have pulled over on the sidewalk.

Somehow I can't bring myself to regret all those shouldn'ts.

"Good night, Tess." I grab her doorknob once she's safely

inside. "If you want…next time you're in town…" I press my lips together. She's stone-still. Expressionless. I nod, leaving my words where they lie. "Sleep well."

I close the door and walk back to my car, which I drive around the perimeter of the property before leaving, even if leaving is the last thing I want to do. I might as well be on duty for the night, because I don't rest until the sun rises and exhaustion sweeps over me, finally drowning out thoughts of Tess's mouth on mine.

Chapter Six

Tess

No, I'm not sure.

That's what I wanted to say. Words I desperately willed my lips to form, my vocal cords to speak. But self-doubt settled like a cloak over me, and nothing came out. Now Kit's gone, and all I can think is that I've made some kind of mistake.

Whether that was kissing him or letting him leave, I couldn't say.

What the fuck am I doing? I'm here to spend time with my uncle. To explore what's left of the family I have in this world. This was not the time for some tryst, no matter how irresistible I find the dark, sarcastic deputy now driving away from me into the night.

I can't even blame it on being drunk, unless you count my double dose of ice cream today. A sugar high. It still courses through my veins, making my heart beat so fast I can feel the pulsing in my ears. It drowns out everything else. The hum of the AC unit. The distant rumbling of what little traffic is left on the roads. The ringing of my phone in my purse.

Crap. I fumble for it, catching a glimpse of Alicia's picture before I swipe to accept the call.

"Hello?" I sit at the edge of the saggy motel mattress, sinking into my own bones like I might dissolve entirely. Can my best friend hear how breathless I sound? How freshly kissed?

"I don't know why I bother texting anymore, when I know you'll never answer." Dishes clang in the background. I picture Alicia—dark hair, doe eyes, some vibrant lipstick color despite the fact that she's just doing late-night chores—bent over the sink of the little cottage in Alabama that she shares with her husband, Destin.

The familiarity eases some of my panic, and I flop onto my back, staring up at the pattern-stamped ceiling. "Sorry. It's been such a hectic weekend. I haven't texted anyone back, if that makes you feel any better."

"It does," she chirps. "So how's it going?"

I hold a clammy palm to my flushed cheek, leeching some of its warmth. "Really good."

"Yeah, your tone screams enjoyment." Meanwhile hers drips with sarcasm.

"Sorry, it's just…been a day." I normally tell Alicia everything, but for some reason this feels too fragile. I don't know how *I* feel about it yet, so I'm not ready to hear her thoughts on the matter. I swallow a deep breath and tuck away the doubt. The insecurities. The desire still electrifying my skin. Then I slip into the version of me everyone else gets, even if I can't give it to myself. When I open my mouth again, my voice jumps an octave. "We've had the best time. It feels like I've always known him. And the whole town is so friendly." *So friendly they offer good-night kisses after giving you a ride home.*

"I'm happy for you, Tess." Alicia, savant that she is, is not fooled. "Are we going to just skip over how bedraggled you sounded when you picked up the phone?"

Shit. "Oh, it's nothing." I gnaw on my bottom lip, searching the swirls and loops of the yellowing ceiling for an excuse that's believable. "There's this guy, a friend of my uncle's, who's decided I'm the exciting catch of the day. Had a hard time taking no for an answer." I chuckle, but it's hollow. Guilt rings in my ears at throwing Kit under the bus, even if Alicia will never meet him. He deserves better, and I know it.

There's no time to reel in the words, though, because Alicia is already howling. "Why am I not surprised? Tess Monroe strikes again, bringing men and women to their knees in every city from sea to shining sea."

"Ha ha," I say flatly. Time for a change in subject. "Why are you up so late anyway?"

"Destin's on rotation tonight at the hospital. Figured I'd check on my best friend instead of binge watching *The Office* for the thousandth time."

"I'm honored, truly."

"As you should be." She chuckles softly. "When do you land tomorrow?"

That reminds me, I need to check in for my flight. I put Alicia on speakerphone and toggle screens to pull up my airline app. "Not till late. I imagine I'll be back to Fly Hollow by nine or ten, depending on delays."

She clicks her tongue. "So no catch-up drinks, then."

"Maybe later this week?"

"That would be nice." There's a muffled scraping, like she's shifting her phone from one ear to the other. "Actually Delilah Ridgefield moved back to town recently. Would you wanna do a girls' brunch with her? I think she could really use it."

The name rings a distant bell. I rack my brain, finally pulling up an image of a girl who was in Alicia's grade, with light brown hair and a father who taught music at our school. Said father had an affair with another teacher a year or so after I graduated, which became the town's gossip topic of choice for months on end. I'm ashamed to say that, at the time, I was just grateful to share the tragedy spotlight for once.

No wonder she stayed away till now.

"Sure, I'd like that," I say finally.

"Great!"

I glance at the glowing red numbers on the clock beside the bed. It's close to midnight, and I'm supposed to meet Gary bright and early at his place. "I've got to go, Alicia. I'm already exhausted *for* me tomorrow."

She chuckles. "Sounds good. I'll text you once I figure out a day that works with my schedule. I'm almost done packing up the classroom for renovations, so should be available later this week. Love you big, you charming monster. Try not to steal the hearts of any more unsuspecting people before coming home, yeah?"

My throat constricts, but I force my words out in what I hope doesn't sound like the nervous squeak it is. "Yeah. See you soon. Love you."

"Good night." She makes a kissing sound into the phone, which I return, and then the line is dead. It's just me, the leaky faucet dripping in the bathroom, and my thoughts, which circle like vultures.

I have no faith I'll be getting any sleep tonight.

Gary arranged for an impressive array of treats from the coffee shop downstairs, which he somehow convinced the owner, Rose, to hand deliver for him before my arrival. They sit alongside two to-go coffees adorned with the 8th & Main logo on his time-worn dining table in the small living space of his apartment.

I peer out one of three tall windows on the far end of the room, which overlook Main Street from a prime vantage point above Nomads. The perfect spot for some young student from the nearby college town, wanting nightlife at their fingertips, but all I can think of is how annoying it must be on Friday and Saturday nights when the bar stays open late and music vibrates the floors.

"Oh my God." I turn to Gary, whose gaze sparks with amusement at my sudden outburst. "Am I getting old? All I can think about is how loud Nomads must get on the weekends, and how hard that would make it to sleep."

He sucks on his teeth, leans forward on both elbows, and meets my gaze resolutely. "Not old, but perhaps a fuddy-duddy."

I snort, disturbing the surface of my latte. "God, you sound like my parents."

"An honor." He dips his chin, his snowy beard nearly submerging in his cup.

"You say that," I tease. In reality, I can't imagine better people to emulate.

Silence settles between us. He's studying me, perhaps smiling, though it's hard to tell with the beard. It doesn't feel uncomfortable. There's no need to fill it like there is with everyone else. I'd forgotten how nice it is, to just sit in the acceptance of family. Not something everyone gets from their bloodline, but I had it in spades.

How many mornings did I sit with my mom before school, her sipping coffee while I picked at a frozen waffle and pondered my plans for the day? Something I took for granted, thinking I'd have a lifetime of mindless mornings to spend with her. Turns out lifetimes aren't always the lengthy measurement you think they are.

"What are you thinking about, Tess?"

I bite at my bottom lip, gaze lifting from the scratched wooden tabletop to meet his gray eyes. "It's going to bring the mood down."

He chuckles dryly. "Try me."

He's right, I suppose. If I can't be honest here, where else can I be? Aside from Kit's car, apparently. "I'm wondering why my parents had to die. They were so good, you know? Just genuinely wonderful people. They deserved better."

He nods like he understands completely. And perhaps he does. He lost his wife, Wendy, far too soon. Cancer, I think. We don't talk about the details of their deaths often. Only the holes they created in our lives.

Age spots riddle his hand. It settles over mine, taking up a soothing pat on my knuckles. "If I've learned anything, it's that the universe doesn't give a damn what we deserve. If you want better, you have to take it for yourself. *Today.* Because that's all the time you can be sure you've got."

I press my lips into a firm line. For a moment I can sense Kit's hands heating my lower back. His mouth slanted over mine. Then it disappears, replaced by the forlorn resolution in his gaze when I froze on the spot. "I'm afraid I haven't been doing that very well lately."

"You came here, didn't you?" Gary grins around the lip of his cup. Coffee dribbles onto his teal fishing shirt, which I'm beginning to suspect is the only kind of top he owns. "You took the DNA test. That's something."

I try to see myself through his eyes. A woman with no family of her own, late twenties, no career to speak of, who put herself out there and flew halfway across the country for just the shot at building a bond with the uncle she never knew. I like to believe I'd find that woman brave, too, if I didn't see her in the mirror every day.

"That's something," I echo.

"Speaking of, I was thinking of visiting in the fall, if you don't mind. And you could come here for Christmas, if you don't have any plans."

Christmas last year was spent working retail to keep my mind off the empty rooms of my house, a sprawling ranch-style home that once belonged to my grandparents. I can't seem to convince myself to sell it, no matter how impractical it is for just one person.

I'm about to agree, but then I imagine running into Kit. What will I say to him? I can't avoid him forever, not if I want to continue being a part of my uncle's life. But just the thought of his wounded expression before he masked it over brick by brick and shut the door at my feet, has me wavering.

"Er, I might not get that much PTO with this gig." The truth is, Harvey lets me have free rein of his gym and my schedule, so long as the dues keep coming in. But what Gary doesn't know won't hurt him. And besides, who knows how long I'll be at the job anyway. "If you'd be up for spending Christmas with me, then maybe I can see about coming back here late next summer?"

A year feels like a good enough buffer. Kit will have long forgotten me by then, surely.

"Sounds like a plan." Gary's eyes glint as he smiles, crow's feet forming webs on either side of his face. "I promise to be all healed up by then so I don't have to pass you off to the kids to be chauffeured."

"I could've easily rented a car."

"You shouldn't have to." He shrugs one shoulder. "Besides, they all owe me for the endless entertainment I provide to their otherwise mediocre lives."

We both gaze at his foot where it's propped on a pillow in his other chair. He grabs a wooden spoon off the pony wall dividing the living area from the kitchen and slips the handle inside his boot, eyes rolling back when he scratches what must be a bothersome itch.

I wrinkle my nose. "Sure, I guess gore is entertainment to some."

He swats at me with the spoon, and I squeal, lurching away.

"You're a menace." He yields the spoon like a waggling finger, admonishing me with a grin on his face. "But I love you."

My heart is all at once too big for my chest, yet so small I'm not sure I have enough room for the way I feel to fit in it. I practically leap across the space between us, loop my arms around his neck, and plant a kiss on his polished head. "Love you, too, Gary. Thank you. So, so much."

"Anytime, kiddo." He pats my arm. His voice is thick. Strangled. He clears his throat and presses on. "Zoey will be here any minute to pick you up. I'm sorry I can't come with you. Going that long without my leg propped up is, quite frankly, hell right now."

I sit back. "I know you'd be there if you could be."

"Sure would. I'd scream and jump up and down. Embarrass both you and Zoey without hesitation." He smiles. "I really am sorry, though. I wanna make sure I'm doing this uncle thing right, and being tied down by this old boot doesn't help."

"You're doing it perfectly. An old pro," I say, forcing my voice to stay steady.

"Who are you calling old?" He narrows his eyes, squeezing my arm where it rests on his clavicle. "I'm not the one complaining about the youths and their late-night partying."

We dissolve into laughter, the bubble of emotion popped. We remain that way until Zoey arrives and I pile into her car, headed for Denver. It distracts my heart from thinking about Kit and how different this drive was with him by my side.

It's for the best.

Chapter Seven

Kit

I SPEND four months swearing under my breath that I'll forget her. A single drunken evening researching the resort she mentioned visiting every summer. Two months reminding myself that it's a bad—and quite frankly, creepy—idea to show up there when she's most likely forgotten our kiss even happened.

One mulling over the fact that *she* invited *me,* after all.

At three months out, on a night of profound weakness, I book the flight.

A week before, I tell myself there's still time to cancel the reservation. Who wants to go to some resort in the Gulf chasing a girl he can't forget anyway? I've got two weeks of PTO to waste. I can go anywhere in the world.

But when the day comes, I'll be damned if I don't get on the plane.

May

Chapter Eight

Tess

THE FIRST TIME Ted and Marissa Monroe stayed at the Carmen Beach Resort, they knew it was something special.

It was their honeymoon, and because they'd married young, a trip to the nearby Gulf Coast was all they could afford. The resort was little more than an oversize shack at the time, with clapboard siding and a rotten back porch that led to the sea. It wasn't a bad thing, though, because they were in that kind of love that makes even the most humble date nights feel like a grand affair. They played in the surf, ate jumbo Gulf shrimp and oysters until their bellies were nearly bursting, then stayed up all night chatting while huddled close beneath sandy sheets as they dreamed of the life they'd build together.

One that, a few years later, would grow to revolve around me.

The Carmen grew bigger, too, but maintained its charm. My parents had a regular room on the top floor with a view of the water. It was jokingly named the Marilyn Suite, golden plaque and everything, as a riff on our last name and my mother's gorgeous blonde hair. When I picture Mom and Dad, he's wearing a Cuban-style linen shirt and her sundress billows around toned, suntanned legs. They're leaning against the white railing of their balcony, laughing at some joke that only makes sense to them.

My grandparents continued bringing me here after my parents were killed, but staying in that room was too difficult for them. Too many memories, especially for my grandmother, who never quite got over the loss of her daughter and son-in-law.

It wasn't until she, too, was gone and my grandfather became too sick to come with me that I reclaimed my parents' room. Mauricio, the operations/maintenance/a little-bit-of-everything manager, was overjoyed. The room still smelled like them. Or maybe my memories of them are so wrapped up in this place that, to me, they smelled like the room. They were everywhere, from the pergola covering the rooftop bar that they helped the owners, Alex and Jenna, select to the mimosa tree the gardeners let Dad and me plant by the entrance when I was six.

Even now, as I walk through the sliding glass doors into the lobby, I swear Dad's booming laughter is echoing from the hall that leads to the elevator bay on my right. Mom's espadrilles slap the seashell-colored tile just to my left, at the edge of my vision. I turn, half expecting her to be standing by the coffee counter with her arms wide open, welcoming me home.

Because that's what the Carmen is to me. Home. With all its pain and comfort wrapped up in an ocean-blue bow.

"*Mi querida Tessa.*" Mauricio sweeps me up in his cigarette-and-cologne scent before I've even spotted him. I squeeze him back, peppering kisses along his cheekbone as he does the same to me. "*Te extrañé.*"

"I missed you, too, Mo."

We retreat to cupped elbows, scanning each other for new scars or fashion movements (I'm not sure which). He smiles, folding his tan face into joy. I mirror it, though my heart is still throbbing with nostalgia.

It's a relief, knowing if some of the grief leaks through my facade that I won't be judged for it. The Carmen is the one place where I can be honest. Where I don't owe anyone my composure. I just exist here, in this limbo at the edge of my real life. For the rest of the year, the staff here do not know me. So what does it matter if a tear falls in their opalescent lobby even as I smile?

Mo swipes my cheek clean without faltering. "How beautiful you are. More like your mamá every day, Tessa." His accent is thick, landing firmly on each consonant. He's also the only person in the world I'd let add an *A* to the end of my name. "So grown up I can hardly bear it."

"*Gracias, Tío.*" Despite his persistence through the years, my Spanish is abysmal, but he loves it when I try. Even my simple phrases earn a wash of pride over his expression. "I'm literally thirty, though."

He mock spits on the ground to my right, his left, then says, "Not possible. Because that would make me old, and I do not feel old, *querida.*"

I rub a thumb over the wrinkle between his dark, bushy brows. "You're not old, Mo. Simply experienced."

He blows a raspberry that trickles into laughter. "Come; the ladies will not allow me to keep you to myself much longer."

With an arm around my shoulders, he takes control of my ratty suitcase and guides us both toward the check-in desks in the far left corner of the room. Every surface here is white or beige or some shimmery shade of almost-pink or almost-blue that gives the impression that you're gazing at the inside of a conch. Couches and tables arranged haphazardly throughout the space allow people to enjoy the view through the windows along the back wall, which face the pool deck and, beyond that, the Gulf.

The desks—three stand-alone pods forming a half circle—are framed with driftwood boards harvested from the beach. Exposed wooden beams traverse the lofty ceilings overhead, with fans constructed to look like palm fronds dropping from them. They circle lazily, stirring up the Florida humidity that gets swept in each time the door opens behind me.

I tug my blouse away from my chest, allowing some of that air to cool my sweat-dampened skin. It's not busy season yet. A few regulars, whom I acknowledge with a nod, pass through the lobby on their way to the half-empty parking lot. Give it two weeks, though, and the place will be slammed with every tourist along the I-65 corridor.

The desks on either end are empty. In the center pod, two familiar women huddle close. Jenna glances up from a paper she's been studying on the raised counter that shields the computer from view, her brown gaze finding mine and instantly illuminating. "Tess!"

Jenna co-owns the Carmen with her husband, Alejandro, who is Mauricio's older brother. Their daughter, Xiomara, is poised in front of the computer to her mother's left. She started working here officially when she turned sixteen two years ago, though she, like me, has been around the place since infancy. Mara tears her gaze from the key jacket she'd been scribbling on and squeals at the sight of me.

Mo barely releases me in time for the women to envelop me in an embrace that's all pointy limbs and long, dark hair.

"Ouch!" I pull away, laughing while rubbing my sore boob. "Someone nailed me with an elbow."

"Can you blame us?" Jenna squeezes her daughter since she's been rejected from squeezing me. "We're just so excited. Tess time is our favorite time of year."

Despite a forty-year age difference, the two women could be twins. Short and thin but strong, both built like gymnasts. Ears that poke out from their lush, dark hair and skin that's always kissed by the sun. Jenna struggled for years with infertility. She finally got pregnant with Mara by accident just when she figured her fertile days—if she'd ever had any—were long behind her. I remember the summer we showed up to find a rosy-cheeked and swollen-stomached Jenna, and all the summers after where I pretended Mara was the baby sister I never had.

"Can't blame you at all." I stick my tongue out at Mara. "Wasn't sure if I'd get to see you this year or if you'd be too busy with college prep."

"If you had social media, you'd know I deferred a year." She flips her hair over her shoulder as she circles her mother, returning to her spot in front of the computer. "I'm going to travel the world first."

My rounded gaze meets its match in Jenna's. "Is that so?"

Jenna crosses herself but doesn't comment. I can't imagine it's easy to loosen the reins on a baby you never thought you'd get to have.

"Yep. Some friends and I are going to backpack through Europe. Have you ever been?"

I tug at one of Mara's curls. "I spend all my vacation hours with you, you dork. When would I have been to Europe?"

Mara shrugs and types something, probably my name, into the computer. I unzip my purse and reach for my wallet, but a firm hand lands on my wrist, stopping me.

"Not a chance," Jenna says, glaring.

"You know the rules. Monroes stay for free at the Carmen." Mauricio pats my back, his eyes crinkling at the edges. "Though I wouldn't say no to help if you feel like folding sheets."

"I'd rather give you my next paycheck," I tease, bumping him with my hip. Internally the realization that I'm the only Monroe left carves out a notch in my heart that I'll be nursing for days.

We all seem to think it at once, because a silence falls between us save for the click of Mara's nails against the keyboard.

Discomfort settles in the nape of my neck. No matter how hard I try to make returning to the Carmen a happy occasion, somehow the sadness always leaks through. I clear the lump from my throat, plastering a smile on my face to remind everyone I haven't actually forgotten how to make the expression. "You know what's crazy? I actually found out last year that I have an uncle. Mom had a half-brother that she never knew about."

"That's amazing!" Mo says just as Mara adds, "When do we get to meet him?"

My smile thins, and I glance from Mo to Mara to Jenna in turn. "Well, he lives in Colorado, so even I haven't seen him since Christmas. But next summer, maybe."

I try to picture Gary here, in one of his fishing shirts and a pair of cargo shorts, surrounded by the shimmering lobby. Enveloped in an embrace by the Ortiz family. Witnessing me floating down the halls like a waif or saturated with grief as I lie in the same room where my parents made plans for the years that lay before them, never realizing how few there would be.

A haze of tears like fogged glass clouds my vision. My friends become a blur of colors before me. Funny how easy it is to only remember the sunshine and salty skin and sand-ridden carpets when I'm away from here. The minute I step through the door, it's like I become a different version of myself. A truer one, I fear.

"Is that where you met your man?" Jenna asks, completely missing whatever mist has suddenly turned my eyes overcast.

I blink once, twice, to clear it. "My man?"

She laughs. Mo hip checks me. Mara places my key card on the counter, and even she is smirking.

"No need to play coy with us. Christopher arrived yesterday, and Mara here had the pleasure of checking him in, but we all watched the security footage after." Jenna's full lips curve wickedly. "Very handsome, Tess."

"I'm sorry." I shake my head, trying to reel my thoughts back to a place where what they're saying makes sense. "Christopher who?"

Mo scratches his temple. "Something with an L?"

Mara's nails clack rapidly, the light reflected on her face changing as a new screen loads. "Llewellyn."

"He was asking for you. Said he was meeting you here." Jenna's eyebrows rise. "Is that not— Did you not invite him?"

My chest flutters like my heart has grown wings and is desperately attempting to fly away. Or I'm having a heart attack. The odds are fifty-fifty, favoring no one. In a matter of seconds I'm thrown from grief to something else entirely, with no way for my body to make the journey between the two.

Heaviness settles in my limbs as the image of a dark, broody cop fills my belly with unwelcome warmth. Kit is here. *Here.* Either in a room that looks too similar to mine or at the lima bean–shaped pool where I learned to swim or in the ocean, the water tousling his hair and making his skin at once sticky and deliciously salty. He's at the Carmen. *Right. Now.*

Did I invite him? Well, yes, I guess I kinda did. In a joking way, though, right? I was being flirtatious, drunk on ice cream and the scent of his hair gel and filled with the kind of confidence that only comes from conversations held in the dark cabin of a car. I never thought he'd actually show up. Never actually *hoped.*

That's a lie, if only a small one. For that brief moment after the words spilled from my lips and before they tripped into other, more scandalous thoughts, I allowed myself to imagine it. Lying close to him in a cloud of white bedding, the sound of the waves drifting through a cracked balcony door. But in my wildest dreams I never thought it would feel so thick with terror and vulnerability. That beneath it all would be a thread of anticipation, bubbling up like an unwelcome illness in the midst of the overwhelm.

"Tess? Should we be concerned?" Jenna asks.

"I'll call the police on him if you'd like," Mara offers with a shrug.

"No, no." I suck in a breath. When I open my mouth again, I

pray my voice comes out level. "I'm just…surprised, is all. We haven't talked in a while, and I… I guess I assumed he wouldn't come." *Haven't talked at all, actually.* Not since that night outside the Horseshoe.

Everyone is staring at me. Even if I couldn't see them, I'd feel their gazes on me like a thousand tiny pinpricks in my skin.

I stuff fisted hands into the oversize pockets of my boyfriend jeans. Grip. I need to get a fucking grip. "Sorry, what room is he in?"

Never mind that I don't know what I'll do with that knowledge. I'm teetering between avoiding him like the plague and hunting him down to rip him a new one for not calling first.

"We're not really supposed to say—" Mo starts.

"It's 326," Mara interjects, eyebrow raised.

Fuck. *Fuck.* "Okay." I grab my key packet from the counter and force a smile. "Thank you." Mo fights me for control of my bag, a question still in his gaze, but I pry it away in the end. "I've got it, *Tio.* See you all around?"

Jenna takes a step toward me. "Tess, if—"

"So good to see you again! Really!" I toss over my shoulder, already making a break for the elevator bay down the hall. An alarmed family plucks their toddler from my path. I don't slow down. Don't apologize. Heat is flooding my face, my throat, my head until I can hardly see to press the button that will summon the elevator.

By some miracle of the universe, it's already on the ground floor and closes behind me blessedly fast. I want to sag into the railing, but I can't, because realization is sweeping over me like a splash of cool water. Kit has to leave. I can't trust myself to be levelheaded when that man is around, if our making out on the porch of the Horseshoe Inn is any indication. The raw, aching grief that I only allow this close once a year… I can't do that with him here, distracting me. Because there's no doubt in my mind that he will if given the chance.

I press the button for the third floor. My spine is rigid. My stomach twists with anticipation. I'm going to see Kit again for the first time since our kiss. A fist closes around my heart, whether to protect it or wring my feelings dry, I couldn't say.

A bell chimes and the doors slide open. I spill from the elevator and turn right, then left, climbing the spine of the L-shaped building. My feet move without needing instruction on where to go. Of course they don't. We've walked this path a thousand times before.

At the end of the long hallway, I stop, the wheels of my suitcase nearly taking out my ankles in the process. I become my pulse. Every nerve ending in my body flickers with its beat. With a trembling hand, I knock. It doesn't take long. Almost like he could sense me coming.

He appears from behind the opening door like an apparition. The way my parents would still be standing in the kitchen in the days after their funerals. Something I willed into existence. Now I have to will him right out of it.

Our gazes meet, green grass and the earth that lives beneath it, and he smiles, stealing my breath away. "You're here."

"I am." My voice is surprisingly calm. Stronger than I feel. I stand taller, even as I white-knuckle my suitcase handle. Every ounce of fear, I siphon into some sense of authority, praying it hides the truth well enough. "But you shouldn't be."

Chapter Nine

Kit

I'VE SPENT the last twenty-four hours thinking I made a huge mistake. Pacing my living room. The airport. Fuck, even this long hallway after I realized the woman at the registration desk knew Tess. And why wouldn't she? It's not like Tess has been coming here for God knows how many years or anything.

I've had ample time to stew over my bad decisions. To wonder what in the hell I was thinking, being so confident as to show up here without a single word shared between us since that night last July.

But that all disappears when I lay eyes on her beautiful face.

It doesn't matter that she's clearly upset. It should, but I'm too damn excited.

Ten months is a long time. Enough to wonder if I imagined what we shared. Enough to question every word, every touch, until I've dissected it into nothing more than a bunch of coincidences. But this… this *relief* that washes over me the minute I see her. That cannot be a coincidence. Even if I don't know what the hell to make of it.

Because this desire, these feelings… they're the opposite of everything I've said I want. No attachments, right? That's how I avoid a repeat of my failed marriage and all the pain that came as a result. But one look at Tess and I can't help it. Regardless of the red flags waving in my mind, I want to see this through.

She does, too, even if she won't admit it. She may be scowling, but I've been trained to read every impulse. Every hint that someone is faltering. And in that millisecond after I opened my door, before her walls could go up, I saw it. Just as I felt it.

Relief.

"Hello? Earth to Kit." She jabs a pointed nail into my chest. "Did you hear what I said? You have to leave."

"Sorry, the jet lag must have affected my hearing," I say, dramatically digging a knuckle into my right ear canal. "Could you repeat it one more time?"

I'm goading her, and I know it. But a part of me can't resist. The part that loves how she looks all hot and bothered. Emphasis on bothered. She narrows her eyes, not honoring me with a response. I rest a hip against the doorframe, a sly grin stretching my lips north even as hers curve due south. At least if she's irritated, she can't be whatever it is that I keep catching glimpses of when she forgets she's putting on a performance. Scared? Hurting? Two things I don't know how to fix.

But an angry woman is my specialty.

"I know you heard me," she says flatly.

Okay, so she's not in the mood for banter. "You do recall that you're the one who invited me in the first place, right?"

Her arms cross. I doubt she knows it pushes her cleavage into view. I drag my gaze from her chest back to her face, which is painted red with agitation. She huffs a breath, and it's a bit like watching a golden retriever prepare to fight. She's cute when she's mad, and although I'm sure she *could* kill me, I also know that she won't.

"I'm sorry, regardless of how much of a cocky bastard you are, there is no way you thought that showing up without a single text or call ahead of time would be received *warmly*," she bites out.

Point made. "I certainly didn't think it'd be received this poorly, either."

Her arms fly wide, then slap against her hips. "You have to go, Kit. You can't be here."

"Why not? Is your boyfriend on his way?" It's a cheap, immature shot. One I'll be cringing over later. But it's out now. No reeling it back in. Best to just own it.

She deflates into herself, the corners of her eyes crinkling slightly. "No. I just… can't do this. Not here. Not with you."

Sadness coats her words. Never mind I don't know what *this* is; I desperately want to find out just so I can take that feeling away from her. It's dangerous territory, a landscape I recognize only after I've blown past the warning sign. The last time I cared this much about a woman's feelings, I'm the one who ended up broken.

I stand up straight and measure the space between us with an upturned palm. "Clearly we get along. What's so bad about spending this vacation with me? Or, worst-case scenario, on the same property as me. Surely you can avoid me if you want to that badly."

Please don't want to.

We're standing so close I could reach out and brush the stray wave from her face. She's wearing a flowy white tank top, and I can see that she's covered in goose bumps despite the heat. She hides so much of what she's feeling behind her facades. First the vivaciousness in Colorado, and now frantic irritation. I'm so tempted to touch her. To read her thoughts like they're written in Braille on her flushed skin. I curl my fingers into a fist, knowing better than to give in to that particular inclination.

"Not possible," comes out in a pained whisper. She punctuates it with a wince.

Something like hope springs up in my chest. Perhaps staying away is as hard for her as it is for me. "And why not?"

She stares at me for so long I'm afraid she may never answer. Finally, with a heavy sigh, she jabs a thumb over her shoulder. "Because that's my room."

My gaze lands on the golden plaque mounted next to the door perpendicular to mine. *The Marilyn Suite.* I noticed it last night. Briefly considered how much better the view must be, with mine facing the pool deck and that one seemingly angled toward the ocean. Then I promptly forgot about it as I downed five beers and tried to imagine how this reunion would go.

Safe to say, this wasn't one of my favored scenarios. Cocky as I am, I do have enough self-awareness to feel a stab of guilt that I've invaded her space this thoroughly. "Shit. I'm sorry, Tess."

She softens at the sound of her name. Almost imperceptibly, if I weren't already so attuned to her body language. Her shoulders slump. Cheekbones lose their tension. She sucks in her plump bottom lip and bites down, sending stars across my vision.

"I can ask to be moved? I'm sure they have other rooms open." The place hasn't seemed that busy. I remember her mentioning school gets out in a few weeks, so I imagine the crowds really ramp up then.

She shakes her head softly. I want to be the hair dusting her shoulders. A ridiculous thought, but I feel it in my very core.

What the hell is this woman doing to me?

"I can't do this with you." Her voice is low, but not so much that I can't hear it breaking.

The air around us shifts. In an instant it goes from electric to something heavier. I want to fold her into my chest. Hold her till whatever is fracturing that confident exterior of hers is gone for good.

"Do what?" I say, but what I really mean is, *Let me in.* I'd settle for a fraction of the honesty we shared in my car that night in Loveless. An ounce of the vulnerability.

As though she realizes she's slipping, she sucks in a breath and squares her shoulders. Her cheeks are still flushed, but her green eyes are bright. Glistening, like she's blinked back a few tears she refuses to cry.

She's retreating, and I suddenly, desperately want to bring her back out before she disappears from sight.

"I came to see you, you know."

Her lips part. Close. Then, "When?"

"That next morning, after…" I let my voice trail off, but I can tell she remembers our kiss. Her chest crests and falls on rapid breaths. That pretty blush spreads down her throat. I want to trace its path with my tongue, but I settle for trailing it with my gaze. "I went to the inn. You didn't answer the door, and I was… concerned. So I checked with the front office. Marcy said you'd checked out just thirty minutes prior."

The owner had looked at me like I'd grown a second head when I asked where Tess was. Then, when the realization dawned, she'd smiled ear to ear.

"Then I drove to Gary's place, but you'd already left with Zo for the airport."

If I thought Marcy was perplexed by my motives, Tess's uncle was downright suspicious.

Tess clears her throat, her delicate hand landing there like it might assist her somehow. Her familiar stack of rings glitters in the hall light. "Why?"

"Because I couldn't not." It's the simplest explanation in the world, but the only one I have.

Just like I couldn't not get on that plane yesterday. Whether I understand it or, quite frankly, want to feel it, where Tess is concerned, my actions are more impulse than conscious thought.

A wrinkle forms between her brows. "Gary never mentioned it."

I chuckle miserably. "Yeah, well, that's probably because he essentially told me to fuck off. Said things were tough for you right now, and the last thing you needed in your life was someone like me."

It'd hurt, but I couldn't exactly argue. Not when all he'd ever seen from me was mindless flirtation and brief situationships that ended as quickly as they began. I couldn't tell him how I felt for Tess was different. Not when I could hardly admit it to myself, much less decide what *different* meant in the long run for either of us.

He'll be none too pleased when Tomas reveals where I've run off to.

Tess grabs her suitcase handle and uses her other hand to retrieve a key packet from her pants pocket. Her expression has gone blank. All that heat, all that life has been locked away. She turns, crosses the hall, and reaches for the door to her room. The small keypad beeps and the latch groans. In seconds she's pushing it open, and the blue-white light of the sky floods the hall from the balcony windows I catch a glimpse of on the far end of the suite.

"Tess—"

She glances over the sharp right angle of her shoulder. "You should've listened to him, Kit."

With that, she lets the door fall closed.

You should've stayed gone. A different voice, echoing through the years. I can't help but fear my ex-wife was right even then.

I stumble back into my room. The door shuts with a resounding thud. Through the gap in my balcony door, laughter trickles up from the pool. I pull it open wider and slip outside. Wet heat coats my skin in a matter of seconds. I brace my elbows on the white-painted railing and hang my head.

What *am* I doing here? Did I think I'd just show up and Tess would be overjoyed? That we'd romp in the sunshine for the next two weeks and then she'd finally be out of my system and I could move on?

She deserves better than that. And I'm an idiot if I thought that's how this would work.

Something about Tess makes me lose all sense of reality. I'm not this person. Not anymore, at least. The last flight I got on for a woman, I arrived home just to find her in bed with someone else. It damn near ruined me. I swore right then that I'd never let my heart lead the way again.

And yet, here I am.

Courtney was nothing like Tess, I quickly remind myself. She was selfish. Conniving. She wanted a comfortable life at home, everything she could ever want provided, and not much else. Not from me anyway. From every other airman on base? Well, that was another story.

But I was young and thought myself in love, and the rest was a blur of wedding bells and, when I joined the Air Force, long periods of me being away. She thrived when I was gone, unlike the other airmen's wives. I prided myself on choosing an independent woman. Boy, was I an idiot.

Before I can fall too far into the canon of my own misery, my phone buzzes. I retrieve it from my back pocket, half hoping that a certain blonde has decided to change her mind.

My father's name appears, followed by a grainy picture of his thumb and, in the background, a largemouth bass. He's sent it in a group chat with me and my brother that only the two of us ever participate in, but you can't blame the man for trying.

DAD

Set a personal record today with this guy!

ME

That's impressive, Pops. Looks like you're eating good tonight.

DAD

If you hop on a plane right now, I can have him ready in time for a late dinner. Gage is coming by too!

My chest tightens its vise grip on my lungs. I swallow hard, willing the emotion back from whence it came. I'll have to text Gage separately, to warn him not to hit them up for money. I groan inwardly. How did this become our life?

ME

Not tonight, but soon. I miss you guys.

DAD

Sounds good, son. We miss you more.

I can read between the lines of his text. He's as close to believing my promise as I am to meaning it.

In a new thread, I fire off a message to my brother. Within seconds he reacts with a thumbs-up. So he *is* by his phone, he just can't be bothered to acknowledge our parents unless they're offering a free meal.

A minute later my phone vibrates again.

GAGE

Can you spot me for some groceries? Between jobs right now and money is tight.

ME

When are you not between jobs?

GAGE

You're a fucking prick, you know that?

Apparently no one ever taught my brother about catching more bees with honey.

After I've sent the money, I turn back to the room, toss my phone onto the bed, and retrieve my wallet from the neat pile of keys, wallet, and book to read that I left on the desk. Some autobiography of a veteran that I'll leaf through before dozing off tonight, and every night until I eventually give up and add it to the shelf of would-be-reads in my room back home. All the lives I should be learning from but am sleeping through instead.

With my hand on the door, I hesitate. What if I run into Tess in the hallway? Or worse, what if I don't?

I shake my head and yank the handle. The hallway is empty, much to my relief. And disappointment.

I'm well and truly fucked.

So I do what anyone would in my situation. I take the long hallway in quick strides, then bear right and continue past the elevator bay, to the restaurant at the other end of the floor and, beyond it, a rooftop bar.

If I'm going to be this close to Tess, yet unable to touch her, I'll be damned if I'm not soothing the ache with a drink, umbrella not required but appreciated.

Chapter Ten

Tess

Why didn't you tell me that Kit came to see you after I left last year?

Why didn't you tell me that you were going on a vacation with the boy?

BECAUSE I DIDN'T KNOW. I start to type the words out but hesitate, fingers hovering above my phone screen. Why, even distraught and, honestly, a little bit annoyed as I am, do I want to protect Kit? I blame the Neanderthalian version of me that thought, "*You, Tarzan. Me, Jane,*" and then mounted him like a tree outside my motel room last summer. It's obviously her fault I invited him here in the first place.

That's what I get for going too long without getting laid. The first warm-blooded, delectable-looking creature comes along, offering milkshakes and quick comebacks, and I'm throwing all rational thought to the wind.

When I find myself doing the sad calculation to find out just how long it's been since I last did the naked tango, I abandon my text thread with Gary and my half-unpacked suitcase in favor of the rooftop bar.

Anxiety weighs on my heart and, beneath it, confusion. How can I be so upset that he's here and still find myself hoping he's waiting for me in the hallway when I yank open my door? It doesn't make any sense.

I know I was right. About everything. I can't function with him here. And he shouldn't have come without warning me. But there's a part of me who relished every second we stood a mere foot apart for the first time in nearly a year. The same part that feels vindicated now that I know for certain I wasn't imagining the draw between us. Even with all the shock of seeing him, I feel it now, simmering beneath the surface. I'm simultaneously wishing he'd hop on the next plane back to Colorado, and wondering if he'd bottle up his sandalwood scent for me to spray my pillows with later tonight.

No. I wouldn't give him the satisfaction.

He's already dangerously confident. There's no other way to explain the level of absolute cognitive dissonance it would take to think showing up here was a good idea. I'll give credit where credit is due. The man is really fucking cocky.

Past the elevator bay, the hallway is devoid of hotel room doors. Instead the fogged-glass entry to the spa is on my right and a wall of windows on my left, giving passersby a view into the gym. It's barely more than a few cardio machines and a weight rack, but it does its job.

I wrinkle my nose as I catch a whiff of the plastic-y rubber mats that make up the gym flooring. A year at Harvey's was half a year too long.

My boss didn't really understand when I gave my notice last week. Offered a generous raise for me to stay on, especially since I didn't have a new gig lined up to take this one's place. But I never do. I don't ever know when the timer is going to run out on a job. I just wake up one day and know that I'm ready to move on. Alicia calls me restless. I don't think there's a word for what I am.

I'll find something else. I'm like a cat in that way, always landing on my feet.

The restaurant at the other end of the L-shaped building is suffering from a midafternoon lull. Come dinnertime, it'll be bursting at the seams. Topwater is the only restaurant for a few miles and therefore benefits from the captive audience of the Carmen's guests. Their only other option is driving thirty minutes in summer traffic to the nearby outlet mall, where chain restaurants and fried seafood abound.

It's also Alex's passion project, which is why I'm not surprised to find him behind the bar as I step out onto the patio portion of the restaurant.

He's Mauricio's senior by several years, but the two men are twins in appearance. Dark, coarse hair peppered with gray and brown eyes that warm you up the minute they land on you. The only difference is the goatee he insists on sporting, despite the fact that Mara and I have been trying to convince him it's uncool for years.

"Still haven't shaved, huh, Alex?" I climb onto a rattan barstool and drop my purse on the granite counter. The surface is sticky and stained with red splotches. I help myself to a nearby rag and wipe it clean.

He glances up from the papers he'd been going over with a young bartender I don't recognize, and smiles wide when he realizes who's ribbing him. "*Mija!*" *My daughter.*

There's a reason I keep coming back to this place.

"I swear you look a year older every time I see you," I tease.

"Perhaps that is because I am." He abandons the young man, probably freshly twenty-one if I had to guess, with a baby face to boot, and exits the backside of the square bar through a pony door next to the liquor wall that makes up the fourth side. I stand up just in time for his arms to swallow me whole, and though we are the same height, I sag against him for a moment, all the tension of my run-in with Kit finally hitting me at once.

"Whoa, whoa." Alex pulls back, dark brows pinching tight. "Why so sad, *mija?* You're home! Today is a happy day!"

"You're right. Today is a happy day." I smile, though it doesn't reach my eyes. He's been saying it to me for so many years that I can hardly remember the first time he repeated my father's go-to phrase back to me. The words Dad would reassure me with when I was anxious for a cheer meet or sad that he had to go back to work after a long weekend spent playing together outside while Mom baked cherry pie for us to gorge ourselves on in the evening.

It's been my motto ever since. A reminder that, even when I feel like I'm falling apart, my parents would want me to be happy.

Alex pats my bicep. "That's my girl. What can we whip up for you?" He gestures toward the new guy, who waves awkwardly and tosses his shaggy hair back with a neck jerk that hurts my own. "Sebastian here is in training."

I open my mouth to say hello to Sebastian, but just then he shifts his weight, clearing my view to the other side of the bar.

Where Kit sits, eyebrows raised, with a strawberry daiquiri pressed to his lips.

"No."

Alex's nose scrunches. "No?"

My gaze slices to him briefly. "No, not you, I meant—" Back to Kit, who's smirking. "You." I point a finger at him and ignore the innocent way he splays a hand over his heart to verify my target. "Not here too. The bar is mine."

He wets his lips, and I'm ashamed to say it makes my hands sweat.

"I hadn't realized we were divvying up custody."

Sebastian decides this is the perfect time to collect the rag I'd snatched along with a bucket of Q-San. He slips out of the bar, heading for the array of tables that line the balcony to start wiping their shiny surfaces one by one. Alex points at Kit and me with his respective fingers, then switches, crossing his arms over his chest. "You two know each other?"

"Yes," Kit says, sounding amused. I pinch my lips closed. Much as I'd like to contradict him, Alex knows me too well to buy that lie.

Alex scratches at his goatee with his thumb and forefinger. "Hm. All right. Interesting."

"We aren't divvying up custody because the whole resort is mine. You can find somewhere else to stay." I gesture broadly. "It's a big fucking beach." I'm ashamed to say my voice cracks on the curse, stealing any heat from it.

"Now, Tess," Alex says. He raises his hands palm out like I'm a horse in need of steadying. "We could use the revenue—"

"How many times do I have to remind you that you invited me here?" Kit's jaw is taut, his thin lips flatlined. Gone is the easy confidence from earlier, and damn, am I ashamed to admit that I miss it.

Though perhaps I like this version of him better. The intensity in his gaze. Tightly coiled muscles visible beneath a linen shirt. It feels more real, somehow.

I don't acknowledge his question. Can't, because it pulls the rug right out from beneath my already flimsy argument. Desperation crackles in my veins. I turn to Alex, whose gaze is wild with confusion. "Surely you can do without one room's worth of revenue, *Tio*." *Uncle*. He and Mauricio will do anything for me when I start reminding them we are family, if only the kind you find rather than being born into.

Kit huffs, "Excuse me—"

Alex clicks his tongue. "Can't, *Mija*. We're renovating the pool deck at the end of the summer and need every penny we can find."

A stone plummets from my chest to my stomach. "What do you mean, renovating the pool deck?"

His gaze softens at the corners. "All the concrete's finally getting torn up. We're replacing it with these really nice pavers Jenna found from a wholesaler out of Defuniak Springs."

"Can we please discuss—" Kit starts.

"Not now," I bite out, sounding more like a scared, feral dog than the strong woman I'd like to be right now. I just don't have the energy to devote to this petty argument when I'm struggling as it is to process Alex's words. "But the handprints?"

"I know, Tess. I'm sorry. But it's time. The concrete is cracked and unstable. It needs the upgrade badly. Your parents would understand."

They would, maybe, but do I?

"What handprints?"

This time both Alex and I turn to Kit. "None of your business," I say, exasperated.

A woman I hadn't noticed sitting at a nearby table, next to the one Sebastian has washed at least five times by now, turns in her chair. It screams against the slate flooring as her weight shifts. She scans all our faces but narrows her eyes at me specifically. "Do you mind? Some of us are trying to have a peaceful afternoon, and you two bickering certainly isn't helping."

"Yeah, get a room," is the extremely valuable addition the man opposite her offers.

Heat floods my cheeks. I turn back to Alex. "I'm sorry, I—"

"I'll move closer." Kit pushes back from the counter, grabs his drink, and is closing in on me before I have a chance to object. He slips into the seat beside the one I abandoned for my Alex hug, and drags a sip from his daiquiri. "Where were we? Oh! The handprints."

Alex eyes me carefully. I feel his gaze burning my temple. I know he's looking for a hint at how much information to withhold, but I'm too busy regaining my footing to offer much.

"Er, Tess was little when we redid the pool deck last. She and her parents stamped their handprints in the concrete the day it was poured."

I remember it clearly. Dreary gray clouds blotted out the sun. They feared it would rain, so the construction workers—friends of Jenna's—almost didn't pour it. In the end, after a lot of radar watching and tense conversation between grown-ups, they forged ahead. I was upset that it meant no pool time for an entire week, but Jenna and Alex sweetened the deal with their offer to permanently memorialize ourselves in the pool deck we'd visit every summer.

Permanent, as it turns out, only equals about twenty years.

"And now you're going to tear that concrete up?" There's no attitude left in Kit's voice. Only concern, and based on the way his hazel gaze cuts from Alex to me and softens, it's all for me. "Tess," he breathes, and then he's reaching for me.

I step back just as his fingertips brush my bicep. The touch shrink-wraps my lungs, which are already struggling in the damp Florida heat. I duck my head, hoping I can hide what he does to me and how this news has me reeling, in one fell swoop.

"I'm sorry, Tess. Really." Alex steps closer, and I allow him to loop an arm around my shoulders. More for his comfort than mine. "We will still have their picture in the lobby."

Ah, yes. The memorial plaque. I avoid it like the plague. A black-and-white photo pulled from their obituary, that the Ortiz family surprised me and my grandparents with the first summer we returned after the accident.

I know they meant well, but every time I see it, it's like a shard of glass gets lodged in my heart. The handprints are different. They are proof that my parents were living, breathing people who loved this place so much they left their mark on it. It's a physical reminder that they really were here. I didn't just imagine all those happy years before the really, very unhappy one.

I can't say all this to Alex, though. He and his family have been nothing but kind to me. If their resort needs updating, I can't expect them to refrain forever on my behalf.

"Sure, Alex. It's totally fine." I shrug, lifting his arm along with my shoulders.

Kit's expression is unreadable. His lips part, but he's cut off by the nasal voice of the woman whose bad graces we've earned.

"Can I please get a piña colada?" she asks, having hobbled over to the bar while her husband waits at their table, nose buried in his phone. They're in their midsixties, likely snowbirds who'll head back North in a week or two, based on the visor holding back her bouffant hair and his Hawaiian print shirt/tall white socks in sandals combo, if not her unmistakable Boston accent.

"*Mierda.* I haven't taught Sebastian how to make those yet." Alex's gaze dances from me to Kit as his arm slips from my shoulders. "Can I trust you two to behave?"

"Yes, sir," Kit replies with a salute.

"No promises," I add with an honest eyebrow raise.

Alex pinches my chin. "Why am I not surprised?" Then he's gone, cutting back into the bar alongside Sebastian and making a beeline for the blender on the opposite countertop.

"Can we declare a truce long enough for me to ask if you're all right?" Kit asks.

"I'm fine. Why wouldn't I be?" I climb back into my chair and fold my arms onto the counter. "Besides the fact that I still haven't gotten a drink."

Without hesitation, Kit slides his half-empty daiquiri in front of me. "Don't do that."

I take a sip of the too-sweet cocktail and wince as the cold hits my teeth. "Do what?"

He leans close. So close that his sandalwood scent is making it hard to breathe, let alone swallow my next sip. "Pretend you're okay when you're not."

My mouth freezes on the rim of the glass, and not because of the cold. He has no right. He thinks he can waltz in here, not knowing me from Adam, and pretend in the minuscule amount of time we've spent together he's learned to read my tells?

Nuh-uh. No way.

"Good night, Kit."

He glances toward the beach, where the sun is nowhere near setting. "It's, like, five p.m."

I grab my purse and lock eyes with Alex, who has a million questions in his eyes and enough courtesy not to ask any of them. "Catch up soon, Alex?"

I'd be lying if I said I didn't get a little thrill from the daggers he starts shooting Kit. "I'll have dinner sent to your room. It's just you, right?"

Okay, so he let one question slip. Can't blame a man after the show we put on. "Yes. Just me."

"Tess—" Kit starts to rise from his barstool alongside me, but his movement is halted by the hand I place on his forearm.

I'll have to boil that hand later, if the way it's tingling is any indication.

"Stay." I must glare convincingly enough, because his ass finds the seat again. "Good boy."

He scoffs. I turn away, remind Alex of my usual (scallops and his signature pasta recipe, a pink sauce I've never been able to recreate at home), and then push into a blast of air-conditioning. The restaurant is filling up with early bird diners. I dodge their curious glances, practically jog back to my room, and flatten my spine against the door once I'm safely inside it.

I'm sticky from the humidity or the nerves of being around Kit or both, and my heart is about to beat out of my chest. I quickly strip off my tank top and jeans, which I leave in a pile by the door with my discarded purse, and step into the bathroom.

A cold shower. That'll fix all my problems, right? It works for the athletes I see on TV, at least.

Wrong. So wrong. Within a second, I'm turning the water two degrees shy of blistering. Why the fuck would anyone subject themselves to the misery of a cold shower?

The tension melts from my muscles. For the longest time, I don't even bother with the shampoo or soap. I just wither beneath the stream of boiling water, hoping this is the thing that will fix me. Praying it'll wash away the sadness and desperation both, leaving behind some version of me I can actually be in front of Kit, since he's obviously not going anywhere.

When thoughts of him standing before me in the sea-green glass-tiled shower, all long, muscled limbs and bare, steam-pinkened skin fill my mind, when the temptation to touch myself just to ease the ache between my thighs becomes all consuming, I realize all hope is lost. There's no fixing this kind of insanity.

There's no choice but to endure. Or to get out of the shower.

I'm ashamed to say I choose the former.

Chapter Eleven

Kit

TESS IS the perfect amalgamation of her parents. Not just their names (Ted + Marissa = Tess, if I were a guessing man) but also in appearance. The black-and-white photo is cast in an orangey glow that spills through the windows onto the wall where it's hung, just to the left of the hallway that leads to the elevator bay. The sun has only just risen, and the lobby is quiet save for the gurgle of a coffee machine coming from the opposite corner of the room. A bored barista looks on while the girl who checked me in stands next to her, mixing up a concoction of epic proportions, complete with a mile-high whipped cream topper. She pops a straw in before returning to the middle registration pod, drink in hand.

I turn back to the photo, noting Tess's small face and twinkling eyes mirrored in her mother. Her father is tall, and I'm guessing she gets her sharp wit from him given the open-mouthed smile he's aiming at the person behind the camera. Each parent braces a hand on a little Tess's shoulder. While they pose for the picture, she's busy staring up at her dad with a gap-toothed grin.

In Loving Memory, the plaque reads. *Ted and Marissa Monroe.*

A quick Internet search brings up articles about the tenth anniversary of their passing. The *Fly Hollow Chronicle* notes their lasting impression on the community. A photo of two wooden crosses in the grassy margin just before a bridge concludes the write-up. They're draped with flowers, and an elderly man who vaguely reminds me of Gary stands behind them. *Marissa's father, Ron, passed last year,* the photo caption reads. I check the date on the article. It's already been a couple years since it was released.

They're all gone. That's what Tess said when I asked about her family last year. She truly meant everyone. I push a palm to my aching chest. She stands so tall for a woman carrying so much. Part of me wonders if anyone ever told her she shouldn't have to.

I snort under my breath. What a fucking hypocrite I am. Here I stand, wishing she'd open up and let someone (me) take care of her, and yet I've spent God knows how many years trying to handle everything—my failed relationship, a high-stress career, my brother's issues—all by my lonesome. Pot, meet kettle and all that.

Courtney was the only person I ever opened up to about my brother. Had to, since a big portion of our savings went to his last rehab stint. I couldn't burden my parents with the stressors his addiction caused, not when the entire reason I was handling things was to keep them from having to. But my ex-wife was sure to throw even that in my face, there at the end. All the more reason to keep it locked up inside.

Maybe the reason I've been unable to resist Tess is because I sense, deep down, how similar we really are.

I peel off my baseball cap and place it over my heart, meet Ted Monroe's eyes as though he were standing right in front of me, and smile. "Your daughter is amazing." My gaze slips to Marissa, with a face so similar to her daughter's that I feel like I know her. "You both would be so proud." A guest walks past, casting a curious glance my way, but I ignore him and press on. "She's stubborn, but I'll find a way to be there for her. Just give me some time."

I dip my chin toward the photo and replace my hat. As I turn toward the door that leads out onto the pool deck, I lock eyes with the girl behind the registration desk. She smiles like she knows what I was doing. I wink, and hope she gets the message that this is to be our secret.

It's early yet, but the air is already balmy. Immediately, sweat pools in every crevice I have. Some I didn't even realize were there. Heat in the Gulf has a way of seeping into your very bones and then turning them sopping wet.

It'll make for an interesting morning jog on the beach.

The gentleman skimming the pool waves, and I return the gesture. On the water's surface, the reflected sunrise is split in two by his net. It looks more like sherbet than pool water, and I'm already craving a refreshing swim when this run is over. Maybe I could even convince Tess to join me.

Fat chance, given how things went at the bar last night.

But if she thinks for one second that I missed the way she responded to my touch, however brief, she's got another thing coming. I'd recognize that little gasp anywhere. The way her skin pebbled before she pulled away. All the details that have been seared into my brain since our kiss at the Horseshoe. I doubt she's even aware of her reactions, that's how primal they are. But I want more of them. More of her.

And despite every alarm bell going off in my brain, I want to take care of her. This place clearly means something even deeper to her than I realized, and the pain wrenching her face over the changes being made gutted me. Tess's features are hardwired for joy. Her white-blonde hair, her sun-kissed skin. Lips that curve into a smile like a flower blooming. Seeing sadness take root not only hurt, it felt wholly unnatural.

My shoes hit the sand and sink in. I wobble like a newborn deer for a moment. That's how long it's been since I've come home. Stepped foot on the beach. It's hard to believe my brother and I were once water babies, nearly addicted to it for the week we'd spend at Orange Beach each summer while growing up. Our mother had to pull us from the ocean by our ears when it was time to head home back then.

I don't know what it feels like to be Tess, but when I think of my brother and how life used to be, I imagine it comes somewhat close.

Once I'm on firmer ground near the surf, I take off. The beach is empty save for a few surfers testing the measly waves kicking up this early in storm season. It doesn't take long before my limbs grow heavy and my lungs squeeze tight. I push through the burn and, on the other side of it, find the type of quiet my brain only encounters on a run.

The sun is baking my neck by the time I've looped around a pier a few miles from the resort and made it all the way back. It's still early, but I spot several people enjoying their breakfast on the wooden patio that juts out from the pool deck. To my left, a woman floats on the still surface of the ocean, a few yards out so she's clear of the waves breaking. My steps falter without me realizing why. Then she shifts to a standing position, and as the water sluices from dark blonde hair onto the narrow wings of her shoulders, recognition slaps the back of my head like a gong.

"You do realize sunrise is, like, prime feeding time for sharks, right?" I call out.

Tess spins around, but she can't fix her face into irritation fast enough to hide the fact that for a moment, I made her laugh. "Mama always said they'd spit me back out. Too bony." She flaps her arms for emphasis.

"I'll bet she did."

Never mind that the last word I'd use to describe Tess is *bony.*

She's all softness. From the curve of her hips to her ample breasts, which are on mouthwatering display in a blue string bikini. I'm mesmerized by every inch of her, right down to the sexy swell of her lower belly that makes me want to grovel at her fucking feet.

She tilts her head and, as though I've spoken these thoughts aloud, blushes crimson.

She's the first to break eye contact, dropping her gaze to the water swirling around her hips. "You know, you're failing miserably at keeping your distance."

That's because I don't want to. I clear my throat and lock my hands together behind my head. "What? How was I supposed to know that blob floating in the ocean was you? I just thought I'd impart my ample knowledge of shark behaviors on this random passerby, in case they didn't know. What kind of asshole would I be if I didn't and you got eaten because of it?"

"Ah, yes, if you hadn't mansplained marine life to me, I'd be screwed," she deadpans.

I arch a brow. "I noticed you're still in the water."

"How astute." She half-heartedly splashes in my direction, though she's too far out to even come close to hitting me. "I prefer the sharks' company to yours."

"You know I can also eat you, right? If that's what you're interested in." The words are out before I can second-guess them. For a moment the air between us is fully charged. I'm bracing, and also kicking myself internally, when she holds out what I'm expecting to be a middle finger.

Instead it's a thumb, which she turns straight down. "*Booooooo!*"

Nervous laughter whooshes out of me. Then it grows, changes, until it's a full-on guffaw. Because she's referencing our first day together, and that can't be anything but a very good sign.

Finally she begins wading toward me. Just as she's about to step out of the worst of it, a particularly strong wave hits her backside, and she's vaulted forward. I rush to catch her. My shoes are immediately soaked. She falls into my arms, and we stumble back, my moment of attempted heroism going south at the same time our bodies do.

We hit the sand in a tangle of limbs, but I've managed to take the brunt of the fall, with her landing on my chest. Our gazes meet, and her surprised gasp turns into a wrinkled nose and a tap on my forehead. "You stink, you know that?"

"Yeah, well, I just ran for the last hour." I make no move to get up, even as another wave blankets the sand we're lying on. For however long she's willing to remain like this, I'll be here, savoring every place where our bodies meet. "What's your excuse?"

She smells like her signature coconut sunscreen and the sea. I bet if I kissed her, she'd taste like sugar. Which means I'm lying through my damn teeth, and by the look on her face, she knows it.

"You are insufferable," she says, but there's no bite.

"And yet"—I release my hold on her long enough to gesture to our entwined bodies—"you're here."

Her green eyes narrow, and before I can lift a hand to protect myself, she's dropping a handful of sand right onto my face. A knee nearly connects with my balls as she pushes to her feet. By the time I scramble upright, she's halfway to the stairs.

So I jog after her.

Hopeless. I'm so damn hopeless when it comes to her. "What do you have planned for the day?"

"Nothing," she tosses over her shoulder. "Just going where the wind takes me."

I shudder internally. That sounds like my worst nightmare. I catch up to her, grab her hand, and spin her toward me. Sand coats her skin, and I'm overwhelmed with the desire to bathe her. To wash all the evidence of my bungled rescue attempt from her gorgeous skin.

I swallow hard, and she notices. Her gaze darts to my throat and lingers. Is she breathing faster? Or am I?

We both glance at our joined hands, but neither moves to separate them.

"Spend the day with me," I offer. "Let me make this whole thing up to you."

"Let you make up for the fact that you crashed my vacation… by further crashing my vacation?" She glances up, amusement sparking in her gaze. Her face is open this morning. Less guarded. I try to savor it as much as possible while it lasts.

I shrug. "Pretty much."

She shakes her head and laughs, which feels like progress. "Did you seriously not have anything better to do than go on a trip with a stranger?"

One light squeeze of her hand and that laughter dies on the breeze. "You're not exactly a stranger, Tess."

She slips from my grasp and takes a step backward. Away from me. "Couldn't visit your parents?"

My flinch is involuntary and hopefully imperceptible. "Too busy."

Her brow lifts. "Siblings?"

"Just the one, and definitely not."

She throws her arms wide. "Friends?"

I suck air through my teeth, and she pinches her lips closed. Pink lights up her cheeks in an instant. Apparently we're both embarrassed for me.

"Wow. I don't know how you did it, but now *I* feel bad for *you*." She crosses her arms and shakes her head. Drops of salt water spill from her waterlogged hair down her torso, and it takes everything in me not to trace their path—with my gaze *or* my tongue.

I lick the salt from my lips instead, not missing the fact that she watches me do it. "What an honor. If you're done, can we return to my original offer?"

For a moment all I can hear is the rush of waves and my own rapidly beating heart. She has no reason to say yes, and after the way she's reacted to me the last twenty-four hours, I don't expect her to. But hope is a stubborn bastard. He's hanging on for dear life, even though I'm starting to wonder if we should've given up already.

Her gaze is low, settled on the ground behind me, when something in her expression softens. "Okay."

My stomach leaps into my throat. "Okay?"

Tess lifts a brow, gaze darting to mine, as though daring me to keep questioning this olive branch.

Right. "Okay." I dust my sand-covered hands off on my sopping wet gym shorts and grimace. "Should we change first?"

"That depends. What are we going to do?"

Of course. I need a plan. Something that will get her out, get her living, so that hopefully the changes happening here will hurt a bit less. It's what works for me, anyway.

Something I saw on my jog flashes in my mind, and I grasp onto it like the life rope it is without a second thought.

"How about parasailing?"

Chapter Twelve

Tess

THIRTY MINUTES later we're loaded into the back of a ski boat by
a guy named Jimmy and his teenaged son. The sun is blistering
overhead, and with every wave the boat hits, Kit and I rock into
one another, bouncing like pendulum balls. Sticky skin meets
sticky skin. His black board shorts brush my exposed thigh, and I
jerk away. He glances toward me, smirking, but I avoid his gaze.

Being here was my one concession. He's not off the hook
just yet.

My mind drifts to the sand dollar sitting on the desk in my
room back at the Carmen. A perfectly whole one, with nary a
crack and a smooth, water-worn surface to boot. I spotted it in the
soft sand just past Kit as he asked me for a chance to make things
right. It was too much of a coincidence not to be a sign, like Dad
himself was sending me some kind of message. So I agreed to
spend the day with the guy, because it seemed like I should. And
because it's the least I could do after he broke my fall with his
own body, saving me from a face-plant of epic proportions. I can't
say I'd have been as kind had the situations been reversed.

I hope you know what you're doing, Dad.

Sand dollars were our thing. Mom was never an early riser,

but he and I always woke up at the crack of dawn, even on vacation. It was as if someone had injected our veins with espresso while we slept. We'd spend those early mornings strolling the beach together in search of cool shells to show Mom. Once every few years, a whole sand dollar would appear like magic, and our entire day would be better because of it. The weather perfect, the food extra delicious. Dad called them our lucky charms, and he kept every single one. I still have his stash in a box back home, including a shell no bigger than a quarter that he found the year they discovered they were pregnant with me.

Every year since they passed, I've scoured the beach, but not a single one has made an appearance. It was as if Dad took them all with him when he went.

I smile softly. If spending time with Kit brings the sand dollars back, then so be it.

A particularly rough wave knocks our shoulders together. I pull back, attempting to rub the sore spot, though my life jacket makes it difficult. Kit studies me, gaze roaming from the crown of my head to the tip of my lavender-painted toes. Somewhere in the middle, his face falls a bit. "You changed."

"You're just now noticing?" I glance down at my black one-piece—a little sturdier than a bikini, should things get squirrely up there—and denim shorts, all covered by a bright red life jacket. Then I narrow my eyes at Kit. "What? Are you disappointed?"

He inflates his cheeks, then slowly lets the air out while shaking his head. "Nope. You look amazing in blue, that's all."

I choose to ignore the butterflies taking flight in my abdomen. They've been hanging around since he appeared on the shoreline this morning, skin slick with sweat and face flushed from exertion. I can't think about it too much without things turning into a frenzy.

"Are you saying I look bad in black?"

His answering sigh is two parts exacerbation to one part… nerves? I think? "Tess, you'd look good in a trash bag."

"A black one, specifically?" I'm picking, but it's too fun not to when his reactions are written so plainly on his face. I can only hope I have a better hold on my expressions.

The skin between his dark brows folds. "Yes? No? I have no clue what the right answer is to that." The sunlight glints off his watch face when he flips his wrist and grimaces, then turns to face the back of the boat. His leg starts bouncing. "Is now a bad time to mention that I'm terrified of heights?"

We both watch as Jimmy and his son shake out our sail, prepping it for takeoff. Kit's biting his bottom lip, and upon further inspection, sweat is beading on his forehead that apparently has nothing to do with the unbearable humidity.

"You do realize you picked this activity, right?"

He mutters something like, "I panicked," but doesn't reply otherwise.

I place a hand on his knee and squeeze. His skin is hot to the touch, with flecks of sand still stuck in his leg hair. He changed, too, and likely showered, based on how good he smells. But I know better than anyone that it's nearly impossible to get every granule off, no matter how thorough a scrubber you are.

"We don't have to do this if you don't want to." I keep my voice low and steady. Rub my thumb in slow circles on the side of his knee. "I'll tell them I got seasick."

"We're ready for you!" Jimmy hollers.

Kit sighs, and I swear every ounce of oxygen leaves his body. He's that deflated. "It's fine. It was a childhood fear. I'm sure I'm over it by now."

My lips flatten. "Not sure that's how fears work."

But it doesn't matter, because he's already on his feet and striding toward the end of the boat. It takes a few minutes to get strapped into the harness, but they feel like hours when all I can do is study Kit's gorgeous face for hints of green. His hair is gel-free today, and I think I prefer it like this. The fluff softens his angular features, reminding me of the boy band crushes of my youth. If we'd met as teenagers, I imagine he would've been the quarterback to my cheerleading captain. What a pair we'd have made.

It's very rare these days that I wish for my life before the accident. I gave up the fruitless practice years ago in exchange for running so fast that the feelings couldn't catch me. But for a moment, as Jimmy flashes us a thumbs-up and Kit turns to me, seeking comfort, I let myself long for it. That other life, where we met while I still knew who I wanted to be, before circumstances decided who I had to become.

I offer my hand, palm up, to Kit. He grabs on tight without hesitation.

A mechanical whir overtakes the sound of surf and seagulls calling overhead. Soon air replaces the hard surface of the boat beneath our feet. A laugh bursts from my lungs. My hair whips hard and fast around my face, too short after my latest cut for a pony to contain it well. The boat grows smaller and smaller, while the world seemingly expands around us. Or maybe being above it all is the only way to realize we're not actually the center of the universe. Not even close.

"This is incredible!" I yell. When Kit hasn't responded after a few pounding heartbeats, I tear my gaze from the ant-size people on the beach. I find him with his eyes closed sucking in lungfuls of air like he might be plunged underwater at any second and need the reserves. "I take it you're not over the fear?"

He shakes his head. Possibly gags.

I squeeze his hand and he squeezes back. It feels awful to be grateful for a moment like this when he feels so absolutely ill, but I am. I'm glad I said yes, so I could see all this. Glad, even, that I'm here to hold his hand.

Would you look at that? Turn me into a balloon and apparently I'll float away from all my resentment, if only temporarily.

"What would help?"

One eye cracks. Just enough for a flash of hazel to peek through. "Just talk to me. Distract me."

I say the first thing that comes to mind. "Tell me about your parents. Why don't you visit them?"

He snorts, which feels like a good sign. "Your idea of a distraction is dredging up my family trauma?"

I wince. "Is there trauma?" Of all people, I should've known better. It's just hard for me to fathom having parents out there in the world, living and breathing, but never seeing them. No matter how busy, which honestly sounded like a cop-out the minute he said it.

A strong gust catches the parasail, yanking us higher so quickly it's like God himself plucked us up with his giant forefinger. I let out an involuntary whoop. Kit groans.

"Okay, not trauma, per se." He's pale as can be, dark eyelashes standing in stark contrast to his sullen cheekbones as he squeezes his eyes shut tight. "Just… I haven't really gone back since my divorce."

"You're *divorced?*"

He releases my hand to wipe his palm on his shorts. If he was sweaty, I hadn't noticed. But the absence of his touch? Now that grabs my attention.

"I think this is my worst nightmare."

"Being divorced?" I can't help how squeaky my voice is. Is this jealousy? Why the fuck am I jealous of a woman he's not even with anymore?

"Discussing it with you," he grumbles. "While hovering one hundred feet above the ocean."

"Technically that's not the ocean. It's the Gulf of Mexico."

That earns an almost smile. "And besides, weren't you in the Air Force? This is literally your area of expertise, no?"

"I worked on base. Which is on the *ground.*"

Oh. I swallow against a dry throat. The boat is getting close, which means they're reeling us in. And while a part of me is hoping that being back on steady footing will cure whatever momentary insanity this is, another part wants to remain suspended in the air with Kit awhile longer.

Though, by the looks of it, much longer and he'd be emptying his stomach.

"So I get that this whole thing is miserable for you, but it's almost over. They're pulling us in. And it'd be a damn shame if you didn't open your eyes long enough to see how freaking beautiful this view is, Kit."

For a moment it seems like he's going to ignore my advice and keep his eyes plastered shut until he feels something other than air beneath his feet. But then, a little miracle. His eyes fly open, and our gazes meet for the first time since takeoff. I expect him to glance away. To take in the powdery strip of beach dotted with brightly colored umbrellas and the array of resorts visible from here to the pier. To land on the vast expanse of the ocean, so he could feel even a portion of what I'm feeling now. Like if we're so small in the grand scheme of things, maybe something like being drawn to someone you shouldn't be in the midst of your pain isn't so big a deal after all.

But instead he holds my gaze the entire way down. And just before our feet hit the stern of the ski boat, he smiles. "You were right."

I try to laugh, but the sound gets caught in my throat. "You didn't even look."

"I saw everything I wanted to see."

My lips part, but without words to form, they stay that way.

Agape and useless as my heart, which does a happy dance that resembles nothing of the pulse that's meant to keep me alive.

"What'd you think, you two?" Jimmy's son, who can't be older than sixteen, holds out a hand to steady me as we touch down.

I take it, finding my legs surprisingly wobbly as they try to adjust to bearing my weight again. "Amazing!" I say, distinctly aware of how breathless I sound.

"It was…high," is Kit's answer.

After we're both released from our harnesses, I lead the way back to where we sat before. My steps are still unsteady, though, and the water is choppier now. All it takes is one slick spot and suddenly the sky is beneath my feet and my head is connecting with the bench meant for my butt.

A solid thud reverberates through the chasm of my thoughts. The sun flares bright, and ringing fills my ears. I'm not sure if I'm upright, or even if I'm still on the boat. Not until the flash of light subsides and I see Kit's face, concern lining every hard plane.

Calloused fingers smooth my cheeks more gently than should be possible. The sound of lapping water returns, and then his voice. "Are you okay?"

"Hm?" I hear myself mumble. I blink rapidly. Then the pain sets in. "Fucking *ouch.*"

He chuckles, and it sounds a bit like relief. "Fucking ouch is right."

I'm sitting on the floor of the boat, and when I glance around, Jimmy is speaking into a radio and his son is watching me like I might've just died and risen again all before his very eyes. I laugh nervously and try to stand, but Kit holds me still.

"Maybe just stay put until the EMT from the lifeguard stand can check you over." He runs his fingers through my hair. I have to fight the moan of pleasure that hits the back of my throat. That is, until he touches the spot where my head made contact with the hard plastic seat. I swat his hand away on instinct and he scowls. "Hey, I'm just trying to make sure you're not bleeding."

"Yeah, well, it hurts."

His lips are thin, but I still remember how warm and full they felt against mine. Now they're a breath away. Turning down at the corners, like I've wounded him by admitting I'm in pain. "I'm so sorry, Tess." His hand moves to cup my jaw instead, and he leans forward, brushing those lips against my forehead. "I'd take the hurt for you if I could."

I melt faster than a dropped ice cream cone on the sidewalk. And I'm pretty sure I hurt less, too.

We make it back to the marina in record time. As father and son work to tie down the boat, Jimmy says, "Radioed the lifeguard station. EMT is en route."

Kit glances over my shoulder. "I can see them coming down the dock."

I try to look, but he pinches my chin and raises a brow at me.

"I already feel better." The dizziness has subsided, and there's just a knot on the back of my head that throbs dully, save for when I reach back to touch it and the pain grows sharp. Tongue to teeth, I suck in a breath.

Kit grimaces like he can't believe I touched it after I chastised him for doing so. "That's a good sign. Maybe don't push it, though. I don't think you're concussed, but I'd appreciate a second opinion to be safe. Let's just see what the EMT says."

"Yes, sir." I mock salute him.

He clicks his tongue. "Terrible form."

I snort. "What are you going to do, punish me?"

His gaze darkens. A thick lock of black hair falls onto his forehead as his gaze drops to my lips and he swallows. Audibly. "On second thought, maybe you do have a concussion."

Chapter Thirteen

Kit

Tess's dad stares me down. And although he's smiling, there's a hardness to his eyes. Like he knows exactly what I did.

"It's not a concussion. Just a bump on the head. The EMT said she'll be back to normal in a day or two. I'm really sorry, sir." I bite down on the inside of my cheek. The iced latte in my right hand is sweating, so much so that condensation pools at my wrist and drips down my arm. In my left hand, a hot mocha has *me* sweating. "I didn't know which kind of coffee she liked, so I got both."

"Are you expecting the picture to talk back to you?"

"Jesus Christ!" I nearly throw both drinks. Still shaking, I place them on a nearby coffee table, then turn to find the girl from the reception desk standing behind me. Her curly hair is the color of midnight, and her equally dark, carefully sculpted eyebrows are raised. She crosses her arms, expression incredulous, while I work to get my pulse back to its normal rhythm. "You scared the shit out of me."

"Sorry," she says, sounding like she isn't really. Her fingertip joins my gaze on her name tag. "Xiomara. But everyone calls me Mara."

"Right. Mara." I push the condensation-slicked hand through my hair. "Sorry, I was just—"

"Apologizing to Ted for injuring his daughter? Yeah, I heard." She retrieves one of the beverages from the coffee table and holds it out to me. "She drinks iced coffee. You're welcome."

I take the drink from her. "Thanks."

She grabs the hot mocha and takes a sip, her bright pink lipstick leaving a print on the white lid. With a long, similarly magenta-colored fingernail, she points to the picture. "I was really little when they died, but my parents tell stories all the time. For what it's worth, he would've thought Tess falling like that was fucking hilarious."

I glance around, like said parents might jump out with wagging fingers at any moment. "Are you allowed to say fu— I mean, the F word?"

"I'm eighteen," she deadpans.

"Right." I'm horrible with kids' ages. From ten to twenty-one, they all blur together at this point. "Sorry."

Her shoulders bounce in a half-hearted shrug. "So, apology coffee?"

"Excellent guess. Do you think it'll work?" The whipped cream is melting into the beige liquid. Even with the AC cranked high, a nasty thunderstorm overnight brought with it a wave of particularly thick heat. I can't even see the pool deck for the dense layer of condensation coating the windows.

"It's a start."

Across the lobby, a middle-aged couple approaches the left registration desk. When one of the men offers his wallet to the woman behind it, I have to blink twice. For a second I think I'm seeing double. She looks that much like Mara. But upon further inspection, I realize this woman is older, with a few silver streaks in her dark hair that occasionally sparkle in the light. Mara's mother, then.

My mind flickers to the man at the bar the other night. Alex, if I remember correctly. He and Mara don't look alike, per se, but he's there in her facial expressions. Even the surly ones.

"How long has your family known Tess?"

Another shrug. *Teenagers.* "Her whole life, I'm pretty sure. At least, I've known her for all of mine." She purses her lips, and her gaze travels the length of me like she's taking my measure. "You know, if you really want to make it up to her, you should take her to the aquarium."

"The aquarium?" I snort. "What is this, a fourth-grade field trip?"

She rolls her eyes so hard her dark irises nearly disappear. "Just trust me, 'kay?"

With that, she spins on her heel and waltzes back to the desk, drink in hand. Guess it's hers now. Her mother glances up from her conversation with the gentlemen. She spots her daughter and then follows the line of her path back to me. Her smile is warm and so contagious I can't help but smile back.

Well, if these are the people who know Tess best, who am I not to listen? The aquarium it is. Of course, that's only if I can get Tess to agree to hang out with me again after yesterday's fiasco.

Tess is beautiful. I've thought it since I first saw her picture on Gary's tiny phone screen, but today it hits me square in the chest. Her short blonde hair, which is tucked back with heart-shaped, tortoiseshell sunglasses, makes the warmth of her skin all the more apparent. Narrow face, body, and features. She looks like she was built for flight. But soft in every place that matters, including the edges of her eyes, which relax as she gazes up at the giant wall of glass before us.

It's painful how much I want her. I don't know that I've ever felt a desire like this, and I'm not quite sure what to make of it, only that it hurts in the way a new PR in the gym does. Like it's breaking you down and growing you at the same time.

"Have you forgiven me for trying to kill you?"

Tess snickers under her breath but doesn't look up at me. "Holding grudges isn't really in my nature." The shifting water in the tank casts reflections around the room which dance like waves of silver on Tess's otherwise serene expression. "Besides, I think you suffered enough to balance it out."

I let out a huff of laughter. "I'm still a little woozy, now that you mention it." I glance down at her just in time to catch the hint of a smile. "But did you have fun?"

A curt nod. "Of course."

"Head injury notwithstanding?"

"Oh yeah, I've had worse." She takes a sip of her coffee and licks a stray drop off her full bottom lip.

Suddenly the massive viewing space we're in doesn't feel so big after all. I clear my throat and face forward, focusing on two dolphins playing with neon-colored rings that remind me of hula hoops. "What was your worst?"

"Are you asking me about my trauma, Kit?" She waggles her finger. "*Tsk tsk.*" I clamp my mouth shut and she laughs. She's entirely too pleased with herself. "Tore my ACL during cheerleading practice my senior year. That sucked *badly.*"

I whistle quietly. "One of my buddies tore his at basic. Not pretty."

"Thought you didn't have any friends?"

Does she remember everything I say? Or in this case, everything I don't. It'd be flattering if it weren't so inconvenient. "I have friends. They all pretty much live in Loveless, though."

"But none from your time in the military?"

I shake my head. "We were all part of a big friend group. A bunch of couples, you know. Their wives took my ex's side in the divorce, and they chose not to rock the boat. We chat if the need arises, but not otherwise. We're friendly. Not friends."

She's quiet for so long that I glance her way just to check she's still there. As if I weren't already aware of her in an unhealthy way. Every millimeter she shifts away from me, I feel its loss.

"So," she says finally. "This divorce. What happened?"

I groan internally. Probably a little externally, too, based on her raised brows. I can't help it though; I'm so tired of telling this story. "She cheated on me while I was deployed. A lot, actually. But I caught her once, when I came home early. And that was that."

I have needs, she'd screamed. *You're always away. What was I supposed to do?*

How about keep your fucking vows? I'd snarled it right in her face. I'm not proud of it, but in the moment the only thing I knew to do with all the hurt was to turn it into anger.

"How long ago was that?" Her voice is quiet but not full of pity like I've come to expect. There's sadness there. The kind that comes from empathy. Like she knows how it feels to have her whole life imploded in an instant.

"Over four years now." I cross my arms and settle into the railing along the wall. People stroll in and out of the room while the dolphins play on, completely unbothered. It's soothing. Like life is on pause for a bit. I find I can breathe a little easier because of it. "I'd planned to re-up, but after that… I waited until my contract ended and got out. Found the job in Loveless and never looked back."

She studies me carefully, like she might find the answer to some unspoken question if she looks close enough. "Have you seen anyone else? Since the divorce, I mean."

I laugh, but it's a tad self-deprecating. "Ironically, Zoey and I went on a few dates when I first moved to Loveless."

"Zoey as in *Gary's* Zoey?" When I nod, her mouth forms a perfect O. "She seems like she'd eat you alive."

I give her a pointed look. "I think that's my type."

She drops my gaze to take another sip of her coffee.

"Anyway, she had feelings for Aaron, and things never really felt right between us anyway. We make better friends." Speaking of, I owe her a phone call. She's been blowing me up since word got out about where I am. Part of me just isn't ready to share what's happening here. Mostly because I don't *know* what's happening, or if anything ever will.

"So." Tess drags the toe of her Birkenstock across the low-pile carpet, focusing on its path as she speaks. "What about those other ice creams you mentioned sampling?"

I snicker at the forgotten metaphor, and she glances up. If I were a betting man, I'd say she's fishing. For what, I don't know.

"Nothing more than a sample." I press my lips together, considering my next words carefully. "After my marriage ended the way it did, I decided casual was the way I'd keep things. That way no one feels let down. No one gets hurt."

The way I figure it, if you don't try to be someone's whole world, you can't be disappointed when you find out you aren't. A sad truth, but a necessary one.

The corners of her mouth dip. She's wearing some kind of gloss that makes them so enticing, so full that I can't bear to look away as she speaks. "You afraid of feeling tied down?"

"It's not me I'm worried about."

One of the dolphins does an impressive flip, head over tail, that has a nearby family cheering. Drawn by the enthusiasm, a few more clusters of people press into the room. What was once a foot of space between Tess and me becomes mere inches. I can smell the sunscreen on her skin. The sweetness that is so distinctly her. I draw in a deep breath and try to stow it away for safekeeping.

"That's sad," she whispers. "If more is what you want, then you should go for it."

Much as I wish it were so, I know she's not inviting me on her behalf. So I change the subject. "What about you? Any failed relationships you want to divulge?"

She sighs, letting her shoulders go limp. "First of all, I don't believe in giving relationships a pass-or-fail rating. I consider them all a lesson learned, if nothing else. Same with your divorce. Hopefully you learned something, even if it was just what you don't want in a future partner.

"But no, not much to report on that front. I get antsy if I stay still too long. It's hard to maintain anything steady. I think my longest relationship lasted about a year. Her name was Samantha. She wanted to settle down, and I wanted to keep running. So we ended things."

Panic clamps down on my gut. I'm re-running the kiss we shared all those months ago for the millionth time, but now through a different lens. Did I misread her signals? Push for something she didn't really want?

"Go ahead and ask whatever question you're chewing on over there."

"So…bisexual?" I say hopefully.

She shrugs. "I've never felt the need to label it. I love who I love." She points to the show being put on. "I could probably date a dolphin if it were respectful and liked the same things as me."

"Ah, so *that's* what you were doing in the ocean yesterday. Looking for a date."

Her laughter cuts the tie binding my nerves so tightly. The blood returns to my organs in a rush that leaves my head spinning. The crowd slowly begins to dissipate, but we don't move apart. If anything, we're closer than ever.

"To be clear, I wasn't asking because it bothers me or anything. I just wanted to make sure I wasn't barking up the wrong tree."

"Oh, you definitely are," she says, expression suddenly morose. "For reasons that have nothing to do with my sexuality."

I kick the toe of her Birkenstock, and she kicks me right back.

I like this openness between us. And I'd like to keep it going for as long as I can, so I stoke the flame, hoping it'll burn.

"How was that? Growing up in a small town and all."

"Not great. But not as bad as it is for some." She takes another sip, this time hitting bottom. A harsh gurgle of liquid sucked through ice interrupts the hushed conversations around us. A few heads snap in our direction. Tess releases the straw on her coffee, does that frown/shrug thing one must when they know they messed up, and mutters, "Sorry."

The passersby return to their own pods of discussion, the interruption already forgotten. Tess's wide gaze meets mine, and she mouths, *Can we get out of here?*

I nod. She tosses her empty coffee cup into a nearby trash can and reaches for my hand. "Come on, I'll show you my favorite part."

She does it so naturally that I almost feel stupid for forgetting to breathe. I'm not entirely convinced she didn't knock her head so hard she's forgotten why she's mad at me. It barely took any convincing to coax her to join me today. I'd question it further, but I'm so desperate for it to last that I don't want to rock the boat. If she's happy with me for now, then I want to exist in this moment for as long as she'll let me.

She pulls me into a space that's long and narrow, with glass walls curving into a ceiling that creates more of a tunnel than a room. All around us, fish weave in and out of artificial coral reefs. Up ahead, a shadow moves eerily across the gray carpet. When I glance up, I'm met with the belly of a shark.

"Holy shit."

"Right?" Her grin is infectious. All straight white teeth and almost-dimples. She releases my hand to step closer to the glass. "My parents brought me here every summer growing up. The sharks were always my favorite."

Thank you, Mara. "Of course they were." Beautiful yet untouchable. That's Tess all right.

It's brighter here. I can see the column of her throat working as she gazes up at the sharks passing overhead, their movements reflected in her glossy eyes. "To answer your question, I'm sure people in town blamed the whole dating-women thing on the trauma I went through or some shit like that. Anything but it just being who I am. Luckily I got very good at blocking them out early on, when I couldn't escape the questions about my parents dying. I often felt more like some juicy tabloid feature in the local newspaper instead of a real, grieving person."

Anger ripples through me, but with nowhere to send it, I trap it in closed fists that I shove into my pockets. I want so badly to fix it for Tess, even if it's something that can never truly be repaired. The only thing I can do is be here now. Listen, if she'll let me.

"It was a car accident, right? With your parents."

"Yeah." Her gaze tracks a smaller shark that sails down the arch of the tunnel and levels out with us. There are spots along the top of it, barely visible until you really focus, which Tess does, narrowing her eyes on the creature. "I'd just turned seventeen. Drunk driver crossed the middle line. They were killed instantly."

"And the driver?" I ask.

Her eyes drift closed. "Died en route to the hospital."

My God, the magnitude of her grief. I can feel it from here, rolling off her in waves. And yet she gets up each day. Makes jokes. Smiles her big, sunshine grin. You'd never know how much she's endured just by looking at her. And I realize in that moment how lonely it must be, burying your own feelings to make sure no one else ever knows they're there.

I realize it because, in a way, I've been doing it for years.

"Is that what you meant by running?"

Her eyelids flutter open. When she glances my way, her irises gleam with unshed tears. "Do you want the honest-to-God, pathetic truth?"

I hold out my hand, palm up, the way she did for me on the boat yesterday. She takes it. Inhales sharply when I thread our fingers together and squeeze tightly. I offer what I hope is a reassuring smile. "That's my favorite kind of truth."

Her snort is harsh, like it hurts to laugh in this moment. Then a somber pain sobers her expression. "When it comes to my parents… my mom's childhood home, the town where they lived, hell, even their annual vacation… I can't seem to let go. Can't move on. Not because it's what I want, necessarily, but because I'm afraid I'd be failing them somehow by doing so. In that way, my life remains completely stagnant. But for my choices? My relationships? The burden of another thing that could be lost is just too much to bear."

I graze my teeth across my bottom lip, turning her words over in my mind. "And so you run."

She swallows, gaze drifting to the tank overhead. "And so I run."

There is so much longing in that simple statement. What it is that she longs for, I can only guess. I can't fix her past. Can't even predict that the future will be better. But I can see her, right now, for exactly who she is—happy facade completely set aside. And my God, she's still so beautiful. More so because she's honest.

I bring our joined hands to her cheek, gently swiping a stray tear from her skin. When she smiles up at me limply, my heartbeat stutters.

"May I offer you some advice?"

Her green eyes glisten in the watery light as she nods.

"I know what it is to be afraid of letting down your parents. But I find it hard to believe yours would ever be disappointed to see you living your life on your own terms." I take a small step toward her, bringing us closer. "So it's okay to let go. It's okay to run, if that's what you want. But if standing still would make you happy," I say, my voice raw in my throat, "then just stand still."

Her body is so perfectly poised, so lovingly crafted that I'd believe she was made of glass if someone suggested it. I take another step. We're so close now that our chests are brushing, but she doesn't move. I thread my other hand into her loose curls, gingerly brushing the place where she hit her head.

"Does it still hurt?"

Her tongue slips over her bottom lip. "Not so much now."

"Good." Then I lean in and capture that shiny lip between my teeth. The sigh that spills from her lungs urges me onward, and I'm nothing if not a gentleman, so I oblige. Our mouths fuse together, unspent hunger and months of desire all rolling into a kiss so deep I could drown in it. And I do. I lose all sense of time, of space, of the crowds around us and the sharks swimming above. There is only Tess.

Tess and her sighs. Tess and her soft, warm skin. Tess and her sugar-and-sunshine scent. I could get drunk off her. It's likely I already have, because I don't hear the staff member trying to get our attention until Tess pulls away. Her lips are swollen because of me. Cheeks flushed, limbs loose, smile lazy. I did all of that.

"Do you mind? This is a family establishment," the woman in a Gulf Coast Aquarium polo chides.

"Sorry, ma'am," Tess replies, her accent a little stronger now that she's gotten in trouble. "Won't happen again."

We get a look in return that feels a hell of a lot like *I'm watching you.* Then the woman turns back to the trash she'd been emptying, and Tess's knees buckle beneath her.

She swats my chest, but she's laughing. When her hand drops, one of her straps slips from her narrow shoulder, and she pushes it back into place. I'd recognize the buttery yellow sundress anywhere. It's the same one she had on last July. If I close my eyes, I can feel the fabric piling against my hands as I pushed it higher, reaching for her hips. Her ass. Anything and everything I could touch. Whatever would bring me closer to her.

I'd like to feel it again.

"What are you thinking about?" She asks it in a way that implies she already knows.

I clear my throat and glance pointedly down at the ridge forming in my khakis, then back at Tess. "You look amazing in that dress."

It's hard to tell in the haze cast by the water overhead, but I think she blushes.

"Even if it isn't blue?"

I click my tongue and sigh dramatically. "I suppose."

"Ah, well. Don't be too kind." She flips a hand through the air like she's wiping away my compliment. A few gold bracelets dangle from her wrist, and when she moves, they clink together, making music.

"Don't worry, it's not in my nature."

She rolls her eyes and bites down on the inside of her cheek. The smile she's fighting so hard is winning, whether she likes it or not.

"Would you like to go someplace else?" I ask, nodding toward a sign beside the exit on the opposite side of the long room. "Maybe the turtle enclosure?"

Her hands smooth down the front of her dress just to gather two fistfuls near her hips. She shakes her head, gaze round and thoughtful, and not in an entirely positive way. "What are we doing, Kit?"

I recognize that she's overthinking. Spiraling. The fever

dream of our kiss has worn off, and she's moved to analyze mode, which didn't work out well for us last time. So I do the only thing I can. I grab her hand and start walking.

Chapter Fourteen

Tess

IT'S BEEN at least fourteen years since I last needed to sneak out of my hotel room without alerting anyone. To say I'm rusty would be the understatement of the century. But despite my lack of practice, I like to think I manage to shut the door and slip down the hall expertly, leaving Kit completely unaware.

I'm not hiding from him, per se, but this is a moment when I most definitely need space.

Somehow one reluctant agreement to go parasailing with him spiraled into spending every waking moment of the last few days together. I realized it this morning when I found myself already up and brushing my hair at the crack of dawn in anticipation of his familiar knock and the iced coffee that would accompany him when he returned from his daily run. I sat down on the bed and stared out the balcony window, wondering how in the hell I went from resenting his presence to having our own damn routine.

It's been one of the best weeks I've had here since my parents were alive, which should be a good thing, right? But each night when my head hits the pillow, shame slices through my center like a hot knife. Shame that I haven't thought of them all day. That for a moment I was happy having forgotten.

So I resort to the only thing I can think to do—I visit my parents. Or the closest I can get to them these days.

It's the middle of the night when I exit the cool air of the lobby in favor of the boggy outdoors. The worst of the heat has leached from the pool deck, leaving it comfortably warm against my skin as I sit down beside our handprints. I feel each sharp ridge of the concrete pressing into me through my thin flannel shorts. A nearly full moon peers down on the Carmen, bathing me in its white light. Distant thunder competes with the sound of waves lapping at the shore.

I rest my hand inside the print my mother left, nearly filling it perfectly. It's as though I made the impression myself. To the right, my father's dwarfs hers. And there, in the middle, lies the little handprint I made. Proof that I was once small and safe between my parents. That we were happy.

Above them all, true to my father, is a whole sand dollar, forever memorialized in the concrete slab. My chest constricts. To think that by the end of this summer this snapshot of our lives will cease to exist makes my stomach turn.

Grief swells in my chest, fueled by all the love I still feel but am unable to give to them. To anyone, really. I meant what I said to Kit at the aquarium. The risk of not just pain but true suffering is too much to bear.

Warmth like a fever floods my cheeks as I picture him leaning in beneath the blue glow of the overhead tank. As I took his advice and stood very, very still.

I shake my head while mentally shoving thoughts of him as far into the recesses of my mind as I can. What kind of daughter am I? Wasting the time I'm meant to spend remembering my lost family on some guy I barely know. Shame rejoins the grief, becoming so thick I'm certain I'll suffocate from the weight of it pressing on my lungs.

It hurts. The effort it takes to hold on to it all.

"How do I let you go?" I whisper, though there's not a soul around to hear me speak.

With tears blurring my vision, I snap a photo and send it to Gary, alongside the caption, *Can you believe my hands were ever so small?*

I expect him to be sleeping, but within seconds, he responds.

GARY B

Yes, mostly because they aren't that much
bigger now!

For some reason when I laugh, it sounds sadder than if I'd let out a sob.

ME

Miss you, Gare Bear.

ME

Sorry I didn't tell you about Kit. Are you mad?

GARY B

Never, Tess. He's a good kid and so are you.
Though I can't wait to hear how all this
happened when you find some time.

I promise to call, and he wishes me good night, not once questioning why I'm up so late in the first place. It's how I managed to keep from spilling my guts about what happened with Kit when my uncle visited at Christmas. Even if he's always down to listen, be it to gossip or a true undressing of the heart, Gary doesn't prod. So I didn't mention it, much as Kit had been weighing on my mind since I left. It was over, anyway. A one-time ordeal. Or so I thought.

My lips are soft to the touch. Warm. There's no evidence of the way Kit burned himself onto me, and yet I feel it. Haven't been able to stop feeling it since that moment in the aquarium. Yet he hasn't pushed for more, or even another kiss. I get the sense that the ball is in my court, and he's waiting for me to make the next move. Too bad I'm waiting for me, too.

Waiting to figure out what the hell I want from this life, beyond surviving it with minimal pain from here on out. If I stand still like Kit suggested, what will catch up to me? How much hurt have I been evading by never settling long enough for it to float to the surface? What little leaks through is bad enough. Anything more and I'd be incapacitated.

"Tessa? *¿Qué haces?*" Mo steps into my line of vision just as I glance up, startled. His gaze settles on my palm, still resting in the outline of my mother's, and the wrinkles at the corners of his eyes soften. "Oh, *querida.* My brother told you, didn't he?"

I nod. "But it's okay; I mean, I understand—" I'm interrupted by my own hiccuping sob. A sound that says it's very much *not* okay and I most definitely do *not* understand. I bat away the tears slipping over my cheeks and draw in a ragged breath. "I'm sorry; I don't know why I'm crying."

"I think I do." Mo lowers himself to the cold ground and wraps me in his embrace, that familiar tobacco scent soothing me like nothing else does. "It is okay to be sad. I was, too, when they first told me it was a possibility."

"They're just handprints," I say, though the words are interrupted by more tears, followed by sniffling.

He rubs the goose bumps decorating my bicep rapidly, like he might kindle a fire. "I know. But they belonged to people you loved."

It's the past tense that splits my heart in two. "People I love," I correct weakly.

I feel his chin brush the crown of my head as he nods. "And whom I love as well."

We sit there, tangled in a haphazard embrace, for what feels like hours but may only be minutes. Long enough that he eventually releases me to remove a cigarette from his pocket, which he lights before offering it to me. I accept it, and he retrieves a second for himself. I've only ever smoked while drinking, which has been infrequent as of late, if the pack of Camels gathering dust in my underwear drawer back home are any testament. But it feels right to do this with Mo, under a mostly starless sky thanks to a bright moon casting everything else in its shadow. It gives me something to focus on rather than the erratic breaths still struggling to find their pace in my lungs, or the tears that have dried sticky-taut on my cheeks.

Mo releases a plume of smoke that climbs the air above us like a chimney. Our gazes meet, and he purses his lips the way he always does before asking a question he shouldn't. "How are things with your *novio?*"

I narrow my eyes at him and take a long drag. When I finally speak, my voice is threadbare. "If that means anything close to *lover,* I'll fight you."

He chuckles around his cigarette.

"We are friends," I clarify. "Just. Friends."

Somewhere above us, a balcony door closes. Neither of us reacts. Mauricio watches me for so long that my skin begins to itch. He must notice me squirming, because he finally relents. "Did you know Alex and I have a cousin who works at the aquarium?"

No fucking way. My eyes close in a grimace against my will. I have to pry the left one open to peek at him. "Are you related to everyone around here?"

He huffs a laugh. "She said a young couple put on quite the show a couple days ago. You went on Wednesday, right? I wondered if you saw them."

I smoosh the tip of my cigarette into the concrete and then let my body follow suit, becoming one with the rough surface. It chills me to the bone, but it's better than facing a man who might as well be family as I admit to making out with someone in public. "It's very complicated, *Tio.*"

He sinks onto the pavement beside me, though a guttural groan gives away our age difference. "Love is always complicated. That's why it's wonderful."

"Says the perpetual bachelor," I grumble.

"It is because I love to fall in love that I remain alone, Tessa. I can never give it up."

"Ah." I turn to look at him. His face is cast half in shadow and half in stark moonlight, like he's wearing the mask from *The Phantom of the Opera.* "And here I thought it's because no one could put up with your shit."

He flattens a palm over his heart. "You wound me."

Our soft laughter is quickly caught and carried away by a breeze coming off the Gulf. We sit in silence until that silence fills my chest to the point of bursting. I need someone to talk to, someone who is unbiased. All Alicia has been telling me to do is go for it. Get laid and get it out of my system. But it's deeper than that, even if I can't bring myself to explain that to her, though I don't know why not.

"I can't let him be more than a friend to me."

"And why's that?"

I chew on my bottom lip. Though it offers no solace, it buys me time. After a minute and some intense eye contact with the moon, I crack open the door to my heart ever so slightly. "I'm scared he'll be another split decision I make that I can't come through for, because it hurts too much. And where will that leave him?" Then, softer: "Where will that leave me?"

There. I did it. The thing I couldn't admit to my best friend, because it felt too much like admitting it to myself. Now out in the open air for him to call ridiculous. Inconsequential.

But he doesn't, of course. Mo would never.

"It leaves you with us," he says.

In the quiet that follows, I swear I can hear the fissures of my heart cracking and splitting apart. A feeling like a fossil appears through the cracks. Something I didn't even realize was there, waiting, just below the surface. It's painful to look at. Impossible to ignore.

An invisible fist closes around my throat, and my stomach twists in on itself. I grab Mo's hand and hold it tight so he can't leave, even though that's exactly what it feels like I'm doing by voicing the terrible feeling aloud.

"What would happen if I stopped coming here, Mo? To the Carmen, I mean." I focus on the lone palm tree swaying in the breeze, caught somewhere between me and the glowing moon. "I just— What if it's time for me to move on? To figure out what I'm supposed to be doing with my life, beyond grieving."

He doesn't panic. Doesn't argue. He simply squeezes my hand twice and sighs.

"I've been running in circles," I say, quieter now, like I'll offend the universe if I speak my doubts too clearly. "And I don't really know how to stop. Only that I need to, if I ever want to be able to hold on to anything or anyone long enough for it to matter." The image of Kit rushes back to the forefront of my mind. Just as quickly, it's replaced by that of my parents, whose handprints I can still feel beneath me in the concrete. My words catch up to me, roaring like a betrayal in my ears and in my heart. How ungrateful am I? How selfish?

I turn to Mauricio, pleading leaking into my voice. "I'm so sorry. I don't even know what I'm saying. Please don't tell Alex or Jenna or Mara. They would be devastated."

Mo meets my gaze, brown eyes wide open and serene. The exact opposite of what I expected. "You want to know what I think, Tessa?" I nod, and he does, too. "The Carmen is just a place. But the memories you have made here, and how my family feels for you, will never change, *querida.* You could go anywhere in the whole world, and both of those things would still be with you." He lifts our entwined hands to catch the stray tear that escapes my eye, smudging it with his thumb. "If you're looking for something steady, let that be it."

I swallow, but it doesn't fix the thousand knots suddenly tying my throat. So instead I offer a trembling smile. My weakest yet. I'm a terrible actress tonight, and something tells me Mo never bought my performances anyway.

"*Gracias, Tio.*" I release his hand to pinch his cheek. "You are so wise."

"It's the gray hairs." His white teeth flash in a quick smile. "You'll see some day."

I offer a close-lipped grin in return. "One can only hope."

At that, I'm offered a second cigarette. And I accept.

Chapter Fifteen

Kit

WHEN I LEAVE for my jog in the morning, a Do Not Disturb sign swings from the brass knob on Tess's door. It's still there come lunchtime, long after I've showered and placed an overdue call to Zoey, who both accuses me of being a lovesick idiot and tells me how proud she is in the same long-winded speech. I'm not surprised that Tess is still in bed; the sound of her door closing at two in the morning woke me from a dead sleep. I don't know how I knew, but instinct led me to the balcony, and there she was. Palm pressed against the dark pool deck and shoulders hunched. I watched long enough for a man I recognized from around the resort to arrive, and then returned to my bed to give them privacy.

Sleep wouldn't take me back, though. Not until her footsteps thudded down the hall and the telltale squeak of her doorknob turning informed me she'd returned safely to her room.

By the time I spot her at a stool by the outdoor bar in the late afternoon, chatting with the resort owner in hushed tones, I'm feeling off-kilter. My days so quickly adjusted to revolving around her. I don't know what to do with myself without Tess. Any other woman and I'd consider that a problem. But the syrupy-sweet relief that floods my veins upon seeing her takes up too much space in my head, leaving no room to overanalyze why everything's different when it comes to her.

I step fully onto the patio, letting the glass door to the restaurant fall shut behind me. She hones in on me instantly. She mutters something to the owner, and his gaze tracks to me. If I didn't know any better, I'd say that's pity on his face. And I've never been accused of knowing better.

Tess braces her ring-laden fingers on the countertop as she slips from her seat. She's wearing flowy, white linen pants that shift and stir around her long legs as she crosses the bar to meet me where I'm standing. Waiting. Because I know an, I-need-to-talk-to-you face when I see one.

"Look at you, finally up and at 'em," I say when she's a few feet away. My joke lands like a cracked egg on pavement. She doesn't offer so much as a courtesy laugh as she closes the rest of the distance, stopping only when there's a respectable foot or two of awkward silence hanging between us. I cock my head, studying the tight set of her mouth and her wringing hands. "Is everything all right, Tess?"

She rocks onto her toes and glances sheepishly down at her brown woven leather sandals. Even if her absence today hadn't been a dead giveaway that something has shifted, her complete lack of sarcastic commentary—or any commentary, really—would do me in.

So this is the part where she pulls away. I knew things were going too well, that I'd won her over too easily. Or if not won her over, at least convinced her that spending time with me wasn't the end of the world. Now it seems even that fragile belief has been damaged.

The most masochistic part of me doesn't want to accept it. I blame him for asking, "Do you want to talk about it over dinner? There's a place close to the aquarium that's got great reviews—"

At the mention of the aquarium, her gaze flashes to mine. Her eyes are glossy with tears. The sheen dulls the Sprite-bottle green of her irises, giving them the appearance of tempered sea glass.

Her lips part, then close. Part again. This time, with a breathy voice, she says, "I've been thinking…"

I wait a few seconds, but nothing follows those words. So I try for humor. "Well that's never good."

Her gaze hardens, nose wrinkling, and for a second anxiety loosens its grip on my throat. If I can get that kind of response out of her, then the Tess I know is still in there. She's just reverting to old habits, if her self-diagnosis of being a chronic restless soul is to be believed. We aren't doomed. Can't be.

Her posture stiffens and she lifts her chin. "I'm sorry. I shouldn't have let things get away from me at the aquarium. Or the past couple days. It's given you the wrong impression, and that's my fault."

I scoff. "It's very much not."

"You're right. It's *your* fault," she deadpans. "Can you just let me talk?"

I mime zipping my lips and tucking the key into my pocket. She sighs so heavily the man she'd been talking to raises an eyebrow in our direction, but when he notices me noticing him, he returns to the glass he's been polishing for the last five minutes, this time with more vigor.

Tess follows my line of sight, and when her gaze returns to mine, some of the tension has left her expression. "This trip means a lot to me, Kit. Probably more than it ever has, now. And when it's over, I've got to figure out some things. A lot of things. There's no space in my life for a fling, and respectfully, a fling is exactly what you said you prefer."

"I never said that's what I wanted with you."

"Oh yeah?" She crosses her arms and settles her weight on her left leg. "So what *do* you want with me, Kit?"

I don't know seems like an even worse answer than what she's assumed. Her gaze settles on my pursed lips, and she nods like I've confirmed her suspicions.

"We can be friends. That's all I can offer you. Take it or leave it."

A distinctive type of nausea swirls in my gut at the thought of never tasting Tess's smile again. Never feeling her warm skin beneath my fingertips or hearing the little gasping sound she makes when I roll my hips against her core. I physically ache with the withdrawal of it. But more than that, the idea that I might lose her entirely? When I've just gotten her back? Impossible.

"Okay, Tess." I hold out my hand, pinky erect. "I accept your terms. Promise I won't kiss you again until you ask for it."

She balks, pretty pink lips popping open audibly. "I'm not going to ask you to kiss me."

Her cheeks burn bright in response to my shrug. The truth is, I'm scared as shit to lose her. Scared as shit to have her and not know what to do with her. But I believe my instincts when they say this isn't it for us. All I have to do is convince her to believe it too.

So I match her stance, arms folded over my chest, and try not to revel in the fact that her eyes immediately dart to my biceps. I smile tartly. "Beg, then. Or politely demand. Whatever you want to call it. Until then, friends."

"Has anyone told you that you're the worst?"

My whistle scares a seagull off the patio railing. "It's come up a few hundred times."

"Not shocking."

Nerves coat my throat, but I chuckle through them. My commanding officer once told me during a particularly rough deployment that no one was truly that brave, they were all just faking it to trick their nervous systems into believing it was true. I might've taken it to heart, and then promptly applied it to every aspect of my life. But it's paid off more than it hasn't. If I have to fake it till I make it where Tess is concerned, then so be it.

"So…dinner then?"

She chews at her bottom lip. I want so badly to thumb the damage. The temptation is so intense that I have to shove my hands into my pockets to be sure I won't succumb. Just then, my phone starts ringing.

Her slightly sunburnt forehead wrinkles as she lifts both brows. We can blame that on a particularly long beach session yesterday, which I spent the entirety of trying not to ogle her in that tiny blue bikini.

"Who still keeps the volume up on their ringer these days?"

"Me, and, like, so many other people." I remove my phone from my pocket and grimace at the familiar area code. "One sec."

I plug one ear to block out the ambient noise of the other patrons chatting around the patio, and hold my phone to the other once I accept the call.

"This is a collect call from Inmate Gage Llewellyn at Jackson County Jail. To accept the charges, press one, or say, 'I accept.'"

Shit. My spine goes rigid. Tess raises her eyebrows, and I quickly scramble to regain the easy posture I'd had only moments ago. Before my brother fucked up yet again. I cover the speaker with my hand and gaze at Tess as casually as I can. "Sorry, gotta take this. Catch up with you in a bit?"

She stiffly waves me off, an unspoken question in her gaze. Probably the same that's hidden in mine. Something like, *What the fuck is going on?*

I take the long, L-shaped hall back to my room with clipped strides as my brother is connected through the line. When his familiar voice drifts through the phone, tired but otherwise unaffected, a bit of the stress I'd been carrying in my chest shakes loose.

"Hey, Kit. How's it going?"

The keypad on my door blinks green, and I turn the knob to enter my room. "Oh, you know, just shooting the shit. What's up with you, bro? I imagine you're having an amazing day, considering you're calling from the county jail."

He mutters a curse, and I shove a clammy palm to my forehead. He doesn't need me to get snarky with him, but my God is it hard not to when we keep finding ourselves in these positions. I want to reach through the phone and shake some sense into him, but I've lost all hope that it would help.

"What happened, Gage?"

"Man, I swear it wasn't my fault. Zack and Easton were fucking around with some speed, and I was just in the room. But we all got arrested."

I sink onto my mattress just as my stomach plummets to the floor. "Meth? You have got to be fucking kidding me. What were you thinking?"

Before he even speaks, I already know the answer. He wasn't. He never is. Since the first time he got busted with drugs in the eighth grade, he's continued on this endless cycle of acting without considering the consequences. So much so that my junior year of college, when he was still in high school, I got the call that he'd overdosed on some pills he'd gotten from a friend that were unknowingly laced with something much more potent. He got his stomach pumped, then our terrified parents dumped their life's savings into a rehab facility that they really thought would work. Took out a loan when he had to go a second time while I was away on a deployment.

By the third go-'round, he called me first because he was terrified of their reaction. I'm not sure mine was much better. But I made him swear right then and there that he'd never bother our parents again. It was killing them to watch him struggle, and it was killing me to watch them give up everything for a kid who couldn't see how his addiction issues were hurting everyone around him. Or if he could see it, he simply didn't care.

Every time, it's the same excuse. His friends. Some stranger at a party. Not him. Never him. He was just a victim of the circumstances, and could I please bail him out yet again?

"It's the last time. I swear, Kit. I'm not gonna talk to those guys no more. I'll get a job. Get clean. Just please don't let me rot here." His voice is as frayed as my nerves. And despite the rage boiling in my veins, it cuts me to the quick. At the end of the day, he's my little brother. When he calls, no matter how much trouble he's gotten himself into, I can still hear Mama the day they brought him home from the hospital and placed him in the pillow nest on my lap.

"He's your responsibility now, Christopher. You're his big brother. You gotta show him the ropes. Make sure you look out for him. Always. You promise?"

I've been keeping that promise all twenty-six years of his life. At this point, I can't even tell if it's helping or hurting him that I'm always there to catch him when he falls. Only that it's killing me.

I scrape a hand through my hair, focusing on the flickering red glow of the clock on the bedside table. It's late in the afternoon, and a weekend no less. I can get a bondsman, but it'd be no use. The earliest Judge Carson will set bail is Monday. Ask me how I know. "What are your charges?"

"Possession."

I grind my molars to the precipice of breaking. "How much?"

The line goes dead for so long I pull the phone back to be sure I haven't dropped the call. The seconds are still ticking past on my phone screen, so I return it to my ear. "Gage, how much were you caught with?"

"Hardly any, man, but they're also accusing me of intent to sell." His voice is smaller than it's ever been.

I'm off the couch and pacing, the only thing that helps temper my racing heart. "That's a *felony.* Do you realize that? How could you be so stupid?"

"It wasn't mine!" he whines. "You have to believe me."

"I wish I could." Except experience is a hell of a teacher, and everything we've been through to this point tells me he would, in fact, do this. Working in law enforcement, especially in a town as sleepy as Loveless, where drugs are the entertainment of choice among the less savory crowd, I can see it all play out. The dollar signs rack up behind my eyes, like the world's worst lottery. This is bad. The worst it's ever been.

And it's never going to get better. Not for so long as I keep saving him when he's headed up shit creek at breakneck speed without so much as a plastic spoon for a paddle.

"I'm not paying it. Not this time." I pause at the glass door to my balcony, gazing out over the swaying palm trees around the pool to try and steady my swimming head. "If you keep going in this direction, you'll be dead by the time you're thirty. I'm doing you no favors by saving you from the consequences of your actions, and quite frankly, there's not much I can do to save you from these. You'll go to jail, Gage. Might as well aim for time served."

"Fuck you," he seethes. The wounded-puppy act drops instantly, and I'm reminded of the time he blackened my eye when I caught him stealing pills from our parent's medicine cabinet after Dad's back surgery. The day I truly realized this was not just a young kid messing around, but a man with a serious problem. "If you don't post bail, I'm calling Dad. He'll come get me. He's not a self-righteous asshole like you."

I hook a hand on the back of my neck, suddenly feeling half my age. I want to volley this problem to our parents. Let them fix it for once, when I'm so weary from doing it for years. But then I think of our mother crying softly while we sat in court for his first misdemeanor, and I blow out a resigned breath.

My baby brother. My responsibility.

"The earliest we can do anything is Monday. You know that."

Just like that, we're friends again. In his mind, at least. "So you'll get me out first thing?"

"It doesn't work like that. You'll have to see the judge for your bail hearing. Only then can I get you out." My gaze drifts to the rooftop bar on the opposite end of the building, where I can just make out the faraway shimmer of Tess's blonde hair. "Do you have a place to go after? That isn't with those guys?"

He hesitates, and my heart sinks.

"You can't go to Mom and Dad's. That's an absolute hell no, do you understand?"

"It's not like you'll be able to stop me, Kit," he says pointedly. "They're my parents, too."

I bite back a growl. My brain is working overtime, cycling through options. But there's really only one. I study Tess as best I can from here, as though committing her to memory. How will I explain that I'm leaving? Will she even care at this point? "I'll be with them. And I will not hesitate to kick your ass if you show up. You may be my brother, but I will not let you bring that shit into their house. Not again."

His rage seeps through the phone. Silent but so sharp I can feel it lancing my already frayed nerves.

"Whatever, man. You act like you're so much better than me, but you're just a prick who couldn't keep his own wife satisfied at the end of the day. Mom and Dad ain't much more proud of you than they are of me, huh?"

I close my eyes, shuttering off the world and the emotions his words invite all at once. "I'll see you on Monday. Okay?"

His response is a guttural curse punctuated by the sound of the phone being slammed into the receiver. I've seen inmates do it a thousand times. Imagining my brother in their place has my skin crawling.

My phone lands on the covers with a muted thud. I follow suit, flopping face down into the white comforter. It does nothing to dull the ache now pressing at the backs of my eyes. I feel sick. Terrified. Guilty, for whatever fucking reason. But mostly I feel anxious. Because there's no going back now. I have to face my parents, like it or not.

Chapter Sixteen

Tess

I WAIT AROUND for Kit to return from taking his phone call for longer than I'd like to admit. By the time the sun has melted like an orange creamsicle into the Gulf, and I'm still refusing to order dinner, Alex starts stealing suspicious glances at me when he thinks I'm not looking.

"Just send my usual to the room," I say, gathering my room key and purse from the countertop as I scoot off my stool.

He quirks a brow but doesn't look up from the inventory form he'd been filling out. "What happened to the restaurant near the aquarium?"

I stop midstep, toe to the ground, and turn to pin him with a glare. "No one likes an eavesdropper, *Tío.*"

"Hardly an eavesdropper." He places the paper on the stainless-steel prep counter and glances at me, the quirked corner of his mouth just visible beneath that awful goatee. "I'm the one who told him about the place."

"So a meddler, then." I point at him. "That's worse and you know it."

He grimaces. His gaze drops back to the spreadsheet, and he mutters, "*Metí la pata,*" under his breath.

"That's what I thought," I snipe, though I have no clue what he's saying.

Food service comes and goes. My half-eaten dinner grows cold while I sit in bed, knees to my chest and HGTV on the television, waiting to feel better about the situation. I did what I needed to do. Laid down the boundary that will keep both our hearts safe, and yet I feel like absolute dog shit. I retrieve my phone from the piled-up comforter on my right and navigate to Alicia's contact, hoping for a quick confidence-boosting bit of validation from my best friend.

ME

I officially shut things down with Kit.

In no time at all, my phone vibrates with an incoming text. I laugh at the mental picture of her fingers flying over the phone while her tongue peeks out from between her lips the way it does when she's focusing on something intently.

ALICIA

RUDE. Why was I not consulted first? Don't you know I, as an old married woman, must live vicariously through you?

ME

...you're two years younger than me.

ALICIA

and YOU'RE no fun.

I kill the screen and toss it back to the pile of covers from whence it came. So much for that.

Time passes slower without Kit around to fill it. I knew this, had experienced it while avoiding him all day, but it turns out that it's much worse when I'm the one being ignored. Sleep is a welcome reprieve, but when I wake, it's not to a knock on the door, but a seagull squawking on my balcony railing. I even double-check to be certain I removed the Do Not Disturb sign. The empty brass knob confirms it: the tables have turned. Which is basically what I asked for, so why am I so upset about it?

No. I asked to be his friend, not to cut off contact completely. This feels like he's just being petty. In a huff, I strip my clothes from the day before, now wrinkled from sleep, and change into my bathing suit. I'm not going to sit around all day waiting for him to get over the fact that I don't want to sleep with him. He's taken up enough of this vacation as it is.

I told him this trip was important to me, and I meant it. If there's any chance that this is going to be the last time I come here, I have to make the most of it. Have to imprint everything on my heart so I can never forget this place, no matter how far I go. So I can never forget *them*.

I spend the morning in the water, till my fingertips are prunes and I've found two partial sand dollars. Then, freshly showered and rose-colored from the sun, I drive to the sandwich shop thirty minutes away where Dad used to insist on dragging us at least twice each trip. I eat a Baze in his honor—their specialty chicken salad sandwich with banana peppers and some secret sauce I can't identify—but dip it in their homemade ranch for Mom. After a quick trip to the street market near the boardwalk, something Mom always loved to meander on good weather days, my collection of rings is freshly topped off with a mother-of-pearl piece that she would adore.

I soak it all in. Then spend an hour on my balcony trying to imagine what life would look like without it. Maybe I could move abroad. Work as a sherpa in Nepal, despite how much I loathe hiking. Or move to California, where there's endless sunshine to enjoy without any of the humidity. It's hard to pick a destination when I have no idea what I'm truly seeking. Freedom from my past, maybe? A hard restart? Some metaphorical equivalent of slapping the computer so it stops glitching and instead becomes something you can depend on. Unbroken and functional once more.

There's a fine line between continuing my restless wandering and finally seeking the path meant for me. And boy, do I walk it like the tightrope it is.

A distant banging pulls me from this reverie. I blink back the haze of tears I hadn't realized were falling and peer over the railing, half expecting to find Mo and the maintenance crew messing with something on the deck below that leads to the water. Just then, the banging sounds again, only I realize now that I'm focusing that it's coming from inside my room.

As I pass it, I kick the tray from last night's room service under my desk, then grab my bra from the back of the armchair and stuff it into the cushions. The key will be not to forget it, otherwise it'll make for quite the shock of Magdalena's life when she cleans my room next.

I'm breathless by the time I yank open the door to find Kit with his hand braced on the frame above it. The slopes and sinew of his muscular arm loom over me, and the sleeve of his tee rides up, bulging at his shoulder. I attempt to gulp quietly as I avert my gaze only to meet his where it rests on my face.

"Hey." The word takes effort from him that I didn't expect. He grins sheepishly. His hair is damp, his scent fresh and strong. The crook of his once-broken nose is accentuated by the dark purple bags beneath his hazel eyes. One look at him and all the anger I'd been feeling at him for avoiding me slowly packs its bags and slips out the emergency exit of my brain. He's hurting; that much is apparent.

I step to the side and sweep an arm toward my room. "You want to come in?" The door opens into a living area with a desk, armchair, and fold-out couch that I always slept on when I came with my family. Plenty of places for us to sit without the temptation of sharing a bed.

He doesn't bother tearing his gaze from mine. Not even when he dips his chin in resignation. "No, I won't impose. I just wanted to let you know I'm leaving tomorrow. Not permanently or anything. But I—" White teeth flash as he bites down on his lip, interrupting himself. Through the open balcony doors, a breeze rushes in, tousling my hair. He sighs, and I feel the weight of it in my bones. "I've decided you're right."

"Always am," I quip. It's a sad attempt to cover up my disappointment. My heartbeat ceases, like a fist has closed too tightly around it to keep on pulsing. "But about what, specifically?"

The corner of his mouth lifts, though I'd hardly call the expression joyful. "I'm going to go see my parents."

I glance at the gold watch that dangles from my thin wrist. "Right now? How far is that?"

"Not now. Tomorrow. It's about a two-and-a-half-hour drive, so I'm heading out bright and early. I wanted to give you a heads-up so you didn't think I just up and left you."

I'd never think that.

I don't know where the thought comes from. It flits into my mind like a memory you'd much prefer stayed forgotten. Unwanted. Confusing. Why wouldn't he leave? I've given him every reason to. And yet I never considered the possibility that he might.

I fold my hands over my stomach, suddenly queasy. His gaze tracks the movement. Sometimes it feels like Kit notices everything, even the things I wish he didn't. Perhaps especially those.

But I notice things too. Like the tension in his shoulders. The nervous dart of his tongue over his bottom lip. And his eyes, so dark now they could hardly even be considered brown. More like the color of a tumultuous sea. The color of something raw and aching beneath the surface.

I think of his outstretched hand as I cracked open the window to my pain for the first time in years. Of how safe it felt when I finally took hold.

"Do you want some company?"

"Right now?" he asks, one brow rumpling his forehead.

"No." I say it too quickly. Too succinctly. He winces. I shift my weight from one leg to the other and tilt up my chin. "I mean, sure, but I was referring to tomorrow. I could ride with you."

I have no clue why I'm offering. All I know is that he looks like he's lost sleep over this already, and if I can somehow make it a tiny bit less nerve-racking by being there, then I will.

All I know is that today, without him, was the first day since arriving where the grief felt close enough to drown me again. So much for focusing on remembering.

Kit captures his shaking head by raking a hand through the nearly black strands of his hair. "Oh, no. That's okay. I'm probably going to stay the night if they'll allow it. But I'll be back on Tuesday."

I hold up a palm, my brow furrowed. "What do you mean, *if?* Do they not know you're coming?"

"Not exactly," he says, grimacing.

I drop my hand to my side and try pinching my thigh to remind myself it's not my business. But then I think of how much it sucked today, suffering alone. How much better it was with Kit by my side, even if it felt like a weakness at the time. I shake my head at him. "If there's a chance you'll be turned away by your own flesh and blood, I'm not letting you face that alone, Kit."

Besides, isn't that what friends are for?

His features soften, some of that heavy stress slipping away tangibly. But he shakes his head once more. "I can't let you do that. You just told me how important this trip is, and this would take even more time—"

He's right. I did say that. And I meant it. But this feels important in a way that I can't explain. All I can do is trust my instincts. "I'm going. No debate. No complaining. From me, that is."

I expect him to argue some more. To put up a fight. But the moment the words leave my mouth, his entire body sags with relief. He ages in reverse right in front of me, going from a self-assured grown man to a young boy who's just grateful to shuck off some of the weight on his shoulders. He seems fragile now in a way I've never noticed before. Breakable.

I watch as if it's someone else's hand that reaches out to cup his jaw, someone else's thumb that smooths the edge of a sleepless bruise beneath his eye. But I feel him melting into that hand as if it were mine. The warmth of him, the strange familiarity leaves my palm stinging like it's a once-sleeping limb now finally waking up.

The buzzing doesn't stop even after I've dropped my hand. I gather the hem of my cotton shorts and hold on for dear life. My mind is struggling to catch up with my words and actions, and as I begin to grasp what I've gotten myself into, I feel the urge to spiral.

"So, now that it's settled," I say, swallowing back the nerves constricting my throat, "how about we check out that restaurant you mentioned?"

Uncertainty dances in his gaze as he studies me—checking for any sign of doubt, I imagine. Even if he sees one, he doesn't let on. Eventually he sighs, straightens his spine, and gazes down at me with his best impression of a relaxed smile. "Sure. Dinner sounds nice."

If I thought Kit was tense yesterday, this morning he is downright stressed-out. It's palpable, leaving a bitter taste in the air of his rental car. I do my best to combat it with upbeat music and a hodgepodge of snacks I snagged from the pantry at the Carmen, but he doesn't eat a single Teddy Graham. His back remains ramrod straight, his jaw set, for the entire drive. In fact, the only reason I know he's alive in there is because I can see his chest rise and fall with every breath.

His foot finally eases down onto the brake pedal as we take an exit somewhere just over the border of Mississippi. A stilted drumbeat rattles from his fingertips onto the steering wheel. We roll to a stop at a blinking red light, and he glances left, then right, repeating the motion three more times despite no oncoming cars in either direction.

"Do you remember how to get there?" I ask, trying not to sound judgmental. I know it's been a few years, but this town appears to be only slightly bigger than Fly Hollow. I could probably navigate to half the homes of my high school classmates, though I'd never have a reason to. Kit seems even more capable than me. So what gives?

His fingers still, and he crumples forward, head landing on his knuckles. "We have to go somewhere first. And I just— I need—"

Some of the crackling energy dissipates when I settle my hand on his curved spine and begin long, steady strokes along its length. "Whatever you need, it's okay. It's going to be okay." I say it with less confidence than I feel. Something big is upsetting him, bigger than just seeing his parents. I want to yank the burden off his shoulders, but I know firsthand how things like that cannot be taken. It's something he has to give away. Piece by piece. Maddeningly slowly. Until at last, he can breathe again.

He draws a deep breath, and when he speaks, his voice is an octave lower. "Just promise you won't ask any questions, okay?"

My mouth pops open, but I snap it shut, my teeth clacking together. I run my tongue over them. Swallow thickly. When the silence stretches too long to be comfortable, Kit glances sidelong at me, and I nod hesitantly.

"Promise," I breathe. "No questions from the peanut gallery."

He doesn't laugh. Doesn't even exhale. He turns back to face the road, cranking the steering wheel to the left as we pull forward at last. We pass through a town not unlike my own, with old red brick and shotgun houses and railroad tracks that vibrate our bones as we cross them. After about ten minutes, the buildings give way to a tall chain-link fence topped with coiled barbed wire. He pulls up to a security booth, where a portly man with no hair on his head and too much hair on his upper lip leans out the open window and grunts a greeting when Kit rolls his down in turn.

I try not to listen, but I'm right next to him. When he tells the guard that he's here to bail out an inmate, I grit my teeth against every question that bubbles to the surface.

We park in a cloud of dust kicked up by our tires in the gravel lot. Before he gets out of the car, Kit meets my gaze only briefly. When he squeezes my hand, I'm not sure if he's giving strength or taking it.

He's gone for about thirty minutes. Long enough for my bladder to be near bursting and my curiosity piqued. When the main door to the jail opens again, and Kit spills out of it, I forget to breathe. A man trails behind him, equal to him in height but far thinner. His black hair is shaggy, and his clothes—a T-shirt for a band I don't recognize and dark-wash jeans—are equally so. He avoids Kit's gaze, studying the ground like there'll be a test later. Kit's arms are crossed over his chest. Every muscle in his body is locked tight. This is Deputy Llewellyn. Kit as a cop for the Air Force. All the versions of him that existed long before our brief time together.

My window is cracked. Dust and Kit's voice are carried on the breeze, both spilling into the car. Words like "disappointed" and "rehab" find my ears. Then, as Kit breaks stance to throw his arms around the other man, "baby brother" drifts in, tinged with heartbreak.

They part, and this anti-Kit slinks over to a beaten-up taxi I hadn't noticed waiting. Kit watches it leave, then stands there for so long I'm convinced I'll have to retrieve him. Just as I reach for the handle, he moves. His steps, which are normally so sure, carry him back to me like it'll be their last act. He collapses into the car, slams the door shut behind him, and folds his arms over the steering wheel to catch his forehead.

I watch. And I wait. I don't ask a single question. Not even, *How are you?* because I hated being asked that in the weeks that followed my parents' deaths. Still did when each of my grandparents passed. I wanted to scream, *How the fuck do you think I am?* Broken. That's how I was. And that's exactly how Kit is now.

After what feels like a small eternity, his shoulders begin to shake. In the quiet of the car, parked in the lot of the Jackson County Jail, Kit Llewellyn lets out the most heart-wrenching sob I've ever heard. And I let him cry, the way I always wished someone would've let me.

Chapter Seventeen

Kit

TESS DOESN'T ASK a single question. Not for the extent of my pity party. Not when I finally shift the car into reverse and back out of the parking spot over crackling gravel. I stop at the only fast-food restaurant in town, a burger joint that was once a McDonald's that went out of business my senior year of high school. When it reopened a few years later, the new owners named it McNamara's so the golden arches didn't have to be swapped, only painted. Their last name was actually Sorensen. In fact, I have no clue where McNamara came from, but points for resourcefulness I guess.

Tess and I get out of the car in silence, order our food without looking at each other, and then she disappears into the bathroom with a muttered, "I'll be right back."

I shouldn't have allowed her to come. What on earth was I thinking?

The truth is, I wasn't thinking. It was pure instinct, primal and urgent, that held my tongue when she insisted on joining me. Because even if I knew this was going to be bad, I also wanted her by my side more than I've ever wanted anything in my life. The idea that I could walk away from my brother into the safety of Tess's presence was too enticing to ignore. If I were a better man, I'd have told her to stay. But I'm not. Never will be when it comes to her, I'm afraid.

I collect our order, one greasy paper bag and two Cokes, from the acne-prone cashier. Tess waits for me by the door, right hand nervously working the hem of her cotton button-down. I hold out her drink, and she takes it without a word.

"Okay," I say as we each shut our car doors behind us. The scent of fried food quickly fills the cab. I'll have to leave the windows cracked tonight, otherwise we'll smell like a deep fryer by the time we get back to the Carmen. "I'm ready to talk."

She swallows a fry and shakes her head. "You don't have to. It's fine."

"It's not fine. You just watched me bail my brother out of jail without so much as a flinch."

"So that *was* your brother." It's not a question. Merely an observation. She takes a long pull from the straw in her Coke, then deposits it in the cupholder and rests her chin in an upturned hand, elbow braced on the center console. "I'm not going to pry, Kit. It was a surprise. But I'm glad I was there. You didn't need to go through that alone."

My chest physically aches at her words. I'd be convinced I'm having a heart attack if the circumstances were different. But they aren't. Gage is currently on his way back to his normal life, without an inch of remorse for what he did. And I'm in a car with Tess, thinking she looks more beautiful, yet unattainable, by the second.

After all, how could she want to be part of a mess like this? A mess like me?

She breaks eye contact first, and probably for the better. I don't fully trust that my brother won't go back on his word and head straight for our parents' house. I crank the car and say a prayer of thanks for whomever invented air conditioning, because

I'd be fainting without it. From the sweltering Mississippi heat as well as the pain of being back under such awful circumstances.

It's not that I thought I'd never come home. I just wasn't ready. Still am not. But like is so often true for him, Gage didn't give me much of a choice.

"Gage is his name." I say it mostly to fill the silence, but once the faucet's on, it's hard to stop. "He's my kid brother, six years younger than me."

Out of the corner of my eye, I see her lips form a limp smile. "I always wanted a little brother."

My brows knit together. "Parents didn't want more kids?"

She shakes her head. "Said they nailed it the first time. I never appreciated the euphemism, but it's a sweet sentiment nonetheless."

A laugh scalds my throat. I take a sip of my Coke to soothe it, swallowing hard. "Well, take it from me. They saved you a lot of headaches."

"Still, it would've been nice." She hums thoughtfully, gaze trained out the window at a swath of trees smothered by kudzu on the side of the road. "When they died, I would've done anything to have a sibling. Someone who understood what it was like to be me."

At a stop sign, I let my eyes close and try to imagine a world in which my parents are gone and Gage is all I have left. When I speak again, my voice is limp. Lifeless. "He's a drug addict. Has been for a while now. Rehab, scared straight programs, AA. None of it helped."

Her palm settles over my knee. Even through my jeans, and despite the heat outside, her warmth is soothing. "I'm so sorry, Kit. I can't imagine."

I roll through the intersection, past a few run-down houses, then turn right down a familiar two-lane highway. "My parents can't know about today. Promise you won't say anything?"

A quick glance tells me she's blinking in shocked confusion. "Do they not know about his drug problems?"

"Oh, they do. But I made him stop calling them for shit like this years ago. He was bleeding them dry. Financially and emotionally. They're getting older, and I just couldn't stand to watch it break them down every time he relapsed. So I handle things now. It's better this way."

"For whom?" she asks quietly, almost as if she doesn't expect an answer. And there's no time to give her one, because my childhood home has come into view.

I gaze up at the familiar facade, trying to see it through her eyes. The faded brick that's more pink than red these days. The sagging carport my dad added on in '99. They've built a shed since I last visited, which I know from our texts is meant to hold all Mom's gardening supplies. It's bright purple and looks so garish next to the '70's ranch-style home that I let out a harsh laugh. Tess raises a brow at me, and I just shake my head.

"Are you sure you're ready for this?" I ask while gnawing at my bottom lip.

She shrugs. "Parents love me. I'm pretty sure Samantha's mom wanted to keep me in the breakup."

This time my laugh is genuine. Who wouldn't want to keep Tess? "Come on, then. No time like the present."

With her lunch in one hand, Tess meets me at the front of the car and loops the other around my arm. She traces imaginary shapes into the crook of my elbow the entire walk up, and it gives me the courage I so sorely need to knock on my parents' door.

"I just cannot believe you are here, son." Dad slaps his knees and pushes to a stand. "You sure you don't want a beer?"

"I'm good," I say, waving a hand. I glance to my right at Tess, who's leaning away from me to gaze adoringly at the photo album my mom is holding out for her to see. "Do you want one, *shnookums?*"

She rolls her eyes and gives a breathy laugh. "No, *honeybun,* I'm already drunk on the high of seeing your naked baby tush."

My jaw slackens. "Mama, you promised no tush!"

"I can't help it! You just have the cutest little butt." Mom elbows Tess gently, and winks. "I'm sure you agree."

Tess presses her lips together, cheeks flushed pink, and nods while holding back laughter. Satisfied, Mom goes back to flipping pages. Tess meets my gaze and widens her eyes in an expression that screams, *You owe me one.*

We spent the first thirty minutes trying to convince them we weren't a couple. I'm not sure who gave in first, realizing resistance was futile, but soon artificial honey coated our voices and increasingly ridiculous pet names started slipping out. It's a welcome reprieve from the heaviness of the morning. I convince myself that's why Tess is going along with it—to make me feel better. Not because she enjoys pretending it's real even the tiniest bit.

It's me. I'm the one enjoying it.

The inside of the house remains largely unchanged. A red brick hearth dominates the living room, even though it's rarely ever cold enough in southern Mississippi to justify a fire. Folded TV trays are stacked against the wood-paneled wall by the opening that leads to the kitchen, and the vague scent of Pine Sol clings to everything, even the cat.

Bringing Courtney here was different. Her family came from a well-to-do area just outside Atlanta. They had more money than they knew what to do with, and spent a metric ton of it on their three children. My ex-wife was the youngest, and spoiled as such. Whenever she stepped foot in my childhood home, she kept her nose turned up till we left. Too dusty, too dated, too dark for her. Even before the divorce, my visits home had grown infrequent at best, between work and her distaste for it all.

But I feel none of that uneasiness with Tess. She snuggles beneath the threadbare afghan Mama draped over their legs to keep warm, while the window unit works hard to keep the room at subzero temps. Her fingers are buried in Petal's butt fluff, which has the calico purring like mad. This couch is as old as I am, covered in a floral design that would announce its age even if the holes in the arms didn't. Tess pays the exposed padding no mind. Or if she does, she's good at hiding it.

"So what have you two kids been up to? What brings you to our neck of the woods?" Dad asks as he settles back into his recliner with a grunt and the hiss of an opening can of Bud Light. Age is creeping up on him in a way that pictures didn't convey. His skin folds easily. His arms are littered with sunspots. He still has all his hair, but it's more salt than pepper these days.

I open my mouth to answer, but choke on the lump in my throat. I've missed him. Missed both of them so much. And now that I'm here, it's hard to imagine why I stayed away so long. I'd built up in my mind that there'd be a lecture waiting for me about the sanctity of marriage. An accusation that I didn't try hard enough to save it.

It could still be coming. They may not want to say anything in front of Tess. And while it's probably pathetic, I'm happy to use her as a human shield for as long as I can.

"Kit came with me on my annual summer vacation. I'm origi-nally from a small town in Alabama, and I grew up visiting a spot on the Florida panhandle every year." Tess reaches over to pat my knee. Her drawl is thicker than it's ever been, drawn out by my parents, who have the dialect of two people who've never been farther north than Memphis. "We made a deal that if he came with me, I'd come to see y'all with him. Isn't that right, pumpkin?"

Oh, she's good. My mouth curves into a grin even as I'm shaking my head nearly imperceptibly. "Sure is, teapot."

Teapot? she mouths. I shrug.

"Oh surely y'all aren't driving all this way just for lunch from greasy old McNamara's?" Mom asks, eyebrows drawn tight around the wrinkle between them.

I rub my palms over my knees to dry them. "Actually, if it's all right with you, we were going to stay the night? Spend a little time catching up?"

Mom squeals and claps so loudly, Petal darts from beneath Tess's hand and disappears under the solid oak coffee table. Dad raises his can in a toast. "Of course you two can stay. I've got a butt roasting in the smoker. Plenty of food for everyone."

Eyeballing the wrought-iron cross hanging over the mantel where a TV would go in anyone else's home, I say, "Okay, great. Tess can have my old room. I'll sleep on the couch."

Dad clicks his tongue and shakes his head. "No can do, son. Couch is my domain."

"Since when?"

"Since he refuses to get a CPAP for his apnea. Keeps me up all GD night," Mom says. She's the only person I know who uses initials instead of curse words, like she'll get to heaven on that technicality alone. She nudges Tess, who laughs politely. I can see the panic in her eyes. The tightness at the corners of her mouth. But Mom goes on, completely oblivious. "I'm sure your parents know all about that, Tess. Getting old is for the birds."

Tess's lips cinch together, and her gaze drops to her hands where they rest in her lap. "Oh, I'm sure they wouldn't have minded."

Mom's gaze cuts from Tess to me, a question in her muddy-water-colored eyes that are nearly identical to mine.

I grab Tess's hand on instinct. "Tess's parents passed when she was in high school."

"Oh, Betty!" Dad chastises, though Mom had no way of knowing. Still, my mother flushes scarlet and looks halfway to tears.

"It's really okay." Tess glances up, locking eyes with my mom and then Dad in turn. "It's been a long time. I'm all right."

"Hon, my mama passed when I was thirteen. Cancer. She was gone so quick I could hardly believe it." Mom takes Tess's other hand in hers. "I am so sorry. You don't ever have to be okay 'round me. I know that hurt doesn't go away. No matter how long it's been."

Tess meets Mom's gaze for a long beat. I can only see her profile; the slight warble of her bottom lip and the tears that dampen the corner of her lashes are all that gives her away. Finally she whispers, "Thank you," in a fractured voice I've rarely heard from her.

Damn. Less than an hour, and my mom has broken through to a part of Tess she guards like it's a matter of national security. I squeeze the hand I'd been holding, willing her to look at me. And she does. But not before the happy mask slips back into place.

"So anyway," Dad says, clearing his throat. "Gage's room is now our home storage unit. But we put a queen in your room, so you ought to have plenty of space for the two of you." He narrows his gaze when I turn to look at him, and adds, "Just no funny business, you hear me?"

Tess cackles, startling all of us. "Oh, sorry," she says when we glance her way. "It's just—we promise. No funny business. Right, Kit?"

Before I can answer, Mom inserts, "Your father and I were young once, too. We know how those hormones rage. We just ask that you be respectful, is all."

I glance between the two strangers who've body snatched my parents. "I'm sorry, where are the people who threatened military school if I was ever caught having premarital sex?"

Dad shrugs. "We've gotten mellow in our old age. You'd know that if you ever came around."

Well, shit. That stings. Tess flinches, meeting my gaze with hers wide and apologetic. I duck my chin, averting my eyes to the family portrait on the wall between the two front windows. "I'm sorry, Dad."

"It's okay. We know you work hard, and it's such a long distance from Colorado," Mom says, always the one to smooth things over when she can. "Heck, Gage lives in town, and we hardly see him. That boy has no excuse."

I study the version of him from the portrait, still gap-toothed and gangly. The summer before it all went to shit. "I'm sure he's just busy."

"He's doing good lately," Dad says sternly, almost like he's trying to convince himself. "Staying clean."

I nod but don't comment. Tess rubs her thumb over my knuckles. I drop my gaze to our joined hands, a lifeline I'd intended for her to use, not the other way around. "Well, I guess Tess and I should unload our bags and get cleaned up. Then I can help with dinner prep?"

"Christopher Llewellyn, are you offering to cook?" Mom flattens a hand over her heart. "As I live and breathe."

"Yeah, yeah," I chide. "Keep being sassy and I won't help at all."

"So no different than the usual?" she quips back, and Dad lets out a raucous laugh.

"Come on, dear. Let me show you my room," I say pointedly. I gather Tess's and my bags from the pile where I left them by the door and guide her down the hall. The house is evenly divided, with a large master on one side of the living space and two bedrooms and a guest bath lining the opposite hallway. We duck into the farthest room, where I shut the door behind us before flipping on the lights.

It's exactly as I left it all those years ago, save for the queen bed that's replaced my old bunks. Dallas Cowboy Cheerleader poster and all.

"Great taste," Tess says, laughing at the artwork. The smile dies a second later, when her gaze falls on the bed. "What are the odds you'll share a bed with your mom?"

I shudder. "Not great."

She props her hands on her hips and sighs. "If I suspect you're trying to get fresh with me, I'm telling Pete."

My laughter bounces off the walls but is quickly punctuated by a pillow to the face.

"I'm serious," she says, pointing a finger at me. "Your dad would help me kick your ass."

"Oh, I have no doubt." I flop onto the mattress, letting my bones disintegrate for a second of sweet relief. The comforter blocks half my vision as I roll my head to gaze at Tess, but I wink with the one good eye and pat the empty space beside me. "I promise no funny business," I say, quoting my father. And then, because things have been far too serious between us today, I add, "Unless you ask for it."

It earns me another pillow to the face. But it's worth it.

Chapter Eighteen

Tess

THE AFTERNOON IS SO full of chitchat and easy banter that I almost forget the way the day started. Save for the few moments where I catch Kit looking forlorn, gaze trained on some distant, unseeable point, it's easy to pretend this is a normal occurrence for us. That I always pick fresh cucumbers for a side salad with Betty Llewellyn while Kit helps his father temp the meat, a plethora of crushed beer cans giving shape to the limp trash bag at their feet. That we always gather around the table Pete crafted by hand and chat over pulled pork that's so succulent I'm pretty sure I smack my lips audibly. The same feeling that crept over me while I sat with Gary in Loveless settles deep within me. A feeling like belonging. Like home.

It's only when we finally retreat to the bedroom at the end of the hall that reality hits me square in the face. Namely that there is one bed, two of us, and a whole lot of questions that I've been too polite to ask but now feel unable to suppress.

I quickly grab a few items from my bag and say without looking at Kit, "I'm going to the restroom."

From where he stands, peering through finger-parted blinds that block our view of the driveway, he says, "Sounds good."

The door hinge squeals when I open it, but he doesn't glance my way.

I take my time brushing my teeth and doing my skin care. Mostly because I'm avoiding the too-small room and the too-small bed and the way I should feel uncomfortable about all this but I don't at all. By the time I'm ready to change into my pj's, there's a knock at the door.

"Almost done!" I say.

"Sorry, Tess," Kit's dad mutters. "It's, uh, a bit of an emergency. And Betty's in the other bathroom."

"Oh."

I wad up my clothes and open the door. Pete's red-faced and grimacing on the other side. "Sorry about that."

"No need to apologize." I smile awkwardly and cling tighter to my pajamas. "Good night, Pete."

"Night, Tess." He says it quickly, but with no less warmth, as we swap places in the restroom and the door once again is shut between us.

One step into the bedroom and I have to fight back the instinct to gulp like an out-of-her-depth movie character. Kit sprawls on top of the covers wearing nothing but gym shorts that leave very little to the imagination. One arm is slung over his eyes. His skin, looking so soft to the touch, is a deep shade of tan from a week spent in and around the water.

How has it only been a week? Time—which so often folds in like an accordion for me, making years feel like days—stretches out instead, turning a few bright moments into an entire history.

With each rise and fall of his chest, his muscled abdomen ripples. My gaze dips lower, to the trail of dark hair that disappears beneath his waistband, and the bottom drops out of my stomach.

"You okay over there?" Kit mutters without removing his arm.

"Um, yes." I shuffle a few steps into the room. "Your dad

needed the restroom, so I've gotta change in here. Just keep your eyes covered, okay?"

The corner of his mouth quirks. "Tess, do you think I've never seen boobs before?"

That sobers me up. I kick his foot where it dangles over the edge of the bed and he yelps. "It's truly a miracle that you convinced someone to marry you."

"Guess that's why I'm divorced," he replies, voice melancholic. It sucks the heat right out of the room, and any satisfaction I'd been feeling at my snipe dies a painful death in my hollow chest.

I clear my throat and, with my back to him, begin unbuttoning my blouse. "Things seemed to go well today. Your parents were really happy to see you."

His responding grumble is noncommittal.

My bra tumbles onto the pile of my crumpled shirt, followed by my shorts and underwear. I slip on a pair of drawstring shorts and a matching navy-blue top. "The way you talked, I half expected to be met with burning pitchforks. Here they are letting us sleep together in sin."

That gets him to remove the arm. He sits up on both elbows and quirks a brow. "Does that mean there will be funny business after all?"

I spin to face him, crossing my arms over my chest. "No. And stop avoiding the subject."

His gaze travels over me slowly, so much so that I feel it as it goes, warming me from the inside out. His irises are still more midnight than hazel. So dark I couldn't read his thoughts if I tried. He presses his lips together and shakes his head, suddenly staring through me rather than at me.

"My parents never wanted me to marry Courtney. Thought I was too young to be making such a big decision, when I had my whole life ahead of me."

I perch on the edge of the bed, one hand propped close enough to his leg that the hair tickles my fingertips. "And what'd you say to that?"

He snorts softly. "That I was the same age they were when they got married, and it seemed to be working out for them."

The corner of my mouth twitches. "Never pegged you for a romantic."

The ceiling fan rocks overhead, rattling in its frame. Kit stares up at it, and I stare at him, wondering how we both aren't blinded by what we see. Him, the yellowish light overhead. Me, the tender devastation chiseled into his features.

"Dad told me the night before the wedding that if I went through with it, then it better be forever. That marriage is sacred, and he didn't raise me to be a man who walked out on his family."

My throat becomes sandpaper, coarse and biting as I swallow. Since the first time we met, I've sensed that, despite not really knowing me, Kit could see deeper into me than anyone else ever had. Now I'm finally seeing him—if not to the core, then very damn well close.

He's a man who lives to please others, and does so under the pretense of keeping them safe. Perhaps that's why he feels so familiar. We both know a thing or two about performances.

"Kit." I rest my hand on his shin. "Have you ever considered that it's not your parents you've disappointed?"

His gaze envelops me like a hand grasping onto a life raft. "Who else?"

"No one." I shrug. Then, more gently, I add, "Maybe yourself."

We stare at each other for a long while. Eventually, when I've memorized the few flecks of gold still visible in his eyes tonight, I move on to studying his face. The dark stubble. The high cheekbones and well-maintained brows. His nose, which is bent slightly in the middle and discolored in a way that looks permanent.

Without realizing, I've closed the distance between us, lying alongside him to get a better look. I trace the uneven surface of that crooked bridge with a delicate finger, though I know the physical pain has long since passed. "How did you break your nose?"

He shakes his head, then closes one hand around my wrist and turns over my hand, exposing my inner forearm to the light. "How'd you get this scar?" he asks, pointing to the puckered white skin near my elbow.

"I fell out of a tree when I was nine." He doesn't stop trailing his fingers over it, and I don't want him to. "Your turn."

"Got in a fight with the guy who was in bed with my ex." His nostrils flare, and his eyes close briefly. When they reopen, his features have relaxed ever so slightly. "I had so much anger, but looking back, he didn't owe me anything. He hadn't made me any vows."

"Eh, he owed you human decency," I correct, and he lets out a raw-sounding chuckle. "But I know what you mean. Sometimes you feel so much inside you that you have to do something physical to get it out. For some people that's fighting or working out or getting tattoos. For others, it's all three."

"Oh yeah? And what kind of person are you?"

"The kind who never sits still." I flatten my lips. "Also, the tattoo kind. But only one!"

This time, his laughter is genuine. It shakes his whole body, and the bed in turn. "What tattoo did you get?"

I roll my eyes, then hook a thumb in the waistband of my shorts and pull it downward, exposing just enough that he can see where my tan line ends and the small blot of ink begins. "Namaste symbol. Had a brief stint where I was convinced I wanted to become a yogi."

"As in the bear?" he quips. I reach for a pillow to slam down on him, but he captures my arm and pins it to my side as he clicks his tongue. "I thought you weren't the violent type."

I rip my arm from his hand and pull back the covers, climbing underneath them and giving him my back. "I don't know, Kit. Something about you just demands it."

The mattress shifts and sags as he rolls to his feet, pads across the room, and turns off the light. When he returns, he tucks himself into the blankets. Even with a foot or so of distance between us, his heat seeps into me, heightening my senses until I swear I could map his body on instinct alone.

We lie there without speaking, the sound of our breathing its own conversation, as I try to forget how his hand felt locked around my arm. Pinning me. The warmth of it, like fireworks beneath my skin, simmers for so long I'm afraid I won't be able to sleep.

"Thank you." Kit whispers the words into the dark, so softly I'm not certain I really heard him. But when I roll over to investigate, there he is, a breath away, eyes glittering in the dim glow cast by the moonlight leaking through the blinds. "For today. For being here."

His breath smells like mint, and it mixes with the headiness of his hair cream to create something delectable. Something like a memory. The scent of our kiss at the aquarium. At the Horseshoe.

My exhale stalls in my throat, forming a knot that I can't swallow past. I told myself I could do this. Be his friend. Even psyched myself up to share his bed without succumbing to this feeling. But now that he's so close that it'd take no effort at all to close this gap and sink into him, I'm suddenly not so sure of my ability to resist.

Then he bridges that gap, tucking a stray hair behind my ear, and I loose that breath like it's on fire.

"Penny for your thoughts, Tess?"

I shake my head against the pillow, the flannel sheets scratching my cheek. "You can't afford my thoughts."

He huffs a laugh. "I think I've been saving up for this moment my whole life." I can feel his gaze roving my skin, heating every nerve ending that it touches until I'm flush right down to my throat. "What if I promise you an entire carton of mint chocolate chip ice cream?"

My pinched smile bursts apart in a laugh. "You're ridiculous."

"And you're beautiful." He says it like he can't help it. Like the words were poised to leap from his tongue whether he parted his lips or not. "Not even beautiful. That word doesn't do you justice. You're magnetic, Tess. I can feel your pull as sure as my own heartbeat."

"Sounds dangerous," I breathe. My brain is short-circuiting. All I know is Kit's presence and the amount of effort it would take to touch him, which is so very little.

His lips part, and his tongue traces them, leaving them glistening. Kit is always handsome, but something about his face cast half in shadow, painted only by moonlight, has my blood on the verge of a simmer. I haven't felt an awareness like this since my first crush at thirteen, and even then, I don't remember it being nearly this intense.

My clit throbs between my legs. I pin them closed, trying to soothe the need rising there like the tide. Kit's nostrils flare, as though he can scent my desire, and when he speaks, it comes out more like a growl. "Feels more dangerous to ignore it."

I don't want him to be right. I want to be perfectly in control and so firm in my convictions, but my damn body hasn't gotten the memo. My hand finds his, and I guide it back to my hip, where those fireworks spark an inferno that scalds me from the inside out. He tugs me closer, till our bodies are flush against one another. The hard plane of his chest is firm against my breasts. I can feel his length pressing along my lower abdomen. Then his hand slowly slips from my hip, along the exposed skin of my thigh, to hook around my knee and draw it over his leg. If he couldn't tell I wanted him before, the heat of my core against his cock is probably a dead giveaway.

"Kit—" I whimper.

"Just ask me," he says wickedly. "I'll take all that aching away if you'll just say you want me to kiss you."

Through the haze of desire comes the memory of his vow not to cross that line until I ask him to. Pride rears up inside me. The only emotion strong enough to squelch this hunger. I push off him, severing the connection that had me near drunk with its effect, and retreat to the far end of the mattress, which is admittedly not far enough.

I still feel him. Smell him. Still want him so badly my fingers tremble, until I bite them down on the edge of the comforter and clutch it to my chin.

I don't turn away from him. If I do, I'm afraid I'll forget that I'm trying to prove a point, and we'll be right back where we started in no time flat.

"Good night, Kit," I say through gritted teeth.

He chuckles darkly, lifting one arm to tuck his hand beneath his pillow so he can stare at me over the slope of his bicep. "Good night, shnookums."

It takes forever for me to actually fall asleep. And when I do, it's only because Kit wiggles his way across the divide and folds me against him. *It's one night,* I reason. And we're only cuddling. Come tomorrow, with a little distance, I'll be right back to standing on firmer ground.

Half-awake, I swear I feel his lips brush my forehead, but by then I'm too far gone.

Chapter Nineteen

Kit

THE EARLY AFTERNOON air sits on my skin like a damp washcloth. Sweat pools on my upper lip, my hairline. In the bends of my knees and the hollow of my spinal column. Dad swipes a shop rag across his forehead and grunts in disgust at the wet mark it leaves on the faded red cotton. He and I watch from our place on the rickety front porch as Mom and Tess say their goodbyes, hugging like old friends. Mom tucks her into the passenger seat of my rental, waving at her through the condensation-coated window once the door's shut.

Dad lets out a gruff laugh. "That woman could make a friend out of a houseplant in about five minutes, I swear."

I nod, amusement ticking my lips into a smile. "Yeah. Tess, too."

"She's a good one, Kit. Lot better than that ex-wife of yours." Dad rests curled fists against his leather belt. Even in this heat, he's wearing jeans and a short-sleeve button-down he got at the Walmart in Pascagoula. If he hiked up his pants leg, I bet there'd be tall white socks damp with sweat coating his calves. "How long you two been dating, d'ya say?"

"We aren't." Tess and I lock eyes through the windshield, and she lifts a brow. I smile and hold up a finger, letting her know it'll just be a minute. "We told you guys that when we first arrived. Tess is my friend."

Dad scoffs. "Poppycock. I know my son." He claps my shoulder, and when Mom clocks it on her approach, she smiles. Out of the corner of my eye, I note Dad returning the gesture. "You got feelings for that girl. Don't even try to deny it."

"Oh, is he still on about that?" Mom chides. Her hair has formed a shape that is neither curly nor straight, just big. She retrieves a claw clip from the hem of her blouse and pins back her bangs. The porch groans beneath her weight, and I glance down at the sagging boards.

"Y'all ought to fix this before it caves in on you." I kick the nearest board with the toe of my shoe. "You're getting too old to risk it. Might break a hip."

Mom swats me on the chest. "You hush with that nonsense."

Dad's forehead crumples beneath lifted brows, but he doesn't glance at me directly. "Sure'd be easier to fix it if my sons came around more often to help."

My chest throbs like it's been cut open. I cross my arms over it to stop the bleeding, but all it does is increase the amount of sweat flooding my shirt. "I'm sorry, Dad."

My thoughts drift to lying next to Tess last night. Beyond the feel of her leg straddling my hip or her breath hot and blustering against my throat. Instead it's her words that settle over me, cooling me as if they were made from ice water. We're not the kind of family to talk much about our feelings. There's no part of me who thinks now, on this front porch, is the time to air all my grievances about Gage, my fears about letting my parents down. But how many times do they have to lament my absence before I accept what Tess implied? That perhaps they aren't as disappointed in me as I may have led myself to believe.

Mom hooks an arm around my hip and lays her puffball of

graying hair on my shoulder. "We just love you, Christopher. I know it's been hard on you since everything with Courtney, and that you and Gage don't get along much these days, but is it so bad that we'd love to see you more often?"

"Your mother almost bought plane tickets to see you this coming Christmas," Dad mutters.

I glance down at her, eyes wide. "You're terrified of flying."

She shrugs. "I'm a desperate woman. I'd do it for you."

My lungs seize, suddenly unable to take on air. I wrap her in my embrace, cradling the woman who once cradled me. "I promise I'll come down. Don't waste your money on me. I'll be here for Christmas, if not sooner."

Dad pats my back gently, right above where Mom's palm rests against my spine. "Better get on, son. Even with the AC, that sun's probably baking your lady."

I bite back a rebuttal that she isn't my lady; partly because it's a wasted argument. Partly because, despite everything, she sure feels like she is.

"Love you both." I plant a kiss on Mom's forehead. As she pulls away, I turn to Dad, biting back all the words I *should* say and instead slapping a hug against his shoulder blades. "I'll be back soon."

"Better be. Don't make me hunt you down," he warns, but there's amusement in his dark gaze.

"Wouldn't dream of it." I step off the porch, onto the loose dirt of their walkway, and wave once more. That heavy feeling still sits like a pit in my chest, but it's lighter now, if only infinitesimally so. "Bye, y'all."

"Bye, baby!" Mom folds into Dad's side, smiling at me with sun-warmed cheeks and a few tears glistening at the corners of her eyes. It's an image that burns itself into my brain, a snapshot I'll hold on to forever. I file it away right next to the one of Tess, laughing freely with white-blonde hair whipping around her face, the whole of the Gulf at our feet.

The air-conditioning fills the car with a dull roar that takes my ears a few seconds to adjust to. By the time it fades, I catch the tail end of Tess's words. "…was sweet."

"Yeah." My voice cracks. I don't have to hear her entire sentence to guess the sentiment. I shift the car into reverse and clear my throat.

"You're lucky to have them," she says pointedly, gaze aimed straight ahead.

I squeeze my eyes shut. When I open them, stars burst across the image of my parents waving to us from the porch. Why is leaving just as hard as arriving? "I know I am."

She picks absent-mindedly at a loose thread hanging from her shirt hem. All the while, her attention never drifts from Mom and Dad. "You should make an effort to visit them more often, Kit. You can't take for granted that they'll always be here."

I know she's only speaking from a place of experience, from firsthand knowledge of just how shitty the alternative is, but it adds salt to the wound that makes the pain of driving away especially unbearable. She's right, of course. I have two wonderful parents and she has none. It feels completely unjust, and yet it doesn't ease the ache in my chest any more than rubbing my sternum with a balled fist does.

"I'll do better," I manage to force out. "I'm trying to do better."

She nods, a tiny jut of her chin. The only way I know to get out of my own mind is to focus on someone else, and so I zero in on her. The fragile tilt to her neck. The warble of her bottom lip. An inhale that rattles and shakes.

I reach for her hand, stilling it on her shirt hem. "Are *you* okay?"

Her thin throat works over a hard swallow. I half expect her to be vulnerable with me, considering everything she's seen over the past twenty-four hours, but after one brief glance in the mirror to check my blind spot, all traces of sadness have been wiped from her expression.

I tighten my grip on the scalding leather surface of the steering wheel. If we're going to be no-holds-barred honest with each other, then it has to go both ways. "You know you don't have to do that, right?"

Her gaze cuts to me, eyes green as the trees that pass outside her window, and as innocent as sin. "What?"

I should let it go, but I can't. Maybe it's because seeing her bridle that hurt is a bit too much like staring down a mirror. Or perhaps it's because this is the same woman who let me splinter into a million pieces in front of her and still wanted to be seen with me afterward. Either way, I bite down on the inside of my cheek, realizing it's too late to backtrack. On any of it.

"You bury your feelings so deep," I say, then draw a breath in, stretching my aching lungs to max capacity. "Everything negative, you push it away like you've somehow convinced yourself you're not allowed to feel anything but happy. What are you afraid's going to happen if you let the world see who you really are? If you let *me* see it?"

Save for the low hum of the engine and the cry of the overworked air vents, silence settles between us. She doesn't answer, and I'm done pushing. She gave me space when she called me out last night. I can do the same for her now.

I turn up the radio. Something somber, with a plucked-guitar melody and a singer whose voice has been raked over the coals. Tess stares straight ahead, still as stone, as we drive away from my hometown.

It's not long before, in true Southern summer fashion, the sky splits in half. In seconds, the blue expanse gives way to black, and then the black gives way to a deluge. Rain pummels the windshield. It falls in thick sheets, blurring the road ahead. I slow to a crawl, and with a quick sidelong glance, I note Tess white-knuckling the armrest on her door.

"Joys of southern living, am I right?" I shout over the cacophony.

Her chin jerks in what I assume is a nod. "I never go out at three p.m. for this exact reason."

"*What?*" I say, cupping my right ear.

"I said—" she starts but cuts herself off. Her waving hand slices my periphery. "Never mind. Just focus on the road!"

I lean forward and squint into the wall of water. "What road!"

That gets her to laugh, and despite the tension of navigating the storm, it eases something in my chest. Neither of us is any good at staying serious for long. The pressure of it would crumble everything we've built up as a testament to the fact that we're doing fine, thank you for asking. Just fine.

I continue my slow crawl forward, watching for taillights in the rain. The interstate has been largely empty since we got on a few miles back, but tourists who aren't used to the weather like to flip on their hazards and stop in the middle of the road when faced with a storm like this. I learned that the hard way as a teen, when I nearly rear ended a couple from Minnesota.

The great thing about these storms is that they pass just as quickly as they come on. After a few harrowing minutes, the drumming softens to a dull roar and the charcoal sky takes on a lighter hue, promising the end is near. I relax back into my seat just as Tess's hand flies across my chest. "Stop!"

I slam down on the brakes. Up ahead, flashing hazard lights blink against the downpour. They sit at an odd angle, a few feet into the margin. I click my tongue. "Looks like an accident."

Slowly I lift my foot off the brake. With every yard we creep closer, the damage becomes more apparent. They didn't simply lose control and hydroplane off the asphalt. The back quarter panel on the driver's side has caved in, drawing the midsize SUV's hood unnaturally close to its trunk. I turn on my hazards and pull a safe distance off the road, then reach for my buckle.

Tess's hand meets mine there, and when I glance up, panic flares in her gaze. Her skin has lost all its color, looking far too ashen for my sunshine girl. "You can't go out there. It's too dangerous."

"I have to." I press my lips together, drawing in deep breaths through my nose to calm my racing heartbeat. Without realizing it, the pounding of the driving rain has been replaced by my pulse in my ears. I shake my head, and it eases ever so slightly. "Someone could be hurt. I need to check on them."

"Please," she cries, her hand closing around my forearm. Tears pool in her lower lashline, spilling in mascara-darkened drips onto her cheeks. "Please stay."

"I will be right back, Tess." She's panicking, and while I want nothing more than to stay here with her and comfort her through this, my sense of duty overwhelms even this most demanding of instincts. I pop the seat belt free and lean forward over the center console. Her skin is clammy beneath my lips when I press them first to her forehead and then her nose, drawing her scent in like the anchor it is. "It'll be okay. You just stay here and call 911."

Her stricken expression as I pull away will haunt me for far longer than many of the horrors I've faced in my career.

I'm soaked to the bone within seconds of exiting the vehicle. While the storm has weakened, the rain still falls in thick rivulets, pouring from the crown of my head and blurring my vision. I curse myself for not at least grabbing a ball cap from the back seat.

Water splashes up my calves as I jog to the driver's-side

window. They're tinted way darker than they should be, and the rain makes it too hard to see past even with my hands cupped over the glass. I knock, hoping whoever's inside will let me know they're fine, just waiting on a tow truck. But when no one responds after about twenty seconds, I suck in a waterlogged breath and yank on the handle.

To my surprise, the door flies open. Airbags fill every corner of empty space. Garish red brushstrokes mar their white surfaces, immediately flooding my nose with the heavy tang of iron. Slumped in the driver's seat is a woman just a few years older than me, bleeding from her nose and hairline. I duck under the cover of the car as best I can and press two fingers to her throat. Her pulse is weak, but blessedly present.

"Ma'am, I'm Deputy Kit Llewellyn. I'm here to help."

There's no flinch in response to my loud voice. Just a muted cry that barely reaches my ears. I narrow my eyes at her slackened jaw, realizing it's not the woman making the noise. Through a gap in the headrests, which are crumpled far too closely together, I catch a glimpse of a small boy in a booster seat with tears pouring down his reddened face.

Shit. "Hold tight; I'm coming!" I close the door as gently as possible and circle the hood. To my surprise, Tess is already there, opening the child's door.

"What are you doing?" I shout, covering her hand with mine and curving over her in an effort to shield her from the rain.

When she glances up, her eyes are wide with fear. "I had to— to help. Had to help."

I reach past her to the boy's balled fist. He's no more than six, with a Paw Patrol sticker slowly peeling away from his instantly rain-slicked forearm. He wails earnestly now, calling for his mama. I squeeze his trembling hand in mine. "Mama is resting. She bumped her head. But help is on the way. What's your name?"

His bottom lip quivers. He has thick black hair that's plastered to his forehead. Big, blue eyes blink up at me. "Brayden."

"Hi, Brayden, I'm Deputy Llewellyn. You can call me Kit, though. Like a Kit Kat. Do you like Kit Kats?"

He nods. His gaze cuts briefly to Tess, then back to me.

"Good. Me too." I offer him what I hope is a reassuring smile. "I'm a policeman, Brayden. That means I'm a good guy. More good guys are going to come, too, and they'll help you and your mama. I promise."

Tess's nails bite into my shoulder. I glance back at her, and she's white as a sheet. Her hair sticks to her neck in thick, rain-darkened clumps. With her gaze trained on the front seat, she sways on her feet.

I pull her into my side and lean close, so my lips brush her slick ear as I speak. "Get back to the car. I will stay with him. It's okay, Tess. His mom is alive; she's just hurt. Did you call 911?"

She retreats enough to face me, pink lips parted. "She's alive?"

I nod. She's going into shock, and it's imperative that I get her out of the rain. "Yes. Did you call 911?"

This time it's her that nods, a deep wrinkle forming between scrunched-up brows.

"Good. Now go get warm." I kiss her softly, without thinking. "It won't be like your parents."

At that, tears pour from her eyes, blending with the rain. "You promise?"

"Cross my heart."

I don't know if she fully believes me, but it's enough for her to walk away. Or stagger, more accurately. When I turn back to Brayden, he's staring at his mother. There's a laceration on his temple, likely from hitting the window. But it's superficial. As I quickly check over his body for other injuries, I scramble for something to talk about to distract him. "Brayden, are you from here? From Mississippi?"

"No," he says, and his gaze cuts back to mine. "But I can spell it. Mama taught me how."

"That's so impressive," I say as distant sirens finally reach my ears. "I've been struggling with it myself. Would you teach me?"

A missing front tooth splits his hesitant smile in half. He spells it out the way my grandmother taught me, years ago on a sloped front porch with stray kittens curled up in my lap. *M-I-crooked letter-crooked letter-I-crooked letter-crooked letter-I-humpback-humpback-I.* I hum it with him, replacing that bloody tang with the memory of Grandma's powdery perfume as he goes.

On the tail end of the final humpback, a fire engine breaks through the wall of water, and I exhale fully for the first time since the rain started falling.

Chapter Twenty

Kit

A HIGHWAY PATROL officer drops his cigarette butt and kicks it to death in the dirt. "Fuckin' hit-and-runs, am I right?"

I can't blame him for being surly. It's his job to conduct what I imagine will be a fruitless investigation. He pushes a set of mirrored aviators up the bridge of his nose, despite the fact that it's still overcast in the wake of the storm. They leave me staring at my own reflection anytime I look at him, so I try not to. He's twenty years my senior, with a gut he can rest his hands on, which he does now. I grimace, both in commiseration and dread that I'm looking at myself in the future.

The ambulance gives a final *whoop* before taking off, en route to the hospital. Traffic crawls past the scene, necks turning to rubber as everyone steals glances at the mangled SUV.

I grunt my agreement with the officer. He's right. It's bad enough to drive recklessly and cause harm to another innocent family. What's worse is not even sticking around to make sure they get help.

He thumbs the notepad in his other palm, perusing what he's written. "There's a special place in hell for 'em, I swear."

I peer over my shoulder to check on Tess, who's curled up in the passenger seat with her gaze trained anywhere but at the wreckage. "Look, if you've got everything you need, mind if I get back to her?" I jerk my chin toward my rental. "This whole thing has her really upset."

"Oh, sure," he says, slapping his notepad shut and slipping it into his uniform shirt pocket. His sunglasses slip down the bridge of his nose slightly, revealing the tan line they've painted around his eyes. "I've got your number, so may call if we have any further questions. You know how these things are, though. Rarely go to trial."

I do know, but I can't bring myself to acknowledge his statement with any level of commiseration. Ever since backup arrived, all I've been able to think about is how Tess must be feeling. How badly I want to go to her. It's not like me. I'm always calm and collected on the scene, whether it be an accident or a full-blown crime. But with her near, I've felt like I'm suffocating for the last hour. Like the only thing that'll fix it is holding her and making sure she's all right. I'm practically vibrating with the need to go to her even as every bit of my military training tells me to act with an ounce of decorum toward a person of authority.

"Thanks again for stopping, man. Bad situation could've been a helluva lot worse if you hadn't gotten here when you did." He offers his hand, and I take it. His shake jolts me, nearly enough to yank me from my thoughts.

Nearly.

I clear my throat, swallowing back the need that threatens to choke me. "Happy to help. And I pray for their sake"—I point to the mangled wreckage—"that you find the bastard responsible."

He barks a laugh that contains no humor. "You and me both, kid."

After a few more pleasantries, I'm finally free to go. What feels like an eternity is probably just a few long strides before I reach the car, bypassing the driver's side to go straight to Tess.

When I yank open the door, she starts. Her eyes are red-rimmed, her nails chewed to the quick. Her knees are pulled to her chest, and she rests her chin there, not looking at me as she whispers, "They took them in the ambulances."

There's an accusation in her voice. And how could I blame her? From where she sat, it looks a whole lot like everything is not okay.

I squat in front of her, forcing our gazes to align. "It was just a precaution for Brayden. His vitals were great. His mom—her name's Amber. She woke up as they were loading her in. Looks like a bad concussion and a broken nose and collarbone, but nothing major that they could find at first glance. She should recover just fine."

Tess's eyes remind me of an algae-coated pond. So still at first glance, but one hint of movement and that water spills from underneath. She blinks, and a single tear escapes. "Like you promised," she whispers.

I take her hand in mine, pressing her knuckles against my lips. "I'll always keep my promises to you, Tess."

At that, she comes unraveled. Her entire body shakes. Each gasping breath is a battle. I rise, hooking a hand under her knees and another beneath her shoulders to lift her from the seat. Then I settle us both into it, with her on my lap and her head against my chest. I breathe in her sweet scent. Her hair tickles my chin. I stroke each drying tendril back from her forehead, then press a kiss against her clammy skin.

She sobs so hard that I'm certain her throat will be raw by the time she finishes. The kind of weeping that's been held back so long, contained in a shoddy dam, that when it finally breaks, it buries an entire town beneath the flood. I'm not sure who clings to the other more; only that when I finally am forced to let go, there will be claw marks in us both.

Eventually the tears give way to short hiccups of breath. Her spine stiffens, and she pulls back, giving herself room to wipe her eyes. "I'm so"—she sucks in a breath—"sorry."

My heart sinks low in my chest. "For what? You have no reason to be sorry."

For a long moment her head remains turned away from me, eyes glazed over. Finally, a shuddering sigh spills from her lips. She folds into me once more, though I sense this time it's more about hiding than anything.

"This is what happens, Kit." Her fist closes around the pocket of my shirt and she beats the handful of fabric against my chest. "You asked me what happens if I show who I really am? *This is what happens.* I fall to fucking pieces."

I lean back so I can look her in the eye. Fury has replaced her sadness. But a second look tells me it's guarding something. Fear crouches just behind, in the folds at the corners of her eyes. In the tremble of her downturned lips. She's afraid, so she's lashing out. And boy do I know how that feels.

"Do you think that scares me?"

She freezes, every feature turning to etched stone. So I push on.

"Tess, if you think seeing you broken, seeing you honest is going to run me off, you're sorely mistaken. I want you. All of you." I cradle her chin, swiping a tear that dives for my thumb. Her cheeks are sunken, her mascara a pair of black bruises beneath each eye. When she blinks, she winces, like my kindness is her own personal brand of punishment. I tilt my forehead to meet hers, capturing her gaze with mine and not letting go. "It's okay to be scared. It's normal to be upset. We've all got demons, love, even if we're good at hiding them. What scares me isn't that you have them. It's the thought that you're suffering all alone in there, when I'm right here begging you to let me in."

When she speaks, her desperate words steal my breath. "And what if I don't wanna be let in to my own shit? What if I want to spend my life pretending none of it's there so I can have a Hail Mary shot at being normal? What then, Kit?"

I bury my fingers in her tangled hair, cradling the nape of her neck. She's here. She's real. And even with her body pressed against mine at the hotel that night in Loveless, or curled into me at the aquarium, I've never felt as close as I do right now. It hits the back of my throat, tasting a lot like need. I want more. I want everything she can give, and then some.

"I wish hiding from it worked, Tess. I really do. But I'm living proof that it doesn't." I gently massage the base of her skull, and her eyelids flutter closed. "You can't outrun a pain like that. It always finds you in the end."

Her whimper brushes my lips. I want to close the minimal space between us. To take all that hurt and make it something that feels good instead. But I can't fix it. I know that. All I can do is be here, and hope she comes to me when she's ready. If she's ever.

"Let's go back to the Carmen, okay? We can make it in time for dinner. I'll bet I can have your favorite dish waiting in your room for you when we arrive with a single phone call."

She sighs, her entire body deflating into me. "They're too good to me."

I smile because she doesn't even see it. Doesn't realize how many people would get on their knees and crawl for her, if only she asked. Myself included. "Nah. They're on to the same thing I am: Tess Monroe deserves the world. We're all just vying for a chance to give it to her."

Her playful swat meets my sweat-slicked bicep with a wet thwack. Turns out the minute the rain disappeared, humidity rushed in with a vengeance. I'd kill for a towel right about now.

When she pulls away, her nose is wrinkled. "You need a shower."

"Is that an offer?" I ask, raising a brow.

I catch a glimpse of her rolling her eyes as she scoots off me, freeing me from her seat. By the time I make it around to my side, she's buckled in and ready to go. Exhaustion tugs at her puffy lids. As I signal to merge into the long line inching around the remnants of the accident, Tess reaches for my other hand. I expect her to let go once we're past the scene, but she doesn't. She holds on until her hand goes limp in mine, her lips parted as she drifts off to sleep. And then it's my turn to hold her.

And I do, the whole way back to the Carmen.

Chapter Twenty-One

Tess

WHEN WE STEP into the lobby of the resort, it's absolutely bustling. Five o'clock is prime check-in time, and the crowd of new arrivals threads through that of those headed out for the evening, whether that be for dinner or some other off-property activity. Flip-flops thwack against the opalescent tile. Voices echo from the high ceilings. I'm shocked that Jenna even spots me through the masses, but before I know it, her thin arms encircle me, competing with Kit's hand at my back to give me warmth.

She pulls back, cupping my face in her hands. "Tess, are you okay? Alex said there was an accident."

One sidelong glance of Kit's sheepish shrug tells me he made good on his promise to order dinner ahead. Must've been while I dozed off. I sigh, then turn back to my friend. "We're okay. It wasn't us. We came up on a hit-and-run on the interstate. A mom and her young son had totaled their car." I don't have it in me to try to be convincingly unaffected, and it shows. I sound every bit as bedraggled as I feel.

Jenna's brown eyes are wide, her lips bracketed by deep frown lines. "Is everyone okay?"

"They're going to be fine," Kit inserts. He offers the hand

that's not holding up the base of my spine to Jenna. "I'm Christopher, but most people call me Kit. You're either Mara's mom or her sister, right?"

Her olive cheeks turn a deep shade of rose. "She mentioned she'd chatted with you," she replies warmly, taking his outstretched hand. "Jenna. Nice to finally meet you. And yes, Mara's my daughter. Her father and I own the resort." She smiles, pride bubbling from her words. Her gaze dances between us as she adds, "I'm so glad the woman and her boy were okay."

"We are, too." I can feel myself wilting with every second that passes. As happy as I am to see Jenna—and even, deep down, to introduce her to Kit—I'm not sure how much longer I can maintain this conversation. Not since the events of this afternoon have effectively chewed me up and spit me back out again.

She must sense it, because a wrinkle forms between her brows as she measures me from head to toe. "I won't keep you two. Just had to be sure you were all right. Alex said your dinner would be waiting for you in your room, Tess. Let me know if I can send anything else. Some bubble bath, perhaps?"

Kit chuckles softly, and I shake my head. "Not this time, Jenna. But thanks for offering."

She pinches my side playfully. "Any time."

The wheels of my suitcase click over the tile as Kit pushes it toward the elevator bay. His bag is slung over his shoulder, leaving his hand free to continue guiding me down the hall. It should feel overbearing, but it doesn't. In fact, I'm already dreading the moment we part ways and that steady pulse of warmth leaves me. That bit of contact that anchors me on this side of my sadness.

Before the elevator door has even closed, Kit is smirking at me. "Bubble bath?"

I press my lips together. "There was an incident when I was

nine. I may or may not be the reason the whole hotel got upgraded carpet that year."

His laughter drowns out the hum of our upward climb. It's a welcome buoy after hours spent below the surface, struggling for gasps of air. I somehow manage to giggle in return, though it sounds weak even to my ears. We spill out onto the third floor, and despite the fact that both of us were blessed with long legs, we make our way slowly to the very tip of the building where our rooms await our return.

I was so sure when I walked out of here with him just a day ago that I was only tagging along to support him. So how is it that I'm crawling back wounded, and he's the one who picked up my pieces in the end?

We pause awkwardly outside my door. The Marilyn Suite placard has been freshly polished, welcoming me with its gleam. I thumb through my purse, find my key card at the very bottom, and try to ignore the ache in my throat when the mechanical whir of the lock announces I'm free to enter.

The moment I've been dreading comes. Kit's hand slips from my back to open the door. I walk through the gap he's created like I'm leaving home rather than returning to it. The wheels of my suitcase make hardly any noise as he pushes the bag across the plush carpet. He opens the door that leads to the separate bedroom, where he deposits my suitcase right next to my bed. When he returns to my side, his gaze follows mine to the room-service table sitting in front of the armchair in the corner of the living room. After a long pause, Kit clears his throat.

"Well, food's here. So I'll give you some privacy." His tongue wets his bottom lip, and he draws in a ragged breath. "If you need anything—"

"Stay with me."

His mouth clamps shut with an audible click. We both wince at the sound. The truth is, I can't eat right now anyway. The bottom has dropped out of my stomach. I can't think about food, or a shower, or anything else besides what I *should* do and what I *want* to do, and how those two things never seem to overlap. Especially not now, when the thing I want most is to not be alone. One glance at Kit's rain-mussed hair, and suddenly the sensation of his muscular arms encircling me while I fell apart after the accident reappears like a phantom limb.

He may be a bad idea, but I'm tired of pretending like I'm known for making excellent choices.

His Adam's apple bobs as he swallows. "You got soaked out there. You probably need a shower. I know I do. I can come by after…"

"Shower with me." I don't know whose voice that is. So sure of itself. So quietly desperate. A shudder runs through Kit, then finds its way to me. Soon I'm outright shivering. The cranked-up AC in the room hits my clammy skin, pimpling it with goose bumps. I mindlessly rub at my forearms, unable to look away from Kit's wild, tortoiseshell gaze.

He shakes his head slowly, disbelief pulling his jaw taut. "You don't mean that."

"I do, though." I chance a step forward, knowing very well that if my legs give out, he'll catch me. "I don't know what it means, or how much it will change things between us. But I do know that you're the only person in the world who makes me feel even a little less alone. So please don't make me beg, Kit."

Every hollow in his angular face is painted in shadow. His back is to the sliding glass door that leads to the balcony. Orange afternoon light gilds him at the edges, making him look more like a dream than a man. And hasn't he always been, at least a little bit? Exactly what I needed, even when I didn't have the words to give the request shape. Someone only my subconscious could've contrived, all while I wasn't paying attention.

He swipes a hand through the mess of his hair, his forearm

flexing as he tightens a fistful in his grasp. "Okay." His voice cracks, splitting the word in two. "If you're sure."

I'm tired of speaking. Words feel so heavy right now, so cumbersome. Instead I tug my shirt over my head and let it fall to the floor. Let that be my answer. My shorts follow after, and when I'm standing in front of Kit with nothing but a pair of underwear and my bralette to cover me, he jolts into action, yanking his own T-shirt off in one smooth motion.

"I'll get the water warmed up," he says. I'm standing between him and the bathroom, though, so his escape brings him right past me. Our skin brushes, and I've never been more aware of every nerve ending in my body. Of how they burst and fizz when they make contact with him. Somewhere behind me, the glass shower door slides open. Seconds later a faucet shrieks to life.

I get to work unclasping my bralette. Shucking my underwear. Kit's back is to me when I step through the bathroom doorway. Steam billows from the shower, coating my skin in warmth, but even so, I shiver when he turns.

"Tess." My name comes out as a low rumble. A warning, almost. Even with shorts on, I can see how much the sight of me affects him. His thick length strains against his zipper, and I have to force myself not to reach forward and free it.

Desire pools low in my belly. An ache builds between my thighs, pulsing with need. I have to drag my eyes back to his, heavy-lidded with lust. "Aren't you going to undress?"

He shakes his head. "You know, it's really difficult to be your friend when you look like that."

My nipples pebble at his praise, aching with the need to be touched. And it is praise, of that I have no doubt. I can't quite put a name to the look in his dark gaze, but gun to my head, I'd call it worship.

"I don't want to be your friend, Kit." As soon as the words are out, my chest inflates with relief. I hadn't even realized how much the lie was weighing me down. Hadn't admitted to myself it was a lie in the first place. But of course it was. How could someone feel the way I do when he is near and mistake it for anything so mundane as a friendship?

I draw in a steam-soaked breath. "I have tried so hard to convince myself I don't want you, and that only makes you harder to resist. I'm tired of fighting it." I shrug, letting my hands slap my thighs in exasperation. "I give up."

A single brow lifts. "What are you saying?"

"I have no clue," I say, laughing harshly. "I don't know what this feeling is, or where this could even possibly go. All I know is that it's what I've wanted since the very first time I saw you." My chest is on fire, scalding me from the inside out. I swallow hard. "Isn't that enough?"

He smiles like it's the most painful thing in the world. "Yeah, Tess. It's enough." Then he holds out his hand.

I take it. Let him guide me into the onslaught of steaming water. He quickly strips, then joins me beneath the downpour. His body is perfection. Studying him is like tracing my fingers over a topographical map. The line carved from his sternum to his navel is a river I want to float down. The ridge of his hip bone, a precipice I want to lounge upon. A valley of muscle draws my gaze downward, and I swallow thickly at the sight of his length, so hard for me already.

"Uncircumcised," I note, sounding so unlike myself. "Nice."

Laughter rattles the cage of his ribs. His shoulders dance, and he throws his head back into the flow of water, mouth wide open and gasping. "I can't believe that was your opener."

I flush crimson, embarrassment licking all the way from between my breasts up to my temples. "Sorry. I don't know why I said that."

His lips seal in a wry grin, and he reaches for me, capturing my hand and tugging me close. Our bodies meet, his cock pressing into the softest part of my abdomen. Dark chest hair scrapes my breasts, making my nipples ache. He presses a kiss to my forehead, husky laughter brushing my skin. "It's fine. It was cute."

"I can't believe we're touching. Naked."

"I know. You think *you've* wanted this since we first met. You have no idea how often I've imagined this exact scenario. You know, minus the circumcision comment."

"It just surprised me, that's all!" I try to pull back to face him, but he squeezes me tighter, shaking with laughter once more. Over the spray of water, I can hear the rasp of it in his lungs. The sound melts my core until it's molten and full of yearning. After a second he relaxes his grasp, and I lean back to meet his heavy-lidded gaze with one of my own. "When you thought about it before, did you touch yourself?"

His expression hardens. I can tell he's chewing at the inside of his lip, probably gauging how much is too much to tell me. "Tess, if I told you how often you were the reason I had to fuck my hand these past ten months, you'd probably want a restraining order."

A spark runs down my spine, stoking the flame in my core. "Wouldn't it be better if I did it for you?"

A groan rips from his throat. His fingertips trail down my back and dig into the soft flesh of my ass so hard it'll probably bruise, and for some reason that thought thrills me.

"We can't do this right now. You've been through a lot today. I came in here to help you, not to seduce you."

I quirk a brow. "And what if I seduce you instead?"

"Consider me thoroughly seduced." He shakes his head at me. His pupils have dilated, blotting out every shade of green in his eyes. All that's left is the darkness. He looks positively sinful with water pouring from his stubbled jaw. "Need I remind you, you haven't yet asked me to kiss you again."

"Need *I* remind *you*," I retort, since we're apparently going for debate-speech-level formality here. I lock my hands against his tailbone and pull him closer, though there's no space left between us. "You already kissed me today. At the accident. It was a peck, but it counts."

His lips part, an exasperated grin tipping the corners upward. "After all that happened, that's what you remember?"

I shrug. "I'm just saying, bet's off."

"It was never a bet." He says it quietly. More to himself, it would seem, than to me. Then he leans down, and amid the unrelenting stream of warm water, our lips meet. I vault onto my tiptoes, dragging my breasts over his chest as I go. It draws a moan from deep in my lungs, which spills into our kiss. He swallows it like he's a drowning man searching for air. Our lips part, tongues slipping alongside each other. Kit's hands knead my ass, fingertips getting so close to where I want them yet never close enough. He deepens the kiss, and just when I think I will shatter from the pressure of my desire, he drives me backward into the cool shower wall, holding me together with the weight of his body.

I can no longer tell where he ends and I begin. Only that, when a growl rips from my stomach, it rattles us both.

We part on shaky breaths. Not because I want to. In fact, I cling to him desperately. But Kit loosens my grip easily, plucking my hands from his body and placing them at my sides. His cock is hard and pulsing between us, clearly as upset as I am at the turn of events.

"We've got to get you fed." Kit reaches for the tiny hotel shampoo bottle and uncaps it, squirting a dollop into his palm. "Turn around, and I'll take care of you so we can get out."

"Ugh." I do as he says, reluctantly giving him my back just as my grumble bounces off the walls. "I wish that meant the same thing to you as it does to me."

Kit buries his hands in my hair, lathering until the scent of a beach holiday coats the thick air. Coconut and hibiscus and some unique musk that I always associate with the Carmen. He kneads my scalp, drawing a moan from my lips. At that, he uses my hair to pull me into him, so his cock is nestled in the seam of my ass. His lips meet my throat, and he grazes his teeth over my pulse point before whispering, "Believe me, I will take care of you in every way possible. You think it doesn't kill me to see you dripping wet and naked, your perfect nipples so tight with want, your pussy so ready for me that I can feel its heat against me now?"

I gulp, and he licks the hollow behind my earlobe. "It does, Tess. But I can't have you the way I want you if you're exhausted and hungry. So let me do this for you. There will be time for everything else later."

My bones turn to liquid. I dissolve into him, pliable to his every touch. He bathes me thoroughly. Washes and rinses my hair. Drags a washcloth over every sensitive nerve ending, then quickly repeats it all on himself. He towels me down, and even though we both know I could do it, I let him. Because I can tell he needs this, almost as much as I need him.

We eat pasta, eventually trading the sunset for the flickering blue light of shitty cable. I don't bother changing out of my towel, and neither does he. Eventually, when our stomachs are full and my lids weigh heavy, he guides me to the bed and pulls back the covers, gesturing for me to climb in. We curl into one another, every inch of us bare, and drift off to sleep to the distant sound of waves crashing.

It's the best sleep I've had in years.

Chapter Twenty-Two

Kit

T‌ESS STROLLING down a sidewalk in Loveless with the wind plastering a sundress to her legs. Tess painted blue by an overhead aquarium, chin tilted up to take it all in. Tess curled up on a ratty couch next to my mother, cooing affectionately over my baby pictures. Until now I thought I'd seen this woman in all her most beautiful forms.

But waking up to find her sleeping beside me, naked and sprawled out beneath a fluffy, white comforter? Nothing else could ever compare.

I lie completely still, afraid even the slightest movement will wake her and end this fantasy come to life. Golden spools of her hair form a fan around her head. Her pink lips are pursed, skin creamy and smooth in contrast. A freckle I hadn't noticed before mimics a piercing on the shell of her nose. The comforter cuts across her ribs and her arms rest on top of it. Her breasts are exposed, perfectly round and pert with rosy nipples that leave me salivating. I want to devour her as much as I want to leave her be, in order to avoid defiling someone so angelic.

Impossible. It feels impossible that she exists. That I'm here with her now. And yet the rightness of it is something I'm more sure of than anything before in my life. There was a shift between us yesterday. Whatever it was left both our walls down, more so than they've ever been. Now all I can think about is finding a way to keep it like this for as long as possible.

I want to believe that we've really turned a corner. That she won't change her mind again and retreat the moment she wakes. I want to fulfill every promise I made to her in that shower, with her body slick against mine. But apprehension stirs my gut. I'd be stupid not to consider the very real possibility that she'll regret this as soon as the sleep has fully cleared from her eyes. It's the anxiety of that which pulls me reluctantly from the warm bed.

The sun has yet to fully rise. Only a few milky strands of its light illuminate the room. The coffee shop in the lobby won't open for another hour and some change, so I settle for the cheap coffee maker that sits on the counter of the kitchenette in the corner of the living area. It hisses to life, spitting out one and then another cup of black coffee, which I doctor from the selection of sugars and creamers on the tray to hopefully resemble the drink Tess enjoys every morning.

She doesn't stir for the noise of the coffee maker, or me slipping on my shorts from yesterday. When I push open the sliding glass door in her bedroom, it's the sound of the not-so-distant waves that finally pulls her into consciousness. She stretches like a lazy cat disturbed in its nap. Her back arches, the fullness of her breasts shifting. Then I'm the one shifting, adjusting my erection into the security of my waistband.

I half expect her to cover herself when she remembers she's naked, but instead, when her lids crack open and she turns toward me, propping her head on her palm, I'm greeted with an uninterrupted view. She catches me looking, and responds with a bleary smile. "You're up early."

I clear my throat and drag my gaze up to meet hers. "Unfortunately you can take the man out of the Air Force, but there are some things about the Air Force that you can't take out of the man. And also, you were snoring." I wink and hold up two steaming cups of coffee. "I thought we could watch the sunrise together."

She chuffs at the blatant lie—if anyone was snoring, it was me—but rolls toward the edge of the bed and sits up, the comforter falling to her waist. She grabs the nearest piece of clothing, which happens to be the shirt I left on the floor, and yanks it over her head.

Add Tess in my clothes to the list of my favorite views.

"I may snore, but you talk in your sleep." She reaches me in a few easy strides and plucks a coffee from my hand, but makes no move to pass me and step onto the balcony. Instead she leans into me, every curve of hers soft against all my hard, and attempts to impersonate me with an even more affected Southern accent than her usual. "*Tess is so perfect. I've never wanted anyone so much. I can't believe I didn't sleep with her when I had the chance.*"

"If I really said all those things"—I lean down and plant a kiss on the tip of her nose—"then it's only because they're true."

She didn't expect such blatant honesty. I can tell, because her cheeks flush and she glances out to the ocean, which is calm enough to reflect the early dawn like glass.

I tap my cup to hers in the world's laziest toast, earning back her attention. "Hope the coffee is okay. I eyeballed it based off the stuff the barista makes you, but I didn't think adding ice would work well."

She arches a brow, her gaze dropping to the cup she's holding. One barely contained wince later, she swallows her first sip and says, "It's perfect."

My responding snort ripples the surface of my own subpar beverage. "Really testing your acting skills this morning, huh?"

"And?" She holds her arms out as though she's offering herself up for scrutiny.

I shrug. "Needs work."

She scoffs, finally taking this opportunity to step fully over the threshold and fold herself into one of the rattan balcony chairs. The hem of my shirt hits her just below her butt, and pools in her lap when she sits. I can't help thinking about what lies beneath and truly kicking myself for being a gentleman last night, even if I know it was the right decision for us both. If this is the part where she turns tail and runs, then it's a good thing I'll never truly know what I'm missing.

"You coming?" she asks with a tipped brow.

I move silently to the other seat and lower myself, hoping my boner isn't too painfully apparent.

The wind kicks up, stirring a few of her wild hairs. I'm sure I look no different. As soundly as I slept with her beside me, I'm probably littered with sheet wrinkles and matted hair. There's an intimacy to it that knots my throat. I've missed this. Having someone to wake up next to. It's one of the simplest pleasures. A gift you don't even fully appreciate until it's gone.

Tess tilts her head in my direction. "What's got your eyebrows in a bundle?"

I try to relax my scowl, but it's here to stay. I take a sip of coffee, letting the warmth seep from my stomach out to my limbs, easing me deeper into the chair. Then I focus on Tess, squinting against all her bright light. "I'm just trying to enjoy this moment while it lasts."

She draws her knees to her chest and, in a flash of creamy skin, pulls my shirt up and over her knees till they're covered. I can just make out the curve where her butt becomes her thigh. The desire to bend over and bite her there is akin to my heartbeat with its resounding throbbing in my chest.

"You planning on going somewhere?"

"No," I say honestly. "But I'm sure you are."

She wraps her arms around her legs, coffee in hand and

cradled against her shins. Then she lays her head on her knees and peers over at me with a soft expression. "I deserve that."

"It wasn't meant as a dig."

"Good, because I didn't take it as one." The corners of her mouth dip. One finger taps out a steady rhythm against her coffee cup. "I meant what I said, Kit. I don't know what this means for us. What it could ever turn into. My life is in constant flux, and that's only going to get worse after this trip. I told you I couldn't afford to waste this time because it's the *last* time. I—I don't think I'll be coming back to the Carmen after this year."

She pauses for dramatic effect. The thing is, I'd be more apt to believe her if she said it with an ounce of conviction. But I don't say that, not even when her brow furrows in question. Instead I press my lips together and nod for her to go on.

Her lips part on a heavy sigh. She blinks, and when her eyes reopen, they are still trained on my face but unfocused, like she's seeing something else entirely. "My life needs a complete over-haul. I don't know what it will look like when the dust has settled. But as it turns out, resisting you is almost as distracting as just accepting how I feel and letting it all play out. So that's what I'm offering. That's all I *can* offer. Me, for this little window of time before everything changes and I hopefully become someone you wouldn't even recognize as Tess Monroe."

A tear leaks from the corner of her eye and drips onto the bridge of her nose. I set my coffee on a little glass table to my right and then drag my chair closer till I can swipe that tear from her skin with the pass of my thumb. She gazes up at me, and it's like a fist has grabbed hold of my heart. She seems so lost. I remember that feeling. Looking up in the middle of your life and realizing you don't want to be where you've ended up, yet having no clue where to go from here.

I tuck a wild hair back behind her ear, then pinch the lobe before dropping my hand. "I'm all for growth, babe. I fully believe that if you don't like something about your circumstances, then you should go balls to the wall on fixing it. Why do you think I left the only career I'd ever known and started over in Loveless?"

A smile slowly creeps over her wobbling lips.

"But you've got to realize something. You will always be recognizable to me. I'd notice you in any room you walked into, find you in any crowd. There's no changing that. You're like a lighthouse for me. You can repaint the exterior all you want, but the light's what draws me in."

Her eyelids flutter closed, like she's letting my words wash over her and soaking them all in. I bite at the inside of my cheek, wincing as the stinging pain makes my eyes burn. Or maybe it's all the emotion festering in my chest that has me tearing up.

Purples and oranges and dusky pinks illuminate the sky and, in turn, paint Tess's skin the softest shades of morning. I itch to touch her. To reassure her. But the truth is, I'm so far out of my comfort zone that I don't know which way is up, only that this woman feels a lot like true north. I wish I could promise to be enough for her, but I can't. The only thing I'm sure of is that, in whatever form, she's more than enough for me.

"What are you saying?" Her voice is a strained whisper, nearly drowned out by the calls of seagulls waking to a new day and the waves eagerly lapping at the shore.

"I'm saying that, if you'll let me, then for the time we have left, I will not get in your way. I'll help however I can to make this the best trip you've ever had." I pluck the coffee cup from her hand and place it gently on the ground, then draw her hand into mine and squeeze. "And I'll deal with my own broken heart when it's all over."

Her forehead crumples. "Kit—"

"I'm kidding." Deep down, I'm not so sure that I am. But that's my own shit to deal with, not hers. "My flight home is in six days. I will get on that plane and refrain from begging you to join me. I'll be a perfect gentleman. Though I can't make any promises about behaving well on your next visit to Loveless."

She giggles softly. It brightens her whole face, even as another silent tear slips from her eye.

"Do we have a deal?"

A half smile tugs at her lips, but her gaze is hazy. Wistful. Like she's taken every single word I've said to heart. And I truly hope she has, because I meant them with all of my being. She shifts her hand in mine until my kind gesture becomes a firm handshake. "I suppose we do. Pleasure doing business with you."

I let out a relieved chuckle that ends with me clearing my throat. "So what's left on the list?"

That cute wrinkle appears between her furrowed brows. "What list?"

"You know, of things you need to do. Goals for the trip. Memories you wanna make."

"Oh." She sucks in a breath and sits up, dropping her legs from beneath my shirt till her bare feet rest on the concrete balcony. "I, um, don't really have a list. Not really a list kind of girl."

This fits perfectly with everything I know about Tess, so much so that it makes me grin. "Lucky for you, I'm the king of lists." I retrieve my phone from my shorts pocket, relieved to find there's a minuscule amount of battery left. I open my notes app and title the page *Tess's To-Dos for a Perfect Final Vacation*.

She leans close to peer over my shoulder, the scent of the hotel shampoo in her hair making me shiver. "A little wordy, don't you think?"

"Don't bite the hand that feeds you." I add a few bullet points, then glance at her expectantly. "What do you still need to do to make this the best last visit to the Carmen that it can be?"

With pursed lips, she considers this, peering out at the ever-encroaching sun as she does. Finally, she says, "I'd like to find another whole sand dollar."

I type that out on the first bullet point. "Next."

"Dinner, with Mo and Alex and Jenna and Mara. The whole family." She smiles softly and adds, "You can come, too."

Something in her voice when she says *family* effectively knocks the wind out of me, but I recover quickly. "What else?"

"Crab hunting." When I meet her gaze, she holds a finger up in warning. "I'm not explaining further, so don't ask. It's a Monroe tradition that's best experienced without preconceived expectations."

"Got it," I say hesitantly. "Anything else?"

She sighs heavily. "I'd like to figure out what I want to do with my life."

My shrill whistle pierces the morning air, causing a few of the early risers I've been running into on my jogs to glance in our general direction from their spots on the beach. One woman in a precarious downward dog tumbles over.

"What?" she asks, brow furrowed.

"Nothing." I type it out as instructed. "Just a big ask for six days."

"Maybe I'd have figured it out by now if you hadn't been distracting me for the past week."

I wave my hands in a show of innocence. "Hey now, don't go blaming me. You're the one who invited herself to come along to Mississippi. Could've had two days free of me, but no."

"You're right," she sighs. "But then I'd never have seen your T-ball pictures, so I guess it was a fair trade."

I level my gaze with hers and smile grimly, instantly tightening the air around us. "I'm glad you were there."

She doesn't say anything for a long while, so I drop my attention back to my phone. It's a good enough list for the time we have left. I save the note and am about to back out of it when the phone disappears from my hand.

Tess has yanked it into her lap. I try to reach for it, but she evades me easily.

"What are you adding?"

"Just one last thing." Her fingers fly over the screen. When she's satisfied, she saves the note and locks the phone, handing it back to me with a satisfied grin. "There. Now, the sunrise was absolutely beautiful, but I'm still exhausted from yesterday, so I'm going back to bed. Care to join me?"

As much as my muscles are begging for a run, if only to release all this built-up tension, I hesitate. How many more chances will I get to fall asleep next to Tess? I'd be an idiot to give this one up.

"Definitely."

"Perfect." She stands and retreats through the small gap between our chairs, into the opening that leads to her bedroom, then dives headfirst into the covers.

I'm about to follow her when curiosity gets the better of me. I open the note and scroll to the bottom, getting hard all over again when I see what she's added.

5. See if sex with an uncircumcised penis is any different.

I practically leap from my chair and into the room. As soon as the sliding door is shut behind me, she rolls over and smirks. "You promised to help me with all my goals, remember?"

"Am I allowed to pick which one we do first?"

Her smile is wicked when she replies, "I've already got one in mind. Don't worry, I think you'll love it."

A shiver runs down my spine. *I bet I will.*

Chapter Twenty-Three

Tess

MY BREATH COMES IN QUICK, excited bursts as I cut through the lobby, making a beeline for the small cluster of chairs by the door that leads to the pool deck. Kit's waiting for me there. One ankle is balanced on the opposite knee. His chin is tilted up, gaze focused on the photo of my parents. The realization has my steps faltering just a few feet before I reach him. Normally I avoid that picture like the plague. But seeing him there, peering up at it with a half smile on his face, fills me with a happiness that tastes bittersweet on the back of my tongue. It feels like I'm interrupting a conversation between Kit and my parents. Something I'll never get to experience in real life but suddenly want to so badly it makes my chest ache.

Kit turns to take me in over his shoulder, his dark features suddenly intensified by the contrast of a huge, white smile. "You look so much like your mom, you know that?" Then his gaze drops to my right hand, and he laughs. "That's what you just drove forty minutes round trip to get?"

I glance down at the purple sandcastle bucket I'm holding, still a bit off-kilter from his comment. I know I look like my mom. I take pride in that fact. Something about him noticing, though—about the intimacy of it—is so precious it makes me feel weepy. I clear my throat and force myself back into the moment, willing the excitement to creep forward once more and push that aching nostalgia to the back burner.

I take the seat opposite him, keeping the photo at my back. "Unfortunate but necessary. You can't get anywhere quickly around here in the summertime."

Kit nods like he, too, has realized this, then holds up the over-size flashlight he was charged with snagging from Mauricio. "So we hunt them in the dark?"

I point through the window to the sun dipping low on the horizon. "Yes. They're more active at night. Soon as that sun goes down, it's crab-hunting time."

His gaze flickers from the glass to my face. "And do we eat them?"

"Not that kind of crab."

"What do we do with them then?"

I shake the bucket. "We put them in here. And then, when we're done, we set them free."

He narrows his eyes at the bucket for a second, a frown disturbing the hard lines of his jaw. He didn't shave at all during our trip, leaving his stubble somewhere on the border of beard territory. I imagine how it would feel scraping the insides of my thighs, and heat floods my cheeks.

Finally, with a shrug of acceptance, his gaze returns to mine. "All right. But I'm ordering crab legs at dinner, because now that's all I can think about."

My stomach growls as though it heard him and vehemently agrees. I nod on both our behalves. "Sounds like a plan."

He rises to his feet, all those long limbs unfurling, and uses a firm grip on the bucket to pull me from my seat. He plants a kiss on me that steals my breath. For a second I consider cutting the kiss short. Pulling back and ducking my head in case someone sees us. But then I think of his words in the aquarium. I think of standing still. And the very thought of it settles something inside me. That's how I find myself melting into his embrace fully, right there in front of my family photo.

If only that little girl in the photograph could really see me now. Maybe knowing something this good was waiting for her would've made the awful years it took to get here a bit less painful.

Maybe the sweetness of having experienced it will make losing it hurt a little less.

***

"Crab hunting is as much an art as it is a sport."

I can't quite make out Kit's expression in the moonlight, but his snort is translation enough. He's knee-deep in powdery sand, scouring the surface for movement. I'm supervising, while sneaking peeks of his ass when the light hits it just right.

"Brutal way to find out that I am neither artistic nor sporty, apparently." He must spot the little crab at the edge of the flashlight beam at the same time I do, because he dives for it, landing with a huff of breath in a spray of sand. "Damn, they're fast."

I cover my laughter with a swipe of my hand. "You just have to be faster than the crabs, Kit."

"That's what my sex ed teacher said, too."

"And?" I ask with an arched brow, not that he can see it.

He rises to his feet and gets to work dusting sand off every surface from chest to shins. "And what?"

"Did it work?"

He pauses, and I swear I can feel his gaze like a brand the minute it lands on me. "Tess, are you asking if I have crabs?"

I snort. "Among other things. Gotta be careful, you know. Given what's on my list."

I can just make out the shape of his arms folding over his chest. "All clear on my front."

"Same." I try to sound casual, but excitement has both my blood pressure and my pitch spiking.

"Does this mean we can abandon crab hunting and get to work on other tasks?" he asks suggestively.

He takes a step forward, but I bring the flashlight up to his face in an instant, effectively blinding him. "Nuh-uh. We're not leaving here till you catch a crab."

He yanks the flashlight from my hands and turns it on me. I blink against the harsh light, my whole world shrinking to that single beam.

"You've caught, like, thirty-five." He swings the beam to the bucket at my feet. "See? It's so full that they can use each other to climb right out of there. What's one more going to do?"

"Give you the satisfaction of a job well done," I say matter-of-factly. "And get you into my pants."

"Deal." He turns and marches away with renewed vigor, sweeping the flashlight over the sand frantically as he searches for movement.

I can't help but laugh as I tip over the bucket and free my cache. They scramble and scurry, tickling my feet in their misguided attempts to escape. Some are the size of my palm, while others are no bigger than the tip of my finger. They're everywhere at night, making it even more baffling that Kit hasn't managed to capture a single one. For all his measured intensity, when it comes to even this amateur version of hunting, he has no grace. He fumbles through the sand, crashing and stomping so loudly the crabs disappear before he's even made it close.

After another failed attempt, he grumbles, "You make it look so easy!"

I shrug into the darkness, smiling even though he can't see me. "Lots of practice. My dad guided us on at least one hunting session per summer. Sometimes two, if I was being restless. Though I think the second one was to let Mom grab an extra nap when I was driving her crazy."

"You? Driving someone crazy? Impos— oof!"

We fall to the ground in a tangle of limbs, me straddling him from behind and him landing full-frontal on the ground with a grunt. I nip his ear, tiny granules of sand coating my lips. "Take it back."

"Did you just *tackle* me?" He huffs in disbelief. Then he rolls us, careful to disentangle himself so he doesn't squish me in the scramble. In a flash, he has me pinned beneath him, and I'm breathlessly trying to figure out how he managed to turn the tables so easily. The flashlight casts us in stark relief, his left side blindingly clear while his right remains in shadow. "Say you're sorry."

"Excuse me? You're the one who should say sorry!" I squeal.

He shakes his head, and sand rains down from his hair to dust my face. "I was about to catch one when you pounced on me."

"You called me crazy."

"No," he corrects, chest heaving with rapid breaths. "I said you drive people crazy. There's a difference."

"And the difference is…?"

"Crazy would be me scooping you up and dragging you into the ocean in the dark."

My lips pop open, and his gaze drops to meet them. I narrow my eyes at him. "You wouldn't dare."

He goes on like I haven't spoken, still zeroed in on my mouth. "But if I stripped you bare and took you right here on this beach, I bet that'd *drive you* crazy."

My heart soars into my throat. Every bit of pent-up tension coils tightly in my abdomen, begging for release. There's sand everywhere, people with balconies not even a hundred yards from where we lie, yet even with all these impracticalities, I find myself picturing it. Wearing nothing but moonlight while I finally figure out what it feels like to have Kit Llewellyn inside me.

I swallow hard, blinking away the image even as heat grows in intensity between my thighs. "You wouldn't dare."

The corner of his mouth tips into shadow. "You said that already."

He starts tickling my side, and the sound that escapes me is somewhere between a laugh and a gasp. But that's impossible, because his hands are currently occupied with pinning mine on either side of my head. The tickling sensation intensifies and moves, climbing the lattice of one exposed rib and disappearing when it reaches my bandeau. I glance down, and Kit does too. There, in the small space he's left between our chests, a tiny crab has paused to stare at me. Or us. I can never tell what direction their eyes are pointed.

Kit shifts his weight slowly, backing onto his knees and releasing my hands.

"Be gentle," I whisper.

"Always am." The words are dark and double-edged, implying a second meaning that I can't help but ponder at, though I get the feeling I'll find out for myself soon enough.

His hand brushes my breast as he sweeps up the little crab, causing me to ache in more ways than one. He brings it close to take a better look, and from my vantage point, I see both the cradle of his strong hands and the impossibly beautiful smile that breaks up the shadows on his face.

"Hi, little guy," he coos. "You just made me the luckiest man on earth, you know that?" His gaze flickers from the crab to me, and he quirks a brow. "So, can we cross crab hunting off the list?"

I swallow hard and nod, feeling sand bury itself farther in my hair. "I'd say so."

"Good." He lowers the crab into the sand on my right and releases it to scurry free. Then he begins to rise, offering a hand that I gladly accept. We both make it upright while I imagine that little crab running for its life somewhere in the dark.

I sweep a hand over my body. "I'm covered in sand."

"You won't be in a second." He gathers the bucket, the flashlight, and finally, my hand, then starts toward the wooden walkway leading back to the Carmen.

Our footsteps thud over weather-worn wood, still warm though the sun set hours ago. Light from the pool deck spills down the path, stopping just a few feet short of the outcrop where several showerheads were installed for rinsing off before returning to the resort. Kit sets our bucket on the railing, then clicks off the flashlight and sets it inside the container. He kicks off his shoes and turns to me. "Anything you don't want getting wet, you better take it off right now."

He says it wickedly. Teasingly. I quickly unbutton my jean shorts and lower them to the ground, revealing bikini bottoms beneath. My bandeau top is white and will be made see-through the moment it gets wet, but I don't have any alternatives, so I leave it in place. Kit's eyes glitter in the near-darkness as he takes me in, a guttural sound vibrating his throat. He strips his shirt off and shucks his flip-flops, leaving him bare-chested in a pair of board shorts with no more than a five-inch inseam.

He really is beautiful. My eyes have adjusted to the shadows, and despite them, I can make out the lines of muscle and sinew carving out his abdomen. Broad shoulders swell into firm biceps, then hollow out to form valleys between the corded veins of his forearms. My gaze drops to his legs, and the taut thighs that fill out the hem of his shorts. Every hour spent running, training, whatever else it is he does to stay in shape for his job—it has paid off. Royally.

The pipes squeal as he turns the faucet on. Lukewarm water spews from the overhead spout. Kit pulls me beneath the spray, instantly dousing us both. His hands roam my skin under the guise of wiping off sand, but I know better. He palms my ass. Cups my breasts through my top. Turns me toward him and pulls me in close to stroke my spine.

His hands are warm everywhere they touch me. I find myself craving the rasp of his fingertips, arching into it like a cat seeking affection.

"Feeling clean yet?" he whispers against my hair.

"Mm," I hum. "I think you might've missed a spot."

He pulls back enough to lock eyes with me. "And where's that?"

I turn, aligning my back with the hard ridges of his muscular chest. He's facing away from the resort, which leaves me blanketed in his shadow. With my gaze trained on the dark, undulating ocean, I grab his hand and guide it over my abdomen, to the seam of my bottoms, then slip it beneath. How long have I imagined this moment? How it would feel? Countless times, even when I knew I shouldn't. But I never could've imagined the delicious scrape of his calluses brushing my sensitive skin. I sigh at the sensation, letting my head loll as his hand dips lower of its own accord.

His fingertips brush my throbbing clit, drawing a shocked gasp from my lungs. His hips surge forward as though on instinct, pressing the hard ridge of his desire into the hollow at the base of my spine. "*Fuck.*"

He delves lower, spreading me to test my desire. I'm soaked. I don't need to touch myself to know it. He strokes my wetness, coating his fingers, then plunges into my aching core. First one finger, then two. I bite my lip to swallow my cry. So good. He feels so good. Even like this, which is nothing compared to what I want from him. But he handles me perfectly, curling his fingers to stroke me in a steady rhythm, drawing me to an edge I hadn't even realized was so close.

Straddling his hand, I rest my head against his collarbone and groan his name as loud as I dare. "Oh God, Kit."

"You're so wet for me, gorgeous. So ready."

And I am. Because for all my teasing, I probably want this even more than he does. So I surrender myself to the feeling of his fingers sinking into my aching core. Every nerve ending in my body is a live wire. From the warmth of his hard palm against my hip to the rivulets of water spilling over my pebbled skin to his breath, hot and quick as it brushes my throat. It stokes the flame higher. Demands my attention. I forget my surroundings and lose myself in him, riding his hand the way I want to ride the man attached to it, biting my bottom lip so hard I'm certain it'll bleed. In a matter of seconds, any worry that someone will see is lost to the feeling building in my belly, like a wave of pleasure surging toward a break.

"You're so fucking beautiful, Tess. Taking your pleasure. Are you going to come for me, baby? Right here, where anyone could see. Are you going to fuck yourself on my hand until you scream?"

His words are as tantalizing as his touch. I soak in every sensation: The hard press of his palm against my throbbing clit. The burning heat of his other hand moving to grip my breast and pinch my nipple through the thin fabric of my bandeau top. And finally, the whisper of my name against the hollow behind my ear that sends me skyward, exploding like it's the Fourth of July and I'm the show everyone came to see.

I choke on my own cries, fighting and failing to keep quiet. Kit helps. He releases my breast to cover my mouth, grip so tight on my jawline that I come harder, riding his hand until my legs feel like they'll collapse beneath me if I try to take one single step.

"That's right, baby. You did so good." He nips my shoulder at the same time he removes his hand from beneath my waistband, then brings his fingers to his lips and sucks them clean. "You taste like heaven."

On wobbly legs, I turn to him, rising on my tiptoes to take a taste for myself. Our tongues tangle and dance, mixing the spice that is him with the flavor of my desire. At some point he reaches back to kill the spray of the shower, replacing its warm blanket with a breeze that has my nipples aching against my top.

Kit steps back, bracing me with a hand on either shoulder, and smiles. "You're incredible, you know that?"

I nod, smiling breathlessly up at him. "Can you take me to your room? *Now.*"

He chuckles darkly. "So bossy." Then his gaze drifts lower, and he arches a brow. "What will we do about this?"

A quick glance downward confirms my suspicions. My top is completely transparent, dark pink nipples making themselves known through the fabric. I suck in a breath through my teeth and peer up at Kit. "Looks like I'm borrowing your shirt."

He retrieves it from the railing and tosses it my way with a wink. "Not for long."

We dress quickly, gather our things, and run hand in hand up the boardwalk.

Chapter Twenty-Four

Kit

WE TAKE THE EMERGENCY STAIRWELL, having no patience to wait for the elevator. I've already got my key card out, droplets of water coating it from being in my pocket while we rinsed off. I silently pray that it still works as I hold it to the keypad. A beep answers my prayers, and the mechanical lock whirs. I push the door open into the darkness of my room. When I reach for the light switch, though, Tess swats my hand.

"No direct overhead lighting," she deadpans.

"Yes, ma'am," I say, chuckling.

She crosses the room, skirting around my bed to grip the curtains and yank them open, allowing meager amounts of moonlight and shimmering fluorescence from the pool lights below to filter through the windows. I'd fuck the woman beneath a spotlight if it meant I could see every inch of her on display, but if it's mood lighting Tess wants, then mood lighting is enough for me.

I don't give her a chance to turn around, instead hooking my arm around her waist and dragging her to the bed. We land on top of the covers, our wet hair shedding droplets with the impact. She moves to straddle my hips, breathlessly giggling as she gazes down at me. My shirt is off her in a matter of seconds, exposing the delicious view of tight nipples pressing through the tiny top she's been teasing me with all afternoon. It knots at the back, and I make quick work of untying it and tossing the damn thing across the room.

Her breasts are perfect. I hold still for a moment, soaking in the sight of them after so long spent imagining it. I test their weight in my hands. They're full and pert, tipped with hard, rosy nipples that beg to be sucked. And so I do, sitting up and taking first one and then the other into my mouth, nipping and flicking and sucking until she's writhing against me, burying her hands in my hair and whimpering my name like a desperate plea. Her skin is so soft and warm against my tongue. I swear I could come from this alone: the taste of her filling my mouth while she grinds her hot center against my aching cock.

"So needy," I whisper against her taut nipple. Her back arches, and I lick her from sternum to throat to chin, punctuating her sigh with a kiss. "So perfect."

"Kit, please," she begs. Her nails carve ravines into my back. I'll be wearing the marks for days, and I don't even care. I'm half tempted to never wear another shirt if it means showing the whole world that I was branded by Tess Monroe. That I'm hers, and hers alone.

"What do you want, baby?" I say as I flip her onto her back, where I hook my fingers into her waistband and tug. The bottoms come away easily. I slide them down her mile-long legs, and once I've tossed them to the side, grab her knees and push them apart. Her pussy is so perfect, a pristine dirty-blonde landing strip guiding my gaze to her glistening lips. "You want me to eat you?"

"Yes," she hisses, and it's so fucking hot that she isn't ashamed to ask that I don't hesitate to oblige. I kneel between her legs and bury my face in her pussy the way I've fantasized about doing since the moment we met.

She's even more radiant like this, grinding against my mouth with her head thrown back and my name a barely audible chant spilling from her throat. I suckle her clit, then flick it with my tongue. She likes that. I can tell by the way her legs clamp tightly on either side of my head, holding me in place so I couldn't move even if I tried. But fuck, I'd never want to escape this. She grinds wildly, taking all the pleasure she wants, and I gladly deliver. I continue lapping at her clit as I slip two fingers into her and stroke in the same come-hither motion that made her come on my hand mere moments ago. At that, she screams, not a care in the world spared for who might hear. She loses herself to the pleasure, and the sight of her so unabashed has my cock throbbing in my shorts.

"Fuck, I want you," she groans, fingers tangling in my hair and pulling. She's rough, and I love it. I want her to tear me apart until I'm nothing but a man on his knees before her, ready to worship. When I don't let up, don't retreat, she releases me to prop herself up on her elbows. "Kit, I need you inside me. *Now.*"

"But I'm having so much fun," I say, punctuating my sentence with a long lick up her center that has her sucking in a gasp.

I meant what I said. She tastes like heaven. I find myself licking her wetness from my lips, savoring the flavor of her ecstasy.

She locks eyes with me, expression at once so wild and yet completely controlled. "I'm begging you."

I couldn't argue with her if I tried. I nip her clit once more, then relent for now, crawling forward to cover her swollen mouth with mine. We crash into one another, finding a perfect rhythm instantly. She ebbs and I flow. I draw her bottom lip between my teeth, and she arches into me, begging for more. Her skin is smooth and supple against mine, so divine I could spend days exploring her every curve and never grow tired. Everywhere we touch, I'm engulfed in a heat that can only be satiated by stoking the flame higher.

"Let me grab a condom," I rasp, pulling away ever so slightly. It's as much as I can bear.

"No need." She meets my questioning gaze with a raised brow. "You said you're clear. I am too. And I'm on the pill."

My heart, which had stopped beating, restarts at a gallop. "Are you sure?"

Tess nods, her salt-tousled hair tangling on the bed beneath her. "Absolutely. I want to feel you. *All* of you."

I bite down on my knuckle with a groan. "Woman, you are going to be the death of me."

"So long as I get to feel you come inside me first," she teases with a shrug.

I rip my shorts off as quickly as I can. A moment away is still too long. I surge forward, my hand fastening to her jaw so I can tilt her head to align our mouths once more.

Then I wipe that smirk from her lips with a roll of my hips, bringing my cock into her wet heat. Just the tip, but it's enough to still her breathing, to dilate her pupils till there's no green left glinting in the moonlight. Her breath spills onto my lips, and I draw it into my lungs, soaking up every part of her that I can.

I trace a finger from her mouth to her throat, then close my hand around its base. Not too tight, just enough to earn that thrill in her gaze. "Are you going to take my cock like a good girl?"

She nods, wrapping her hand around my wrist and squeezing. "Yes, sir."

"Good." I squeeze her throat once for good measure, then I bury myself to the hilt.

"Fuck fuck fuck," she murmurs, rolling her hips wildly against me. She's so tight, so warm that I have to grind my molars to keep from coming instantly. Damp heat envelops my cock. Over and over again, I slam home, earning gasps from her parted lips. Her breasts bounce with every thrust. Her skin is perfect and creamy in the pale light. Now that my eyes have adjusted, I can see it all. And it's everything I could've wanted and more.

"You look so good with me buried inside you." And she does. Her pussy has me in a death grip, her lips parted around my base in a way that is deliciously sinful. I rock forward with a steady rhythm, feeling her walls tighten more with every thrust. She's so close, as close as I am. Not much longer and we'll be unraveling together.

Her nails scrape my forearm, her throat bobbing beneath my grip as she swallows a gasp. "Come for me, Kit. I want to feel you."

"So soon?" I drawl.

"Won't be long before I'm begging you to do it again."

Begging. That word again, spilling from her pretty mouth, is my undoing. I lose control, thrusting wildly into her, taking every-thing for myself. She calls out my name, again and again until it's the pulse that roars in my ears as I empty myself inside her with a guttural moan. Her walls tighten around me, and soon she's arch-ing, grinding, stealing back every ounce of pleasure I took for myself.

We collapse in a heap of slick limbs and gasping breaths. For a few heartbeats, I can't even think. My mind is blank save for Tess's face as she came, the most breathtaking sight I've ever seen.

When I've gathered my strength enough to move, I slip from inside Tess and rise to my feet on trembling legs. From my spot at the edge of the bed, I watch as my come spills from inside her, and the sight is enough to make me hard again. I have to force myself to walk away. To gather a washcloth from the bathroom and wet it, then return to wipe her clean.

She rolls onto her side, and I crawl into bed behind her, cradling her body against mine and sighing when at last we're aligned perfectly. This is how it always should be. Tess and me, together. Nothing has ever felt so right.

"That was everything," I whisper into her hair, because it's the only word that comes close to describing how I feel, without touching on something I cannot name. Not now, when I've only just convinced her I can keep my emotions at bay. Even as I promised it, I knew it was a vow I could not keep. When I get on that plane, my heart won't just be broken. It'll be fucking shattered. But that's my burden to bear, not hers. And I'd gladly do it a million times over to experience the type of bliss I'm feeling right now.

"It was," she says with a sigh. The heaviness of sleep tugs at the edges of her voice. "I can't tell if it's the uncircumcised penis that made the difference, though."

My chest vibrates with laughter. I bury my face in her hair, but it's no use. I laugh so loud I'm sure the walls shake with it, and so does she. When one of us has nearly come to grips, the other snorts, and we fall back into it all over again.

"You're something else," I tease when at last I'm able to catch my breath.

"Something special?" she asks, turning to gaze at me over her shoulder. Her eyes are bright with the remnants of laughter. Hair a mess. Lips swollen from my kisses. Absolute perfection. The death of me, I'm nearly sure of it.

"Definitely something special." I force the words out through a tight throat, and her responding nod is nearly imperceptible as her gaze drops to my mouth with a heaviness I sense as much as I see. I kiss her in an attempt to bring the lightheartedness back, but I fear it's gone for good.

We fall asleep above the covers, beneath the weight of all the things we don't dare say. But I feel it, and in my dreams, she says it clear as day.

Chapter Twenty-Five

Tess

TODAY IS A HAPPY DAY. So why do I feel so sad?

I wake with emotion coating my throat like cough syrup. All those years jumping up at the crack of dawn with my dad have finally shown their hand. I lie in the quiet cradle of the morning, watching Kit sleep while grieving a loss that hasn't happened yet.

I may not love him now, but I could, probably a lot sooner than I'd like to admit. The mere possibility terrifies me. I know better than anyone where all that love goes when the object of it is no longer around to receive it. It festers in your heart like infection in an open wound. The kind that never really heals, instead becoming a burden that weighs you down for the rest of your life.

Last night was incredible. It's everything I didn't know I was missing and then some. And my God, do I wish I were the type of person who could let that be it. Let myself be happy with what I was given without yearning for something beyond it. But I'm a woman whose bankroll lies in wishes for more: more years with my parents. More time to be a kid. More of an idea of what the hell I'm supposed to do with a life that could end at any second.

That's the crux of it. The part I don't tell anyone. When your parents, the people you look to for your own sense of self, die young, logic tells you that you will too. I can't imagine myself outliving my mother. Can't fathom anything beyond a fortieth birthday candle to blow out.

It's why I've never quite gotten around to really growing my own roots, beyond those I inherited from my family. Why bother, when they'll be ripped up soon enough?

As I trace the crooked bridge of Kit's nose with my fingertip, noting the freshly bronzed skin from our time together in the sun, I can't help the longing that overwhelms my every nerve ending, every cell. I'm transformed by the want. It's in my tightly squeezed lungs that cling to a breath of his warm, weathered-wood scent. It's in the kiss I press to his sleep-ruffled hair, grown long enough to now brush his ears when it's not gelled properly.

It's in my prayer, silent and pleading, as I beg the universe not to take him from me, too.

I hadn't realized the tears were falling, nor that my eyes had drifted closed. Not until Kit's thumb scrapes the peak of my cheekbone, coming away damp, and he whispers, "Tess, are you all right? Did you have a nightmare?"

I peel my lids apart with some effort, after they'd been glued by my tears. "Something like that."

A waking nightmare. Story of my life.

"I'm so sorry." He leans forward to kiss me, but I dodge him, covering my mouth in a flash.

"I haven't brushed my teeth yet."

"Convenient, because neither have I." Then he plucks my hand easily from in front of my mouth and fuses his lips to mine. Suddenly I don't give a shit about morning breath. In fact, I'm able to bury every negative thought, every deep-seated fear, in the ever-tightening space behind my sternum, allowing happiness to float up in its place.

Because I'm here now. I'm happy today. And since that's all any one of us is guaranteed, I decide it's enough for me.

After he's effectively stolen my breath away, he relents, shifting instead to tuck my head into the curve of his throat before wrapping his arms around my shoulders. Neither of us is clothed, and why would we be? Every moment one of us finally started to drift off in the night, the other would stroke a soft patch of skin or whisper a confession made possible by the scant moonlight, and soon we'd be entangled once more, exploring new and newly favorite parts of one another till just a couple hours before dawn.

"What would you like to do today?"

I catch sight of the rings glinting on my finger and smile. Tilting my head up slightly, I make my request to the hard edge of his jaw. "Permission to stray from the list, sir?" I murmur, savoring the sting of his stubble against my lips.

An exasperated groan rumbles in his chest. "Permission granted."

I push up onto my elbows so that we're face-to-face, ignoring the grunt earned from a misplaced appendage to his chest. "There's a market my mother loved. All different vendor stalls with everything from jewelry to fresh vegetables to a hot dog stand that serves the best devil dogs this far from LA."

"What do you know about devil dogs? Or LA?" he asks, quirking a brow. His hazel eyes are framed by sleep-darkened lashes, making them stand out in stark relief. So beautiful. And currently, so confused.

"I worked briefly as a personal stylist for a B-list singer from Foley. Spent many a weekend trip with her in LA."

His expression is momentarily unreadable, followed by a mesmerized smile. "What haven't you done?"

"Hmm." I tap a finger to my lips, pretending to contemplate the question far longer than I truly need to. "Never been to space."

"We'll work on that, then."

"Adding it to the list?" I ask, both brows raised.

He taps my nose and grins. "Look who's coming around to the list."

I roll my eyes. When I move to shift my weight off his chest, he stops me with a vise grip around my midsection and snarls a kiss into the bend of my shoulder. I shriek and try to push away, but he only squeezes me tighter, play-nibbling at the sensitive skin of my throat.

When laughter saps me of my strength to resist, Kit takes the opportunity to steal a kiss. His head flops back onto the pillow, and he gazes up at me adoringly. "Fine, we shall abandon our list. But only for today, because we have dinner plans tomorrow night at the Ortiz household."

My mouth pops open. "You did that?"

He shakes his head. "I'm pretty sure I barely got the words 'dinner' and 'with you' out before Jenna was running with it. If anyone deserves your gratitude, it's her. I'm merely a vessel."

I kiss the corner of his mouth. The space between his dark brows that is much less manicured now than it was the day he arrived. The harsh line of his jaw. Finally I lick his earlobe and follow it up with a gentle bite. "Thank you. So, so much, Kit."

I feel his muscles go limp around and beneath me as his gaze turns somber. "It's the least I can do after everything with my brother. My parents. The accident..." His voice trails off, suddenly unstable.

"Have you heard from him?" I ask softly.

"No. And I probably won't until he needs money again. But that's nothing new." Kit's hand trails down my spine and settles at the curve of my ass, which he pats lightly. "Do I have time for a run?"

I pretend to consider it for a moment but quickly nod. "Absolutely. Wouldn't want to have to report back to Tomas that you're slacking on your vacation."

"Mm, don't worry. He's already scheduled a sparring match

for the day I get back to assess me for any weaknesses." Kit pokes my side, causing me to roll off him in an effort to escape the sensation. "Imagine his surprise when he finds a you-sized hole in my defenses."

"Boooooooo!"

The corner of his mouth ticks upward. "I'll win you over eventually."

My heart seizes. I can only pray my next words come out sounding casual. "Perhaps. But it won't be owed to your incredible pickup lines, I can tell you that much."

He mock-pouts as he shifts my weight fully off his body and sits up in bed. "You're mean in the morning, you know that?"

"What can I say? I hardly slept last night. I'll be nicer once I've had my coffee."

"Is that a request?

I shrug. "It certainly can be."

"Deal." After a quick kiss, he rises to his feet and pads over to the blonde-wood dresser, where he rifles through the drawers, removing articles of clothing that he dons one by one until he's fully dressed for a run and I'm just the naked woman in his bed. When he returns from brushing his teeth, his gaze moves slowly over my every curve, and he grins. "Is it too much to hope that you'll be waiting for me exactly like that when I return?"

I toss a pillow his way, which he easily dodges with a laugh. Never mind that his blatant desire has me heating up from head to toe. "Not a chance, lover boy. I'm going to go shower in my room. I'll see you in a bit?"

He sighs dramatically, then deposits an earbud in each ear and leans forward to steal a final kiss. "No running this time, okay?"

I'm tempted to turn the mood back toward humor with a quick remark about his intended jog, but there's a layer of earnest pleading in his tone that stops me in my tracks. He needs reassurance. I know that feeling better than anyone. So who am I to deny him this?

"I'll be here." I tip my head toward my room across the hall. "Well, there, but you know what I mean." I bite my lip, noting the way his gaze darkens when it lands there. "I'm not going anywhere." *Not yet, anyway,* I think, though I can't bring myself to say it aloud and risk hurting him. We both know the ugly truth. No need to discuss it any sooner than required.

He nods and, without another word, heads for the door, leaving me to wonder how on earth I'll move on when this vacation is over. Or worse, if I even want to.

"Why, it wouldn't be my favorite niece interrupting her wild vacation to phone her frumpy uncle, now would it?"

"I'm your only niece," I gripe into the receiver.

Gary chuckles dryly through the line. "Semantics. How are you? How's Kit? Keeping his hands to himself?" After a seconds-too-long pause, he adds, "Never mind! I don't want to know!"

I giggle around a sip of water, swallow, and set the bottle down on my balcony table, next to the coffee cup from my first morning with Kit that I've yet to dispose of. It makes me smile even more than I was already. I miss him, and he hasn't even been gone for thirty minutes.

"I do want to know how you're doing, for clarity. Just not… the other stuff."

"Got it." I laugh again, and it feels good. Like a tight muscle finally being stretched. "I'm doing well. Only a handful of days left in this trip and it's a bit bittersweet, but I'm trying not to think about it too much right now."

Gary clicks his tongue. Dishes clang in the background like he's loading the washer as we speak. "Well, there's always next year to look forward to. Maybe I could join you then, see the place that meant so much to my sister."

I bite my lip, reasoning with myself that he isn't intentionally guilt-tripping me. How could he, when he doesn't even know that I've been considering stopping these trips? Suddenly the idea of telling him fills me with dread. Though I have no clue if it's from a lack of conviction or simply the fear of letting my uncle down.

He tuts again, growing silent—and I imagine, still—on his end. "Something you wanna talk about, Tess?"

His ability to be observant even through a phone call is unnerving, to say the least.

"I don't know," I say honestly. Sucking in a much-needed breath of fresh air, I squeeze my eyes shut, cutting off the familiar image of the blue-green waves lapping at the shore. "You remember how I quit my job?"

He hums his acknowledgment. I know he was confused when I first broke the news right before this trip, asking me what was wrong with Harvey's and what I planned to do instead. Imagine his surprise when I admitted I had no reasons and, frankly, no clue about next steps. But Gary, being the way that he is, recognized an untouchable topic even from miles away. So instead of prying, he pivoted to floating the option of me moving to Loveless. Even offered up his couch.

I said no, of course. Mostly because I didn't know then what I still don't know now: what I want my future to look like. All I can fathom is that I want one at all—and, I now realize, that I don't want to spend it alone.

It's a terrifying feeling, to desire the one thing that's most painful to lose.

"I've been thinking... Well, I'm not planning to come back here. After this year." I pause, waiting for an objection that never comes. Then I clear my throat. "I've been trying to figure out where I go from here. Not the literal here, but the metaphorical one. You know?"

He remains silent, save for a grunt to let me know he's heard me. Deep down I know he's not judging. Maybe it's my inner critic, or perhaps it's no one at all. Either way, I find myself jumping to my own defense.

"I love the Carmen; don't get me wrong. My parents are everywhere. Hell, *I'm* everywhere. This place has been the backdrop of all my favorite memories for as far back as those memories go. I know it seems stupid, wanting to give that up on top of everything else. But it hurts, too, Gary. I see her here. I see them both here. They're in every room, at every corner. They're playing in the water and cracking jokes at the bar and slow dancing on the balcony to the sound of the waves. It hurts so goddamn much.

"Every good memory I've ever made here is tainted by that one really bad memory. The one where they're dead, and they'll never not be dead, and coming here summer after summer without any sort of forward momentum feels a bit like I'm just following in their footsteps, marching toward the inevitable end."

My chest is heaving with the effort it takes to breathe through the pain. My lungs prickle and sting. Tears burn the backs of my eyes. I don't know where all these words came from. Only that they've been living inside me far longer than I even realized—since long before Gary's name popped up on that DNA test.

Finally he lets out a somber sigh. "First of all, there's nothing stupid or foolish or wrong about the way you're feeling. The only thing wrong with grief is that it has a reason to exist in the first place. If the people we loved hadn't bothered dying, we wouldn't be having this conversation at all, now would we?"

I sniffle my agreement. He presses on.

"When Wendy first died, I lived in limbo for an entire year. Couldn't go forward. Couldn't go back. It was all I could do to hold completely still and hope another wave wouldn't knock me down while I was catching my breath."

That's how my grandparents' deaths felt. Like one wave, and then another, crashing over my already bruised and battered soul. Then a swath of relief when I'd finally buried them both, if only because I knew there would be no one else left to lose. I'd never have to endure that type of pain again. I felt horrible guilt afterward, for managing to be relieved that they were gone. Then I quit my job as a stylist and went to work as a server in a food truck for a while, distracting myself with the change of pace.

Always distracting. Pretending. Putting on a smile and swearing I'm fine, when I'm not even sure what *fine* means anymore.

Gary inhales deeply like he's steadying himself. "After that year, I took down all the art she'd hung on the walls of our place. I couldn't bear for it to look the same as it had when she was here. My world had been permanently altered inside. How could it still look the same on the outside?

"But eventually, after years and years of living in that silo of grief, I started letting people in. The patrons at the bar. Zoey and her friends, those heathens. I found people to love and be loved by, and I thought, man, I wish they'd known Wendy. That she could've known them. So one day I dug those old pieces of art out of storage and one by one, gave them away. A painting for each of my newfound family. A way for Wendy to know them, and for them to know her. For us to share the burden of my love for her, when it had nowhere else to go for so long.

"It's okay if this is your last summer there, Tess. Whether that's forever, or for just a little while, until you find people you love that you want to share your parents with. Or share with your parents."

Just as he says it, Kit jogs into view. He pauses at the shoreline, hands on hips, and peers out at the horizon with an unnatural stillness that I envy. He looks wholly present. Or perhaps just whole. Not lacking in the ways I've always felt I am. Lacking a family. Lacking a future. Simply existing in the present, rowing fast from one buoy to the other because it's my only guarantee.

"You still there?"

"I am," I croak. I'm crying in earnest now. The teardrops blend with the damp splotches my freshly washed hair has left on my blouse as they fall, and I'm grateful for the disguise. "I'm just taking it in, that's all."

"I'm sorry I made you cry," he says with a sigh. "I just love you, kiddo. And I want you to be happy more than anything."

Just like my parents. Such a seemingly simple ask, but one I struggle with so fiercely.

"I love you, too, Gary. Thank you for everything."

"Oh, I did nothing but wax poetic about my own heartache. You'll find your way. I promise you that. And whatever it looks like, I'm here for you. You know that, right?"

"Yeah. I do," I whisper. More to keep my voice from cracking than anything. "Any souvenir requests?"

He chuckles softly. "Surprise me. Something my sister would've liked."

I nod though he can't see me. Smile, because I hope she can. "You've got yourself a deal."

"Bye, kiddo."

"Bye, Gary."

Kit begins his final stroll up the beach toward the wooden walkway that will lead him past the showerheads, a sight that has my heart skipping a beat, and to the Carmen, where he'll take an elevator back to me.

And, just like I promised, I'll be here.

Chapter Twenty-Six

Kit

WE ARRIVE at the market just after noon, when Tess assures me that the rush of locals grabbing a bite to eat will have finally died down. The tourists, however, are still out in abundance. Not that we have any room to judge. Though it's hard not to look at the swaths of folks wearing neon T-shirts spray painted with beachy designs tucked into their fanny packs and feel some sense of superiority. Sure, we aren't from here either. But at least we aren't arguing over the price of a jar of shells from one of the more kitschy stalls rather than walking down to the nearby beach to collect some ourselves.

Sun-bleached cobblestones warm the ground beneath my flip-flops. Tess's hand is slick in mine, but not once do I consider letting go. I'm not sure if she even realizes that she's smiling, but it's there in the swollen apples of her cheeks. The slight crinkle at the edges of her eyes. Her gaze dances from stall to stall, taking it all in like it's the first time she's seen it rather than the hundredth.

"You said your mom liked this place?" I ask, squeezing her hand to punctuate my question.

Her gaze flits to meet mine, and her smile takes on a weary air. "She did. She'd insist on coming to visit this one particular shop owner who makes handmade jewelry." She holds up her free hand and wiggles her fingers, causing the sunlight to reflect off her many rings. "Some of these were hers. A lot of them are mine. I still get a ring every summer in her honor."

"From the same shop?"

She nods. "The very one."

Seagulls shriek overhead, announcing their demand for a dropped fry or a discarded ice cream cone. Between the sunlight beating down and the thrumming mass of bodies, heat presses in like a physical front, slowly shrinking the available free space. But Tess either doesn't notice or doesn't care. She's in her element, smiling at shopkeepers. Waving to babies in carriers. She gives away so much happiness. Sometimes I wish she'd learn to keep a little more for herself.

I clear my throat, drawing her attention away from a street performer dressed in Statue of Liberty regalia. She lifts a brow, and I tilt my head slightly. "How are things going with the 'figuring out what to do with my life' task?"

She shakes her head as she turns to face forward again. "All quiet on the western front."

I elbow her ribs as best I can without releasing her hand.

Her responding laughter is half-hearted, a flash of brilliant white teeth that's here and gone again in an instant. "That was a bit of a lofty goal, I'll admit. It's like Einstein coming up with the theory of relativity in a week."

"Bold of you to compare the complexity of your life to theorizing how gravity affects the fabric of space and time."

This time it's my ribs getting elbowed. I huff a laugh, knowing I deserved it. At least she's smiling now, in a way that almost feels genuine.

I pinch my lips together and let her stew in silence for a few minutes as we stroll past a hot dog stand and a snow cone cart that have my mouth watering for different reasons. Finally, when we reach a set of benches, she tugs me toward one and drags me down beside her.

She folds our joined hands together with her other in her lap. The scent of sugar and sunshine wafts off her exposed skin, smelling more delicious than any food we've passed. I have to force myself to focus on the intensity carving out her features. Turns out, now that I've tasted her, any time spent without a sampling leaves me ravenous.

"I talked to Gary about it, actually. While you were on your run." She grazes her teeth over her rosy bottom lip, staring straight ahead even though I doubt she's seeing any of the people who cross her path. "I think I spent so long running from my grief that I'm just now processing it at thirty years old. Thanks to you and Gary and everything else, I'm taking a hard look internally and realizing just how much of who I am is made up of what happened to me, whether directly or as a result of trying to seem fine in spite of it. And you know what? I kind of hate it. I don't want to be a product of loss. Or at least, not only that. I'd like to become a different, better version of myself. Something that resembles who I might've been if my parents hadn't gone and died on me when I needed them most."

She draws in a deep breath and drops her gaze to our folded hands. "You probably think I'm dumb. Sold on New Agey bullshit about reinventing oneself with the help of a crystal and a few affirmations."

I swallow a painful laugh, catching it like a knot in my throat, which is somehow both incredibly dry from the heat and also drenched in humid air. "I never once thought that."

Sunlight dances in her wavy hair as she shakes her head. "And why wouldn't you? I mean, how much can one person really change?"

I scratch my freshly shaven jawline. My gaze drifts to the not-so-distant Gulf, its surface a mesmerizing shade of emerald. "I like to think I've changed a lot. That I've learned from my mistakes."

"Oh yeah? Like what?"

I smile as a boat glides past, disturbing the peaceful surface of the water. "I let you go once without a fight. Not so much this time."

"I'd hardly call you inserting yourself into my vacation a fight." She inflates her cheeks, then lets the air out slowly. "Persistent, for sure. But not a fight."

"Point is, we're here now. Something I would've missed out on completely if I hadn't kept trying." I bring her knuckles to my lips and savor her sweet scent.

She half scoffs, half snorts, then yanks her hand from my grasp to fold it over her chest. I relax into the bench, stretching out my limbs to soak in some additional sun. All too soon, I'll go back to rotting away my days inside a vehicle, turning pale as the snow-capped Colorado mountains come December.

"Do you know what I want more than anything?" she starts, voice laced with purpose. "I want to be a tree. In my childhood home, we had this ginormous live oak out front. So big you could stand beneath it and not see a lick of sky. The thing had roots so deep and so wide that it tore up part of our driveway one summer. Dad was so annoyed." She lets out a breathy laugh while shaking her head at nothing, gaze pinned somewhere far away. "I want to be like that. To land somewhere as nothing more than a seed and then grow and grow and grow. I want to have roots so big and bountiful that you couldn't dream of moving me. I want the whole shebang: a home and a family and a long, beautiful life, none of which are framed around what could've been or what should've been.

"I want to take my children to the store without people tutting about how it's a shame my parents aren't here to see them. I want to go on a vacation with my family and not feel haunted by my memories at every turn. Then I want to return home to said beautiful life and find no evidence that it was ever anything less." She whimpers softly, but I hear it all the same. Then, quietly, she adds, "I've been alive all this time, Kit, but it doesn't feel like I've really been living."

Her words resonate deep in my chest, causing a sickening ache for something, *anything* that'll make the yearning go away. I felt it once, back when Courtney and I first fell in love. I truly believed we'd grow old together. Have children and grandchildren. Sit in rocking chairs on our front porch sipping tea till the end of our days.

After the divorce, I resigned myself to the fact that it was all just a fairy tale. No one really has that life. Least of all me. But now, sitting here with Tess, I catch a glimpse of it again. It's almost more painful than having written it off in the first place, to want it again and have no guarantee of it happening. After all, while I'm seeing Tess in that imagined future, she could be seeing anyone. Or no one at all. Just a blank slate to strive toward, with no pieces of the past still hanging around.

I clear my throat, forcing the images from my mind. "So not traveling the world? Sampling the ice cream bars in, say, Italy? For example."

Her eyes, glassy with unshed tears, roll from that distant point to me. "I believe they're called gelato bars in Italy."

I hum an acknowledgment. She snorts gruffly and shakes her head.

"I know it seems stupid. I've stayed in the same small town for my whole life. Sure, I've visited places and had a million and a half odd jobs, but I've had what most of the world would consider strong roots. They don't feel like they belong to me, though. They're just a continuation of what my parents left behind. But they feel poisoned, in a way. Tainted by everything." A line forms between her brows, and her bottom lip wobbles.

"The problem is, I don't know how to have a life they wouldn't recognize."

I rest my hand on her knee, feeling the rough linen fabric of her pants scratch my palm as I squeeze. "Tess, they'd recognize any life you choose to have."

She blinks hard, pushing a tear over the brim of her eyelashes. "How?"

I brush it away. First with my knuckle, then with my lips. Finally, I press a kiss to her temple. "Because you'll be in it."

She releases a shuddering breath, like I just confirmed something she never once believed could be true. There's so much pain in the sound, so much unspent grief. I want to shoulder it however I can, if only to ease a little of the weight she carries.

It hits me then with the impact of a two-ton semi: I want to be the one she tells everything. The one she admits these fears to, shares her joys with. For the first time in years, I'm picturing my own roots and wishing they could be intertwined with hers. I want more than the next few days or a handful of stolen moments when she visits Loveless. I want all of it. And the most terrifying part about it is that it doesn't terrify me at all. It feels easy as breathing to want this. To want her. Like I've been waiting for it my entire life. And I can't bear for her not to know it. To not at least try.

"Tess, when this trip is over… When we go home…"

Her gaze darts to mine, momentarily stealing my words. I wet my lips and try again. "What we have—"

"Kit," she inserts, jolting a hand up like she can physically stop the words.

Just then, my cell starts ringing in my pocket. I grimace, but after everything with my family this week, I can't risk not at least glancing at it. "One sec."

I swear she sighs in relief, which is not a good sign. The number is from a Mississippi area code, but I don't recognize it, so I let it go to voicemail. Whoever it is can leave a message if it's so important.

As soon as the thought passes through my mind, a text alert sounds.

UNKNOWN NUMBER

It's me, bro. Had to get a new number. I need you to call me back. I am so fucked.

Anger vibrates my throat in a low grunt. Where I normally feel a knee-jerk desire to fix his problems, I find I want nothing more in this moment than to shut him out. Pretend that this, what I have with Tess, is my real life. None of the shit with my brother. I set him up with a lawyer. Paid his fucking bail. Whatever happens next should be on him and only him.

"Everything okay?" Tess asks, brow crumpled in concern.

It jolts me from my thoughts. Thoughts better left time to simmer down before I do something I regret. I shove the phone into my pocket. "Yes. Probably." That doesn't help her confusion. I brush it off with a wave and reach for her hand. "It's not as important as what I was trying to say. Tess—"

"Kit," she says again, more firmly this time. "I didn't tell you all that to get some kind of pity confession. Whatever you're thinking of saying, please just don't, okay? Not like this. I don't want any of your feelings toward me to be because you feel bad for me or you think you could save me or something else equally pathetic. The whole reason I want to leave this current life behind is because I'm tired of people looking at me the way you are now. Like you're seeing my past and what happened to me. Not actually seeing *me*."

I want to argue. To explain that I've felt this for a long time, and I'm only just now admitting it to myself. But she's right. She deserves better than some opportune confession. So I swallow my pride along with my words and force a smile in their place. There will be time later for me to tell her what I want, when we're not sitting in the shadow of her freshly exposed grief.

"As you wish." I kiss her temple. Then, when she tips her chin up toward me, I press another kiss against her lips, light as air, just enough to tide myself over until I can get her alone again. "Why don't you take me to the stall your mom loved? Where you get your rings."

A glint of mischief sparks in her eyes. I've never seen anything more beautiful. More welcome, after so much sadness saturated them moments ago.

"You going to start wearing jewelry?"

"Hey, I look great in silver," I tease, pulling her to her feet along with me. For a moment I feel the phantom press of my dog tags against my sternum, though I gave up wearing the things a while ago. I never liked the attention they brought me, the questions. "But no. I was thinking I could pick up something for my mom."

At that, her lips part in an earsplitting grin. "I think Betty would love that."

Her obvious affection for Mom draws a grin from me, too. "I'm sure she would."

We make our way to a stand at the far end of the walkway, where an elderly Black woman presides over an array of beautifully crafted pieces featuring every color stone you could imagine. I pick up a necklace decorated with tiny teardrops of jade. I've already got a feeling, but when Tess bites her bottom lip and nods with glittering eyes, I know I've found the one.

As she turns to talk with the daughter of the stall owner, I finish paying for the necklace. At the last minute I grab a small piece that catches my eye, tucking it into my pocket with a wink sent the owner's way. She takes my discreetly passed wad of cash, then hugs me tightly like we're old friends.

By the time we make it back to the Carmen, exhaustion has us slinking through the lobby at a snail's pace. Without a second's hesitation, Tess follows me into my room, where we shower and make lazy love on freshly pressed bedsheets. We fall asleep like that, clothed only in the afternoon sunlight drifting through a gap in the curtains, leaving all thoughts of what happens when this vacation ends tucked away in the shadows.

Chapter Twenty-Seven

Tess

I'VE ONLY BEEN to the Ortizes' house a handful of times, but as I crane my neck to peer up at the teaberry-pink siding through my window, the memories are as clear as day. I see my dad and Alex on an expansive back patio, decorated with tiki torches and several large lounge chairs, perfect for entertaining a crowd. The smell of freshly charred shrimp and bell peppers wafts off the grill. Mom and Jenna are enjoying tequila sunrises at the kitchen island, casting cursory glances my way while I work to entertain a toddling Mara.

Our tires rasp over the sand-covered driveway. Then we're opening our doors and stepping into an evening that's thick with static. My hair grows wilder by the second. A storm is forming in the distance, an ominous darkness on the horizon that could be mistaken for nighttime if you weren't observant enough to note its purple hue. We'll get drenched in the next hour or so.

Kit strides around the front of his rental car, meeting me before I've even had a chance to shut my door. He does it for me, then leaves his hand braced on the roof of the car. His gaze travels the length of me, taking in a sundress whose color reminds me of the tall grass that grows wild on the dunes. Bright white cuts through the gray haze of evening as he draws his teeth along his bottom lip. "You look beautiful, Tess."

"Not so bad yourself," I say, trying to force nonchalance that I don't feel. The truth is, my knees have gone weak at the sight of him. With his nearly black hair tousled by the wind and his button-down open just enough to reveal a smattering of dark chest hair, my mouth is practically watering. How I ever tried to convince myself I could resist him is beyond me. I was doomed from the start.

He pushes off the car to propel himself into my orbit, looping an arm around my waist and pulling me flush against his chest. Our heartbeats pound in tandem. His eyes glint as he smiles down at me. "Sure you want this dinner on your list? If we run now, we could probably revisit goal number five."

A smirk twists my lips. "I think we've thoroughly investigated it."

"And the verdict?"

"Best I ever had," I say, enunciating each word succinctly. "Though I've definitely decided that it has nothing to do with your penis."

More to do with the fact that I'm falling for him faster than I can reason myself out of it, but I'm not going to tell him that. Not when our separation looms ever closer, threatening as that not-so-distant storm. So I tell him, and then what? I walk away like none of this ever happened? Like my life hasn't changed irrevocably, and all due to what should have been an inconsequential summer fling?

He sighs heavily. A wash of minty breath flows from his lips onto mine, pulling me back to the present, where his proximity alone is enough to flood my cheeks with warmth. That and his cheeky grin. "It was the double-jointed thumb, wasn't it?"

I cough up a laugh. As I move to swat his chest, he captures my wrist and instead folds my hand in his and presses it to his sternum, where the resounding thud of his heart vibrates my palm. Then he leans forward and covers my lips with his. He takes his time with the kiss, like we're the only two people in the world. And for a moment I'm nearly convinced we are.

"Kit! Tess!"

We break apart like waves. Alex leans over the porch railing above us, a bright bulb behind him rendering his features unreadable. The house, like all others this close to the water, is on stilts. The tall wooden beams keep the home safe from rising flood waters in the event of a hurricane. I can just make out Alex's white linen shirt billowing in the strong breeze. A nearby flag whips and snaps against its pole, piercing the evening with its hollow clanging.

"Hey, Alex!" I call out, hoping he can't hear just how breathless I sound.

Under the cover of dusk, Kit slips his hand from my lower back to my ass and squeezes. Hard enough that I'm reminded of the print he left in that exact place after our early morning balcony session earlier today.

"Later, then," is all he says. But I feel it like the promise it is, seeping all the way down to my bones.

He releases me and makes quick work of the few feet between us and the stairs. It takes me a moment to kick into gear, but finally I do, and I'm flying past him, taking the steps two at a time.

Alex meets me at the top of the staircase. He holds out a hand and, once I've taken it, uses it to pull me into a hug. "So glad you got here before the storm!"

I pull back, cupping his biceps and grinning at him. "Hope you built a cover over that back patio since I was last here. Otherwise your second shower of the day will be happening in T-minus thirty minutes."

"Ah, you assume there was a first shower."

"Gross," I say, wrinkling my nose. But I'm laughing, and so is he. His dark eyes narrow at a point over my shoulder, likely that foreboding cloud. From the way he clicks his tongue and nods, I can see he agrees with my assessment. Still, he shrugs as his gaze meets mine once more, as if to say, *What can you do?*

Alex is relaxed here in a way he never is at work. Free to enjoy himself without trying to keep the world afloat around him. The man in front of me is wearing cuffed chinos and a Cuban-style linen shirt that my dad would appreciate. He appears years younger than the version I see most often, who spends his days running a luxury resort that he and his wife built from scratch.

He tosses a playful wink and then releases me to embrace Kit. "Nice to see you, Mr. Llewellyn. Jenna tells me this was all your idea."

Kit pinches my side gently. Enough to provoke the colony of butterflies in my stomach. "Please, call me Kit. And your wife is being too generous. I barely got a word out before she had the whole menu planned."

"That's my girl." Pride softens Alex's features. "Come, let's get inside. How many years has it been, *mija?*"

"Too many." I allow myself to be guided to the front door, with Alex at my side and Kit bringing up the rear. Once inside, I kick off my shoes at a familiar Turkish-style rug and watch as Kit does the same. The entryway opens right up into a kitchen and dining area, with sliding glass doors that lead to the back patio straight ahead on the far side of the house. A dividing wall splits the level down the middle, with an open archway leading from the dining room into a sunken living space that was filled with an overstuffed couch and enough cozy, hand-crafted throws to drown in the last time I saw it.

Mo sets a beer bottle on the kitchen island with a clink and marches across the small distance between us in his signature quick clip just to sweep me off my newly bare feet for a hug. "*¡Qué hermosa eres!*"

"*Gracias,* Mo." I kiss his cheek and draw in his familiar tobacco scent.

"Don't mistake my lack of rushing you at the door for me not loving you as much!" Jenna calls from her place at the stove. She winks at me as I step fully into view, pointing a finger that she drags over my entire person while whistling. "Love this dress. Though if I looked as good as you, I swear I'd never wear any clothes."

"Ma!" Mara cries. She's standing at the counter, stirring a bowl of what looks to be coleslaw. Her hair is pinned at either temple, reminding me of the way she'd wear it when she was younger. Disgust curdles her expression.

"Oh, pfft." Jenna waves a hand dismissively at her daughter. "You came out of this body, thank you so much. And I wasn't wearing clothes at the time, believe you me."

Mara rolls her eyes. Mo and Alex chuckle. Kit accepts the beer Alex offers with an easygoing smile of his own. And at the center of it all is me. For a moment I'm so focused on taking a mental snapshot of this feeling, of these people, that Jenna's words don't quite register.

"Did you hear me? I said that I made your favorite." She lifts a tray of freshly browned griddle cakes. "Pupusas. I got the recipe from Magdalena."

I shake my head and smile breathlessly. "I haven't had them in years." My lungs grow tight in my chest as a wave of gratitude rushes over my belly. It's the distinct sensation of being loved, and more importantly, of being known. I suddenly wish I had all the time in the world to revel in it.

I can sense that my face has fallen, only because it takes more effort than normal to force my lips back into a grin. Jenna notices, because of course she does. I can tell because her own smile droops at the corners, the wrinkles there deepening with the fall.

"What's a pupusa?" Kit sidles up to me and wraps an arm around my shoulders. I sink into his warmth, and when he presses a kiss to my temple, a ripple of surprise flutters through the room.

Jenna is the first to recover, giving me a look that says, *We'll discuss this later,* before audibly replying, "Think of a flatbread stuffed with different things like cheese or beans. It's an El Salvadoran thing, or Honduran, depending on who you ask." Jenna shrugs. "Since Magda is from El Salvador, that's what we're going with tonight."

I hip check him. "They're delicious. You'll love them."

He rubs his stomach with the hand not holding me. "There are very few foods I've met that I didn't like."

Mara finishes what I now realize is curtido and starts heading for the table with the bowl. "What's your least favorite?" She drops the question on a drive-by.

A shudder runs through Kit. "Mushrooms. Can't fucking stand them." He blushes when his words hit his ears, and his gaze cuts right to Jenna. "So sorry, ma'am," he utters quickly, drawl thicker in his panic.

"Amen," Mo inserts. "Slimy bastards."

At that, the room erupts with laughter, and I feel more than see Kit relax into relief. As Jenna passes him with the tray of pupusas, she rises onto her tiptoes and kisses his cheek, which thoroughly melts him. Mo pulls my chair out for me at a dining table crafted from local driftwood, and he and Mara fight for the seat on my other side. Kit sighs good-naturedly and gives his chair to Mara, moving instead to sit between Alex and Jenna on the opposite corner of the table.

Alex whispers a quick prayer over the food before crossing himself, and then we dig in. There are plates passed, silverware clinking, and a dollop of salsa ends up splattered on Mauricio's lap. It's messy and chaotic and beautiful, just like the storm that finally unravels outside.

Once our bellies are round and tight, Kit and I make quick work of clearing the table and tag teaming the dishes. Halfway through, he doubles over with a groan. "Why did you let me have that fifth pupusa?"

"Overeating pupusas is a canon event," I say, shrugging, before depositing a rinsed plate in the dishwasher. "I couldn't interfere."

He grumbles a response that I can't make out. When all is done and put away, he stumbles toward the living room like a woman in the eleventh hour of pregnancy, sparing a glance over his shoulder to make sure I'm watching. I shake my head and laugh as he calls, "You did this to me!"

Where the kitchen and dining space is painted a pale yellow and decorated only with the occasional photograph, their living room is a menagerie of color. I stand in the archway with my head tilted upward, taking in the vaulted ceilings and the windows of pure black night, interrupted only by the occasional burst of lightning. The rain has subsided for now, but thunder still grumbles its promise that the storm isn't over yet.

On the opposite wall, various artworks Jenna and Alex have collected over the years from their travels leave very little of the seafoam green wall exposed. Scenes of Parisian streets and Costa Rican rainforests grapple for attention. In the end I let my eyes go hazy, which creates a blurry abstract of the whole world.

Mo and Alex are seated in either of two oversize recliners bracketing the same plush couch I remember from years ago. Kit has made himself at home there and is animatedly telling Mara about his own travels during his time in the military. Turns out, he was in Germany for a time, and that's one of the stops she's planned for during her gap year. I lean against the threshold, crossing my arms over my chest as I watch him gesticulate, eyes bright and mouth never straying from a half smile.

"He sure is handsome, Tess."

I glance over my shoulder. Jenna sidles up to me, her bare feet sticking slightly to the tile floor with each small step. She leans against the opposite side of the threshold, our bodies brushing from shoulder to elbow to hip, and smiles at the scene before us.

"He's aware," I deadpan. But I can't help the way the corner of my mouth twitches.

Her laugh is more of a sigh. I turn to study her and find she's already looking at me. In a lowered voice, she says, "You want to talk about what you plan to do next?"

My brow furrows, even as my heart skips a beat. "What do you mean?"

She shrugs. "You know, since you aren't planning on coming back here."

My gaze darts to Mo, who's laughing hysterically at some story Kit is telling.

"He didn't tell me anything." Her hand flattens over her heart. "Though *ouch,* you told Mo and not me?"

I grimace. "It wasn't a planned thing. He caught me at a vulnerable moment."

"Ah, I see. I can accept that."

"If Mo didn't say anything, how did you know?"

When our gazes meet again, there's a sad crinkle to the edges of her dark brown eyes. Not pity, exactly. More like regret.

"You've seemed different this year. And not just because you brought along a guest for the first time since your grandparents passed." She nods toward Kit, who is now on his feet, giving Mara a self-defense lesson from the looks of it. Or perhaps he just likes to be kicked in the shins. "I don't know if you've realized, but every year you grow more and more subdued. Alex and I were getting very concerned, actually. It was like we could see the light inside you dying out."

Now it's my turn to say ouch.

Her hand curls around mine, soft from the cocoa butter lotion she applies religiously. "I don't mean that to hurt you, Tess. I only say it because lately I've been catching more and more glimpses of the old you, in the moments where you forget to be sad." She tilts her head, catching the fluorescent light from the kitchen on the sharp curve of her delicate jaw. "Where he reminds you how to be happy."

"I've been happy," I say in an attempt to come to my defense, but the words are so hollow it does the opposite. "Or, I haven't been sad. I've been mostly numb, I guess."

Her lips thin and she nods her head sympathetically. "I'm not sure that's better."

My throat grows dry. I force a painful swallow. "I'm not either."

"Did you know that I have a baby sister?" Jenna's looking at Mara with sparkling pride, but there's a wateriness to it that tells me where this story is going before we've even begun the journey. "She was the light of my life. My hero. Most of my friends wanted nothing to do with their little siblings, but I loved Carmen fiercely. We did everything together.

"She died of an undiagnosed heart condition when she was only seventeen. I was away at college. When my mother called, I couldn't believe her. I'd just seen my sister the day before." A tear slips down her cheek, but it's caught by a watery smile. "You see, every Friday after class, I'd drive an hour to meet her at this little diner halfway from my hometown to the college I was attending at the time. It was our tradition. A way for us to stay close, back before cell phones and Facetime and all that.

"After she died, I still made that drive every Friday. It

confused Alex when we first got together, because he could never take me out on a Friday night. I'd come home exhausted and weepy and shut myself in with a boxed-up order of her usual that'd never get eaten."

I picture Jenna at Mara's age, carrying the burden of grief that I know so well. I'm shocked I never noticed it on her shoulders.

"Part of it was habit. Part of it was my silly attempt to keep her here with me for longer. Even though all it really did was remind me she was gone." She releases my hand to wipe at her cheeks with the ball of her palm. "When Alex and I got serious about starting the resort, I had to make a decision. I knew it was time. That she'd understand.

"And what a gift it has been. This place that I love so deeply. That she's very much a part of, even if she's never seen it. It has brought me immense joy, and I'd have none of that if I'd stayed stuck in that old routine, never allowing myself to move forward."

I open my mouth, not entirely trusting my voice to be there when I reach for it. "That's beautiful, Jenna."

I never once questioned where the resort's name came from. I guess I assumed it was a grandmother's name, or maybe Jenna's middle. Perhaps just a place somewhere that Jenna and Alex loved. But Carmen was someone who mattered, whose life ended too soon. And in creating this place, Jenna has allowed her legacy to be more than just the sum of her years. It's every memory made here, each trip that became tradition. Her legacy is me and my family. Both the one I've lost, and the one I'm realizing I have here, with the Ortizes and even Kit, if only for the time being.

None of that would exist without Carmen. And I tell Jenna exactly that. Seeing her, but also seeing my past and all my possible futures, I smile at Jenna. "Thank you for sharing her with me. With us."

In the quiet that follows my words, I realize that Kit and Mara have given up on sparring. Mo and Alex are snoozing in their chairs. Kit's gaze drifts to mine, surprise flitting across his expression, like he hadn't realized I was watching this entire time. His brow furrows, and I quickly shake my head to let him know I don't need him quite yet, but I'm sure I will soon enough.

He relents, but the tension remains in his shoulders like he's ready to come for me the moment I call.

"Moving forward doesn't mean moving on," Jenna says.

My brow crumples. "What do you mean?"

"They'll always be with you, just as my sister is with me." She squeezes my hand one final time, then lets it go. "And wherever you go in this great, big world, just know that my crazy little family is there with you, too."

I smile, remembering Mo said something similar that night by the pool. It makes that great, big world a lot less terrifying, when I know there are people somewhere in it who love me. Who are rooting for me.

"Did you ever go back?" I ask because I can't resist. "To that restaurant?"

She brushes a strand of hair from her cheek with the back of her hand and nods. "Yes. Many, many years later. I wanted Xiomara to meet her *tia.*" She laughs self-consciously, ducking her chin. "I know that sounds ridiculous, but it felt right at the time."

Our gazes meet, and I shrug. "Makes perfect sense to me."

She nods. "I thought it might."

We say our goodbyes shortly after. By the time Kit shuttles me home, the small part of me that was filled with dread for this one of many lasts has instead been balmed by pupusas and the warmth of my conversation with Jenna. I take Kit's hand gladly as he guides me toward the entrance to the Carmen, feeling lighter than I have in months.

"Was that everything you hoped it would be?"

The smell of wet asphalt is thick in the air. A layer of

humidity coats my skin. Where our palms meet, sweat pools, but neither of us seems to care. I grin up at him. "It was even better. Thank you. I needed that more than I realized, I think."

The cool lobby AC hits me like a cold front, sending a shiver down my spine as we step inside. Kit points toward the hall that leads to the elevator bay. "Ready for bed?"

I glance in that direction, but my gaze catches on the glowing blue pool on the other side of the wall of windows, and my steps falter. "Could we stop and visit my parents for just a sec?"

He doesn't hesitate. Doesn't ask questions. Doesn't even lift a brow at my seemingly absurd request. Kit switches directions on a dime, guiding me to the pool deck, where the handprints await.

I tell them all about our night, and he chimes in with his own side of the story. We chatter till we run out of words to say. And then, we sit still and listen.

Chapter Twenty-Eight

Kit

IT'S NOT long after we make it to Tess's room that the sky reopens. With the curtains flung wide, every flash of lightning fills the space, illuminating the patterned carpet and the crisp white sheets. The strikes are reflected in the glass surface of the bedside tables. Overhead, the rain picks up. Drumbeats of rainfall drown out our hearts, which pulse in tandem as I pull Tess close.

She is so beautiful. Watching her tonight, surrounded by people she loves, felt like catching a glimpse of her that the rest of the world rarely sees. It felt like a fucking privilege. And now that I've got her alone, I can't resist showing her just how grateful I am.

"Take off your dress."

Her brow arches, but she doesn't argue. She steps out of my embrace and gathers the fabric at her hips, then lifts the pale green gown over her head. Her breasts bounce as she drops it to the ground. She's not wearing a bra, and the sight of her pert nipples already standing at attention for me is enough to leave me hard and aching.

"Anything else?" she asks, her tone teasing. With two thumbs hooked in the waistband of lace panties, she knows exactly what I want, but she's going to make me say it.

Very well then. "Take off your panties and put them in my pocket."

She drags them slowly down her endless legs. In a brief flash of white light, I can see wetness darkening the pale fabric. It nearly makes my knees buckle.

She holds them out for me to examine. "Front or back?"

"Front. And unzip my pants while you're at it."

"Yes, sir."

A guttural sound tears through my throat. She knows exactly what she's doing to me as she trails the tip of a finger over my length, the touch at once exquisite and yet not nearly enough with the layers of fabric between us. She slips her underwear into my pocket for safekeeping, and then slowly, painstakingly, draws down my zipper. She doesn't wait for my next command. I watch, enraptured, as Tess tugs at my shorts and then my underwear, freeing my cock from its confines. It falls forward, into her waiting grasp.

"Mm, was it the dress that did it?" she asks with a titillating tilt of her head. "Or the fact that I ate three pupusas in one sitting?"

My laugh sounds more like I'm choking. "Is now a bad time to mention that dirty talk is not your strong suit?"

Her fist tightens around my hard length, sending stars across my vision. "Maybe not. But you know what is?"

I shake my head, fighting to keep myself from coming right into her hand.

Instead of elaborating, she drops to her knees.

Her lips part and I catch sight of her glistening tongue as she leans forward and drags it along my length from base to tip. Then, those perfect lips close around my head and she sucks. Hard. If I thought my knees might give out before, it was nothing compared to this. The draw and pull of her suckling. The swirl of her tongue. Pleasure arcs up my spine like a live wire, electrifying my thoughts. There is only Tess and her beautiful green eyes gazing up at me. Only Tess and her hands working in tandem with her throat to take me deeper.

"You're so fucking perfect," I growl. "If you don't stop, soon you'll be drinking my come."

Her responding hum of pleasure gives way to the primal sound of her choking on my cock as she grabs my hips and pulls me toward her, burying me in her throat. My vision explodes in a kaleidoscope. I rock backward, slipping from her hold. She whimpers like I've stolen her favorite toy. And honestly? From the way she was devouring me, that just might be the truth.

"Not tonight." I meet her halfway to standing and scoop her up by the thighs, wrapping her legs around my hips as I march us toward her bed. We fall gracelessly. Somewhere in the midst of it, she pulls my shirt over my head and I kick my shorts and boxers away from my ankles. Our bodies tangle together, all slick skin and heat as we move like we've been doing this forever instead of a single, short week.

I want to do this forever. The thought comes unbidden as I slip into her wet heat. Not just sex. I want late-night swims and dinner parties and chatting about her favorite memories by the pool. I want to taste every gasp like I'm capturing this one, our lips pressed as tightly together as the rest of our bodies, moving in perfect tandem.

She tastes like sunshine and sweetness. Like the whipped cream Jenna sprayed on strawberries for us to have as dessert. Tess's body is so warm, so perfectly soft everywhere I grab her. She clenches around me, already approaching the precipice. I want to take her there now, and once she's had time to rest, again. To drive her mad with desire. As mad as I feel inside.

"Fuck, Kit!" she cries out, digging her nails into my shoulder blade. "Don't stop."

"Never," I groan. I keep my rhythm. Stroke her cheek with my thumb. Draw each exhale of hers deep into my lungs like a drug. As she loses herself to the pleasure, I lose myself in her. Soon we're both free-falling into oblivion, where there is nothing but this intangible feeling between us. Satisfaction and desire and something else, something so much deeper, that I've felt since the very moment we met.

As soon as I collapse, I crush her to my chest and roll. We land with me on my back, head sunken into her plethora of extra pillows courtesy of a staff that dotes on her. Her curtain of shoulder-length hair falls just short of my face, shielding me from the lightning strikes and even cocooning me from the noise of the storm overhead. She is all I can see. All I ever want to see.

This is going to hurt a lot more than I thought it would.

"Tess," I breathe, reaching up to stroke her chin. I pinch her there and draw her lips to mine, something gentle to rectify the bruising kisses from a moment ago. "How am I supposed to let you go when this is over?"

She stills on top of me like she's bracing for a blow. "What do you mean?"

I stroke the hollow beneath her cheekbone, savoring the soft warmth of her skin because, with a confession like this, it may very well be the last time I get to feel it. "I don't want this to be it. Not for us. And I can't leave here on Monday and walk away without knowing I tried my damnedest to show you that I can be a part of your future, no matter what that future looks like. I'd fight for my place. Be whatever—*whoever*—you need."

A fresh sheen of tears coats her blown pupils. The corners of her eyes crinkle. "Why would you want me messing up your life, Kit? Your stable, perfect, figured-out life."

My laugh is harsh. Scalding. "My life is nowhere near figured out. Who the hell's is? I'm telling you I don't care about the uncertainty. It doesn't scare me because I'm certain about you, and that's what matters."

Hard breaths are rattling her shoulders. Then her weight is gone, and suddenly she's sitting up on the edge of the bed facing the window. She tilts her head toward me but keeps her gaze low. "What changed?"

I hook an arm around her waist and, using a firm grip on her leg, turn her to face me in the bed. "That's the thing, Tess. I don't think anything's changed. I think I've felt this way, known this was how it'd end up between us, since the second I spotted you at that airport. I just had to wait for it to be the right moment. And I'm pretty sure this is it. This is our shot."

She shakes her head so sorrowfully, so surely that a piece of my heart splinters, but at the same time there's hope gleaming in her eyes. She's scared, but she wants this. I'd bet my life on it. The realization brings with it a bone-deep ache in my chest, so strong that it steals my breath away.

"Kit, I—"

Over the cacophony of the downpour and the warbling of Tess's voice, the ringtone I specifically assigned to my parents sounds. Tess starts, letting her words falter. I keep waiting. Urging her to continue with my gaze, with my touch, even when I'm terrified that what she's about to say will hurt like hell.

I ignore the call until I can't anymore, because Tess is scooting off the bed and marching over to the pile of clothing on the floor, where she plucks my cell from a pocket and tosses it to me. "It's your parents."

"I'm not answering this right now." I reject the call and set the phone aside.

Following a brief silence, the ringing starts up again.

Tess gathers her dress and pulls it over her head. She perches on the edge of the bed, as far from me as she can, and nods toward the screaming phone. "Just pick it up. They wouldn't call unless it were important."

"*You're* important."

"Kit." Her voice contains a warning. It's protecting something fragile, something so close to breaking. And I realize then that she's stalling. "Answer. The. Phone."

We're locked in a battle of wills, both of us too stubborn to break, when the phone falls silent. Moments later it starts up again.

"Goddamn it." I rip the phone from the bed and slide my thumb across the screen to answer. "Hello?"

"It's Gage," my dad bites out, voice fraught with panic. "We can't find him anywhere. Have you heard from him?"

"Not today, but"—my brow furrows—"it's not unusual to go a while without talking to him." My parents know that. So why the panic? "Is something wrong? Why are you looking for him?"

"There's a warrant out for his arrest."

My entire body stills. Tess's gaze roves my face like she can measure how bad the news is by what's reflected there.

"Kit? Are you there, son?"

I picture my brother's text from a new number. The one I left unanswered, more focused on spending time with Tess than once again being tagged in to clean up his messes. "What are the charges?" I croak while mentally preparing myself to break the news that this is my fault. That I covered for my brother, thinking he'd be scared straight. At least for a bit.

My dad's sigh sounds more like a freight train's approach. Thunderous. Exhausted from a long haul. "Hit-and-run, on the interstate a few days ago. He nearly killed a woman and her small child, then left them to rot."

"Hit-and-run, on the interstate," I echo, trying to make it make sense. It's too specific to be a coincidence but too coincidental to be true. At least, that's what my aching brain insists. "That was *Gage?*"

A sob breaks through the call, so loud even Tess must hear it. My father's cry, a sound I haven't heard in years. It fractures something in me. Or perhaps it finds a piece of me that was already splintered and splits me wide open. I can't speak. Can't breathe. My gaze meets Tess's, but I find no solace there. Turns out, we're both drowning, looking to one another for a life preserver that neither of us has.

"I just don't understand. He'd been doing so well." Dad's voice shakes. "What on earth happened?"

My heart stutters to a stop, then drops like a stone into the chasm of my stomach. "Dad," I rasp, clutching the phone to my ear. Tess's hand moves to cover her lips. "There's something I have to tell you."

Chapter Twenty-Nine

Tess

I LISTEN with balled fists grinding against my thighs like aching mortar and pestles as Kit tells his Dad just how much he's been shouldering for years.

I knew it was bad. But this is so much worse than I thought.

And even though every instinct in my body begs me to reach for Kit, to pull him against my chest and hold him through this, I am also frozen in shock. Images of that woman bloody and slumped against the airbag flash in my mind. Every time I blink, it's my mother's face I see in place of hers. Mine instead of that little boy's. I grind my fists harder.

This is exactly why we cannot work, no matter how much Kit insists otherwise. In this moment where he needs me most, I can't get past my own grief to be of any comfort. Hell, I can barely keep from collapsing in a heap of panic the way I did at the site of the accident. And while he is so certain he can be what I need, the problem is, I clearly can't do the same.

After what feels like ages, he hangs up the phone. I missed their parting words. Surely his dad, the jovial man I met who absolutely adored his son, was understanding? But the look on Kit's face would suggest otherwise.

The thunder has quieted to a soft rumble. I fold my arms around my middle when all I want to do is gather the broken man before me into an embrace. For a brief, shattering moment I wish desperately that my mom were here. She always knew what to do to stop my tears.

Kit leans forward to gingerly place his phone on the bedside table, staring at it the entire time like it's a bomb that might obliterate us all. And didn't it? Or were we already breaking before the call ever came in? I only had a heartbeat to consider that Kit's confession might be everything I never knew I wanted, right before the universe reminded me why that would be impossible.

Too much brokenness, too much heartbreak to go around. It's a wonder anyone makes it out of this existence unscathed.

Finally his eyes lift to mine. In our short time together, I've come to count on their color as a gauge to his mood. More golden-green when he's being playful. A deep, rich umber when his gaze roves my bare skin. But this dappled camouflage, made even more pale by the soft moonlight, is foreign to me. I don't know how to read it any more than I would Ancient Greek.

"I'm in love with you, Tess."

All at once the room is both vastly too large and incredibly small. My ears ring like I've lost consciousness, though I never lose sight of Kit. My pulse pounds out a rapid staccato, fueled by each shallow breath I manage to drag in. I'm undeniably present, and yet I've spun off into my own world with no idea how to get back to him even if I tried.

"Say something." His words are firm. There's no desperation. Only a strong, electric current pulling them taut. It's as close to a command as he's ever given me. Even more so than, *Get back in the car.* "Good or bad; just talk to me. Tell me what you're thinking."

Somewhere in the rubble of my thoughts, I find my voice. "Y-you're confused. And emotional. Everything with your brother… The crash…"

He shakes his head. "Don't discredit my feelings just because you don't understand yours."

My jaw goes slack. I hadn't fully registered that he was still naked, but as he rises to walk over to his pile of clothes and yank on his shorts, my cheeks heat. I have to duck my head. It's too much. All of it is too much.

"Kit, why are you doing this?" I whisper, gaze trained on my hands. They've gone white from blood loss as I continue grinding them into my aching thighs.

He crouches in front of me where I sit at the edge of the bed and gently places a hand over each of mine, stilling them. His brows are screwed up against the ravine of concern that crumples his forehead. He is everything earnest and beautiful, framed in nothing but bluish-white moonlight that bathes his skin in an ethereal glow. So breathtaking it hurts. And oh, do I hurt.

"Because I just spent half an hour explaining myself for all the years I spent keeping secrets simply because I thought it was what was best for everyone else. Spoiler: it wasn't." His mouth pinches into a firm line, bracketed by regret. "I'm in love with you whether I tell you or not. And there will never be a perfect moment to lay that on the table, not for so long as you keep being terrified that saying it aloud means it can be taken from you. I know you're scared to let someone in again, but baby, that's not living. That's just being alive."

The room is shaking. Or really, it's my head that's shaking and the room is my Etch A Sketch. I keep thinking if I try a little harder, it'll all become something I recognize again.

Because this room, this place, even the pain that arises each time I step foot in the Carmen: it's all predictable. Familiar. How I feel for Kit is anything but.

Hot, sticky tears spill over my cheeks as I meet his gaze,

searching desperately for any solution to this hollow aching. "This wasn't supposed to happen."

His grasp on my hands tightens, pulling me imperceptibly closer. "Nothing is *supposed* to happen. Your parents weren't supposed to die. My brother wasn't supposed to be a shithead who only acts in his own self-interest. There was no reason for you and I to meet. But we did, and I'm so fucking glad. What matters is what we do with all that shit that just happens. So I'm telling you I love you. Telling you I choose you and I want you and I will do everything in my power not to die on you because I need a whole, long life with you. That's my truth, Tess. What's yours?"

Our own small eternity passes before he realizes that I won't —*can't*—answer. In that time I see it all play out. The life in which my parents never died. One where I grew up, graduated, and left my small town. Somehow found my way to Colorado at the exact same time as this man before me. Maybe I was still seeking Gary; perhaps in this other life my mother and I found him together. Kit and I would have met some other way, like at Zoey's bar over a couple of drinks. We'd have fallen quick and heavy, with none of my ghosts around to hold us back.

He'd give me an uncomplicated confession at a nice dinner. I'd smile instead of cry. It would be a happy day.

My throat constricts. His eyelids close tightly. We're both making ourselves smaller in our own ways, vital organ by vital organ, until we're back to our shrink-wrapped selves, protected from the kind of love that makes you consider if it's worth changing your ways to keep it.

I try to reason that he's in shock. In pain. That his confession is a knee-jerk reaction, one he'll regret in the morning. But as I study the sharp ridges of his cheekbones and brow, the soft waves of his dark hair, tumultuous as an undulating ocean, I know in my soul that he meant it. Every single word. I'm sure one day I'll be on my deathbed, thinking of the man who professed his love for me on his knees. I'll scream at this younger version of myself who slipped her hands from beneath his and watched him break, if only beneath the surface, rather than open herself up to the possibility of getting hurt.

Without a word, Kit rises to his feet, every exposed muscle rippling, then shrugs into his shirt. His broad, callused hand sweeps under my jaw, thumb testing my bottom lip. Resignation settles into his expression. Then he releases me, and I feel the loss right down to my toes.

He stops in the doorway to my bedroom and glances back. "For what it's worth, I don't think it's over between us. Not yet." A small, sad smile. "It probably never will be."

Then he turns on the living room light as he goes, so I won't be left alone in the dark.

Chapter Thirty

Kit

STEPPING out of Tess's room is the hardest thing I've ever had to do, but it's also necessary.

When I make it back to my room, I realize the second hardest thing will be cleaning up this mess. I pull up Gage's last message to me and dial the unfamiliar number. It rings endlessly until finally succumbing to a robotic voice that informs me the voice-mail box has not been set up yet. I drop onto the bed, completely boneless, and type out as succinct a text as I can manage.

ME

Mom and Dad know about everything, including the accident. You need to turn yourself in.

ME

Please answer me.

The second message slips out before I realize I've even typed it. That familiar desperation to fix things for him, always leaking through. But old habits die hard, so I dial him once more. This time it goes straight to the nonexistent voicemail.

So he's ignoring me. And I'm ignoring my feelings by

focusing on tasks that mean shit all in the end. Guess neither of us has really changed.

It's late, even in Mountain Time. But to my surprise, Tomas picks up on the second ring.

"Is this the call where you tell me you're actually eloping on a beach tomorrow and I need to get my ass on a plane?"

What's supposed to be a laugh comes out as more of a haggard cough. "Not exactly." I sound wrung out, even to myself, my voice as raw as a pubescent boy's. "But I will be missing my flight on Monday."

Thank God I booked refundable tickets, in case I misjudged Tess's arrival time completely.

There's shuffling, followed by the click of a light switch. "Indefinitely or just for now?" The jovial tone is gone from my boss's inflection. Now he's all business.

"A couple days. I should be back by the weekend." My gaze roves the ceiling, searching for shapes in the shadows. A distraction. Anything.

I don't know what I can do to fix this, and I doubt my presence will make one iota of difference, but I've run from this confrontation long enough. I need to look my parents in the eye and say I'm sorry. Own up for all the ways I've let them down. Just the thought of my dad's heartbroken voice on the phone is enough to collapse my lungs under the weight of the guilt.

"Everything okay?" Tomas asks.

I rack my brain for the answer to that question. Is everything okay? No, absolutely not. My brother has gone AWOL, I've finally and thoroughly scared Tess off, and I've failed the two people in the world who mean the most to me. It all feels so overwhelming and large, and I don't know how to play the cocky bastard against an enemy when I'm this outmatched.

But I also don't want to worry Tomas any more than I already have, so I say, "It will be," without a hint of conviction.

He curses under his breath. "Anyone ever told you you're a cagey son of a bitch?"

It reminds me of Tess's question the night I told her I'd wait till she asked me to kiss her. *Has anyone ever told you you're the worst?* Despite the pain still radiating behind my sternum, I smile. "Not in so many words, exactly."

His responding harrumph is about as masculine as my dejected sigh.

"All I want to know is if I'm going to have to hold that old man back from coming down there to kick your ass."

That earns a genuine laugh. One that ends with me biting down hard on the inside of my cheek and blinking away my suddenly blurry vision. "It's family stuff, Boss. Tell him his niece is just fine." At least I hope she will be. Eventually.

I meant what I said to her. We're not done. Not even close. At the height of my love for my ex-wife, I never felt the way I do with Tess. She is ever-present in my mind. There isn't a meal I eat that I don't think, would Tess like this? Every sunrise I've witnessed on this trip has been beautiful, but it wasn't until I watched one with Tess beside me that the sight truly took my breath away.

She's everything I've been walking toward since the day I stepped out of my old life. Perhaps even before then. Like it was all a labyrinth I had to trudge through to get to her. Even knowing that she'd eventually leave my love on the table, I'd do it again in a heartbeat and consider myself lucky for the suffering.

"Family stuff," Tomas repeats, then clicks his tongue as though tasting a flavor he can't quite identify. "Are we talking, like, your parents? That kind of family stuff?"

I find myself nodding before I remember he cannot see me. Then I clear my throat. "The very same."

"It's about damn time. I'm proud of you, Rookie." And he genuinely is. I can hear it in his voice. Still cautious, like he knows he's treading on sensitive waters, but warm with the pride of someone who's watched you struggle for far too long to figure out what everyone else already knew. "Listen, it's late, and the wife hates when I take work calls in bed. But you take all the time you need. We'll be here when you get back."

We share quick goodbyes before I can tell him he has no reason to be proud of me. I drop the phone on the comforter. It feels too cool to the touch without Tess here to warm it. I push off the crumpled bedding to stand in the middle of my room, the only light coming from the pool deck below, and wonder what the hell I'm supposed to do now.

I can't sleep, that much is certain. But I can't leave without saying goodbye to Tess. So I do the only other thing that remotely calms my nerves like her presence does: I put on my running shoes.

The lobby is quiet. Even the wall-mounted television by one of the sitting areas is muted. I pause at the mouth of the hallway, listening to the quiet whir of the palm-frond fan overhead and the dull tap of the night receptionist's pen against a notebook he's perusing. The windows facing the pool deck frame a scene familiar to anyone who grew up on the Gulf. Blue light from the pool flickers and flows across the leaves of the palm trees. Someone must've put up the chairs to save them from the wind, because aside from displaced fronds that lie scattered around the concrete, the deck is otherwise empty.

My gaze flickers to the photo of Tess and her parents, and another pang of guilt twists my stomach. I step closer and, with my voice low and arms crossed, mutter my apology.

"I hope you know I meant every word I told her. And I'm not giving up. I promise. I just need to take care of my family and give her some space. There was too much pushing on my part and not enough waiting for her to pull. I'm sorry about that. About all of it." My voice breaks, and I swallow past the fault line to clear it. "But I'm not sorry about loving her."

"Who could ever be?"

I glance up, only to lock eyes with Mauricio, who's smiling at me warmly. At first I hardly recognize him in the dark gray mechanic's jumpsuit he's wearing. His name tag sits lopsided atop his chest pocket, but I can just make out *Facilities Manager* in fine print underneath his name. His gaze tracks mine, and he turns the label to rights. "Leak in a guest's room. They trust you more when you come in uniform." His gaze lifts to mine and he shrugs. "I knew when the storm rolled in to be ready. There's one every season, no matter how new the roof is."

How has it only been a few hours since we all sat in the Ortizes' kitchen stuffing ourselves and laughing over one of this man's many ridiculous tales of guests' antics? It feels like a lifetime ago. Before the world and all its contents flipped upside down, turning into something I don't recognize anymore.

You'd think I'd be no stranger to it, the upending. But it turns out, no matter how many times it happens, you don't get desensitized to it. It hurts just as damn much every single time.

Whatever Mauricio reads in my expression, it flattens the smile in his. He turns to the photo and shakes his head. "The most beautiful family. Every year, we looked forward to their arrival. It was like the resort came alive when they showed up."

I picture Tess on the beach the night we hunted for crabs, all laughter and giddiness and sunshine, even in the dark. "I can imagine."

"It killed that little girl to lose them. And we—Jenna, my brother, and I—felt so powerless. To know Tessa is to love her. And to not be able to fix the heart of the one you love… That is its own special hell." He sniffs, pats his pocket, and removes a cigarette that he leaves dangling between his fingers. "Thank you for bringing her back to us. It makes it so much easier to let her go."

My gaze drifts from Mauricio back to the photo. "Do you really think she won't come back?"

The corner of his mouth turns up, wrinkling his deeply tanned skin. "I think that whether she does or doesn't is a matter as fluid as time. Always up for debate. Always able to change, sometimes in the blink of an eye. Either way, we will be here."

"Has anyone ever told you that you're awfully wise?" I say with a raspy chuckle.

He nods toward the picture. "Only Tessa."

Of course. She always could see the best in people. She certainly saw the best in me. I drop my gaze, frowning at the pearlescent floor. "She didn't get to finish her list."

"What list?"

I pull up the note on my phone, but I can't bring myself to erase her salacious addition, so I refrain from showing it to someone who might as well be her family. "Of what she wanted to do with her last trip here." The truth is, I looked for a whole sand dollar on every morning run, but all I could find were a bunch of pieces. It felt like a metaphor I didn't want to look too closely at. And as far as figuring out what to do with the rest of her life, well, I think that one's a lot like time. As Mauricio said, always changing. Always in flux.

Hard to give advice when I, too, remain largely unsure. For the last few years, the rest of my life looked a lot like my daily reality: go to work, go to the bar, perhaps have some meaningless sex, then rinse and repeat. Ever since meeting Tess, that all changed. Now it's a blank slate save for her face, her name, her everything.

"Anything I can help with?" Mauricio asks, eyebrows perched high on his forehead as though he was tracking my thoughts.

God, I hope not.

I return my attention to the list, feeling hopelessness rise like a wave in my chest, until I catch a glimpse of something through the window, just barely peeking out from the shroud of shadows surrounding the pool deck.

"Mo, you wouldn't happen to own a jackhammer, would you?"

He follows my gaze, a smile slowly creeping over his face. "No, but I do have a masonry blade and chisel."

I'm not handy enough to know if those tools will work, but if Mauricio is suggesting them, that's enough for me. "Perfect. Will you go get them, please?"

Chapter Thirty-One

Tess

Despite thinking *it'd never happen, I must eventually succumb to one of the waves of exhaustion that rises up between each bout of tears. The sound of a door snicking shut pulls me from sleep, and I bolt upright, half expecting to see Kit standing in my doorway.*

But it's not him, and I'm not where I expect to be. I'm in the living area, where the pull-out couch has been made up into a bed just for me. And my dad is taking a seat at the edge of the thin mattress.

"Daddy?" I blink twice in confusion, expecting him to disappear. Why? I don't know. There's just some voice in the back of my mind whispering, insisting his presence here is impossible.

The milky morning light brings out the silver that's beginning to fleck his brown hair. He offers his signature smirk and reaches forward to ruffle my hair. "Good morning, sleepyhead. I figured you'd be awake by now."

The strangest sense of déjà vu sends a shiver down my spine. "Did we have something planned?"

"No, but then, we never do." He smiles, flashing the same effortlessly white teeth that my friends at school envy me for.

Or used to? Why does it seem so long ago that I last saw

them? School only let out for the summer a couple weeks ago, right?

Dad's silver-blue gaze roams my features, and the corners of his mouth dip. "What's wrong? Today is a happy day."

I shake my head. Nothing inside me feels happy. "But why?"

"Because"—he claps his hands together quietly—"we're going home!"

I glance at the clock on the microwave, as though it will orient me to the right day rather than time. "I thought we didn't leave until tomorrow?"

He sighs and folds his hands over one knee. "Sometimes you have to go before you think you're ready. But it'll be okay, kiddo. I promise."

Confusion settles like a fog over my mind, submerging all my thoughts in heavy syrup until it seems as though I'll never be able to pluck them out.

"I don't understand," I say, sounding younger than I expect to now that I'm listening to myself more intently. "Why is it a happy day if we're leaving? You love it here."

"I love it here because it's where you and Mom are. Here's the thing about that, though, Tess: you're also everywhere else."

My mouth tries to form a response, but before words can trudge from my mind to my lips, another voice interrupts.

"My two early birds."

Dad and I glance up at the same time. Mom leans in the threshold that leads to their bedroom, arms folded over some faded T-shirt of Dad's that she's using as a nightgown. Her long legs are bare and tan even in the pale light. For some reason the sight of her makes my heart ache. I reach up to rub at the knot in my chest, and something on my hand glitters. Rings. My fingers are covered in rings, just like Mom's.

She notices at the same time I do, shaking her head thought-

fully. "Isn't it crazy, Ted? There's so much of us in her, and yet she's become someone else that's all her own."

Dad grumbles his agreement in a low timbre that's heart-wrenching in its familiarity. "And all those parts that are so different are the ones I love the very best."

I'm startled by a sudden knock. Mom's fist rests against the doorjamb, and she looks just like me when she says, "I'm really sorry, Tess."

"For what?" I ask, pulling the blanket higher up my torso.

"So sorry," Dad adds. Mom knocks again.

"It's okay. I'm okay with leaving. Just don't go." I don't know why I add the last part. They wouldn't leave without me, would they?

Of course not. It's always been the three of us. Sometimes more, but never less.

"Sorry, but it's time to go," they say in unison, sounding at once so close and yet very far away. I squeeze my eyes shut so I won't have to watch them go.

When I open my eyes again, the room is different. Right, but in its rightness, so wrong. My parents are gone. I'm back in the king-size bed in my normal room. And it's Kit's voice, instead of theirs, that drifts through the closed door to my hotel suite.

"I'm sorry, Tess. For everything."

I wait, but only silence and my thudding pulse follows. Tears spill down my cheeks. I leap from the bed and pad over to the bathroom, where my blotchy, stricken face greets me. I haven't dreamed of my parents in years. Not like that, where it felt as though I were living in a memory and the present all at once.

Cold water stings my puffy eyes. I splash my face quickly and wipe it down with a soft, white towel, then stumble from the room in search of something to wear other than my dress from last night. I peel it off my body and replace it with a T-shirt and jean shorts from the floor that seem clean enough, then stumble into the living area without sparing a glance at the couch, for fear and simultaneous hope that my parents will be waiting there.

The hallway is empty, save for a housekeeping cart parked across from my room. In front of Kit's open door.

I'm so distracted by Magdalena's presence, her signature music drifting into the hall, that I nearly trip over something solid and cold as I stumble forward.

A sharp sting shoots from my toe all the way up my leg, drawing my gaze downward. There, amid the blues and greens of the carpet whose pattern I could draw with my eyes closed, are my handprints. Mine and my parents' and a sand dollar, all memorialized in concrete. I kneel on the floor, drawing my fingertips across the jagged edges where the chunk of pavement has been chiseled away from the patio. Then the tears return in earnest.

An envelope with my name scrawled across it sits on top of the slab. I gather both pieces in my arms, surprised at the weight, and slip back into my room. As the door slams shut behind me, I set the stone gently on the coffee table and tear into the envelope.

A simple note written on hotel stationery greets me, and a small flash of gold falls from its grasp.

> You wanted a sand dollar, so I'm giving you two. One from me, but more importantly, one from them. Here's to whatever comes next. For both of us.
>
> -K

I laugh-cry into the quiet morning. My gaze shifts to the floor. What I now realize is a delicate gold ring lies prone in the carpet. I scoop it up and turn it over in my palm. Where there'd normally be a stone, a plate of gold has been engraved to look like a sand dollar, then filled with a shimmery blue inlay. I recognize it immediately as Angela's work—it matches every other piece I've bought from her shop through the years.

All Kit wanted was something true. Something real. Why couldn't I give that to him? Why did it scare me so damn bad to even consider it?

I lay my hand in my mother's print, wishing above all else that I could feel her warmth in the stone. But she's not in this stone, or even in the Carmen. Neither is Dad. They are nowhere and everywhere. They are in me and ahead of me and behind me, all at once. I've spent so long searching for them in my past that I forgot to look ahead. Was too afraid to, in case I didn't like what I'd see.

I glance up at the doorway where she stood in my dream and I weep. I weep for the child who lost her parents, and all her hope right along with them. Who thought the world needed her to always be light and bright and perfect in order to not leave her behind as well.

Kit saw me even at my darkest, and he still chose me. Still loved me. Now I'm filled to the point of breaking with the love that was meant to be his in return, all because I was too afraid to let it happen. Well it happened anyway, and I'm irrevocably changed for it.

I go through the motions of gathering my things and repacking them neatly into my bag. I strip the bed for Magdalena the way I do every summer, throw my towels on the pile of linens, and open the windows to let the light pour in. Sunshine spills onto my skin and I tilt my head back to drink it in. It feels as much like a beginning as it does an ending, the way most important moments in life have a tendency to.

Jenna, Mara, and Mauricio are all huddled around the center desk when I step into the lobby. Alex is nowhere to be seen, probably sleeping off the one-too-many beers he indulged in at our family dinner, but that's okay. Sometimes it's better not to know the last time you see someone will be the last time.

The moment Jenna lays eyes on me, her face crumples into a rueful smile. "I figured you'd be leaving early, once Kit checked out."

So he is gone. I knew as much already from the sight of his room being cleaned, but still, the confirmation that we're no longer under the same roof hurts in a way I hadn't anticipated.

It's for the best. His parents need him right now. And this is one thing I always knew would be done alone.

Mauricio has deep purple bruises under his eyes, which are the shade of bittersweet chocolate this morning. His gaze dips to the slab of concrete held tightly to my chest, and he chuckles breathily. "I see you got your present."

I glance down at it, then back at him. "Mo, how on earth?"

"Do not ask, *querida.*" He nods toward the windows to the deck, where I can just make out a barrier of caution tape warding passersby off from the place the handprints once lay. "I cannot wait to hear my brother's thoughts."

"He'll want to go ahead and rip up the pool deck a few months early," Mara says matter-of-factly. Then she shrugs as she meets my gaze. "That's a good thing, though. I hate dealing with the pool. Some kid poops in it at least once a week."

Jenna elbows her. I laugh. "Have I told you just how much I'm going to miss you, Mara?"

She ducks her head, but I swear I catch a blush. "If you'd get on socials, you could keep up with me while I'm traveling. I'll be vlogging the whole thing."

"Vlogging. Got it," I say while shaking my head in tune with Mo and Jenna, who seem equally as clueless as I do. The truth is, I mostly avoided social media so no one from high school could stalk me on random drunken nights when they pondered what happened to the girl whose parents died. But now I realize I don't really care. Their opinion of me is just that. I shouldn't let it impede my life anymore.

I set my keys on the counter, and Mo blows out a heavy breath. "So it's really happening, huh?" He steps forward and throws his arms around me, his familiar tobacco-and-cologne scent flooding my senses. "Please remember, you do not have to give up every part of your old life in order to create a new one. And we are only a phone call away."

I squeeze him tightly around the middle and draw in another deep breath. Until you've lost someone, you don't realize how important things like someone's smell are. But scent, handwriting, a voice: they're what you lose first. And therefore, what you miss the most.

Jenna tugs me from his grasp. "No hogging Tess." Then it's her turn, with all her pointy limbs, to hug me tightly. Mara joins in from behind, sandwiching me between mother and daughter. "You'll forever be our girl."

"Love you," Mara mutters into my hair.

"I love you all so much." I force the words out through a tight throat. When they finally release me, it still feels like I'm being held. I hope it stays with me the whole drive home. "Give Alex my love as well. And some ibuprofen for the headache this will inevitably cause him." I lift the stone in a shrug.

Jenna's dark eyes glitter with amusement, and Mo huffs a laugh. Mara retreats to her space behind the desk, as much a fan of goodbyes as I am.

"Would you like help to your car?" Mo asks.

I shake my head. "Not this time."

"How about the next?" he says with a wink.

Tears flood my vision, but I smile anyway. "That sounds good."

I walk out of the Carmen without looking back. Under the mimosa tree, across the scalding pavement, to my waiting car, where I load my bag into the trunk and place our handprints gingerly in the passenger seat. Who cares if it dirties up the fabric interior?

As I drive away, I catch a glimpse out of the corner of my eye of the signature green roof, and I decide that's how I prefer it. The Carmen will remain an image always in my peripheral, there if I choose to turn my head. There if I choose to return.

And everything else lies ahead.

Chapter Thirty-Two

Kit

FOR THE ENTIRETY of the monotonous drive to Mississippi, my thoughts oscillate between two points. One moment, I'm beating my head against the gold Marilyn Suite plaque as I pray and pray and pray for one last chance to lay eyes on Tess. The next, I'm envisioning Gage behind bars. I can practically feel the keys dangling from my fingertips, as though it's my fault he's finally created a problem that can't be solved with a little charm and a whole lot of money.

It spares me from thinking about my parents, at least.

By the time their house appears in front of me, I can't remember a single turn I took to get here. Just me, the low crackle of the radio, and an endless internal monologue that insists I've let down everyone who matters in my life.

The first time I brought Courtney here after we'd announced the engagement, I remember sitting in the car buzzing with anticipation. As a boy who'd become a man who craved his parents' approval like no other, I felt like I'd won the lottery. All I'd ever wanted was a love like my parents'. One that stood the test of time and raising two rambunctious boys. Never mind that they insisted we were too young; I was going to prove them wrong. Make them proud.

It's hard to believe we'd have been married nearly a decade by now. At the beginning it was easy to look forward and see a whole life laid out. But from where I stand now, the fault lines are so painfully obvious. We never would've worked. Never should've even tried. Courtney was yet another victim of my need to do everything perfectly. It's hard to admit to myself, but it's the truth. I have no right to blame her for seeking affection elsewhere, just like I can't blame my parents for staring at the car the way they are doing now.

The balmy morning meets me with a firm embrace. I slam the door behind me and march up the walkway like a man headed to the gallows. But to my surprise, Mom meets me halfway. Her arms come around my neck, and she pulls me in so tightly I have to bend to conform to her small stature. "Oh Kit, thank you for coming."

A firm hand slaps my shoulder. I glance up, and my dad has tears pooling in his deep brown eyes. "Two times in as many weeks, huh, son? Careful, now. We're gonna get spoiled."

I straighten up and take a step back from them both. "This is all my fault."

Dad's bushy brows crumple. "Were you driving the stolen car?"

I blink. "Well, no, but—"

"Did you abandon it in a Greyhound parking lot in Mobile and skip town?"

"Obviously not." I shift my weight. Glance from him to Mom and back. "But I—"

"But nothing, Kit." Dad places a hand on Mom's back, then reaches for me with the other. It creates a sort of semicircle out of our bodies, with him at the center of it, staring me down. For a moment I feel like I'm eight years old again, bracing for a lecture.

"Your mama and I appreciate what you were trying to do. You're a damn good brother and an even better son." His voice cracks, and the sound slices straight through my heart. "But that boy is not your responsibility. We brought him into this world. And we may look old and fragile, but we aren't. It's our job to parent him, not yours."

Mom nods, her bottom lip wobbling. "I always let you take on too much when it came to him. That was so unfair of me, Christopher. We should've known something was wrong, what with you staying away and all. But we buried our heads in the sand because we wanted to believe he was better. We let you pull the wool over our eyes 'cause it was better than facing the truth."

I try to swallow, but my throat is in knots. The sun burns like hot coals on top of my head. Sweat beads at my temples. Every instinct tells me they're wrong. That it was my job, and I failed miserably. I don't know how to see it any differently.

"It wasn't just Gage." I manage to force the words out, difficult as they are. "I let you guys down in so many ways. Leaving the military. Getting divorced." I shake my head. "I was supposed to be the easy kid. The responsible one. And I fucked it all up."

"*Language,*" Mom hisses because she can't help herself. But her flattened lips curve into a sad smile.

Dad, on the other hand, lets out a strangled laugh. "'Easy' is the last thing any kid is supposed to be. Exhausting? Sure. Amusing as all hell? Absolutely. But I don't believe any of those parenting books your mom made me read included the word 'easy' as it relates to child-rearing."

Mom rolls her eyes, nudging my father with an elbow before leveling me with the kind of stare only a mother can master, somehow holding love and exasperation in tandem. "All we wanted for you in life was to be happy and safe. Your marriage ending didn't disappoint us. Neither did you changing jobs. What would've been disappointing is you staying with someone who didn't value you the way you deserve because you thought it was the right thing to do. Eff the right thing. It's a load of bologna most of the time anyway."

I choke on a chuckle. My face is wet, I realize, and not with sweat. With tears that have spilled from my eyes onto my cheeks, pouring in rivulets down the column of my throat. Mom reaches up to swipe them from my skin. Her touch is cool despite the heat. It reminds me of being little and her checking me for a fever. Sometimes I'd grab her hand and hold it in place because the iciness was such a reprieve from the fire burning me up inside.

I feel small all of a sudden. Dependent. And my God, it's such a relief. To be a child to my parents, despite being grown. To let myself crumble and trust that they'll be strong for me.

It makes me ache for Tess. For all that she misses.

She must sense the shift in my thoughts, because Mom half frowns at me and nods toward the door. "Should we go inside where it's cool? I made some fresh sweet tea. You can tell us how the rest of your vacation went."

I hesitate, worrying my bottom lip. "Isn't there something we should be doing?"

Dad shakes his head. "We called that lawyer you mentioned. He's coming by tomorrow to chat through next steps."

"Until then?" I ask.

"We wait," they say in sync.

"We wait," I echo, hating how it sounds like giving up. Waiting for my brother. Waiting for Tess. I crave action, to feel like I'm actually doing something to move forward, but maybe that's exactly why this is what's best. If I'd slowed down sooner, perhaps love wouldn't have caught me so unprepared. Then I could've been what Tess needed instead of just another person she felt she had to pretend to be okay for.

"Sweet tea?" Mom repeats while tugging my arm.

I nod. Allow myself to be dragged inside. We talk about Gage intermittently. They ask about Tess, and I surprise myself by being honest. We order pizza for dinner from the only joint in town that delivers, and we fall asleep exhausted and emotionally spent, with enough beer in my system to not obsess over the fact that my bed still smells like Tess.

The lawyer tells us there's not much to be done until my brother is found. We each try to call him, but to no avail. After days of this, I finally relent that I'll have to return to work. When it's time to go, it's much harder than I expect. But I leave knowing the air is clear between us, and for that I stand taller. I'm no longer shouldering the burden alone, and neither are they. We'll face whatever comes as a family, for better or worse.

I promised myself I would give Tess space but can't help texting her a picture as I pass the exit that leads to her hometown. Every mile that passes after feels like my heart is being pulled taut between two points. Where I'm going, and where I belong. With her. Yet I keep pushing forward, knowing it's what's best for us both for now.

Denver International greets me with its usual cacophonic chaos. I retrieve my Hellcat from the parking garage and drive in silence back to Loveless. The familiar streets feel wrong somehow. Like instead of mountains in the distance, there should be an ocean. Like a woman in a blue sundress should be strolling down the sidewalk, rings shimmering on every finger as she waves.

Twilight has settled in by the time I reach my small house on a tree-lined street. At first I don't notice the figure waiting for me on my stoop. I'm too caught up in my own melancholy to be vigilant. It's not until a familiar voice rattles the otherwise quiet night that I look up and my heart stalls in my chest.

Gage steps into the puddle of light cast by a nearby streetlamp. "Man, am I glad to see you."

My professional instincts kick in before my brain can process what's happening. By the time I'm fully online, I've already dragged my brother and my bags into the house and deposited both at my dining room table.

"What the fuck, man?" he grumbles. He reeks of cigarettes and body odor. God knows how long he's been without a shower.

"My thoughts exactly." I plant both hands on the table across from him and stare my brother down. His shaggy hair is even more bedraggled than usual, matted to one side of his head. He peers up at me with bloodshot eyes, and I wonder how the hell he still manages to find a fix even out of his normal environment. Addiction always finds a way; there's no doubt about that. "So you can't answer a damn phone call but you think it's perfectly fine to show up at my house as a fucking fugitive?"

He throws his hands in the air. "What other choice did I have? This is all your fault anyway."

My laugh is threadbare. "Please, enlighten me on how exactly it is my fault that you stole a car and nearly killed someone with it. Two someones, might I add. There was a kid in that car, Gage."

"How the hell do you know that?" He at least has the decency to look horrified for a flashing moment before his walls of anger and indignation fly back up.

"Because I was first on the scene, asshole."

His nostrils flare at the insult. "Well, I wouldn't have been running in the first place if it weren't for you. You wouldn't let me go to Mom and Dad, and Easton's hotshot lawyer had the bright idea for him to testify against me to save his own skin. He kicked me out of his house. Said he couldn't have contact with me."

"So you decided to steal a goddamn car?"

"I *borrowed* his," he bites out. "I was going to give it back. I just needed to get to this girl's house, Chelsea. We'd been seeing each other here and there. She said I could hang with her till it all blew over. But then that bitch came out of nowhere on the interstate. I was in my fucking lane!"

It's fruitless to point out just how unreliable of a narrator he is, so I don't even bother. "I don't think you realize just how big of a deal this is, Gage. That woman could've died. Hell, her *son* could've died."

"But they didn't!" he whines. After a beat, his eyes widen. "They didn't, right?"

"No, and thank God for that. Because instead of vehicular manslaughter now you get to face vehicular assault and hit-and-run charges. On top of your drug charges. You're going to go to prison."

He shakes his head. "But not if you don't turn me in. No one is looking for me here. You could help me. Come on, bro."

I straighten and fist a hand in my hair. "You're kidding me, right? You do realize I'm literally a cop. Or did the sheriff's cruiser out front not jog your memory?"

Gage pales, the gaunt angles of his malnourished face suddenly becoming even more pronounced. Drugs have done a hell of a job with him. He was a handsome kid. Charming, when he wanted to be. If he'd made different choices, I imagine he could be married by now with a good job in something like sales, using his conniving ways to be a productive member of society at least.

"I'm your brother. You wouldn't turn me in." His voice warbles, but the conviction is clear in his eyes. As much as he knows I value my career, he also stands firm in the knowledge that I've always sacrificed everything to save his skin. Why would he think this time would be any different?

Will it be? Could I, honest to God, turn him in, knowing the fate that awaits him? I've worked in and around prisons for years. Gage is not some hardened criminal—I've never let it come to that. He's an overgrown child who wouldn't know a consequence if it slapped him in the face. The prison system would eat him alive.

Sure, my parents were happy to finally be let in on what's happening, but could they ever forgive me for condemning their little boy to that fate?

I feel myself wavering. Falling back into old ways. But all I see when I close my eyes is a mother and son battered and bruised in their car. I think of Tess and her parents, and I swallow hard. This was not a victimless crime. And if I allow him to continue on this path, how long before he destroys more lives than just his own?

I shake my head. It's all too much. Too heavy. And despite everything, I can't bring myself to call our parents. Not when I can barely get a grip on myself.

I grab my keys from the counter and fist them so hard my hands scream for relief from the stabbing pain. "I'm going to get dinner. Don't go any-fucking-where. Do you understand?"

Gage's shoulders slump with relief and he nods vigorously. He thinks the argument is over, that he's won. His big brother has saved the day yet again.

I slam the door behind me, cutting across the driveway to my deputy SUV in several quick strides. If he decides to run, the last thing I need is for him to hot-wire my work vehicle.

I send a silent apology to my Hellcat as I pull out of the driveway and head for the only place I can think to go.

Chapter Thirty-Three

Kit

I'M QUICKLY REDIRECTED to Nomads by Tomas's concerned-looking wife, who answered their door without so much as a question as to why I was frantically knocking at my boss's house acting like I was the one running from the law. At the bar, I parallel park in a miracle of a space in the street right out front. It's Friday night, and the place is rightfully slammed. I pause just outside the door, listening to the thrum of music and blending voices as I steel myself. I haven't so much as gone to the bathroom since I made it back to Loveless—I have no clue how I even look. Though based on the flash of worry in Tomas's eyes as I approach once inside, I'm betting on pretty damn disheveled.

"Rookie." He nods. "Wasn't planning on seeing you till tomorrow." His normally gruff voice is softened at the edges. A line has formed between his dark brows. I feel him taking my measure, so I forcibly school my expression into one of cool indifference. The one I normally reserve for interrogations.

Gary appears from behind Tomas, leaning back in his barstool to lay eyes on me. "Look what the cat dragged in. The silver-tongued snake who seduced my niece!" He cackles at his own joke, clasping his heart with an open palm as he shakes with laughter.

Thankfully Zoey's not on bar duty tonight. It's one of the newer bartenders who doesn't yet recognize us well enough to insert herself into our business. She's busy chatting with a couple seated at the far end of the counter, not sparing us a glance even after Gary's outburst. A small blessing, but a welcome one nonetheless.

The truth is, I've been teetering on an edge this entire week, and with everything that's happened this evening, the mention of Tess is enough to tip me over into outright despair. She never responded to my text. Not that I expected her to, exactly, but it was a further reminder that she's not here with me. That whatever we had is on pause, perhaps indefinitely, and I can't wait around for her soft touch or a disarming kiss to save me from this hell of my own making.

I try to smile at Gary. Really, I do. But my face, my entire body feels like it's made of stone. I could collapse into a heap right here and sleep for days. Maybe by the time I woke, this would all have worked itself out, and I'd be spared from a decision that feels impossible to make.

"I—" I start, but my voice cracks and falters. I wet my lips. Tomas elbows his friend, pinning him with a look that I can't see from where I stand. Whatever it is, it wipes the grin right off Gary's face.

"Sorry, boy," Gary says. "She's a hard one to leave, huh?"

You have no idea, I want to say. I dig a Sperry-clad toe into the wooden floor. "Have you heard from her?"

His bushy gray eyebrows lift. "Have you not?"

I shake my head. It's short. Quick. Heartbreaking enough to admit. I'm not trying to drag things out.

Gary's eyes are a shade of blue so light they might as well be silver. Understanding fills them. Crinkles form at the edges as he winces and nods. "She'll come around. You just gotta give her time."

Tomas clears his throat, drawing both our attention. He quirks a brow. "That's not why you're here looking like someone pissed in your cornflakes, though, is it?"

Leave it to him to cut to the chase. I glance around at the crowd, finally spotting Zoey chatting with a booth full of regulars. She catches my gaze and narrows her eyes, but I shrug off her attention. I can tell she wants to pry, but her hospitable spirit won't let her break away from the conversation.

The bar is far too crowded, and my nerves too raw, to get into this here.

"Can we talk outside, actually?"

Without hesitation, Tomas hoists himself off his barstool, straightening a T-shirt representing a soccer team I don't recognize, and gestures to the door. "After you."

By the time we're disappearing through the entryway, Zoey has rejoined Gary at the bar, and they speak with heads lowered and eyes darting in our direction.

The night is cool and damp. I hadn't noticed before that it was raining. Nothing like the storms in Florida that Tess and I endured, ones you couldn't possibly ignore. But the sidewalks cradle puddles of water that reflect back the streetlamps that line downtown Loveless. The soft pitter-patter of wayward drops falling from storefront awnings supplements the sounds of a busy Friday evening. Tomas takes one look around and gestures for my vehicle. "If you want privacy, that's the only place you're getting it."

I grunt my agreement. We duck into the SUV, and I crank it enough to turn on the heat, which feels like sacrilege in the dead of summer, but my muscles need the encouragement to relax. The familiar surroundings of my dark patrol car and a muted Loveless hustling past just outside the tinted windows helps quiet my tumultuous thoughts. It helps that Tomas doesn't push. It's part of what makes him such a good sheriff. He knows when to shut up and wait. His level of patience makes me look like an overstimulated toddler by comparison.

Until it's my secret in need of keeping. Suffice to say, for that, I can hold out with the best of them.

My hands thaw out first. Probably because I'm wringing them together like sodden rags. "Remember when I said it was family stuff keeping me longer?"

"Yes."

"I don't… I know I don't really talk about them much. My family." My insides feel like they've been turned on their heads. Any second I'm going to spill my guts right here in this car. Either figuratively or literally. Neither will be pretty. "I have a younger brother."

Tomas's eyes glint in the dark. I can feel their weight on my skin. Not pressing but not relenting either. He doesn't say a word.

"Gage is… troubled, I guess you'd say." What am I doing? My brother is a fucking drug addict. Have I never said those words aloud? Surely I have. So why does it feel so impossible now?

Probably because it, like so much else, feels as though it's my fault. No matter what my parents say. I may not have handed him the drugs, but have I not enabled him by giving him a safe place to hide? Have I not thrown money at the problem and pretended that it had any real chance of solving it?

It's Gage's addiction, Gage's life. So why does it feel so intertwined with my own?

Tomas finally decides to take mercy on me. "Your brother had some minor drug charges a few years back. I'm guessing things have escalated?"

I open my mouth to ask, but he cuts me off.

"Background check, my friend. We don't just look you up when you apply. Gotta research the whole family tree."

Of course. I knew that, at least in theory. And here I'd thought I was hiding things so well. Turns out, I had no real reason to after all. Not from Tomas, anyway.

"Escalated is putting it lightly," I say, clearing my throat. "In the past two weeks he's been arrested for possession with intent to sell and then, after I posted bail, he was involved in a hit-and-run that left a woman and her son badly injured. Then he abandoned the vehicle—which was stolen, mind you—and caught a bus to Colorado. And not just anywhere in Colorado. My front fucking door." I tick each offense off on my fingers, then gather them into a fist that I slam against the steering wheel with a dull thud.

Tomas's jaw flexes, and his eyelids shutter briefly. I've seen the expression a thousand times. He's working something out in his brain, and it's best to just leave the man to it. Any attempt to hurry him along will only drag out the process further.

Finally he tilts his head toward me with an expression so morose I'm already bracing for the blow before he delivers it.

"I'll admit I'm not super up-to-date on Mississippi-specific laws, but Kit, I don't have to tell you this is bad. Really bad. We're talking five to twenty years for the hit-and-run alone. That's not even taking into consideration all the other shit you just listed."

I swallow a lump that feels laced with needles. It scrapes my throat the entire way down. My nod turns into violent thrashing that only ends when I slam my head against the headrest and let out a frustrated sound that's more akin to an animalistic howl of desperation.

"I am trying so hard, Tomas. I'm trying to do the right thing by my family and by Tess and now by the damn law, and I just feel like I'm failing everyone."

The rain falls in earnest now, pouring in thick rivulets down my windshield. I stare at it to keep from falling completely apart. I'd give anything in the world to draw in the familiar smell of sugar and sunshine with my next breath. To look over and find a wide green gaze waiting for me without judgment, without expectation.

But all that awaits me in my passenger seat is Tomas, tawny skin pulled taut over a sympathetic frown. His firm grip encircles my bicep and squeezes. "Something tells me none of those people would want you feeling like this on their behalf, man." He chuckles dryly. "Well, except maybe the law, because that's one uncaring bastard. But your family... Tess..." He clicks his tongue, then leaves me to fill in the rest.

The thing is, I know he's right. My parents have said as much. And Tess, having experienced what it is to feel like a burden on others for years, wanted me to see her as absolutely anything else. But it comes as natural to me as breathing, this need to care for everyone else. Like a function my body never had to be taught. Turn air into oxygen for my blood to keep on pumping. Take every problem and place it on my shoulders so that the ones I love can stand a little straighter while I bear the weight.

"What happens when we call?" I ask quietly. Even saying *when,* not *if,* feels like a small step in the right direction. I swear I breathe easier once it's out.

Tomas's expression softens. "Depends on how they want to handle things. Usually we'd arrest and hold him, and they'd send their guys after an order for extradition has been approved."

My lips form a grim line. I nod. "Can I please ask a favor?"

"Anything, Rookie."

"I need to go home and make sure he stays put. If he even suspects I've ratted him out, there's no telling where he'll run. I've got to talk to my parents and let them know what's happening. There's a big difference between knowing what your kid has done, and facing the reality of the consequences of turning them in. I need to prepare them as best I can." My gaze cuts to Tomas's and I grimace. "When the time comes, I'll be the one to bring him in. But Tomas, I think I need you to make the call."

Tomas nods, expression filled with understanding. "Of course I can call, Kit. And I can be there for the arrest, too, if you want. You shouldn't have to put yourself through that—"

"I'm his big brother," I interject. "It's my responsibility to take care of him. And even though he can't see it, that's exactly what I'll be doing. What I should've done a long time ago."

He holds my gaze for a long time without blinking. I hope he sees the truth there. That I'm terrified but determined. That I'm learning to let go, little by little, even if it kills me.

Finally a grim smile tugs at his mouth. "Whatever you need. I'm here for you, man." He reaches for the door but pauses. "Send over what you have for contacts down there, if any. I'll give them a call tonight. You go do what it is you do best: take care of your people. It's what makes you such a damn good deputy and an even better friend."

He leaves me alone in the silence of the cab, listening only to the spitting rain and my own heartbeat. There's so much to do: I need to call my parents. I need to actually get dinner. As trusting as Gage is, coming home empty-handed would be egregious even for him. But for a moment I hesitate. I forget everything I need to do and focus on the only thing I want more than my next breath.

I pull up Tess's contact and, ignoring my last unanswered message to her, fire off another without hesitation. I stare at it for a long time, imagining her in some house I've never seen in a small town a lot like my home, smiling down at the joke.

ME

I don't know about you, but I could really go for one of Alex's daiquiris right about now.

Then I lock the phone and pull out of my spot.

Chapter Thirty-Four

Tess

IF MAY IS the balmy prelude to true summer, then June is the sweltering first act. After straining muscles I didn't know I had to help some pot-bellied gentleman from the next town over load my grandparents' old red couch into the bed of his truck, I'm drenched in sweat. I stumble back into the dimly lit house, make my way to the kitchen, and retrieve a soda from the fridge. Then I lie down in the middle of the living room floor to sip it while willing the cool hardwood to chill my feverish skin.

I'm not sure if minutes or hours pass, but at some point I fall asleep, only to be woken by the sound of my front door slamming shut. Only one person enters without knocking, and soon a flash of pale skin and thick, black hair confirms my suspicions about my intruder.

Alicia flops onto the floor beside me, hair sprawling in an onyx fan around her face, and tilts her petite nose up at the wood-paneled ceiling. "Do I even want to know where all your furniture has gone?"

The floor is unforgiving as I roll my head from side to side, taking in the shockingly empty space. No more red couch or solid oak coffee table. The ginormous rear-projection television was picked up yesterday by a teenage boy obsessed with all things vintage, while I tried not to cringe at the fact that objects of my childhood are now considered as such. The elevated dining room area seems especially bare. My grandmother's dining table—which had had the leaves in for so long they could no longer be removed without excessive force—made a family of six who just moved in on my street very happy.

I turn to my best friend and frown. "I don't honestly know. When I got back from Florida, I looked around and saw so many things that reflected my grandparents' taste, or even my parents', but none of it felt like me. So I started selling things online. Figured I'd use the money to buy things I genuinely like."

It was therapeutic, actually. Watching each piece be carried out the front door. It felt like the beginnings of ripping a Band-Aid off a wound I hadn't even identified yet.

She lifts a brow. "And?"

"And what?"

Her teeth flash as she lets out a bright giggle. "Well, did you have new stuff coming on order? Or did you decide you prefer the minimalist approach?"

I smile, because I suddenly remember how. "You've gotta admit, the floor works wonders on a sore back."

She snorts, reaches for my soda can, and takes a swig. Her purple lipstick leaves a print on the rim. "Speaking of, you missed Delilah and Truett's 5k fundraiser this morning. Turns out I'm a shit runner. And my hip is killing me for some reason?"

I let out a groan that echoes in the empty room. "I forgot that was today. Were they super upset?" Delilah's such a sweet person, and I had every intention of showing up to support her and her fiancé. Ever since her dad was diagnosed with early onset dementia, she's been trying to find a way to make a difference. Raising money for local families unable to afford care for their loved ones seemed like the perfect way to do it. What a shit friend I am for missing it.

Alicia scoffs. "There were over three hundred people in attendance. I don't think they even noticed *my* presence, let alone the lack of yours."

Thank God. My chest deflates with a heavy sigh.

"Are you okay, Tess? You've been so discombobulated since you came back from the Carmen. And now you're giving away all your earthly possessions." She waves a hand toward the room. "The mental health training all the teachers had to go through with the school counselor last year tells me you're a flashing, neon red flag."

"Does the color red come in neon?" My skin squeaks against the hardwood when she shoves me, and I laugh. Both at my friend and the ridiculous sound. "I'm all right. Just trying to figure things out, one baby step at a time."

She's silent for so long that I lift a finger under her nose to ensure she's still breathing, which she swats away with a frown. "Have you spoken to Deputy McHotStuff since you got home?"

His last message pops into my mind. The thought of sharing a drink with him was so tempting that I almost texted him back just to say so. But then I'd scrolled up, back to the photo he'd snapped of Fly Hollow's exit sign moving past in a green blur, and the twisting feeling in my stomach became too much to bear. I'd locked my phone and, consequently, any hint of that feeling was shoved far away.

I shake my head, focusing on the rustle of my hair against the floorboards rather than her tongue-click of disappointment. My lips roll, and I close my eyes. "I saw a listing for a skydiving instructor in Denver."

The sound of fabric shifting, then what I imagine is an elbow hitting the hardwood, tells me she's propped herself up to stare at me. "And why, pray tell, were you looking at jobs in Colorado?"

I squirm beneath her scrutiny but don't answer. Can't, really. All I know is one minute I was soaking in the same bathtub I'd washed my grandmother in for the last few months before she went into a care home, and the next, I was scrolling through a list of very outdoorsy roles that I am sorely underqualified for. Not that that's ever stopped me.

Maybe it was the ache in my stomach when Gary called to see how the job search was going. Or the longing that strangled my windpipe when he mentioned he'd seen Kit at Zoey's bar, confirming he'd made it back to Loveless in one piece. I shouldn't care. I'd made it my business not to. But just the single syllable of his name was enough to bring me back to stage one of grief: denial.

Hence, Colorado.

"Also," Alicia continues, not waiting for a reply that she knows isn't likely to come, "respectfully, how the hell do you afford to live on the salaries from these jobs? If it weren't for Destin being a doctor, we'd be screwed! Teaching might as well be a passion project for all they pay me."

I weigh my options, deciding just how honest to be. But it's Alicia, so of course I go for no holds barred in a way I've only ever been with her. Or Kit. "Being the sole beneficiary of four life insurance policies has a way of floating you for quite a long time."

Her silence is heavy. I feel it pressing on me like a weighted blanket. Through a slitted eyelid, I peek up at her. She's nibbling at her bottom lip.

"It's o—"

"Don't say it's okay," she interjects, her voice no more than a whisper. Her brown eyes shutter for a moment. When they reopen, they're washed with unshed tears. "I know we don't talk about it often. And it's not because it makes me uncomfortable, I can assure you of that. But I try not to bring it up because I see how much it upsets you. Especially this time of year. Especially when you go to the resort."

"Alicia…"

"You're selling their things. Looking at jobs in another city." She shakes her head, the corner of her mouth tilting up. "Something changed for you this summer. And while I'm sure part of it is because of you, I can't help but feel that *he* had a lot to do with it."

I release the breath I'd been holding in a whoosh, feeling my bones melt into the floor beneath me. Wishing I could slip right through, to the cool earth beneath, and let life sort itself out the way it feels so inclined. Letting things begin and end without emotion, without heartbreak. Trusting that each life is exactly as long as it needed to be. That love doesn't have to be spoken aloud to change everything we are inside.

My throat bobs. I gaze up at my friend, vulnerable as I'll ever be, and smile sadly. "I didn't talk about it—*couldn't* talk about it —for a long time because it hurt so badly. Every heartbeat after losing Mom and Dad was a struggle. Every year that passed. Every summer at the Carmen. Every anniversary. While everyone else was growing up and growing older, I was doing the opposite. Moving backward. Becoming less and less, in the hopes that I'd eventually disappear.

"Then I found out I still had family in the world. And that family led me to Kit." I wet my lips and draw in a hiccuping breath. Whisper, so the walls won't hear me. "And I think Kit led me back to myself."

Not the me I'd been pretending to be for so long, but the real Tess. One who could burst into tears if a sunrise was too beautiful, or wallow in sand without caring about the cleanup. One who sometimes needed to be spoon-fed pasta while wearing only a robe to bed because the grief was overwhelming. One who made love, and let love remake her, in the only place she remembered feeling alive.

The Tess who fell in love with him but was too scared to say it when it mattered the most.

"That's wonderful, Tess." Alicia's watery smile quickly turns to confusion. "So what on earth are you doing here with me?"

"You let yourself in," I say matter-of-factly.

She pins me with a glare. "You know what I mean. Why are you here when you could be there? You have no job tying you to this place, and if you think for one second that moving across state lines will keep me from you, you're sorely mistaken. So what gives?"

I sit up, folding my legs in a crisscross, and curse my aching back. So much for the floor helping. "I can't just up and move to Colorado for a man."

"It's not for a man. It's for you." Her hair dusts her shoulders as she tips her head this way and that. "Okay. And a little bit for a man. But let's be honest, Gary's worth it. He killed at Christmas karaoke."

Leave it to Alicia to deflate my very real worries with a pinprick of relentless laughter. The mental image of my uncle, drunk on peach schnapps and brandy, singing "Here Comes Santa Claus" at the top of his lungs in Alicia and Destin's living room will never not win any argument in which it's brought up.

When the giggling finally dissolves, my cheeks ache and my abs are in stitches. I take Alicia's hand in mine and hold it against my heart, which beats in a rapid tempo. "Would it be absolutely insane?"

"Yeah, but that's kinda your MO."

I let out an exasperated sigh, but hope keeps my lungs afloat like a buoy. "Am I really going to do this?"

She nods. For the first time since mentioning it, sadness enters her expression. "You're really going to do this."

"What about you?" I ask, throat raw from blending tears and joy and trepidation all into one. "What will you do without me?"

"First of all, I'm going with you. I'm off for the summer, and a cross-country road trip sounds amazing." She taps my nose with our clasped hands. "Then I'll probably buy this house."

"What?" I scoff.

"Yeah." She shrugs, leaning back to peruse the room. "Lots of potential, and we've been hoping to move closer to town. The commute from Foley is a bitch on school days." Her brown eyes dart to meet mine in a mischievous smirk. "And besides, I know the owner, and she's selling for way below market value."

Laughter bubbles up my throat once more. "Oh, is she now?"

"But only for me. Because I'm her best friend in the whole world." Then she leans forward and throws her arms around me, squeezing the air right out of me. "Don't you ever forget it, either, Tess Monroe."

"As long as you don't forget *me,*" I retort.

She snickers. "As if anyone could."

If only she knew just how heavily I'm betting on that.

Chapter Thirty-Five

Tess

"I should've called first."

Alicia continues thumbing the motel remote, searching for a channel that's at least twenty-five-percent static-free. We've landed at a seedy motel somewhere in New Mexico, where the cable is about as good as any other amenities they offer—such as a half-functioning vending machine that hums so loud I can hear it from our room half a motel away from it. It's a far cry from the Carmen, that's for sure, but oddly reminiscent of the Horseshoe.

Her gaze remains trained on the screen, face awash in artificial light, but she furrows her dark brows. "You called Gary two weeks ago. He was thrilled."

I shift uncomfortably on the mattress, trying to find a spot not completely caved in by previous tenants. "I meant I should've called Kit."

"Oh. Why? It's not like he gave you a heads-up when he crashed your vacation."

I wave my hands frenetically in the air, my feelings put to

motion, then drop them onto a bedspread that will forever reek of smoke. Alicia settles on a show where people have to survive butt naked in what appears to be the Amazon rainforest with nothing but their wits and a small knife about them. I shiver as a man swallows a handful of some questionable-at-best water, knowing dysentery awaits him.

"This is unhinged behavior."

She scoffs. "He started it."

"I meant the show!" My head lands on a stack of lumpy pillows with a muted thud. "Has anyone ever told you that you argue like a middle schooler?"

She drops the remote onto the table between our beds and pins me with a sardonic smile. "Hazard of the day job, I'm afraid."

I stare at my best friend, willing some of her confidence to flow across the divide and fill me instead. Ever since we left Alabama two days ago, she's been unwaveringly excited, certain that this will be the grand romantic gesture to end all grand romantic gestures.

I, however, have been a bundle of nerves.

Turns out, letting my true nature take precedent has had a two-fold effect. It has made me 1) an absolute sop who cries at the drop of a hat and 2) an overthinking mess. With every mile that passes, bringing us closer to Loveless, I play each moment with Kit on repeat in my head, checking for signs that I built it up to be bigger than what it was.

But I always come back to him kneeling before me with his eyes cast in shadow and his jaw set with determination. I see his lips part, thin and expressive, around words that still rock me like a physical push, even in memory.

I'm in love with you whether I tell you or not. But he did tell me, and more importantly, he showed me. By walking away when the pain of doing so was written so clearly in every ridge of his muscled body, because he knew it was what I needed. By leaving the light on for me so I could find my way when I was ready.

It doesn't take long for soft snores to spill from Alicia's side of the room. One glance confirms my suspicions; she's fallen fast asleep with an arm dangling over the edge of the bed, like she's reaching for me. Alone with my thoughts and the flickering light of the television, I stare up at the yellow-stained ceiling and send silent prayers not to God but to Kit.

You were right. It isn't over between us. It never could be. I'm coming. Please be waiting for me. I'll be there soon. Soon. Soon.

Tomorrow, I realize with a jolting heartbeat that pitches my stomach into my throat. After weeks of packing or selling—mostly the latter—all my earthly possessions and getting everything in line to transfer ownership of my grandparents' house to my best friend, it seems impossible that the day has come. That after what feels like a lifetime, but in reality has only been more like a month and a half, I'll get to see Kit again. Almost a year to the date from when we first met.

For the millionth time I unlock my phone and, bypassing a notification of yet another video Mara sent to me via some app she finally convinced me to download, navigate to his unanswered messages.

It brings a strange sort of comfort to reread them. Like for as long as they exist, so did we. Physical proof of some intangible thing that we shared.

Even if Alicia is right, that I'm doing exactly what Kit did by showing up unannounced at the Carmen, it still feels wrong to go from ignoring him to standing on his doorstep, begging for another chance. I don't allow myself to think about it for too long —an Olympic feat that I deserve at least Bronze for. I type quickly and press send before I can consider the consequences. I half expect to hyperventilate, but instead, my racing pulse calms. Just knowing that somewhere not too far from me in the world he's reading the words I've written is enough for me to relax, roll onto my side, and finally succumb to sleep.

Kit

I'd wonder what on earth I'm doing here, but then, what else is new? It seems like every second since I saw my brother carted away by two cops from Mississippi has been spent questioning my sanity for one reason or another.

I know I did the right thing. In time I hope Gage will, too. But even if he doesn't, it has to be enough for me that I did everything I could. I can't let the actions, or inactions, of others define me anymore. That was never my burden to bear.

That's what the new therapist says, anyway.

He'd have a field day with this, I'm sure. Me, posted up on the side of the highway that leads into Loveless, having traded assignments with another deputy just to guarantee I'd be in this exact spot per the kernel of hope that I know what Tess is implying.

I reread her text from last night, half expecting the words to change right in front of me. To prove once and for all that I've gone insane where she's concerned.

TESS

Not quite a daiquiri, but I could sure go for a vanilla milkshake. Say, around three o'clock?

Did I make a gigantic leap from that message to assuming it meant she'd be *here,* in *Loveless,* at three o'clock? Sure. Would a normal person just wait for her to actually arrive and then make plans to meet up? Also sure.

I'm gone for her in a way that I swore I'd never be again. And the kicker? I don't regret it one bit.

A car passes every five minutes or so, each one vaulting my pulse into high gear. I'm searching for something, *anything* familiar. Maybe Zoey slipped out of town to pick her up when I wasn't looking. Or Gary. Or any number of his countless, conniving friends. If she's in a rental car, I'm well and truly fucked, but anything is better than not trying at all.

I'm on the clock for thirty more minutes, but duty be damned. I'm not moving from this spot until I know for certain that she's not coming.

Determined to make a liar out of me, a car darts past me quickly enough that it shakes the SUV. My hands tighten on the sun-warmed steering wheel, knuckles bleaching. I grind my teeth so hard I'm certain my molars will crack. Reasoning that I'll still be able to spot her from a traffic stop is the only way I convince myself to take off after the guy.

It's a rural, straightforward highway, so thankfully I don't have to whip around too many corners to catch up. The speed limit out here is lower than you'd think, and out-of-towners get it wrong all the time. It's not exactly a high-speed pursuit, but adrenaline still pumps through my veins, tightening its grip on my lungs until I let out a celebratory *whoop* when the driver sees my lights and hits the brakes.

Like a wild animal who's given chase, it takes a moment for the fog of excitement and frustration in one to clear from my brain. When it does, I realize that the car is not only the exact make and model that Tess drives, but it has an Alabama license plate. What are the fucking odds of such an unlikely coincidence?

Coincidence. Or fate. After everything that's happened, who am I to question either?

I don't bother searching the plate. Under the glare of a hot July sun, I can make out two heads in the car. The window tint makes it difficult, but I swear I see a flash of white-blonde on the driver's side, and my heart slams against the confines of my ribs.

I rise from my SUV on shaking legs. Though I'd love to blame it on my run this morning, I know it's more than that. If I *were* an animal, I'd have scented her by now. As it stands, even without a predator's senses, my entire body knows that it's her.

Tess is here. In Loveless.

Screw the milkshake currently melting in my center console— mint chocolate chip, which I had to drive two towns over to find, because I know she likes it better than vanilla. Screw the oppressive heat and any cars flying past and whoever else sits in that passenger seat. I stride forward, forgetting every ounce of training in an instant, and rap my knuckles against the driver's-side glass.

I've never seen anything more beautiful than that window rolling down. Like a curtain opening at the beginning of a show, or a magician's hand unfurling to reveal your card. All things hoped and prayed for. Dreamed up, even after convincing yourself it was in your best interest not to.

"Tess," I breathe. How many times have I uttered her name through gritted teeth, making do with my hand when all I wanted was her body beneath me? How many times have I typed it out, because I had something I wanted to tell her. Show her. Ask her. Just to backspace it into oblivion so as not to overwhelm her with this simple fact: she is all I've been able to think about since I walked away from that resort without her.

"Surprise," she whispers, the corners of her mouth tilted down. "Are you upset?"

"Upset? Why the hell would I be upset?"

She shrugs. "I did show up without calling first."

Doesn't she know she could appear out of thin air and I'd praise whatever miracle worker made it happen? "That's kind of our thing, wouldn't you say?"

After a beat, those lips come alive with relief. Her smile is like dawn breaking. Brilliant white teeth. Mouth as pink as a blush, and devastatingly tempting. Dark lashes framing tear-dampened eyes, even greener than I remember them being.

I barely glimpse the woman in her passenger seat—dark hair, fair skin, hands folded together in a giddy clasp—before Tess is grabbing for the door handle and stepping out of the vehicle. Into my space. Where I can finally breathe her in after what feels like a lifetime of waiting.

Her fair brow perks up as she glances at my empty hands. "No milkshake?"

I wish I could wait. Be that kind of gentleman. But I'm not… I can't. I force my hands into her wild hair and pull her to me, covering her mouth with mine. Sweetness floods my senses. Soft, supple skin. Coconut sunscreen. Moans that bring back a litany of images, all with her sprawled beneath me. Long, long legs and tight pink nipples and her. Always her. In the sunshine. In the salt air. In the rain. In shambles, and in laughter. Breathtaking in every form.

Our tongues tangle. She sighs, and I inhale it like the desperate man I am. I drag my teeth along her bottom lip, then kiss it better. Her hands find my jaw and she holds me there, putting an inch of space between us. Enough that our breath mingles and mixes in the emptiness.

"It's in the car." I keep my voice low like I'm saying something sinful.

She gasps a laugh. "What is?"

"Your milkshake."

Sunshine splinters off her white-blonde curls like a kaleidoscope. She throws her head back, throat bobbing with laughter. Finally, when our eyes meet again, her thumb begins a slow stroke over what I know is some serious five-o'clock shadow. I couldn't shave this morning. I was too frantic, too hopeful, for anything involving a razor blade.

"You asked me for my truth that night, Kit, and I couldn't give it to you then," she whispers. Her head shakes. She wets her already glistening lips. "I couldn't give it to you because I didn't know what it was. But I do now. My truth is that I love you. It's also that I'm scared shitless, but I'm not letting that stop me anymore. I'm tired of just being alive. I want to live. I want a heartbreakingly full-to-the-brim life. And I want it with you."

Hope explodes in my chest like a mortar blown sky-high. I kiss her again, because I can. Because she's here and she's within reach and she's everything. *Everything.* How I ever thought I could live without this is beyond me.

"I love you so fucking much, Tess." I cup her delicate jaw with one hand, cradling the base of her spine with the other. "Whatever it takes. I'll move, to you or to somewhere brand-new. We can do long-distance till then. I'll make it work. *We'll* make it work."

She tilts her head to the side, teeth grazing her plump bottom lip as the corners of her mouth twitch. "Here's the thing... I might've already taken care of that part."

My brow furrows. Just then, a singsong voice calls from inside the car. "And she gave her house to me, so no takesies-backsies."

Our gazes meet with a comical snap, and we both burst into laughter.

"You didn't?" I ask teasingly.

She nods. "Figured I'd couch surf at Gary's place for a bit until I find something that's right for me."

I smooth the hair back from her face, shaking my head all the while. "You are something special, Tess Monroe. So damn special. You also fly by the seat of your pants in a way that gives me heart palpitations. But I love it."

"Good." She rises onto her tiptoes to kiss the bridge of my nose. "That part is definitely here to stay."

"Just like you."

"Mm," she hums, lips curling into a feline smile that sets fire to my veins.

Pinching her hip with one hand, I lean over to peer through the window to her friend, who bats a tissue theatrically against her cheeks, then yelps when she realizes she's been caught. "Sorry, I can't help it. I just love *love.*"

I offer my most charming smile, chuckling good-naturedly. "Do you mind if I place your friend under arrest?"

She waves a hand. "By all means!"

"Hey, wait!" Before Tess can protest further, I bend at the waist and snake one arm around her backside, hoisting her onto my shoulder as I rise. She slaps my butt with enough passion to spike my heart rate. "Kit! Put me down!"

I click my tongue as I approach my SUV. "No can do. You were driving way too fast. You're a menace to society. I have to take you in for the good of all."

"I went sixty-five on a straight highway with no other traffic. I didn't even see the speed limit sign," she grumbles. I can practically hear the pout in her voice.

I open my passenger-side door and drop her into the seat. Her skirt rides high up her thighs, a merciless promise of everything I've been missing. Of everything to come.

I fuse our lips together, grasping the back of her head and taking my fill of her until she sags in my embrace. Only then do I relent. And it takes a hell of a lot of self-control.

"Don't you have work?" she says breathlessly.

"Only for a little while longer. And now I've got myself a ride-along."

She smirks, glances over her shoulder, and then shrugs. "So long as I can have the milkshake."

"I will buy you a milkshake every day for the rest of your life."

Her hand flutters over her heart. "My hero."

I lean forward to steal a final kiss. "My Tess."

Mine to claim. Mine to love. For as long a life as we get and as good of one as we make. If that's the only certainty I get this side of heaven, then it was worth every moment spent thinking a love like this couldn't possibly exist.

Because now I know.

Epilogue

Tess

I THOUGHT I'd experienced all the best things the beach had to offer, but that was until I saw baby toes buried in the sand.

Tilly giggles like mad, kicking and squealing, sending little tufts of sand flying into the air. Her Grandma Betty feeds into the excitement by scooping up handfuls to pour onto each chunky thigh. It spills like sugar down into her endless rolls. Bath time will be hell, but isn't that what grandparents are for anyway? That is, if we can ever wake Pete, who's stretched out on a towel a few feet away and snoring so loudly the seagulls leave us be.

I glance up to ensure Kit is seeing the immeasurable cuteness, but he and Gary have each taken one of Asher's hands in theirs and are swinging him high above the waves rolling off the Gulf. Our son, who is the spitting image of his father with all his dark hair and deeply tanned skin, gazes up at his dad over an equally crooked nose. Turns out, he got my sense of adventure but Kit's sense of balance. Last year on our annual family vacation, we went to Europe, and our son managed to break his nose just by tripping over a loose cobblestone in the road.

I shake my head, tutting. My parents would get such a kick out of him.

"Someone's enjoying her first beach trip!" The adoring voice draws my gaze upward. I squint into the bright sky, where Mo graciously shifts his weight to blot out the sun. "I came to invite you all to dinner. Alex is closing down Topwater early so we can use the space." He glances from us three girls, plus Pete, to our male counterparts in the surf. "With so many of us now, we thought that'd give us a bit more room."

"I'd love that, Mo," I say warmly.

"We all would!" Betty adds, elbowing her husband, who chokes on an inhale but otherwise doesn't stir.

"Then it's settled," Mauricio says, clapping two bronze hands together. "See you tonight, *Querida.*" He bends to pinch one of Tilly's fat rolls. "*Gordita.*"

I swat his hand playfully, laughing at his nickname for her. She *is* quite the chunk. And who doesn't love a fat baby? He strides through the sand, which squeaks with each step, back up to the boardwalk that still makes me blush to look at.

"Mama! Mama!" Asher comes careening toward me, collapsing to his knees with his arms outstretched. "Look what I found!"

In the bloom of his small palms, a sun-bleached sand dollar appears. Completely unscathed by the elements. My throat thickens, and I work to swallow past the lump that has formed. I gather Tilly in my arms and stand her up on my thighs so she can see. "Look, Tills, your brother found a sand dollar."

One chubby little finger darts out to stroke the smooth surface of the shell. Asher, who is more patient than any four-year-old has business being, smiles down at us as we admire his prize. I have to blink back tears just to see it clearly.

"Mama?" He tilts his head. "Are you crying?"

Betty leans in to peer down at the shell, not hearing her grandson's question for the wind and shrieking children nearby that drown him out. But Kit appears over his shoulder, eyes trained not on his prize but on me.

"It's okay, Ash. Sometimes people are happy and sad at the same time." Kit smooths a hand over our son's wild hair. "Remember what we always say, buddy?"

Asher nods. He's turning pink on the apples of his cheeks and the precipices of his shoulders. By morning it'll turn to a tan. "Crying is good. It lets the feelings out!"

"That's right," Kit says, grinning with pride. Then his gaze finds mine. "It was sitting right there on top of the sand, like your dad left it out for us to find. I'd say he's happy we came."

I press my lips together and nod, feeling the hot tear streak down my cheek. It took years for me to feel ready to come back to the Carmen. But like Gary once said, eventually I got to the point where I wanted my children to know my parents. To know me, or who I was for such a long period of my life. So when we started making plans for this year's trip, I knew it was time.

It's also the year Gage will go up for parole, a fact so stressful to Kit and his parents that a trip to the Carmen was the perfect distraction. A reminder that, no matter what happens, we have each other. We'll get through it. All of us, Gary included, know a thing or two about surviving hardships, after all.

And Mom and Dad were here, of course, waiting for us to arrive. But I didn't have to come here to find them. They are everywhere else, too. I see them in my children. The way they laugh unabashedly like my dad. In Tilly's fascination with my rings. I don't have to wonder what they'd think of me, or of us and this little life we've built for ourselves. I *know* they'd be so proud. I *know* they'd think it was perfect.

Because I am. And I do. All the good parts are simply sharpened by the bad, honing them into something even more beautiful. Breathtakingly fleeting. Sacred, because it's all temporary.

Betty allows herself to be tugged toward the shoreline by her grandson, where she replaces Kit in their swinging game. Kit flops down in the sand beside me, throws an arm around my shoulder, and pulls me and our infant as close as we can get.

"I love you, Tess." He kisses my temple, that smoldering sandalwood scent of his washing over me. Tilly squawks, and he tousles what little hair she has. "Love you, too, Tills." Then his gaze finds mine, and he smiles knowingly. "Maybe tonight, the kids could have a sleepover with Grandma and Grandpa while you and I go crab hunting?"

"I thought they took care of that at your annual visit," I say, brow crumpling.

He throws his head back in a boisterous laugh. "For the last time, *I don't have crabs!*"

His mom and my uncle glance over their shoulders, casting confused glances our way. Even his sleeping father stirs. I'm too busy hiding my blush behind my baby, but at least Kit waves them off.

"Anyway," he says, still chuckling, "A little crab hunting, followed by an outdoor shower…"

I hold up the seven-month-old in my hands. "Do you want another one of these? Because that's how you get another one of these."

He nuzzles my throat, stealing my breath, and plants a kiss there at the hollow beneath my ear. "I'd gladly make a dozen more babies with you."

Despite the heat, a shiver racks my spine. I try to shoot him a glare, but there's no heat to it. Okay, well, there's heat. But certainly not the malicious kind.

He smirks. "I'll take that as a yes."

Of course he will. I kiss the smart twist right off his lips, then nip him for good measure. Tilly giggles like this is her favorite game, so when we break apart, we each smoosh a kiss against one of her cheeks, sandwiching her between us.

That night, after we've had dinner with the Ortizes—including Mo's fiancée, who finally managed to make an honest man out of him—we gather our bucket and our flashlights. I catch a million of the tiny creatures, and Kit doesn't manage to trap a single one. But he does capture me and drag me beneath the outdoor shower, teasing my body in ways that are both familiar and brand-new all at once. Then he makes slow, intentional love to me with the balcony door open, the sounds of the ocean cocooning us in their rhythm.

It's one of those pristine, rare moments where life happens so perfectly, it could be served up on a silver platter. Like finding a whole sand dollar on the beach. Nine times out of ten, all you get are fragments. Shards. Broken pieces that you have to make beautiful.

But every once in a while, a masterpiece. And this is mine.

Acknowledgments

As always, I can't acknowledge anyone else before taking the time to mention my forever love interest, my lighthouse, my husband. Andrew, this first year of marriage has flown by impossibly fast. I've loved every minute of it, even the hard parts (like moving cross-country), because they brought us closer. Thank you for reminding me every day what true love and kindness looks like. I'm so lucky to be yours.

For our daughter, Halle, who is kicking me in the ribs as I type this. Writing a book while pregnant turned out to be the hardest thing I've ever attempted, but it sure made the feeling of typing *The End* that much sweeter. And I already know the next story, the first I'll write with you earthside, will be even more incredible simply because I'll have you with me all the way through it. I love you more than I ever thought possible, and you aren't even here yet. I can't wait to see your baby toes buried in the sand.

Allie Samberts, thank you for loving Kit and Tess even when I couldn't. For listening to me whine and never complaining. For being an amazing alpha reader, co-author, and, most importantly, a true friend. Jackie Egan, I owe you so much for diving into this story and letting me know it was definitely worth finishing, even though pregnancy brain tried to convince me it wasn't. I can't wait for both our girls to be here.

To my amazing beta readers—Katie, Jennalee, Stephanie, and Linda. Your excitement and love for this story means the absolute world. Thank you for making it better. Kristen, my formatter extraordinaire, thank you for ensuring my stories look as pretty as they sound. Paige, thank you for creating beautiful art that brings my characters to life. Lea Ann, having you as my editor has made me a better writer. Having you as a sister has made me a better person. I love you so much. Thank you for laughing at my many penis jokes.

Finally, to my readers, thank you endlessly for your support in every aspect of this author journey. I could not do it without you. Literally. Every time someone picks up one of my books or tags me in an amazing edit or simply sends over a message letting me know how much a story meant to them, it reminds me why I do this. Why it matters. Thank you for giving meaning to my life. I am forever grateful.

Because of you all, I know I can do anything I put my mind to. And with that knowledge in mind, I cannot wait for you to see what's next.

About Hannah Bird

Hannah's accolades include a second-grade teacher who said her story about bats had "very good potential" and enough accelerated reading medals to sink a body at sea. Her goals in life are to write novels that will make you cry, and to check everything off the bucket list she wrote at seventeen.

Hannah resides in sunny California with her other half and their clingy golden retrievers. When she is not writing, she is trying to outrun her sweet tooth in the gym.

You can travel along with Hannah on her writing journey at her website, hannahbirdauthor.com, and at all the bookish destinations below:

facebook.com/hannahbirdauthor

instagram.com/hannahbirdauthor

amazon.com/author/hannahbird

goodreads.com/hannahbird

tiktok.com/@hannahbirdauthor

www.ingramcontent.com/pod-product-compliance
Lightning Source LLC
Chambersburg PA
CBHW032341310726

48973CB00007B/1795